# DIARY OF AN UNAUTHORISED VAMPIRE

IRIS BEAGLEHOLE

# MAGICAL GIFTS FROM IRIS

Hey lovelies. I have a special gift for you including bonus scenes and other magical goodies, when you sign up to my newsletter!

*The Keys to Myrtlewood include:*
🔑Accidental Magic alternative perspective scene (Perseus Burk meeting Rosemary for the first time)
🔑Accidental Magic Tarot Spread
🔑Seasonal Ritual Mini Guide
🔑Quest of the Dreamcharmer (Dreamrealm Mysteries prequel)

Subscribe to the Myrtlewood Coven newsletter and get instant access to this fabulous selection of special Myrtlewood content: iris beaglehole.com/newsletter

# CHAPTER I

# THE DIVORCE MARGARITA

7:32 AM. Morning routine: chaotic as usual. Children's breakfast: half-eaten. Coffee temperature: lukewarm. Maternal guilt levels: standard operational parameters.

Bloody freezing morning. London winter has no mercy, especially not for someone who oversleeps after hitting snooze four times. Story of my life lately.

I stood in the kitchen, making packed lunches while shouting upstairs. "MERRYN! COAT! NOW!" Why does my voice turn into Mother's when stressed? Mental note: work on calm, empowered tone as suggested by the self-help podcast I'd fallen asleep to the night before.

Emma, my perfect seven-year-old neighbour, walked past the window with her equally perfect mother. Both immaculately dressed with matching scarves. Emma clutching a science project that probably explained climate change to world leaders. Her mother caught my eye. Waved. I waved back with the jam knife, accidentally flicking a glob onto the window. Fantastic.

"We're going to be late again," Merryn informed me as she finally appeared, coat unbuttoned, radiating seven-year-old disappointment in my parenting abilities.

"We're not late until we're actually late," I mumbled, filling a travel mug with coffee that was too hot to drink but absolutely necessary for survival. My hair was doing that special thing where it looked both flat and frizzy simultaneously.

Keyne slid into the kitchen in his socks, a five-year-old tornado of energy. "Mummy, can elephants catch colds?"

"What? I –" The toast popped. The coffee I was pouring overflowed. A lunch box fell to the floor, spraying grapes everywhere. "Shoes, Keyne. Focus."

Ten minutes, one minor mitten crisis, and a last-minute toilet emergency later, we were finally in the car. The heater was blasting but still not touching the chill. My brain was a fog of school projects due, groceries needed, and work deadlines looming.

As we inched through London traffic, the forecast had promised "wintry showers," that delightful British euphemism for "miserable precipitation that can't decide if it's rain, sleet, or emotional tears from the sky."

I absently glanced at the date on the dashboard.

December 5th.

Wait.

My heart did a sudden flip, then started racing.

"Oh my God," I whispered, causing Merryn to look up from her book.

"What's wrong?"

"Nothing's wrong," I said, a smile spreading across my face. "Actually, something's very right."

"What?" Keyne piped up from the back seat.

"Today's just... special. I forgot it was today."

I caught sight of myself in the rearview mirror – my unruly hair and tired eyes suddenly seemed less tragic. There was a glimmer I hadn't seen in quite some time.

As we crept forward in traffic, I noticed a billboard advertising

"NEW BEGINNINGS START HERE" for a furniture sale. A shop window declaring "FRESH START" for January gym memberships. The universe was being rather heavy-handed with symbolism today.

I should remember to text Tilly. She'd been counting down to this day with more enthusiasm than I had, marking off calendar days like we were awaiting parole.

We arrived at the school gates where Mrs. Harrington stood like a Victorian headmistress, clipboard in hand.

"Bye, my loves," I said, leaning over to kiss them both. Keyne accepted graciously while Merryn wiped her cheek dramatically afterward.

Merryn's lunchbox chose that moment to pop open, spilling apple slices across the pavement. Keyne announced loudly that his socks didn't match, as if this was breaking news rather than his daily state of existence.

Mrs. Harrington approached, steam rising from her coffee cup like dragon's breath in the cold air.

"Running a bit behind schedule today, Gillian?"

"London traffic," I replied with what I hoped was a winning smile. "Absolute nightmare."

She didn't smile back. Instead, she made a note on her clipboard, which was definitely not recording my wit and charm.

As I drove away toward the office, I felt a strange tingling sensation. Like the world had shifted slightly. Like something was watching me. Probably just anticipation. Or possibly the three cups of coffee I'd downed in lieu of breakfast.

I glanced at my watch. Needed to be at the solicitor's by two. Needed to pick up the cake for tonight. Needed to remember this feeling – this precise moment when everything was about to change but hadn't quite yet.

I arrived at the office seventeen minutes late, which by Monday school run standards was practically early. The Morrison merger documents could wait another few minutes.

The lift went straight to my floor without stopping – convenient for normal people, terrifying for those carrying precarious coffee cups while attempting to apply lipstick.

The doors slid open and I stepped forward confidently, colliding with Martin from IT. My coffee performed an elegant arc through the air before splattering across my cream blouse.

"Oh God, I'm so sorry!" Martin stammered, frantically offering me a handful of tissues that appeared to have been in his pocket since the last millennium.

"It's fine," I lied, dabbing uselessly at what was clearly a permanent addition to my wardrobe. "Gives it character."

Martin hovered awkwardly. "I could get some soda water from the kitchen?"

"No need," I said, waving him away. "Brown is the new cream. Very on-trend."

I made a beeline for the ladies', where I attempted emergency blouse surgery with paper towels and hand soap. The result was a damp, slightly less coffee-coloured patch that now looked disturbingly like a map of Australia.

Standing at the mirror, I tried to salvage what remained of my dignity. Hair – restyled into what I was calling an "intentionally tousled look." Makeup – enhanced with a strategic second layer of mascara to distract from everything else. Blouse – now artfully tucked into my skirt in a way that mostly hid Australia.

Somewhat restored, I headed to my desk, dropping my bag just as Tilly spotted me and made a beeline across the office floor.

"You're here!" she stage-whispered, in a voice that could probably be heard in Glasgow. "Today's the day!" Her eyes were practically sparkling with vicarious excitement.

"Shhh," I hissed, glancing around nervously. "Yes, two o'clock at the solicitor's. But let's not broadcast it to the entire fourth floor, shall we?"

Too late. Tilly had already perched on the edge of my desk, legs swinging like an overeager schoolgirl. "Six hundred and twelve days of legal faffing about, and finally – FREEDOM!" She did a little shimmy that sent my stapler dangerously close to the edge.

"Tilly," I pleaded, "could we perhaps not –"

"Oh come on, Gill! It's huge! By three o'clock today, you'll officially be free again. No more sharing a surname with the world's most self-important –"

"Is there a reason Accounts is holding court at your desk, Gillian?"

Neville's voice cut through our conversation like a frozen knife. My soon-to-be-ex-husband and unfortunately-still-current boss stood behind us, arms folded, expression suggesting he'd just discovered something unpleasant on his overpriced leather shoes.

"Just discussing the Henderson account," I lied, my voice impressively steady.

"The Henderson account?" Neville raised an eyebrow with practiced condescension.

Tilly slid off my desk with surprising grace. "Just catching up on filing procedures," she offered. "Retention policies. Very dull stuff. I'll get back to my spreadsheets now." She gave me a tiny thumbs-up behind Neville's back before scurrying away.

"The Morrison file needs to be completely redone," Neville said, dropping a folder onto my desk with unnecessary force. "They didn't like the approach." Neville always blamed the client.

"The approach you specifically requested?" I asked, instantly regretting the words.

His jaw tightened. "The approach that clearly isn't working. Fix it by Thursday. And there's something on your blouse."

As he walked away, I resisted the overwhelming urge to throw my half-empty coffee cup at the back of his perfectly coiffed head. Six hours. Just six more hours until I was legally free of him, even if I was still professionally shackled.

I'd applied to fourteen jobs in the last month alone. The problem was finding another firm position – most barristers work in chambers, and I wasn't ready for that leap. Not with school runs and the children needing stability.

Two o'clock couldn't come fast enough.

My phone buzzed with a text from Tilly: "HE'S SUCH A TOOL. Drinks still on for tonight? Bringing party hats."

I smiled despite everything and typed back: "Absolutely. No party hats. One drink only."

We both knew that last part was a lie.

**8:18 PM. Tequila consumed: 4 (possibly 5?). Dignity remaining: minimal. Current marital status: gloriously divorced.**

After-work drinks had never felt so deliciously improper. I raised my margarita glass for what must have been the fifth toast of the night, somehow managing to poke myself in the eye with the cocktail umbrella. Freedom tastes like tequila, poor decisions, and mild ocular trauma.

"To the death of Gillian Bennett and to my rebirth!" I declared, salt rim catching on my fingertip as I brushed a strand of hair from my face. Years of calculated movements and careful words dissolving with each sip.

"Finally!" Priya exclaimed from across our commandeered corner table. "Do you know how long I've been waiting to hear you say that? Since approximately five minutes after I met him."

"Well, I met him at the engagement party," Adrien added extra emphasis to his French accent, swirling his cosmopolitan with practiced elegance. "Where he wrongly corrected the bartender's pronunciation of Sauvignon Blanc, I knew then – this man, he is trouble."

"This is going to be a day to remember," Tilly practically shouted, clinking her glass against mine with enough force to make the bartender wince. Tequila sloshed onto the already sticky bar top. "I can't believe you finally did it. You're finally free of the Beast."

I smiled at my assembled friends. Priya and Adrien had been my voices of reason since university. Priya was a tech consultant who could debug code and bad relationships with equal efficiency.

Tonight, she'd abandoned her usual minimalist style for a spectacular gold dress that made her look like a "celebration goddess," as Adrien had declared.

"Do not forget when he explained my own exhibition to me," Adrien said, raising his cosmopolitan with a flourish. Adrien a renowned curator, had been collecting stories of Neville's insufferable behaviour like other people collected stamps.

And Till, of course - Ten years Tilly and I had worked together at the firm, weathering Neville's reign of passive-aggressive terror. Ten years of hushed conversations by the coffee machine, of Tilly witnessing the slow demolition of my self-worth. Ten years of "Did you notice Neville took credit for your work again in the meeting?"

"I've never felt so terrified and excited at the same time," I admitted, the words sticking in my throat like peanut butter. "Like standing at the edge of a cliff with a really lovely view."

The freedom felt almost as daunting as the thought of staying one more minute in that relationship. After ten years, I'd developed a Neville-radar that anticipated his reactions before I'd even finished forming a thought.

**9:47 PM. Glasses consumed: lost count. Self-reflection: dangerously honest.**

"To Neville Bennett," Tilly announced to the entire bar, swaying dangerously on her stool, "the world's biggest wanker, who never deserved my friend!"

"Here, here!" Priya and Adrien chorused, raising their glasses.

The bartender shot us a look; we'd clearly crossed the line from "respectable working women having a civilised drink" to "potential problem customers who might start a revolution."

"And to my mother's maiden name," I added, "which I am proudly reclaiming as we speak. Goodbye, Bennett; hello, Gillian Spark."

"Does this mean you're officially... re-Sparked?" Tilly asked, then dissolved into hysterical laughter at her own joke.

I drained my glass, welcoming the burn of tequila. How many

nights had I sat at our dining table, reviewing contracts while Neville critiqued my work, my appearance, my very existence? How many mornings had I applied concealer to the dark circles under my eyes, practiced my smile in the mirror, and walked into the office to face him across the conference table?

"You know what the worst part is?" I asked, attempting to signal the bartender for another round but somehow just waving at a confused man by the jukebox. "I still have to see him every day at work."

Priya's eyes widened. "You're not quitting?"

"Can't afford to." I shrugged, the weight of my financial reality dropping onto my shoulders like a wet duvet. "School fees, mortgage, the small fortune I spend on concealer to hide evidence of my general life despair..."

"All those contracts and mergers you handle – Priya interjected, ever practical even after numerous drinks. "Surely other firms would snap you up?"

"I've been looking but everything is in central London, and I still have to get the kids to school."

"You're braver than me," Tilly said, patting my hand and missing twice before making contact. "I would've just burned the whole place down and collected the insurance."

"I did consider arson," I said thoughtfully. "He's not worth the prison time. Though speaking of dramatic exits, my mother's been threatening to leave my father for decades. Always said she'd do it with style."

"Speaking of Delia," Tilly said. "Have you told her about the divorce yet?"

I sighed. When Neville and I first separated, I'd been too ashamed to tell almost anyone, least of all my mother who had complained about my husband since before I'd even married him. I wasn't ready for her I-told-you-so. Instead, I'd been distant. I'd pretended all was well. I'd told myself I'd come clean when it was all final and announce it as a great triumph she could celebrate too. "I guess that's something to think about tomorrow."

"Your mother is a force of nature," Priya laughed. "Remember when she told Neville his tie made him look like an accountant who'd given up on life?"

Adrien raised his glass. "Magnifique!"

"That's Mum," I confirmed. "I love her, but she's not always polite."

I took a moment to check in with myself. I'd built my identity around being reasonable, dependable, and perfectly controlled, and now? This hunger for more was perhaps the most frightening change of all. All those years of being the sensible one, the reliable one, the one who never made waves...

**11:32 PM. Poor life choices: imminent. Support system: exceptional.**

Three more rounds later, I finally checked my watch. "It's after eleven. I should go." My speech was only slightly slurred, which I considered a remarkable achievement given that the room had started rotating gently to the left.

"Stay at mine," Tilly offered, her words considerably more garbled than mine. We can drink more and make a voodoo doll of Neville."

But I shook my head, immediately regretting the sudden movement. "The babysitter will be expecting me." And charging me her special "it's-nearly-midnight-you-disaster" rate.

We gathered our things with the elaborate care of the thoroughly intoxicated. Hugs were exchanged with fierce intensity – Tilly whispering promises that everything would be better now, Priya reminding me I was "brilliant and brave," Adrien kissing both cheeks and declaring me "finally free to be fabulous."

As we made our way outside, the December air hit like a shock of reality. But surrounded by these people who had seen me through the worst, I felt something I hadn't in years: hope.

It wasn't until I left the bar that the terror really set in, compounded by the tap of footsteps behind me in the dark side street. The streetlights were spaced too far apart, creating pools of darkness between each halo of yellow light. I quickened my pace, my heels clicking loudly on the pavement like a metronome of panic.

The footsteps behind me accelerated.

Bloody hell. Of all the nights to be followed down a dark alley, it had to be tonight. Couldn't the universe let me enjoy one single day of freedom before throwing another crisis my way?

I fumbled for my phone, dropping my purse in the process. As I bent to retrieve it, a shadow fell across me.

Mental note for future reference: dark alleys after tequila are never a good idea. Second mental note: really must sign up for self-defence classes.

Before I knew it, everything went black.

The scent of incense. Blood. Chanting.

Waves of cold water flowing over me.

That's all I remember clearly.

**Time: unknown. Hangover status: surreal, like my soul had been put through a cosmic blender and poured back into the wrong container.**

I groaned and opened my eyes. I was in my own bed, but everything was upside down. The ceiling seemed to be below me, the floor above. My head pounded with each heartbeat. This was such an odd hangover. No pain in my head or dryness in my mouth. Only a peaceful calm and masses of confusion.

I closed my eyes again, trying to remember how I'd gotten home. The last thing I recalled was bending down for my purse, and then... nothing. Had I been mugged? Drugged? Had I accidentally joined a cult again? (University was a complicated time.)

I rose from the bed and was startled by how fluid the movement felt. No aching joints, no morning stiffness – none of the perpetual fatigue that had become my constant companion. I glided through the house, wondering if I was still dreaming. The familiar hallway of my suburban home looked different somehow – colours more vibrant, edges sharper. I could see individual flecks of dust in the air where shafts of moonlight cut through the darkness.

Moonlight. It was still night. Not morning.

Wait. How did I get home? Did I drink so much I blacked out? Did I call a taxi? Did I sleepwalk? Is sleeptaxiing a thing?

A scent drifted over me, fragrant and delicious. Something I'd never smelled before yet recognised instantly on some primal level. It drew me down the hallway like a cartoon character floating toward a freshly baked pie.

I pushed open the door to the children's room. Two beautiful cherubs lay sleeping in their beds. Merryn's curls fanned out on her pillow, Keyne's little arm dangling over the edge of his bed. Two gorgeous... delicious...

Alarm bells blared in the back of my mind.

Wait. *Delicious?*

THESE ARE MY CHILDREN!

I shook my head, trying to clear it. What kind of horrible mother thinks her children smell delicious? Not in the normal "baby's head" way, but in a food way?

Images flooded back – school lunches, bedtime stories, the constant juggling act of motherhood and full-time work while Neville claimed he was "too busy" to pick them up from school. The memory of Neville's cutting remark when I'd asked him to watch them for a weekend: "You wanted them so badly, you deal with them."

And yet...their scent was different now. Intoxicating. Overwhelming.

I took a step closer, breathing in the smell, mouth-watering... a sharp pricking sensation on my lower lip, a force inside me driving me closer. I ran my tongue over my teeth and felt something wrong – something sharp, something changed.

Oh gosh. Had I broken a tooth during my blackout? Just what I needed.

I was within arm's reach of both beds when something hard hit my abdomen. I found myself sailing backwards through the air. I reached out and kicked back, to no avail. The world was a blur around me.

I let out a constricted breath as my body landed in something soft.

**Time unknown. Location: definitely not home. Surroundings: suspiciously Gothic. Head: spinning. Status: extremely confused.**

Cold. Stone against my cheek. The scent of dust and old leather.

My eyelids fluttered open to a world suddenly too sharp, too intense. I gasped, my head spinning with disjointed fragments of memory. Children. Hunger. A stranger's voice telling me something terrible had happened.

My fingers clutched at velvet beneath me. Not my bed. Not my house. Panic surged as I pushed myself upright, the room tilting sickeningly around me.

Bloody hell. Have I been kidnapped? Is this some bizarre tequila-induced nightmare?

Stone walls loomed close, adorned with tapestries showing faded scenes of hunts and battles. Carved wooden furniture, dark and oppressive, crowded the space. A candelabra threw shimmering light across a ceiling so high I could barely make out the elaborate patterns carved into ancient beams.

Good god. I've been kidnapped by medieval reenactment enthusiasts. Or possibly time-travelled to a scene befitting a BBC period drama.

"She's awake," a voice said, crystal clear despite its softness.

My head jerked toward the sound. A woman stood before me, tall and commanding. Waves of midnight hair cascaded over shoulders draped in black fabric that seemed to absorb the candlelight. Her dress hugged her figure before pooling around her feet, sleeves nearly brushing the floor. The scent of something floral yet sharp – violets perhaps – emanated from her.

**Gorgeous stranger count: 1. Self-consciousness level: skyrocketing.**

She was stunning. Not normal-person stunning, but impossibly stunning. The kind of stunning that makes you immediately aware you have a smudge of mascara under one eye and possibly something stuck in your teeth.

"Where –" My voice caught, my throat burning with unexpected dryness. God, I sounded like I'd been gargling gravel.

My gaze darted around the room, landing on a blonde man lounging in a high-backed armchair. His casual polo shirt looked jarringly modern against the Gothic backdrop, the bright blue fabric offensive to my sensitive eyes.

**Gorgeous stranger count: 2. Self-consciousness level: astronomical.**

Perfect jawline, perfect hair, perfect everything. The kind of man who would never look twice at me in a bar – unless I was spilling a drink on him, which would be more my style.

"Is this a hallucination?" I asked, though I wasn't sure why I'd be talking to said hallucination.

I looked down, seeing my work skirt covered in a fine layer of grey dust. As I brushed at it, the sensation of fabric against my fingertips felt exquisite, every fibre distinct. I could trace each individual thread, could feel the minute differences in texture where the fabric had worn thinner over time.

Great. Even my skirt was broadcasting its imperfections to my suddenly hypersensitive fingers.

"Have I been drugged?" I asked, trying to organise my scattered thoughts. "Did something happen at the bar?"

"Of course she doesn't know what's going on," came another voice, young and petulant.

My head snapped toward the sound. A girl stood across the

room, her hair pulled into tight pigtails, her face childlike but her eyes ancient. The dissonance made my stomach lurch.

**Creepy child warning bells: deafening.**

"You didn't follow the protocols," the girl continued, arms crossed over her small chest.

"How are we supposed to follow the protocols, Maman?" The dark-haired woman's voice carried a hint of exasperation. "I told you, we found her. We didn't make her."

The room seemed to pulse with tension. My ears picked up sounds from far beyond the walls – wind whistling through cracks in stone, distant voices too faint to decipher, my senses bombarded with information I couldn't process.

**Current sensory overload level: 11/10. Chances of maintaining dignity: rapidly diminishing.**

My legs trembled as I stood, muscles responding with unnerving precision. No ache in my back, no stiffness in my knees. Just smooth, fluid movement that felt foreign in my own body.

"I'm sorry," I said, the polite words falling from my lips automatically, as they always did when I felt threatened. Always apologizing – to Neville, to clients, to everyone. "I better be getting home to my children."

The memory of Keyne and Merryn hit me with physical force. Their faces swam before my eyes – Keyne's gap-toothed smile, Merryn's solemn eyes. Then another memory: standing over them, inhaling their scent, wanting something terrible.

Oh God. My children. My babies.

"Your children are fine, my dear," the dark-haired woman said, her voice cutting through my spiral of panic. "Let me introduce myself. I'm Azalea Burk."

The name seemed heavy with significance I couldn't grasp. She said it like I should recognise it, like she was a celebrity making a grand entrance on Graham Norton's couch.

"This is my husband, Charles," Azalea gestured toward the

blonde man, who inclined his head slightly. "Excuse his poor taste in clothing."

Charles's lips quirked into a half-smile. I could hear the rustle of fabric as he shifted in his chair, could smell something like aniseed and vanilla emanating from him.

"And my mother, Dora," Azalea concluded, indicating the girl with pigtail plaits.

I blinked, certainty growing that this was some bizarre dream. "Your mother?"

The creepy child is her mother? What kind of supernatural family tree nightmare is this?

The room swam around me again. The candlelight seemed to leave trails as my eyes moved, the flames burning too bright, too colourful.

"That's a long and complicated story," Dora said, her childish voice at odds with her weary tone.

"I think you'd better tell her what she's become," Dora added bluntly.

What I've become? What on earth does that mean?

"Excuse me?" My tongue flicked instinctively over my teeth, finding them feeling ordinary if unusually clean, but something felt different. "What's happening to me? Why am I here? Why can I hear everything so... clearly?"

"I'm afraid there's been an incident," Charles said from his armchair. His voice resonated pleasantly, like a cello's lowest notes. "But the good news is you've been given a rather unique opportunity."

"What kind of opportunity?" The words tasted bitter in my mouth.

"Eternal youth is nothing to scoff at," Azalea said, the silk of her dress whispering as she moved closer. I could see every individual eyelash framing her dark eyes, could count the tiny stitches in the seams of her dress.

**Close proximity to impossibly beautiful woman: extremely intimidating. Self-esteem: plummeting.**

I gulped. "Is everyone here this..." I gestured vaguely at her general perfection, unable to find the right words.

Azalea exchanged an amused glance with Charles. "You mean attractive? Yes, it's part of the package. Helps with... persuasion."

"We tone it down for regular people," Charles added with a wink that made something flutter in my stomach. "Otherwise it causes chaos. You'll learn to control it."

Control what? And what does he mean by "regular people"?

"Eternal youth? Right." I stepped backward, my heel striking something solid. I scanned the room looking for a door, an escape. "I need to go home to the kids."

"I'm afraid you can't do that," Azalea said.

"You're not safe around your children."

The words triggered a cascade of sensory memory – the warm, sleeping forms of Keyne and Merryn in their beds, their scent rich and intoxicating, calling to something primal and hungry within me. The way my mouth had watered, an unfamiliar sensation as my teeth seemed to shift.

My hands flew to my hips in frustration, and I heard the sharp sound of tearing fabric. I looked down in horror – I'd somehow ripped my own work skirt, my fingers having torn straight through the material like it was tissue paper. A long gash ran up the side where I'd simply... grabbed too hard.

"What the..?" I stared at my hands, then at the ruined fabric. "How did I...?"

"Oh, how delightfully dramatic!" Azalea exclaimed, clapping her hands together with genuine delight. "Such magnificent strength! Such exquisite lack of control!" She glided to an ornate chest with theatrical flourish, retrieving a sumptuous velvet throw. "Here, darling. Your body is still learning its new capabilities. Fabric casualties are inevitable in the early stages."

I wrapped the heavy burgundy velvet around my waist with

trembling hands, afraid to grip it too tightly. Even my own strength was betraying me now. What was happening to my body?

"I don't understand any of this," I whispered, staring at my treacherous fingers.

The room spun again, colours bleeding into one another, sounds amplifying until the crackle of candle flames sounded like bonfires.

"What's happening to me?" My voice came out muffled behind my hand.

What am I going to tell the kids? What am I going to tell my mother?! "Sorry Mum, can't make Sunday dinner, I've been kidnapped by beautiful people with a creepy child who's actually someone's mother."

"Everything's different now," Charles said. The leather of his armchair creaked as he leaned forward. "You can't go back to your old life. You can only go forward. You'll see there are certain advantages to being one of our kind."

One of their kind?

I shook my head. "You're all mad."

Charles reached toward a small table beside him, lifting a silver object. The soft ring of a bell cut through the room like a knife.

Moments later, the door behind me opened. I whirled, nostrils flaring at a new scent – something rich and metallic that made my entire body tense with sudden, desperate want.

A thin delicious smelling man in formal attire stood holding a silver tray. On it, a single crystal goblet filled with deep crimson liquid. The scent emanating from it was the most exquisite thing I had ever encountered – complex, inviting, delicious.

"Your first refreshment," Azalea announced, satisfaction colouring her tone. "Do enjoy it. It's so rare that we indulge in the traditional source these days, but it is believed to help you settle in."

I tried to step back, but my body betrayed me. My hand reached for the goblet of its own accord, drawn by an instinct as powerful as gravity. The crystal was cool against my fingers, but the liquid inside radiated warmth.

"What is this?" I whispered, even as I raised it to my lips. Something told me I knew exactly what it was, but my mind refused to form the terrible thought.

The first drop touched my tongue, and the world exploded.

**Sensory explosion level: off the charts. Dignity: gone entirely.**

Flavour cascaded through me – rich, complex, alive with history and emotion and life itself. Heat spread from my throat to my limbs, every cell in my body singing with pleasure so intense it bordered on pain. My skin tingled with electric sensitivity, every hair standing on end. Colours intensified, sounds clarified, scents blossomed into sparks of information.

I drained the goblet in seconds, then stood trembling, overwhelmed by the experience. A little moan escaped my lips before I could stop it – How embarrassing.

As the goblet emptied, reality crashed down on me. The metallic taste. The crimson colour. The primal need it satisfied.

Blood. I just drank blood. And I loved it.

I gasped, nearly dropping the goblet. "What have you done to me?"

The room shimmered around me, reality settling into a new configuration. I could see even more details. Everything had taken on crystalline clarity – the individual threads in the tapestries on the wall, the minute cracks in the ancient stone, the complex patterns in the wood grain of the furniture.

I looked down at my hands, startled to find my skin luminous, flawless. I touched my face, feeling the sharper definition of my cheekbones, the smoothness of my skin.

"Come," Azalea said, taking the empty goblet from my unresisting fingers. She led me across the room to an old mirror in a tarnished frame.

I gasped at my reflection. My hair gleamed in copper tones, each strand distinct and perfect. My eyes, once a muted green, now sparkled like peridot. My features remained recognisable but enhanced, as if an artist had taken my ordinary face and perfected every line.

I looked... good. Better than good. Stunning. The kind of stunning that would make Neville's jaw drop and his new 20-something-year-old girlfriend (yes, of course there was one) seethe with jealousy.

"You're still yourself," Azalea said, watching my reaction in the mirror. "Just a new and improved version, as they say on those strange entertainment boxes you humans enjoy. Charles is a huge fan of reality television, of course."

You humans? Wait...

The pieces clicked together with terrible clarity. The enhanced senses. The blood. The supernatural beauty.

"I'm a... vampire?" The word felt ridiculous coming out of my mouth, like something from a teenage novel.

"There it is," Dora said with childish satisfaction. "She's caught on."

"What happened to me?" I asked, unable to look away from my transformed reflection. My voice sounded musical even to my own ears. "Who did this to me?"

"That is a mystery," Charles said from behind me, his reflection joining mine in the mirror, "which we hope to unravel in time. We got an anonymous tip about you and arrived at your house just in the nick of time."

"They do say it's important to wake up in your normal surroundings to adjust," Azalea added, "but it wasn't safe."

The memory of standing over my children's beds returned with visceral clarity – the scent of their breath, the sound of their heart-beats, the overwhelming hunger I had felt.

"Keyne and Merryn," I said, their names catching in my throat. "Are they..."

"They're here in the castle and well looked after. Don't you worry," Azalea assured me, but there was something evasive in her tone.

I spun around, the room blurring momentarily with the speed of my movement. "You've kidnapped me. You've kidnapped us."

"No," Charles said firmly. His heartbeat remained steady, unfaltering. "We've merely rescued you. It would have been devastating–carnage–had we not."

The truth of his words crashed through my defences. My legs gave way beneath me, and I sank to the stone floor. Sobs wrenched from my chest. The tears burned and when I wiped them away, I saw they were red. Blood red. It was all too much. A nightmare. The hunger I had felt standing over my children's beds... the primal urge to feed... I would have harmed them. Killed them, even.

First I become a vampire, then I nearly eat my own children. This is officially the worst week of my life.

"It's enormously dangerous for your living loved ones when you first turn," Azalea explained, her voice softening slightly. The rustle of her dress sounded like waves as she knelt beside me. "There are many tragic stories. We do our best to prevent new vampires from harming their families nowadays."

"The tradition used to be that one killed and took vengeance on all of the living when one turned," Dora said from across the room, her childish voice carrying a disturbing note of nostalgia. "But these days, everything's far too civilised for my tastes."

I looked up at the eternally young face, wondering what horrors those innocent-looking eyes had witnessed. Had committed.

Note to self: Never be alone with creepy vampire child.

"Well, I'm glad my children are okay," I said, struggling to compose myself. "But I can't just leave my life. I have a job. I have a mortgage. I have Pilates on Thursdays. And I'm guessing now I can't be out in the sunshine. Is that true?"

My fingers traced the sharp edges of my new teeth, the physical evidence I couldn't deny.

"It tends to be," Charles confirmed with a sympathetic nod. "The sunshine part, that is. Mirrors, crosses, garlic – mostly human inventions. But sunlight... sunlight remains problematic."

Great. Now I'll never get to use those expensive sunglasses I bought last summer.

As I sat on the cold stone floor, surrounded by strangers who were now my kind, I realised that my life – my human life of contracts and school runs and enduring Neville's criticism – was over.

**Days until I can see my children again: unknown. Supernatural hotness level: unexpectedly high. Existential crisis level: extreme.**

# CHAPTER 2

# JOB INTERVIEW WITH THE UNDEAD

**D**ay 3 of vampire existence. Senses heightened: drastically. Joint pain: gone (silver linings). Children visible but untouchable: excruciating. Ability to exist in physical space without breaking things: still non-existent.

My fingertips traced the cold stone of the windowsill, feeling every microscopic ridge and valley like I was reading braille. Three nights into my new existence, and I still couldn't get over how ridiculously intense everything felt. Perhaps it would get easier if I could sleep but I couldn't – apparently normal for new vampires.

I flexed my fingers, still marvelling at the absence of the familiar ache in my joints – the repetitive strain from years of drafting legal documents gone as if it had never existed. My body felt impossibly light, humming with energy that seemed to have no source. Last night, on impulse, I sprinted down one of the castle's massive corridors, covering the distance in seconds, my feet barely seeming to touch the ground.

Note: Must find stronger writing implements. Already snapped two fountain pens trying to record this madness. Azalea says there's a medieval quill somewhere that's 'vampire-proof.' At least my handwriting speed and attention to detail has improved. Silver linings to supernatural transformation, I suppose.

I'd also accidentally shattered three priceless-looking vases, cracked a marble statue, and torn through a tapestry that Azalea had informed me (with disturbing delight) was "merely six centuries old." My new existence was becoming expensive.

"Collateral damage is part of the rebirth," she'd said, stroking the torn tapestry with affection. "The castle has survived far worse than an enthusiastic fledgling."

The truth is, I both love and hate this new experience of being. It's intoxicating. Terrifying. Liberating.

A far cry from my former life – the crushing fatigue that had become my constant companion, the weight of Neville's criticism pressing down on my shoulders, the perpetual scramble to meet client deadlines while juggling the children's needs and school runs. Now I have supernatural speed and strength, can see in the dark, and possess the coordination of a wrecking ball with anxiety issues.

But the children...

My chest tightened with a pain that had nothing to do with my physical transformation. Keyne and Merryn. I pressed my forehead against the cool glass, watching their small forms in the garden below, visible to my enhanced vision despite the darkness. Merryn was collecting stones, arranging them in patterns on a garden bench while Keyne chased fireflies, his laughter carrying up to my window with painful clarity.

Tilly sat nearby on a stone bench, her bright purple cardigan a beacon in the night. She was reading something on her phone, occasionally looking up to check on the children with surprising attentiveness. The Burks had invited her here, apparently, believing the children would feel better with their aunty Tilly there for comfort. I wonder if she believed the story they'd told about my sudden rare illness. I haven't been able to talk to her. Not yet. Too dangerous. And the children...

So close. So impossibly far away.

I could hear their heartbeats if I concentrated – the quick, light rhythm of Keyne's, the slightly steadier cadence of Merryn's. The sound both comforted and tormented me, calling to a hunger I fought to suppress. At least I hadn't broken the window trying to get to them. Yet.

What did my eternal youth mean for them? Would I ever be safe around them? Would I outlive them? It was all impossible to fathom. I longed for a normal day, a harried school run, a return to the drudgery I used to hate, just to see them again.

"Ah, maternal longing. Such exquisite torture," came Azalea's voice from the doorway, rich with appreciation for my pain.

I turned, unsurprised by the sudden appearance. My heightened senses had detected Azalea's approach – the soft sound of silk against stone, the subtle scent of violets and cinnamon that seemed to accompany her. She glided into the room wearing another dramatic black gown, this one with trailing sleeves that nearly brushed the floor. The neckline plunged just enough to be elegant rather than scandalous, and her hair was arranged in an elaborate updo that defied both gravity and modern hairstyling techniques.

"Will it always hurt this much?" I asked, my voice catching as I gestured toward the window. "Watching them but not being able to hold them?"

"The most delicious agonies are often the most enduring," Azalea replied, her dark eyes gleaming with a strange combination of sympathy and delight. She moved to stand beside me at the window, her dark hair framing her face in perfect waves. "Though the pain does change. Becomes more... manageable. An ache rather than an unbearable torment."

"Manageable," I echoed hollowly. "Like grief."

"Precisely like grief," Azalea agreed, her smile wistful. "You are mourning your human life. Such a beautiful, poignant process. I do envy you that fresh sorrow."

Envy this? How could she possibly envy this? I gripped the windowsill, accidentally breaking off a piece of stone.

I laughed. "Fantastic. Another renovation project courtesy of the new vampire."

"The castle has endured eight centuries of midnight feasts, vampire balls, and the occasional battle," Azalea said with an elegant wave of dismissal. "Your enthusiastic redecorating is hardly cause for concern. In fact, Charles finds it quite charming."

I turned back to the window, watching Keyne spin in circles until he fell dizzy onto the grass. The children's energy used to baffle me, but now? I can relate. "I never expected to feel so…"

"Alive?" Azalea supplied with relish, rather than irony. "Isn't it deliciously paradoxical? Death has never felt so vivid."

"Yes." The word came out almost as a confession. Because despite everything – the loss, the confusion, the hunger – I couldn't deny the exhilaration that coursed through my body. The sensation of power in my limbs, the clarity of my mind, the freedom from the constant exhaustion that had defined my human existence.

For years, I'd been Tired Gillian, Stressed Gillian, Not-Enough-Hours-In-The-Day Gillian. Now I had limitless energy and all the hours of the night. Just not with the people who mattered most.

"You're adjusting remarkably well," Azalea observed, her eyes scanning me with keen interest. "Most new turns spend their first week in a mixture of frenzied bloodlust and catatonic shock. Sometimes it goes on for months with no coherency whatsoever. So dreary and predictable."

"I've had practice hiding my feelings," I said dryly, thinking of the countless times I'd swallowed my rage at Neville's belittling comments, maintained my composure in client meetings while scrambling to fix his mistakes. "My marriage was excellent preparation for containing murderous urges."

Azalea's perfect eyebrows rose slightly, and a slow smile spread across her face. "Perhaps we should invite him for dinner. I do so love a challenging guest."

I couldn't tell if she was joking or serious, or if the delight in her tone was actually about the possibility of eating my ex. The disturbing part was that I wasn't entirely sure I cared.

"I've arranged for you to meet someone," she continued, changing the subject. "Someone who might help give your new existence some... purpose. He's waiting in the drawing room." She clapped her hands together with theatrical enthusiasm. "A new chapter in your eternal night!"

I followed Azalea through the castle corridors, acutely aware of the sensory tapestry around me – the subtle temperature variations between rooms, the complex mess of scents from centuries of inhabitation, the whispers of air currents against my skin. My body moved with a fluid grace, each step precise and effortless. I caught my reflection in a passing mirror and still startled at the sight – my features familiar yet enhanced, my movements carrying a predatory elegance I was still coming to terms with.

**Mysterious visitor imminent. Outfit: borrowed Gothic castoffs that probably witnessed the Black Death. Professional demeanour: attempting to channel despite looking like a Tim Burton character.**

I also kept a careful distance from anything breakable, which in a medieval castle was approximately everything.

"Your preternatural grace is developing nicely," Azalea commented, noticing my caution. "Soon you'll move like you were born to the darkness."

"I used to trip over perfectly flat surfaces," I admitted. "Now I move like some sort of terrifying supermodel, but with the destructive capacity of a tornado."

"A charming combination," Azalea assured me.

We arrived at a set of double doors, and I paused.

"Who am I meeting?" I asked. "The creature from the castle basement that you've definitely been hiding?"

Azalea laughed, the sound like dark velvet. "The basement creature is called Byron, and he's in his winter hibernation. Perseus, who you're about to meet, is my son." She pushed open the doors to reveal what I supposed passed for a drawing room in a medieval castle – though it was less drawing room and more small grand hall. Ancient tapestries lined the walls, and a massive fireplace dominated one end. The furniture was both antique and modern – plush velvet sofas alongside sleek glass side tables.

A man stood by the fireplace, his back to us as he examined what appeared to be an ancient sword mounted above the mantel. At our entrance, he turned, and I found myself face to face with another extraordinarily handsome man. Dark hair perfectly styled, striking grey eyes that seemed to catch the firelight, and dashing features befitting of a luxury watch advertisement.

**Attractive vampire count: increasing. Self-consciousness level: through the Gothic roof. Likelihood of embarrassing myself in front of yet another impossibly elegant immortal: approximately 100%.**

"You must be Gillian," he said, crossing the room with grace. His voice was deep and melodic, carrying just a hint of an accent I couldn't place. "Perseus Burk. A pleasure to meet you."

He took my hand and, in a gesture that would have seemed absurdly formal from anyone else, raised it briefly to his lips.

"Nice to meet you," I managed, acutely aware of my borrowed clothes and generally dishevelled state. "Sorry in advance for anything I might accidentally destroy in your vicinity. My vampire grace is still in beta testing."

Perseus smiled, revealing perfect teeth. "Azalea mentioned your remarkable strength. It's a positive sign – indicates potential."

"Perseus runs a legal practice," Azalea explained with evident pride.

"A law firm? For vampires?" I couldn't keep the surprise from my voice.

Perseus chuckled, the sound rich and warm. "We provide specialised legal services for the supernatural community."

He gestured to a nearby sofa. "Please, sit. Azalea mentioned you were a lawyer before your transformation."

I settled onto the velvet, trying to look like sitting in a medieval castle discussing vampire legal practices was perfectly normal. "Corporate law, yes. Nothing exciting – just contracts and mergers mostly."

Perseus sat opposite me, his movements fluid yet controlled. "Contract law is the foundation of civilisation – human and vampire alike. Agreements, boundaries, consequences for violations... these are the frameworks that prevent chaos."

His grey eyes studied me with interest. "And in our world, contracts carry particularly binding weight. Breaking an agreement can have... significant consequences."

"Your world," I corrected. "Not mine. I'm totally out of my depth here."

"Fair enough," Perseus conceded with a slight incline of his head. "Though you might find integration easier with work to do." He reached into an inner pocket of his impeccably tailored suit and produced a business card. The embossed text caught the firelight: "Clifford and Burk."

"I've reviewed your career history and I'm impressed at your track record. I'm offering you a position at my firm," he stated simply.

I blinked in surprise. "A job? Why would you offer me a job? I know nothing about this world. I'm still breaking priceless antiques just by existing in their general vicinity."

My fingers twisted nervously in my lap. The familiar sensation of being underqualified, of waiting to be exposed as a fraud, washed over me – the same feeling I'd had throughout my legal career, amplified a thousandfold in this strange new world.

**Imposter syndrome: transcends mortality. Current career prospects: potentially supernatural. Likelihood of corporate law experience preparing me for vampire litigation: dubious.**

"Precisely why you're valuable," Perseus countered. "You bring a fresh perspective, extensive mundane legal experience, and —" he glanced briefly at Azalea " – certain... qualities that suggest adapt-ability."

Azalea's smile widened. "She shattered a sixteenth-century vase this morning and didn't even flinch. Such promising composure."

Great. My vampire superpower was apparently breaking things with minimal emotional reaction. Clearly a very marketable skill.

"What exactly does a vampire law firm do?" I asked, trying to regain some professional footing. "Is there a specific section of legal code dealing with bloodsucking and immortality that I missed in law school?"

Perseus smiled, clearly amused by my question. "We handle everything from negotiating territory disputes between covens to creating legal identities for immortals who need to 'die' and be 'reborn' periodically. Property transfers that span centuries, media-tion between magical beings, ensuring our kind remains hidden from human scrutiny."

"And where is this firm?" I asked, already imagining some Gothic cathedral converted into law offices. "The basement of Westminster Abbey? An abandoned castle like this one?"

"You'll be stationed in our Burkenswood office," he said. "We also have premises in New York, Tokyo, and a small branch in Myrtlewood. Our London office is in Canary Wharf," Perseus added with a smile. "Fifty-third floor of the Obsidian Tower. UV-protected glass, of course."

I couldn't help but laugh. "Vampires in Canary Wharf? Among the bankers and financiers?"

"Where better to blend in?" Perseus's eyes twinkled with amuse-ment. "Both groups work late nights, dress in expensive suits, and are frequently accused of sucking the lifeblood from their victims."

"The perfect camouflage," Azalea added, her voice rich with appreciation. "Predators hiding among predators."

Despite everything, I found myself smiling. "Fair point."

Perseus leaned forward, his expression growing more serious.

"The point is, Gillian, we have plenty of work to keep you occupied while you adjust to your new existence. Meaningful work, challenging work." His voice softened slightly. "And work that might eventually help you reconnect with your children."

Hope flared in my chest. "How?"

"Control is everything for our kind," Perseus explained. "The more structure and purpose you have, the faster you'll adapt, the sooner you can safely interact with those you love."

"I need something to do," I admitted. "Mulling about a castle spying on my children and demolishing priceless artefacts is all well and good, but..." I trailed off, thinking of the restless energy that filled my body, the clarity of my mind that now seemed wasted on mere existence.

"Precisely my point," Perseus nodded. "Idleness is the enemy of adaptation."

"And you're clearly not suited for collecting antiques," Azalea added.

A job. Structure. Purpose. Something to fill the endless nights while I learned to control the hunger that surged whenever I got too close to my children.

"When would I start?" I asked.

"Once Azalea confirms you're ready," Perseus replied. "Your control is impressive for a new turn, but we can't have you lunging for the jugular of the mail clerk." His tone was light, but his eyes were serious. "Speaking of training," Perseus said, glancing at his watch, "I believe I've taken up enough of your evening. Azalea mentioned you have your first control session tonight."

"I do?"

He rose gracefully, extending his hand. "I look forward to welcoming you to the firm, Gillian."

I shook his hand, surprised by how normal the gesture felt despite the surreal conversation. "Thank you for the opportunity. I'll try not to destroy too much of your office furniture."

As Perseus turned to leave, a thought struck me. "Wait – how did you know I'm a lawyer?" I asked Azalea. "How do you know anything about me at all? I haven't even told you my full name."

"We make it our business to know about new arrivals in our community," Perseus said smoothly. "Particularly those who appear under... unusual circumstances."

With a final nod, he exited, leaving me alone with Azalea and a growing list of questions.

"Control session?" I asked, latching onto the most immediate concern. "Please tell me that doesn't involve power tools or exorcism."

"Nothing so primitive," Azalea replied, her eyes lighting with excitement. "Training to help you manage your hunger and newfound abilities. Meditation techniques, sensory exercises, methods to channel your energy. The first steps toward mastering your darkness." She actually clasped her hands together in anticipation. "Such a thrilling journey ahead!"

I followed her from the drawing room, my mind racing with questions about Perseus, the law firm, and the mysterious circumstances of my transformation.

"This is all moving very fast," I said as we walked down yet another stone corridor. I narrowly avoided decapitating a bust of some stern-looking historical figure on a pedestal. "Only days ago I was arguing with Neville about the Henderson contracts, and now I'm being recruited for vampire legal services."

Azalea's pace never faltered, her black gown trailing dramatically behind her. "Immortality is paradoxical that way. You have endless time, yet you must adapt quickly. The night waits for no one, my dear."

We reached a simple wooden door that seemed out of place among the castle's more ornate entrances. Azalea paused, her eyes alight with anticipation.

"Are you ready to begin?" she asked.

I thought of the children in the garden, of the hunger I fought to control, of Perseus's offer and the possibility of eventually reclaiming some semblance of a life for myself.

"Yes," I said. What other choice did I have?

**Current status: Vampire. Apparently soon-to-be supernatural lawyer. And desperately hoping that hunger management training isn't as awkward as it sounds. Or as bloody.**

# CHAPTER 3

# MINDFULNESS AND MURDER URGES

**B**lood cravings: severe. Self-control: questionable. Embarrassment level: stratospheric. Vampiric dignity: non-existent. Propensity for destroying furniture: still concerning.

The chamber was a far cry from my expectations. No coffins. No spooky candelabras. Not even a token bat. Just an austere circular room with dark blue walls, a few scattered cushions, and a fireplace emitting light dim enough to be kind to my sensitive eyes but bright enough to see that my borrowed black trousers had somehow collected a constellation of lint despite being worn approximately once.

I tugged nervously at the sleeve of my antique blouse, accidentally ripping the cuff. Perfect. Now I'd be learning vampire meditation while shredding my borrowed wardrobe due to vampire strength. Perhaps nudist vampire colonies existed for those of us who couldn't touch fabric without destroying it.

"Welcome to the Meditation Chamber," Azalea announced as she glided into the room behind me, making even the simple act of walking look like a couture runway show. "So many exquisite transformations have occurred within these walls. So many delicious awakenings."

She turned to me, her dark eyes bright with anticipation. "Learning to control the hunger is the foundation of everything else, my dear. A most intoxicating journey. Without mastery over your bloodlust, you are a danger to yourself and others – particularly those you love." Her voice caressed the word "danger" with disturbing relish.

The image of Keyne and Merryn flickered in my mind, sending a pang through my chest. I straightened my spine. "I'm ready."

"Such determination!" Azalea clasped her hands together. "We shall see how it withstands the first true test." Her smile was both encouraging and terrifying.

"Sit," she commanded, gesturing to a cushion in the centre of the room.

I sat, crossing my legs in what I hoped was a dignified manner but probably looked more like an ungainly pretzel. Despite my new supernatural grace, sitting cross-legged on the floor had never been my forte. Even as a vampire, some things apparently don't change. The cushion compressed with an alarming sound as I settled my weight, and I felt a distinct rip in the fabric beneath me.

"Sorry," I muttered. "Add 'sitting' to the list of mundane activities that now require vampire strength control."

"Destruction is merely transformation viewed from a different angle," Azalea replied with a philosophical wave. "Now, to begin. The first principle of hunger management is recognition."

Azalea began circling me slowly, her black dress trailing behind her like a shadow given form. "You must become intimately familiar with your hunger before you can control it. You must embrace it, dance with it, seduce it into submission."

"I'm already quite familiar with it, thanks," I muttered. "The constant burning in my throat isn't exactly subtle. It's like having strep throat and standing downwind from a bonfire."

"You are merely aware of it," Azalea corrected, her voice rich with amusement. "But you have not truly faced it yet. You've been given regulated amounts of blood in controlled settings. Today, we test your limits. Isn't that thrilling?" Her eyes gleamed with anticipation.

She glided to a mahogany table, opened a cabinet on the side and lifted a tiny crystal goblet. The liquid inside was deep crimson, and the smell that made my fangs extend involuntarily – the scent of iron and ecstasy suddenly filled the room.

"Fresh blood," she announced with obvious relish. "Just a small amount. Your task is simple – resist drinking it for as long as possible."

My throat burned at the very thought. "That seems like torture."

"The most exquisite education often is," Azalea agreed, returning to stand before me. She held the goblet at eye level, maybe two feet away. "Remember – wanting and taking are different things. You may crave, but you must choose."

The hunger slammed into me. Every instinct screamed at me to lunge forward, to tear the goblet from her hands and drain every drop. My hands trembled as I gripped the shredded cushion beneath me.

"I can't," I gasped, already reaching toward the goblet. "I need –"

"Resist," Azalea commanded, though her voice held excitement rather than disappointment. "Count the seconds. Make each one a victory."

I fought against every fibre of my being, my entire existence narrowing to that small goblet and the liquid salvation it contained. Ten seconds. Twenty. My vision was turning red at the edges, my control fragmenting.

"Stay with yourself," Azalea said, softly yet firmly. "Stay centred. Your success in control all depends on your ability to withstand the discomfort of the hunger.

I groaned and tried to do as she said.

"Please," I whispered, my hand extending despite my efforts to keep it still.

At thirty-seven seconds, I broke. I lunged forward, snatching the goblet from Azalea's hands and draining it in one desperate gulp. The blood hit my system like electricity, immediately easing the burning in my throat, but shame flooded through me just as quickly.

"I'm sorry," I said, clutching the empty goblet. "I lasted barely half a minute. I'm hopeless at this."

"Hopeless?" Azalea's eyes were sparkling with genuine delight. "My dear Gillian, you lasted nearly forty seconds! Most new turns wouldn't manage three seconds in your current state of hunger. That was absolutely magnificent!"

I blinked at her. "Really?"

"Really." She produced another goblet. "The hunger you're experiencing right now is quite severe – you haven't fed properly in hours. For a week-old vampire to resist for that long... it's remarkable. Shall we try again?"

The hunger within me growled. The tiny goblet of blood had only whet my appetite, and now I was ravenous.

The second attempt, I managed fifty-one seconds, despite my aching hunger. The third, just over a minute. Each time, Azalea grew more animated with excitement, encouraging me more and more to open up to the pain of my hunger, to embrace it, to feel it so that it did not control me. She did this all the while checking an old pocket watch and making delighted observations about my "extraordinary control" and "unprecedented resistance."

By the fifth goblet, I was lasting nearly two minutes, though each second felt like an eternity of pure torment.

"And once more," Azalea said, producing what I hoped would be the final goblet. "I want to see if you can reach three minutes. That would be truly exceptional."

This time, I focused on breathing – unnecessary for vampires but somehow grounding – and on Azalea's encouraging commentary. "Two minutes... two minutes thirty... such beautiful control!"

After what felt like eternity, I finally broke, grabbing the goblet with shaking hands.

"Magnificent!" Azalea clapped her hands together. "Three minutes of resistance! You're ready for the next phase."

She glided to the door and opened it with a dramatic flourish. "Jenkins. Enter."

The extremely old-fashioned butler I'd glimpsed around the castle appeared in the doorway, his posture rigid and formal. As he stepped into the room, I was struck by several sensations at once: the rhythmic pounding of his heart, the rush of blood through his veins, the scent of life that emanated from him in waves.

My mouth filled with saliva. My gums ached as my fangs extended involuntarily. My muscles coiled, ready to spring.

"Control it," Azalea's voice cut through the red haze descending over my vision. "Observe the hunger, but do not become it. Such a beautiful struggle, isn't it?"

Easy for her to say. She probably hadn't felt proper hunger in centuries, just an elegant aristocratic craving. I gripped the cushion beneath me, feeling the fabric tear completely under my fingernails. Jenkins remained by the doorway, a good six meters away, his face a mask of professional detachment, but I could smell his fear – a sharp tang that somehow made him even more appealing. Like adding salt to caramel.

"He's terrified," I whispered, my voice strained.

"Of course he is," Azalea replied, her voice carrying a note of delighted appreciation. "He's prey in a room with predators. Such exquisite vulnerability! But Jenkins has served the Burk family for decades. He understands his role in the grand dance of predator and prey."

The butler stood perfectly still, but his pulse quickened. The sound filled my ears like a drum, drowning out everything else.

"Focus on your breathing," Azalea instructed, circling behind me like a shark in couture. "Though you no longer need oxygen, the rhythm can centre you. In through the nose, out through the mouth. Feel the air fill spaces that hunger would otherwise occupy."

I tried to comply, but the hunger was overwhelming – a living thing clawing at my insides, demanding satisfaction. Every cell in my body screamed at me to let go, preparing to launch myself across the room and sink my teeth into Jenkins' neck. I could almost taste his blood already. The cushion beneath me was now completely shredded, stuffing scattered across the floor like snow.

"Now, focus on something else about him," Azalea continued, her voice cutting through the hunger with hypnotic precision. "Not his blood or heartbeat. Something mundane. The pattern of his waistcoat. The shine on his shoes."

With tremendous effort, I dragged my gaze from Jenkins' throat to his shoes – polished black leather reflecting the dim light. I counted the eyelets on his shoes. One, two, three, four...

"Good," Azalea murmured, circling closer. "Now find something human about him. A detail that reminds you he is not merely food, but a creature with his own existence. His own precious story."

I forced my eyes upward, past the temptation of pulsing veins to Jenkins' face. I noticed a small scar above his left eyebrow. The slight asymmetry of his features. The wedding band on his finger, worn thin with age.

"He has a family," I managed to say, the words scraping past my parched throat.

"Yes," Azalea confirmed, her voice softening with genuine fondness. "A wife, Eleanor. Three grown children – Thomas, Sarah, and Michael. Seven grandchildren, one of whom – little Abigail – recently won a mathematics competition at her school. Jenkins was radiating pride for days. It was quite touching."

The information didn't eliminate the hunger, but it created distance – a thin barrier between instinct and action. I could still hear Jenkins' heartbeat, still smell his blood, but he was becoming a person again, not just prey.

**10:52 PM. Hunger level: apocalyptic. Not-eating-the-butler success rate: holding steady at 100% (somehow). Damage to meditation cushion: total.**

My fingers were now digging into the floor beneath the cushion's remains, creating small indentations in the stone. Every muscle trembled with the effort of remaining seated.

"That's enough for today," Azalea said suddenly, gesturing for Jenkins to leave. "A magnificent first encounter, Jenkins. Thank you for your service to the education of our newest family member."

*Family member?*

The butler bowed slightly. "Always a pleasure to be of assistance, madam." His voice betrayed only the slightest tremor.

As the door closed behind him, I collapsed forward, trembling violently, my body still screaming for what had been denied it. I had created a small crater in the stone floor with my fingernails.

"Remarkable," Azalea murmured, studying me with undisguised delight. "Truly remarkable! Such control, such presence of mind." She circled me, dark eyes gleaming. "And the way you channelled your physical response into the floor rather than poor Jenkins. Inspired!"

I looked up, surprised by the note of genuine admiration in her voice, not to mention her enthusiasm about what was essentially property damage.

"Most new turns cannot even remain in the same room as a human without attacking," Azalea explained, her hands dancing expressively as she spoke. "They become feral, uncontrollable. Even with the human at a safe distance. Yet you maintained your composure with such delicious intensity."

"I wanted to tear his throat out and drain every last drop," I admitted, still shaking. "I still do. I've destroyed an antique cushion and damaged your medieval flooring in the process."

"Of course you did," Azalea said with a dismissive wave. "That hunger never goes away entirely. It becomes a companion, a whisper in the dark rather than a scream. But wanting and doing are different things." She bent down, tracing a finger along the gouges I'd left in the stone. "As for the floor, this castle has witnessed far more dramatic renovations, I assure you. Charles went through an entire architectural phase in the 1700s. Dreadful business."

"So I passed the test?" I asked, still fighting the burning in my throat.

"Everything is a test," Azalea replied, her smile widening. "Everything is an education. But you've passed this first one impressively. Such promising potential!"

"First one..." I echoed weakly.

"Tomorrow, Jenkins will stand slightly closer," she explained, her eyes bright with anticipation. "The day after, closer still. Eventually, you'll need to touch him without attacking. A most intimate waltz of control and desire." She actually sighed with pleasure at the thought.

Baby steps. Right. Because learning not to eat people should be taken gradually. Like nuclear disarmament or quitting sugar.

"Your first day at Perseus's firm is tomorrow night," Azalea said, rising gracefully from her chair in a fluid motion that made the silk of her dress shimmer like liquid. "I understand no regular mortals will be present, but expect the unexpected when it comes to the magical world. I suggest you rest and process what you've learned. Shadow work can be... taxing, even for vampires."

"Shadow work?"

"Yes, facing your hunger involves facing your darkness, your pain... it's understandable that you're tired. Such delicious exhaustion, though."

I nodded, suddenly aware of a strange fatigue settling over me – not physical exhaustion, but something deeper, as if parts of me, long dormant, had been awakened and were now demanding attention.

"One last question," I said as Azalea moved toward the door. "Why are you helping me? Really?"

"My daughter has always had a weakness for strays," Dora's ancient yet childlike voice cut in. She stepped out of the shadows, pigtails perfectly still. "I enjoyed your performance. You show promise, though I don't imagine you'll survive for long. The advancement of your powers surely will come at a cost."

Azalea tutted. "Now Maman, leave the poor girl alone. Don't let her bother you, Gillian. I recognise potential when I see it. You're not like most new turns. There's something... different about you." Her dark eyes gleamed with genuine interest. "Such a fascinating combination of vulnerability and strength. I haven't been this intrigued by a fledgling in centuries."

Her dark eyes seemed to pierce through my very being. "And in our world, difference is either a death sentence or a path to power. I'm curious to see which yours will be."

With that ominous statement, she swept from the room, her dress trailing behind her like a living shadow. Dora waited a moment longer before melting away too, leaving me alone with my thoughts and the newfound awareness of my own internal darkness.

I sat for a long while, staring into the fire, trying to process everything I'd learned. Not just hunger management but my own personal transformation and the existence of an entirely parallel supernatural society with its own rules and dangers. And somewhere in the castle, Tilly was probably trying to explain to my children why Mummy couldn't tuck them in at night anymore.

**11:27 PM. Training session complete. Self-control: better than expected. Actual self-assessment: marginally less terrified of accidentally eating children. Destruction of property: significant but apparently acceptable.**

A soft knock at my door eventually roused me from my thoughts. Charles entered, wearing a pink polo shirt, his hair styled in a faux hawk, a look befitting a preppy music video rather than an ancient castle. He was carrying a crystal goblet on a tray. The scent of blood hit me immediately, making my fangs extend involuntarily.

"Azalea mentioned you might need this after today's session," he said, placing the tray on a side table.

"Thank you," I managed, trying not to look too eager or accidentally shatter the crystal with my strength.

"She also mentioned you did exceptionally well in your first control session," he added, a note of approval in his voice. "That's rare for one so newly turned. Though the cushion was rather beyond saving."

"Sorry about the furniture casualties," I said with genuine remorse. "And the floor. At least Jenkins escaped unscathed."

"The castle has withstood far worse," Charles assured me with a smile. "In the 1700s, we hosted a particularly rowdy gathering of Transylvanian nobles. Three wings required complete renovation. Azalea still laments that I got carried away."

"I'm still not entirely sure what's happening to me," I admitted. "It all sounds rather..."

"Fantastical?" Charles supplied with a warm smile. "Indeed. The blood part is straightforward enough, but the metaphysical aspects take time to accept. Azalea tends to describe things with more... poetic flourish than some might find helpful at first."

"She does have a flair for the dramatic," I agreed, feeling an unexpected surge of fondness for Azalea's gothic enthusiasm.

"How long have you been a vampire?" I asked, curiosity temporarily overriding my hunger.

"Too many centuries to count," he replied casually, as if discussing a few years rather than a span of time that encompassed more than the entirety of modern history. "It can take decades to adjust. Even now I'm still learning."

"Great," I muttered. "So I'll be a danger to my children for the rest of their lives?"

"Not necessarily," Charles said gently. "Everyone progresses at their own pace."

He moved toward the door. "Get some rest, Gillian. You've done well. Tomorrow night you begin at Perseus's firm, and you'll need your wits about you. Vampire legal practice can be... intense."

After he left, I reached for the goblet of blood, the scent making my head swim with anticipation. As I raised it to my lips, I couldn't help but think how bizarre my life had become.

**Current status: Vampire. Almost-lawyer at supernatural law**

firm. Ravenously hungry but not actually eating people. What a
week.

# CHAPTER 4

# CORPORATE GOTH IS THE NEW BLACK

**8:42 PM. Outfit changes: 7. Suitable attire for vampire workplace: unclear. Blood consumption before leaving: moderate but apparently insufficient. Existential dread: persistent but manageable.**

The sleek black car purred through the night, its headlights cutting through the mist like those dramatic beams they use at film premieres. I sat in the backseat trying desperately not to fidget with my outfit – an elegant black pantsuit (extra strong weave) Azalea had provided after she'd surveyed my wardrobe (collected from my home by Jenkins) with the kind of disdain usually reserved for people who wear socks with sandals.

"This should suffice for your first day," she'd said, which clearly translated to "everything else you own is an abomination and should be burned immediately, possibly in a ritual sacrifice to the gods of style."

I felt more attuned to my hunger, more aware of its presence without being entirely controlled by it.

I could smell the driver's blood – that was unavoidable – but the overwhelming compulsion to feed had diminished from "MUST

CONSUME IMMEDIATELY" to more of a "that smells quite nice, actually" level of interest. Like noticing someone wearing an appealing perfume without feeling the need to tackle them to the ground and lick their neck.

Progress? I'll take it. Though I wondered if I should have had a second goblet before leaving.

"How much farther?" I asked, smoothing down the pantsuit for the seventeenth time. The fabric felt impossibly light against my sensitised skin, yet somehow managed to make me look like I belonged in a boardroom rather than a coffin.

"Nearly there, madam," the driver replied, his heartbeat steady despite having a predator in his backseat. Either he was remarkably brave or remarkably stupid.

I sighed. "You'd think the Burk castle would be closer to Burkenswood..." I'd asked if there was a connection in the name, but Azalea had been vague about the historical details. It struck me how odd it was to be living in an ancient mansion in the middle of nowhere with a family of vampires, and yet it had already become a kind of haven for me, somehow.

The trees thickened around us, ancient oaks and elms forming a canopy that blocked out the night sky. Perfect serial killer territory. Or, I suppose, vampire territory, which was now... my territory? A disturbing thought.

The road narrowed, curved sharply, then opened into suburban Burkenswood. I'd always considered it to be a dull city, but apparently it was crawling with supernatural activity this whole time. We neared the inner city and the car began to slow. I surveyed the large elegant stone and marble building.

Clearly vampires do well financially. Probably all those centuries of compound interest. That and the whole "can't die of old age" thing really helps with long-term investments.

A discreet sign at the entrance read "Clifford and Burk" in elegant, understated lettering.

"It's beautiful," I murmured, mentally comparing it to the dreary grey offices of Bennett & Smith Legal where I'd spent the last decade of my human life being systematically undermined.

"Right on time," Perseus remarked approvingly as the driver opened my door. "Punctuality is a virtue even immortals should cultivate."

I stepped out of the car, concentrating intensely on not tripping over my own feet or accidentally crushing the stone steps with my still-unpredictable strength.

"You survived your first session with Mother, I see," Perseus commented, his grey eyes bright with amusement. "And in remark-ably good condition."

"It was... educational," I replied diplomatically, while thinking, *Your mother is terrifying and made me confront the fact that I apparently have murderous rage buried deep in my psyche, but sure, let's go with 'educational.'*

Perseus laughed, the sound rich and appealing. "A diplomatic answer. You'll do well here." He turned toward the entrance. "Shall we? Your new colleagues are eager to meet you."

Colleagues. Right. Because this was a job. A real job that I was supposedly qualified for despite knowing absolutely nothing about vampire law or any other supernatural legal matters. Imposter syndrome had reached unprecedented levels.

I followed him through glass doors that slid open at their approach. The reception area beyond was a study in understated elegance – polished stone floors, modern furniture in muted tones, subtle lighting. I instinctively placed my hands in my pockets to avoid touching anything breakable, which at this point seemed to be everything.

"Good evening, Mr. Burk," the receptionist said with professional warmth. "The midnight briefing is set up in the main conference room."

"Thank you, Elaine," Perseus replied. "This is Ms. Spark, our newest associate."

Elaine smiled at me. "Welcome to Clifford and Burk. Your

credentials and security access have been processed. Everything should be ready for you.”

I nodded, wondering what “credentials” could possibly have been arranged for me. I hadn’t exactly submitted a CV listing “Recently Deceased” and “Dangerously Craves Human Blood” under special skills.

**9:45 PM. Office tour commenced. Chance of embarrassing self: approximately 94%.**

Perseus led me into a corridor lined with frosted glass. We passed several offices where vampires worked at desks or held quiet conversations. I could tell they were vampires – not just by lack of heartbeat, but by the subtle quality of movement, the uncanny stillness that no human could match.

They all looked impossibly elegant and poised. I, meanwhile, was hyperaware of the run in my tights I’d discovered in the car and had been strategically positioning my legs to hide.

“Our main practice areas are divided by speciality,” Perseus continued, gesturing to different sections as we walked. “Inheritance and Identity Management, Territory and Treaty Law, Inter-Species Mediation, and Shadow Regulation and Compliance.”

“Shadow Regulation?” I recalled Azalea’s words about confronting our inner shadows.

“Indeed,” Perseus nodded but did not elaborate.

We reached a large open workspace where several people were gathered around a holographic display showing what appeared to be a map overlaid with glowing points of various colours.

“This is our analysis hub,” Perseus explained. “I’ll introduce you to some of your new colleagues.”

The group looked up as we approached. I immediately sensed that most were vampires, though with interesting variations in their presence – some felt older, deeper, their stillness more profound, while others had an energy that seemed almost human.

“Everyone, this is Gillian Spark, our newest associate,” Perseus announced. “Gillian, meet the team.”

A tall stunning Black woman with close-cropped silver hair stepped forward first. "Imani Okafor," she introduced herself, her accent carrying hints of multiple continents. "Head of Territory and Treaty Law. I've been with the firm since 1892."

Since 1892. Casual reference to being over a century old. Totally normal workplace conversation.

Next came a pair of identical looking twins, despite being male and female, with copper-red hair and matching charcoal suits. "Alexei and Anastasia Petrov," they said in perfect unison, which was possibly the creepiest thing I'd experienced since becoming a vampire.

They continued to stare at me with identical expressions, neither blinking nor smiling. Right. Clearly they're the office weirdos. Every workplace has them.

A young-looking man with dark hair and a friendly smile offered his hand. "Daniel Kim. Identity Management. Only been a vampire since 1975, so I'm practically the baby around here."

Only since 1975. Only nearly fifty years as a vampire. Just a newborn, really.

I shook each hand, noting the cool texture of vampire skin against my own, the subtle differences in their energies. The firm suddenly felt more real, less abstract – these would be my colleagues, my water-cooler community in this new existence.

"And where will I be working?" I asked Perseus, trying to sound professional and not utterly terrified.

"Initially, you'll rotate through departments to get a feel for our practice areas," he explained. "But given your background in contract law, I suspect you'll eventually settle in either Shadow Regulation or Inter-Species Mediation. Both rely heavily on precise contractual language."

Inter-Species Mediation. Because apparently, I'd be mediating disputes between vampires and... what? Werewolves? Zombies? The Easter Bunny? At this point, nothing would surprise me.

A commotion near the doorway drew our attention. The door

flung open and a new scent hit me – something human yet not human, pulsing with life and power. Something that smelled like... prey.

Before I could process what was happening, my body reacted. The hunger surged without warning, flooding my system like molten metal, burning away rational thought. My fangs extended fully, and a snarl escaped my throat as I whirled toward the source.

A woman stood in the doorway with purple streaked hair matching her outfit – her heart beating strong and steady, her blood calling to me with an intensity I'd never experienced before. I didn't decide to attack; I simply moved, crossing the room in a blur of speed, all thoughts of professional first impressions obliterated by pure, primal hunger.

"Whoa there, fresh meat!" the woman exclaimed, not with fear but with commanding authority, as my face lunged toward her throat.

My teeth were inches from her skin when I hit an invisible barrier – and then my mouth filled with the most revolting taste imaginable. Like biting into a bar of soap infused with industrial cleaning solution and garnished with potpourri. I recoiled violently, gagging, as my senses returned in a rush of humiliation.

"Protective charm," the woman explained calmly, straightening her perfectly tailored purple pin-striped suit. She raised an eyebrow at Perseus. "You didn't warn her about non-vampire staff? Bad form, Perse."

The rest of the room had frozen. Daniel looked shocked, Imani disapproving, and the Petrov twins were watching with identical expressions of clinical interest. Perseus moved swiftly to my side, placing a restraining hand on my shoulder.

"I apologize profusely," I gasped, mortified beyond words, desperately trying to spit out the lingering taste of magical soap. "I don't – I didn't – that's never happened before –"

"I'm Juniper," the woman introduced herself with remarkable composure for someone who'd nearly been vampire lunch. Her eyes

– an impossible shade of violet – assessed me with keen intelligence. "I'm a magical contractor."

There was something about her presence – a crackling, focused energy – that felt entirely different from the vampires around us.

"The enchantment will wear off in about ten seconds," she added matter-of-factly. "Try not to lunge at me again. The second taste is worse than the first."

"I'm so sorry," I repeated, feeling like I might actually die from embarrassment, which would be quite a feat considering I was already dead.

Juniper waved away my apology. "I've seen it enough times. New turns often react strongly to magical blood." She glanced at Perseus. "Which is why senior staff should warn them."

"An oversight on my part," Perseus acknowledged with a slight bow of his head.

The rest of the office was studiously returning to their tasks, pretending they hadn't just witnessed the new associate try to devour a colleague. Office politics apparently transcend mortality.

"Your aura's fascinating," Juniper continued, studying me with unabashed interest now that the immediate threat had passed. "Not standard vampire at all. Much more chaotic energy pattern. You're either going to implode spectacularly or become something remarkable." Her tone suggested either outcome would be equally interesting to her.

I stood perfectly still, the soap taste finally fading from my mouth, feeling rather like a specimen being examined under a microscope. Also, what exactly is a "standard vampire signature"? Is mine defective? Do I have the vampire equivalent of a factory second?

"Juniper," Perseus warned. "Professional boundaries."

"Says the man who just let his new recruit try to eat me," Juniper retorted with a roll of her eyes. "Relax, Perse. I'm simply making observations relevant to workplace safety." She turned back to me, her expression softening slightly. "No harm done. Protective charms are standard practice for non-vampires in this office. Though perhaps some additional hunger management training might be in order."

I wanted to sink through the floor. "I... wasn't expecting..."

"A magically-enhanced being with particularly appetizing blood?" Juniper finished for me. "Yeah, I get that a lot. It's the magical resonance – makes my blood sing to your kind. Like ringing the dinner bell for a particular predator class." She shrugged. "I'd be offended if you *didn't* try to eat me, honestly. It would suggest I'm losing my touch."

Despite my mortification, I found myself appreciating her direct approach. There was something refreshing about her complete lack of either fear or judgment – just practical acknowledgment of the situation.

"Now, if we could prepare for the midnight briefing –" Perseus began, but was interrupted by a chiming sound emanating from one of Juniper's many rings.

The mage glanced down, her expression shifting from sardonic to serious in an instant. "Excuse me, emergency call." She raised a finger. "One moment."

Before anyone could respond, Juniper closed her eyes, muttered something under her breath, and simply... disappeared. Not with a dramatic puff of smoke or flash of light, but a subtle folding of space, as if reality had briefly bent around her absence.

I blinked in shock, accidentally catching Daniel's eye. "Did she just –"

"Spatial translocation," Perseus explained calmly, as if disappearing colleagues were a routine occurrence. "Juniper's speciality. She'll be back momentarily."

The casual acceptance of such blatant impossibility was perhaps the most surreal aspect of my new reality. In my previous life, a person vanishing into thin air would have been cause for panic, therapy, or at minimum, a strongly worded email to HR.

**10:33 PM. Office crisis: developing. Professional contribution**

**so far: attempted to eat new colleague. Feeling of complete inadequacy: overwhelming.**

True to Perseus's prediction, Juniper reappeared minutes later in exactly the same spot, though her expression had darkened considerably.

"Perseus, we have a situation," she said without preamble, all traces of sarcasm gone from her voice. "The Twilight Concordat is missing from the Witching archives in London."

The effect of these words on the room was immediate and dramatic. The Petrov twins exchanged alarmed glances. Imani Okafor muttered something that sounded like a curse in a language I didn't recognise. Daniel Kim's friendly expression transformed into one of tense concern.

I, meanwhile, stood there trying to look appropriately concerned while having absolutely no idea what a Concordat was or why its absence was cause for alarm. Like being the only person in a meeting who hasn't read the brief but is desperately trying to look informed. Also, I was still fighting the residual embarrassment of having just tried to eat the messenger.

Perseus's reaction was more controlled, but I noticed his posture stiffen slightly. "Confirmed missing, or potentially misplaced?"

"Confirmed," Juniper replied grimly. "The containment ward was breached approximately twenty minutes ago. The magical signature is... complicated. Multiple practitioners involved."

"This is serious," Perseus said, his voice low. "The Concordat is connected with the original magic that sealed the covenant between witches and vampires. Its loss could have... significant implications."

"What kind of implications?" I asked, immediately regretting drawing attention back to myself after the lunge-and-gag debacle.

"The kind that rewrite centuries of peace between species," Imani answered gravely.

Ah. Those kinds of implications. Just a total breakdown of supernatural diplomatic relations. No pressure for my first day.

Perseus raised a hand for silence. "This is now our top priority.

Imani, activate the contingency protocols. Petrovs, I need a full surveillance sweep."

They dispersed immediately, moving with the focused efficiency of a team accustomed to crises. I stood awkwardly in the middle of the room, utterly useless and increasingly aware that I had no idea what I was supposed to be doing.

"What exactly is the Concordat?" I finally asked, feeling completely out of my depth.

Perseus and Juniper exchanged a look that I couldn't quite interpret but clearly contained volumes of unspoken communication.

"That," Perseus said finally, "is an excellent question for your first assignment."

My stomach dropped. "My first assignment?" I squeaked, the words coming out higher than intended. "Perseus, I just tried to eat someone. Five minutes ago. I don't think I'm ready for actual responsibility involving ancient magical artefacts and diplomatic crises. I don't even understand why a law firm would be involving themselves in –"

Juniper put her hand on my shoulder. "It's okay, Gillian," she said calmly. "Things tend to be a lot more blurry in the magical world. The Concordat is a treaty, a contract between witches and vampires."

"Can't they just... make another copy?" I asked.

Perseus gave me a look that suggested I'd asked if we could just print more money.

"I'm a firm believer in learning on the job," Perseus replied calmly, seemingly unbothered by my obvious panic. "Most of our colleagues here have been vampires for decades, if not centuries. The age gap alone makes them... challenging to work with for someone in your position. They tend to forget what it's like to be new to our world." His eyes flicked meaningfully toward where Imani was efficiently organising crisis protocols with the kind of brisk authority that spoke of extensive experience. "Juniper, on the other hand, has worked with newly turned vampires before. She's remarkably patient with the learning curve."

He turned to Juniper. "Consider your contract extended with a full focus on the Concordat. Whatever it takes. Gather everything we have on the artefact's provenance and the ward breach."

Juniper nodded. "I'll need to go back to the archive for a proper assessment. Their magical forensics is medieval, and I mean that literally. I'll just have to wait for their investigators to clear out," she turned to me. "Lovely to meet you baby vamp"

"Err, you too," I said. "And... I really am sorry about, you know..."

"Trying to make me your appetizer?" Juniper shrugged. "Trust me, I've had worse first meetings. Last month a selkie tried to steal my skin thinking it was a coat. Now *that* was awkward."

**Current status: Vampire lawyer disaster. Knowledge of current crisis: almost zero. Children: still desperately missed. Outfit: rapidly more dishevelled by the minute. Taste of magical soap: lingering unpleasantly.**

# CHAPTER 5

# SURPRISE! YOU'RE A BEAUTIFUL NIGHTMARE

**T**ime unknown. Consciousness: returning. Dream state: confusing. Reality check: pending.

Warmth on my face. A distant clock ticking somewhere in endless hallways.

*The kitchen shifted, walls bleeding into shadow, and suddenly she was there. Formidable presence. Dark hair flowing like liquid midnight, framing a face of terrible beauty. Her eyes blazed violet. Each step making reality fracture around her like broken glass. "You think you understand power?"*

*Clara...*

*The word floated through my mind, with no purchase, no apologies, just expanding to occupy all the space it wanted to.*

*It wrapped around me like a blanket.*

*Clara...*

*Her name? Who was she?*

*Something about her presence was both infinitely comforting and deeply terrifying, yet I felt soothed, connected...finally like I belong.*

*I floated in that delicious space between sleep and wakefulness, my mind fuzzy with fragments of the most absurd dream. Vampires. A castle.*

*Magic. Blood therapy. A supernatural law firm with creepy twins who spoke in unison and a purple-haired mage who disappeared into thin air.*

I smiled, eyes still closed, savouring the ridiculous details my subconscious had conjured. Neville would have scoffed at such fantastical nonsense. "Grow up, Gillian," he'd have said, that familiar edge of contempt in his voice that made me feel approximately seven years old and caught playing dress-up with his ties.

The dream lingered, vivid and textured. The copper-penny taste of blood on my tongue. The terrifying hunger I'd felt standing over my children's beds.

Quite the psychodrama my sleeping mind had crafted. No doubt symbolic – the hunger for blood representing my suppressed rage at Neville, the newfound strength a manifestation of my desire for power in our divorce proceedings... being unable to see my children reflecting my fears about custody arrangements.

My therapist would have a field day.

I stretched, expecting the familiar resistance of my modest IKEA mattress. Instead, my limbs slid across cool fabric that felt impossibly smooth against my skin, like water made solid. My fingers extended into emptiness where a mattress edge should be.

**Disorientation level: extreme.**

My eyes snapped open.

Colour and texture assaulted my heightened senses. Burgundy silk hangings suspended from an ornately carved canopy. Stone walls the colour of thunderclouds. Tapestries depicting hunting scenes with colours so vivid they seemed to throb. A fireplace large enough to roast an ox, embers pulsing with dying light.

Not a dream.

"Oh blast," I whispered, the words scraping my unexpectedly dry throat.

In one fluid motion, I sat upright – faster than intention, my body responding before my brain had fully formed the command to move. The room spun briefly, details blurring then snapping into hyper-focus. I could see the minute cracks in the ancient mortar between stones, detect the nearly invisible path of a spider making its way along the ceiling beams.

The spider had quite possibly the most complex and fascinating web structure I'd ever seen. I could now understand how it had anchored each supporting thread, how it —

Focus, Gillian. This is not the time to become an arachnid enthusiast.

The scent of dust, old stone, beeswax, and something else — something metallic and organic that stirred a gnawing emptiness inside me.

It was all real. The attack in the street. Waking up changed. Azalea and her terrifying elegance. The Burk family. Perseus and the law firm. The missing Concordat.

I was a vampire.

I had finally slept for the first time since becoming a vampire. That chamomile blood Azalea had offered me after my return from work must have worked.

I pressed a hand to my chest, searching for the familiar rhythm that had accompanied every moment of my life. Nothing. The absence of my heartbeat was a void, a fundamental wrongness that made my stomach lurch. Yet my mind raced with perfect clarity, unhampered by the grogginess that normally clouded my morning thoughts.

No heartbeat, yet still capable of stomach lurching. Vampire physiology is confusing.

But apart from a slight lethargy and a dull pressure behind my eyes when I looked toward the light, I felt surprisingly... alive.

For certain values of "alive" that include being technically dead.

A buzzing sound cut through my thoughts. On the bedside table, my phone vibrated against polished wood, the screen illuminating with "Mum".

**Maternal crisis imminent. Explanation prepared: none. Excuses available: limited and unconvincing.**

The sight of my mother's calling sent a surge of panic through my body. Several missed calls. What could I possibly tell her? The truth was unthinkable. Lies felt impossible to construct.

What was I supposed to say? Hi Mum, sorry I missed your calls. Been busy being dead. How's the play going?

The phone fell silent, then immediately began vibrating again.

Before I could decide what to do, a sharp knock rattled the heavy oak door – three precise raps that my enhanced hearing separated into distinct sound waves, each with its own pattern. The door swung open without waiting for my response.

Jenkins entered bearing a silver tray. His heartbeat was steady and controlled, though a faint tang of fear emanated from him like cologne.

Poor Jenkins. Bringing breakfast to the vampire lady who nearly ate him. He deserves hazard pay.

Behind him came Azalea, her movements liquid and powerful. Her dark hair was pulled back in a severe knot that emphasised her sharp cheekbones and penetrating gaze.

Compared to her, I probably looked like I'd been dragged through a hedge backward. A hedge in the underworld. Even as a vampire, I was a hot mess.

"Good afternoon," Azalea said. "I trust you slept well after your first night at the firm?"

The question seemed absurdly mundane, as if I had simply started a new job rather than entered an entirely different plane of existence.

"I... yes," I managed, the sound of my own altered voice still startling me. "I thought for a moment when I woke up that it had all been a dream."

A hint of amusement crossed Azalea's perfect features. "A common experience among new turns. The mind tries to protect itself from radical change."

Jenkins placed the tray on a table by the window, his movements efficient and practiced.

I stared at the tray in confusion. The arrangement looked like a perfectly normal breakfast – two poached eggs nestled on golden-brown toast, and a steaming cup of tea in a porcelain cup so fine I could see the light through it. But the aroma... beneath the familiar scents of toast and tea lay something else. Something that made my canines elongate and my throat burn with sudden, urgent thirst.

"I don't understand," I said, approaching the tray cautiously, as if it might bite me rather than the reverse. "I thought vampires couldn't eat food."

"This is your first experience of blood-enchanted food," Azalea explained, gliding over to the window. With elegant precision, she drew back the heavy curtains. Sunlight flooded the room through the UV protected glass.

"It's better to try it in the morning," Azalea continued, "get your body warmed up to it."

"Blood-enchanted food?" I repeated, moving closer to the tray.

As I approached, the scent intensified – toast and tea on the surface, but beneath that, a rich coppery aroma that made my mouth flood with saliva. My hunger rose up, a need rather than a want.

"Oh yes," Azalea said with a dismissive wave of her perfectly manicured hand. "It's how we feed these days. Real blood is considered somewhat taboo. Not always, of course. There's the dawn of blood which is approved by the council that you've been having. It can be used for transformations and adapting, but generally, this is how we eat."

I picked up a fork, the silver cool against my fingers. Silver doesn't harm vampires either? How many myths had Hollywood gotten wrong? The weight of it, the balance, the pattern etched into the handle – all registered with newfound clarity. I prodded one of the eggs experimentally. The yolk broke, releasing a stream of yellow liquid that looked entirely normal but smelled... wrong. Or rather, right in a way that scrambled my senses. It wasn't just food anymore. It was sustenance.

"How is it enchanted?" I asked, fork poised above the plate.

"This is part of the covenant between witches and vampires,"

Azalea explained, watching my reaction with clinical interest. "They use their magic for us so that we don't have to eat them... and the other humans."

Her casual reference to eating humans made me wince internally. Not exactly a comforting thought as I contemplated my magical breakfast.

"How does it work?" I pressed, still hesitant to take the first bite.

"Have you heard of the Shadow Covenant?" Azalea asked, seating herself in a nearby chair. "We feed on shadows. Dark matter created within the human psyche, negotiating paradox. All of the stuff, all of the things that humans cannot bear to face about themselves become shadow matter, and witches draw on this to enchant the food."

"The relationship between blood and shadow is fundamental," Azalea explained, pouring blood-tea with practiced elegance. "What Jung called the 'shadow self' in humans – their repressed impulses, their darker nature, their unacknowledged fears – that energy exists in their blood, though they rarely perceive it."

I considered this, watching the steam rise from my cup. "So vampires feed on... psychological darkness in the blood?"

"Precisely." Azalea looked pleased with my quick understanding. "Before the Concordat sealed the Covenant, vampires fed directly on the shadows within human blood. The more psychologically complex the human – often those society deemed 'evil' or troubled – the more nourishing their blood. We were drawn to darkness like moths to flame."

"That sounds..." I hesitated, searching for the right word.

"Intoxicating?" Azalea supplied. "It was. The rush of absorbing shadow cannot be overstated. Fears. Repressed desires. Humanity's darkest impulses – all becoming part of you." Her eyes took on a faraway look of nostalgia. "The more troubled the soul, the more exquisite the feeding."

I shivered involuntarily. "And that's why vampires went too far? Because it was addictive?"

"Addictive and escalating," Azalea confirmed. "The line between feeding and influencing became blurred. Some vampires began cultivating darkness in their prey, creating traumatic experiences to enrich the shadow content." Her voice carried no judgment, only historical observation.

"That's horrifying," I said quietly.

"It was unsustainable," Azalea said, simply. "The witches recognised that vampires were disrupting the natural balance of shadow in the collective unconscious. Too much shadow being consumed too quickly, while simultaneously generating more darkness through violence. A destructive cycle."

She took a delicate sip of her blood-tea. "The Concordat changed everything. Instead of each vampire feeding individually on shadows within blood, witches developed enchantment processes to draw from the collective shadow – the accumulated darkness of humanity's psyche – and infuse it into food and drink. More efficient, more controlled, and far less disruptive to the psychological ecosystem."

"So the blood enchantment is basically... redirecting the shadow energy?" I asked, trying to understand.

"Harvesting and redistributing," Azalea clarified. "The magic gathers excess shadow energy – the overflow of humanity's collective darkness – and channels it into food that satisfies our needs without direct predation. Quite elegant, really. It's why we have to hire a kitchen witch here at the castle."

I looked down at the food with new understanding.

I took a tentative bite. The texture was initially jarring – solid food when every cell in my body craved liquid. My transformed palate rebelled momentarily, sending conflicting signals of disgust and desire. But as I chewed, the food seemed to transform, dissolving into a more liquid essence that slid down my throat with satisfaction.

"Try the tea," Azalea suggested, a hint of amusement in her voice.

I lifted the delicate cup. The liquid inside looked like Earl Grey, amber and fragrant with bergamot, but as it touched my lips, the flavour exploded across my tongue. Not tea at all, but something rich and complex, with metallic undernotes and a strange sweetness that seemed to bypass my taste buds entirely and head straight for the pleasure centres of my brain.

Hunger clawed through me with sudden ferocity. I found myself devouring the remainder of the meal with embarrassing speed, barely pausing between bites, the fork moving faster than I could consciously control.

I'm eating like a starved animal in front of Azalea, who might as well be the vampire equivalent of the Queen for all I know. What happened to all those table manners my mother drilled into me?

The experience was both disturbing and exhilarating – my body taking over, animal need superseding human manners. I finished, momentarily mortified, then oddly energised. Warmth spread through my limbs, chasing away the lethargy that had clung to me since waking.

"There, you see?" Azalea said with satisfaction. "I wanted to make sure you were fed before you saw the morning papers."

"The papers?" I asked, wiping my mouth with a linen napkin that felt impossibly soft against my skin.

Azalea retrieved a folded newspaper from under her arm and handed it to me. The Times. The paper felt different in my hands now – I could detect the individual fibres, smell the ink that had dried just hours ago.

And there, splashed across the entertainment section, was a headline that made me gasp: "THEATER DIRECTOR SETS HUSBAND'S CLOTHES ABLAZE AFTER FINAL BOW"

Beneath it was a photograph of Delia Spark – my mother – looking magnificent and slightly unhinged, standing beside a smouldering pile of clothing on the stage.

"I see your mother is quite the story," Azalea remarked, the subtle shifts in her scent suggesting amusement.

"Gosh," I murmured, scanning the article. The words jumped out from the page with new clarity, each letter crisp and defined. "She's finally done it. She's finally left my deadbeat father."

A laugh bubbled up from somewhere deep inside me, surprising in its genuine mirth. "And what a way to do it."

"You sound proud," Azalea observed, a grin playing at the corners of her mouth.

"I think I am," I admitted, surprised by the warmth spreading through my chest. The sensation was different now – emotions seemed to manifest physically in new ways, bypassing my silent heart to radiate directly through me.

Was it wrong to feel a flicker of envy that my mother had made such a spectacular exit from her marriage? My own departure had been so careful, so measured, paperwork and practicalities. I hadn't told anyone at first. The humiliation had been too much to bear.

Typical Gillian, quietly divorcing while Mum literally sets fire to her marriage on a public stage. We certainly have different approaches to life changes.

**Maternal communication challenge: imminent. Excuses prepared: none. Probability of awkward conversation: 100%.**

"I really need to call her back. I was just thinking this morning, how am I going to explain any of this to her?"

My finger hovered over the phone, tracing the smooth glass surface without pressing down. The device felt fragile beneath my strengthened fingers, as if I might shatter it with careless pressure. What could I possibly say? By the way, Mum, I've been turned into a vampire and I'm living in a castle while working for a supernatural law firm. Oh, and I can't see my children because I might drain them of blood. Cheers!

"Tread lightly, if I were you," Azalea advised, as if reading my thoughts. "People don't always respond well to discovering their relatives are undead. You can imagine."

The scent of Azalea shifted subtly – something darker underneath the perfection, a hint of old sorrow or perhaps regret. It vanished so quickly I wondered if I'd imagined it.

"How do I tread lightly?" I asked, setting down the phone before I could accidentally crush it. "I suppose I can tell her I've gotten another job and I'm moving. Oh, she'll hate that. The children won't be so close by."

The children…how I wish I could see them, myself, but apparently not yet.

"You'll figure it out," Azalea said, rising to her feet in one fluid motion. The air currents in the room shifted around her, carrying complex information my new senses couldn't fully interpret yet. "Just say what you have to, not too much detail. All of that will come out in time. It sounds to me like your mother is on her own adventurous journey."

"You could say that," I agreed, scanning through the rest of the article. The paper rustled like thunderous waves against my sensitive ears. It didn't reveal much more than what the headline suggested – a theatrical exit from both the stage and her marriage.

"I'll give her a call later on when I've got my head on straight," I decided, setting aside the newspaper. My mother's drama would have to wait. "First, it's time for work."

"Indeed," Azalea nodded approvingly. "Perseus expects you at the office at sundown. He's arranged for your first assignment related to the missing Concordat."

The mention of the artefact sent an unexpected thrill through my transformed body. The mystery, the importance, the sense of purpose it provided – it all appealed to something new in my nature, something that craved more than the mundane challenges of my previous existence.

As I rose to prepare for my second night at Clifford and Burk, I caught my reflection in a mirror across the room. My appearance startled me anew. Sharper cheekbones. Brighter eyes – the green more intense, with subtle gold flecks that hadn't been visible before. My strawberry blonde hair gleamed with a more coppery tone. My skin had a luminous quality that no cosmetic could achieve. I hardly recognised myself.

Good Lord. I look like I've had the world's most expensive makeover like Charles had said. Like one of those dramatic reality TV transformations where they ambush frumpy mothers and turn them into glamorous strangers.

But beneath the supernatural enhancements, it was still me. Gillian Spark. Mother. Lawyer. And now, vampire.

As I turned away from my reflection, I felt a strange mix of emotions, each one sharper and more distinct than I'd ever experienced as a human. Overwhelmed by the supernatural world I'd been thrust into. Confused by the complex relationships and magical systems I was only beginning to understand. Worried about my children and how to explain my new circumstances to my mother.

But beneath all that, something else stirred – a thrill that vibrated through my body like electricity. I had indeed stumbled through a looking glass into another world, just as I'd always secretly fantasised about when reading stories to Merryn and Keyne. And as I'd often thought during those bedtime readings, if I ever did find myself in another realm, I wouldn't waste my time trying to get back to boring old reality.

My job as a corporate barrister focused on contracts and mergers had been tedious, but this–learning vampire laws, navigating supernatural politics – this was anything but boring.

And everyone I cared about was still in this world. I just needed to find a way back to them that wouldn't put them in danger.

I straightened my shoulders, feeling the new strength in my transformed body. I had work to do.

**Current status: Vampire mother. Lawyer at supernatural firm. Daughter of theatrical arsonist. Hair looking inexplicably perfect.**

# CHAPTER 6

# CONFIDENTIALITY AND MATERNAL DECEPTION

**6:15 PM. Missed calls from mother: 4. Excuses prepared: 0. Supernatural cover stories: desperately needed. Likelihood of successfully lying to woman who gave birth to me: minimal.**

The office was its usual efficient chaos and I'd barely started work when I pulled out my phone, the screen showing multiple missed calls from "Mum." Guilt twisted in my stomach. With everything happening, I'd completely neglected to contact her. How could I possibly explain any of this?

I'd been dreading the conversation.

I stared at my phone for a long moment, gathering my courage. Finally, I hit the call button.

The phone rang several times before my mother's voice answered, sounding both relieved and wary. "Gilly?"

"Mum, I'm so sorry," I said, suddenly overwhelmed with guilt at how I'd been avoiding her.

"What's going on, love?" she asked, concern evident in her tone.

I froze, mind racing. What could I possibly say? 'Sorry Mum, I've been transformed into an illegal vampire, and oh by the way, congratulations on your dramatic divorce announcement'?

"I can't really explain…" I finally managed. "I mean…"

I glanced down at a pamphlet Perseus had kindly given me: "Explaining Your Transformation to Mortal Loved Ones." The first recommendation: Create a plausible cover story that explains your sudden lifestyle changes without revealing your undead status.

"I've just been offered an excellent promotion, and I'm moving with the kids," I improvised, cringing at how forced it sounded.

"Moving out of London?" The horror in my mother's voice was evident, as if I'd suggested relocating to the surface of Mars.

"Yes, that's right," I confirmed, mentally scrambling for details. "It's an unexpected job offer. I think I was headhunted." The irony wasn't lost on me.

"That sounds nice, dear, but do you really have to move? I mean, what legal partnership worth their salt isn't in London?"

I bit back a hysterical laugh. If only she knew my "legal partnership" specialised in supernatural contract law and was staffed almost entirely by vampires and other magical beings.

"It's rather an old establishment," I replied, which was certainly true – Clifford and Burk had apparently existed in some form since the 1600s. "Well-regarded. And I'm moving to Burkenswood."

"Over towards Cornwall?" she asked, clear judgment in her voice.

"It was just too good to refuse," I said, wondering how many more lies I'd need to stack on top of this initial one.

"And you're taking the kids, but not Neville?" my mother asked, a note of hope in her voice. She'd never been particularly fond of my ex-husband.

"Neville and I are taking a break," I lied. I hadn't told her about the divorce yet, wanting to wait until it was finalised before hearing "I told you so" but now didn't seem to be a great time to reveal I'd been hiding this from her too. There was already too much to explain away.

"Oh, love," she replied sympathetically. "How are Merryn and Keyne coping with all this change?" she asked, her voice softening at the mention of her grandchildren.

My heart clenched painfully. My children, who I wasn't even allowed to see until I mastered my bloodlust. Who had no idea their mother had been transformed into a predatory creature of the night.

"Surprisingly well," I said, forcing warmth into my voice to cover the pain.

"Why don't you come over, and I'll make you a cup of tea?" my mother offered.

I pictured myself struggling to control my newfound hunger while she prattled on about her latest theatrical exploits (and apparently, arsonist tendencies), completely unaware that her daughter was fighting the urge to feed on the neighbours.

"In your tiny flat?" I asked, trying to deflect with humour. "Do you even have room for me in there, let alone the kids?"

"I'm sorry about my inadequate accommodations," she replied with a touch of sarcasm. "How about I come over to your place instead?"

Panic surged through me. My place was currently empty, with Azalea having arranged for my mail to be forwarded to the castle. If my mother showed up there, the entire facade would crumble instantly.

"Oh no, that would be impossible. I...I've already started packing, and it's chaos here." The lies were piling up, each one making me feel worse than the last.

My mother sighed, the sound achingly familiar. "What's really going on, love?"

For a moment, I was tempted to tell her everything – about the transformation, the hunger, the shadow powers. But the risks were too great, for both of us.

"I just need some time alone," I said finally, hating how it sounded but seeing no alternative. "I'll call you later, Mum."

I ended the call before she could respond, guilt washing over me in waves. I flipped to the next page of the pamphlet: "Family Ties: Maintaining Connections Across the Mortal-Immortal Divide."

The headline about my mother's dramatic stage exit lingered in my mind. There was something oddly symbolic about it, a ritual cleansing by fire to mark her new beginning. And here I was, undergoing my own transformation, shedding my human life for something... other.

For the first time since my turning, I felt a strange sense of kinship with my dramatic, theatrical mother. We were both, in our own ways, burning down the structures that had confined us.

**7:42 PM. Hours spent reading ancient documents: 3. Paper cuts: 0 (vampire skin apparently resistant). Comprehension level: minimal. Coffee consumed: 0 (apparently no longer necessary). Blood-tea consumed: 2 cups.**

Three hours into deciphering ancient magical legalese, and I'd developed a nervous tic. My office at Clifford and Burk smelled of leather-bound texts, enchanted ink, and the lingering cologne of its previous occupant – some vampire who apparently bathed in sandalwood and clove.

Even in death, some men overdo the cologne. Impressive, really.

"If I read the phrase 'hereinafter referred to as the immortal parties of the first part' one more time, I might stake myself," I muttered, massaging my temples.

The Concordat files were sprawled across my desk like victims of a paper massacre. Fragments of knowledge about the artefact swirled in my mind – it was ancient, it was powerful, it bound vampires and witches in a complex legal relationship that regulated everything from blood consumption to magical cooperation. But as for what it *actually* was? That crucial detail remained frustratingly elusive.

I picked up a document bearing the firm's letterhead, my eyes lingering on the elegant script: "Clifford and Burk." Something had been bothering me since day one.

"By the way," I said aloud to the empty room, "who exactly is Clifford?"

The door to my office burst open with such force that it slammed against the wall.

"That would be Percival Clifford, founding partner and the longest-napping vampire in Britain," Daniel announced, leaning against the doorframe.

"Napping?" I asked, momentarily distracted from the files.

"Oh yes!" Juniper said, pushing past Daniel and entering my office with a flourish.

The mage looked different today – still vibrant with that crackling energy, but more focused, her purple-streaked hair pulled back in a tight braid rather than its usual waves.

"The Big Sleep," Juniper clarified, stepping fully into the room. "Some vampires, particularly the ancient ones, occasionally enter a hibernation state. Clifford's been under since 1937. Started as a weekend retreat to 'gather his thoughts' and, well…" She shrugged. "His coffin occupies what used to be the executive washroom on the top floor."

"Is that… normal?" I asked.

"Normal enough," Daniel replied. "Perseus manages his affairs and maintains his partnership share. The office joke is that he'll wake up when the firm finally runs out of letterhead with his name on it."

Daniel looked at us for a moment as though he might have more to add, or perhaps he was waiting for a bigger laugh. When none came, he left.

Juniper slapped a folder onto my desk that sizzled slightly on contact. "But enough about sleeping beauty. I've got a lead on our missing artefact."

I leaned forward, instantly alert. "Tell me."

"I've been informed of precisely where the Concordat was stored." Juniper's eyes darted to the door before lowering her voice, "How do you feel about a little breaking-and-entering into the witching archives?"

"Pretty sure that's illegal on multiple counts," I replied automatically. Years of meticulously following legal procedure doesn't vanish overnight, even with vampirism.

"Only if we get caught." Juniper's grin was sharp, calculating. "The residual energy is already fading. By tomorrow, any magical signature will be gone, and with it our best chance of identifying what actually happened."

My new vampire instincts hummed with unexpected excitement. Six days ago, I would have politely declined any activity that skirted legality. Six days ago, I was also boring, exhausted, and utterly cowed by life. Now, the prospect of danger sent a thrill through my transformed body.

"Perseus would never approve," I said, already standing up.

"Perseus is in meetings with the Vampire High Council all evening," Juniper countered. "What he doesn't know won't hurt his perfectly styled hair."

"You're a terrible influence," I said, straightening my suit jacket and checking that I didn't have any embarrassing blood-tea stains down my front.

"That's why you keep me around," Juniper replied. "Now, I wonder if you'll have any delicate constitution issues with spatial translocation... people tend to find it disorienting the first time."

"I'll manage," I said, hoping my bravado wasn't transparent. I silently prayed this "spatial translocation" wasn't as bad as it sounded.

"Excellent!"

Before I could fully process this revelation, Juniper grabbed my hand. The mage's skin felt feverishly hot against my cool flesh, like touching a star that somehow didn't burn.

"Hold tight and don't scream," Juniper advised, her eyes gleaming with something between mischief and calculation.

"Wait, what —"

Reality shattered.

Colours inverted. Space folded like origami. My enhanced senses went haywire – smells became visible, sounds acquired texture, the ground turned inside out. My perfectly steady vampire balance meant nothing as my body existed in multiple places simultaneously.

Then, with a sound like the universe hiccupping, we rematerialised.

I doubled over, hand braced against a bookshelf that stretched impossibly upward. "You might have warned me it would feel like being run through a cosmic blender," I gasped.

"Everyone experiences it differently," Juniper replied with calculated nonchalance. "The last vampire I transported said it felt like being kissed by a thousand butterflies."

"That vampire was clearly deranged," I muttered, straightening up to take in our surroundings.

**8:14 PM. Location: impossibly magical library. Nausea level: extreme. Dignity: severely compromised.**

The witching archives defied mortal architecture. Bookshelves spiralled into infinity, their highest reaches disappearing into a void sprinkled with what looked suspiciously like actual stars. Books floated between shelves of their own accord, reshuffling themselves in some incomprehensible organisational system. The air tasted like knowledge – if knowledge had a flavour somewhere between cinnamon and electricity.

At the chamber's centre, a circle of glowing runes surrounded an empty pedestal. The marble floor around it was scorched with symbols that hurt my eyes to look at directly.

"Is that where –"

"Yep. The Concordat's former home sweet home," Juniper confirmed, already kneeling beside the runic circle. She pulled a crystal from her pocket that hummed audibly when extended toward the pedestal.

"Should I be concerned that we're not supposed to be here?" I whispered, the oppressive weight of the magical knowledge surrounding us making me feel like an intruder.

"Relax," Juniper waved dismissively. "I have clearance – a badge of honour earned through a particularly clever contract last year. The

Witches owed me after I got them out of that whole 'accidentally turning the Prime Minister's cat immortal' debacle."

"But I don't have clearance," I pointed out. "I'm a vampire."

Saying it aloud – the reality of my transformation crashed over me anew, metallic and cold. The words hit me like a wrecking ball. I'm a vampire. Not a lawyer working late. Not a mother who needed to get home to her children. A vampire.

**8:23 PM. Existential crisis: in progress. Location: extremely inconvenient.**

Juniper looked up from her examination, her expression softening slightly. "Having one of those moments, huh? The 'what the hell happened to my life' spiral?"

I nodded, leaning against a bookshelf that hummed in response to my touch. "This is my life now. Breaking into magical archives. Drinking blood-enchanted tea. Never holding my children without wondering if I'll –" I couldn't finish the sentence.

"Listen," Juniper said, abandoning her investigation to approach me. "I can't pretend to understand exactly what you're going through. But I've seen this before."

She touched my arm briefly. "It gets easier. Not because it changes, but because you do. You adapt. You find new purposes. New connections."

The unexpected compassion steadied me. "Thanks. Sorry for the existential crisis in the middle of our crime scene investigation."

"Please," Juniper's expression returned to its usual calculated sharpness. "What's a little breaking and entering without an existential breakdown? Now, put that vampire nose to work. See if you can detect anything unusual while I finish examining these runes."

Grateful for the distraction, I began circling the chamber, focusing on my enhanced senses. The Archives were a mess of magical impressions – books whispering their contents, artefacts humming with power, the residual energy of countless witches who had passed through over centuries.

But beneath the expected, something discordant caught my

attention. A scent that didn't belong amidst the parchment and power.

"Juniper," I called softly, following the anomalous smell to a section of shelving near the empty pedestal. "There's something strange here."

The scent grew stronger as I approached a particular shelf – earthy but artificial, like a laboratory attempt at replicating forest soil. Mixed with chemicals that made my nose wrinkle.

Juniper joined me, eyes narrowing as I pointed to a nearly invisible smudge on the ancient wood. "Is that... potting soil?"

She pulled out another crystal, this one green, which glowed brilliantly when held over the smudge. "This is hybrid magic – organic material enhanced with magical compounds."

"Is that significant?" I asked, leaning closer to examine the residue.

"It's a signature for the Consortium Virentia –" Juniper replied, her voice oddly flat.

"'The Consortium Virentia?' What kind of name is that?"

"The kind chosen by people who think roses should rule the world," Juniper replied dryly. "Botanical extremists with a serious case of species envy. They look at vampires and witches and think, 'You know what this magical ecosystem needs? More photosynthesis, less bloodsucking.'"

I snorted. "So they're environmental terrorists with a plant fetish?"

"That's... not entirely unfair, actually." Juniper's expression had turned thoughtful, almost suspicious. She examined the residue again. "It's almost too perfect, though."

"What do you mean?"

"I mean," Juniper said slowly, "that this evidence is very... convenient. The Consortium is secretive, methodical. They don't leave traces unless they want to." She looked up, meeting my eyes. "Either they're getting incredibly sloppy or someone's trying to plant evidence. Pun absolutely intended."

I groaned.

"Welcome to supernatural politics," Juniper replied dryly. "Where nothing is ever what it–"

She froze mid-sentence, head tilting slightly.

I heard it too – footsteps approaching, multiple sets, moving with purpose.

"Someone's coming," Juniper hissed, grabbing my arm. She pulled me toward a shadowed alcove between two towering bookshelves.

"Why don't you get us out of here?" I whispered, vampire instincts already calculating odds of fighting through multiple magical practitioners.

"I want to listen," Juniper murmured, her eyes gleaming with sudden inspiration. She pressed something cold and metallic into my palm. "Hold this. It's a muffling charm. They won't hear us if we stay perfectly still."

I clutched the small metal disk, which vibrated slightly against my skin. We pressed back against the bookshelf as the massive doors to the archive swung open.

Three figures entered – in formal robes embroidered with arcane symbols. Their voices carried clearly in the vast chamber, seemingly unaware of our presence.

" – insulting that they would even suggest it," one witch was saying, her voice tight with suppressed anger. "As if we would sabotage our own archives."

"The Vampire High Council has officially requested access for their investigator," replied the second witch, older and more measured in tone. "We can hardly refuse without looking guilty."

"Their investigator," the first witch spat the word. "You mean Clara Blackwood. That woman is ruthless. She'll twist everything to suit the vampires' narrative."

I felt Juniper stiffen beside me at the name.

*Clara...* that was the name from my dream. The woman with the dark hair and shockingly violet eyes. Could that be a coincidence?

"She arrives tomorrow night," the older witch said. "We need to prepare. The High Archivist is concerned that having a vampire investigator with her... particular methods... might reveal other matters we'd prefer remained private."

"This whole situation stinks of manipulation," the younger witch insisted. "The Concordat disappears? And now the vampire authorities are falling over themselves to investigate? They're playing us."

"First Elara vanishes, now this," the older witch said grimly. "The timing can't be coincidental."

Elara? I looked towards Juniper to see if she knew what they were talking about but the mage merely shrugged.

"Keep your voice down," cautioned the older witch. "These walls have ears."

One of the witches stepped into my line of sight – a man with a stern expression and practical robes, different from the elaborate garments of the other two. "The warding diagnostics are complete. No sign of forced entry."

*An inside job?* I could feel Juniper's mind working alongside mine, both of us processing this new information.

"See?" hissed the first witch. "This has vampire manipulation written all over it. They create a crisis, send in their pet investigator, and get special access to our archives."

"We don't know that," the older witch reminded her. "But we must be prepared for Blackwood's arrival. Secure all sensitive materials, review security protocols, and for the love of the ancient ones, make sure no one speaks to her without authorisation."

The three witches moved toward the empty pedestal, their voices dropping as they examined the scorched floor and glowing runes. After several minutes of discussion and magical probing that made the air vibrate with energy, they departed, the heavy doors closing behind them with an ominous thud.

Juniper and I remained frozen for several moments longer before I dared to whisper, "Who's Clara Blackwood?"

The name gave me chills.

"Chief Investigator for the Vampire High Council. This situation just got considerably more complicated – when Clara shows up, even thousand-year-old vampires suddenly remember urgent appointments elsewhere. She's got a reputation for being... thorough."

"Thorough?"

"The kind of thorough that makes innocent bystanders confess to crimes they didn't commit, just to make her stop staring at them."

Just as we were processing the new information, Juniper's phone buzzed with an incoming message. Her expression shifted as she read.

"Well, this is interesting," she murmured. "I asked the office group chat if anyone knew about a witch named Elara who might have disappeared from the archive with the Concordat. The Petrov twins just sent me some intel they've been tracking. Apparently our missing witch – Elara Ashwood – was in regular contact with the Helix Coven."

"Also on our suspect list?" I asked, brushing ancient dust from my knees.

"For sure," Juniper said with dark amusement. "Think of them as vampire abolitionists with pointy hats and an attitude problem. They've spent decades whining that the Concordat gives you lot too much power."

"Charming."

"Exactly. They'd have the magical ability to breach these wards, too." Juniper's expression darkened. "They are almost as diabolical as the Obscurum."

"The what now?"

"A secretive vampire group that believes we should return to the old ways. Pre-Concordat feeding practices, shadow dominance, the works. Most dismiss them as fringe extremists, but they've been gaining support lately, especially among vampires who chafe under the blood-drinking restrictions."

"So now we have the plant enthusiasts, the witch activists, vampire zealots...AND potentially the vampire or witch authorities themselves as suspects?" I whispered as we carefully examined the area around the pedestal. "Is there anyone in the supernatural world who DOESN'T want this artefact?"

"The Druids, definitely. Probably the fae," Juniper muttered, her attention focused on the scorch marks. "They tend to stay out of vampire-witch politics. Too messy for their taste."

"How comforting, there are fae...I suspect they aren't cute little garden fairies..." I replied.

Juniper laughed hysterically for a full minute. Then simply said, "no."

A sudden alarm split the air – a high, keening wail that made my sensitive ears feel like they were bleeding.

"Security breach detection," Juniper shouted over the noise. "They must have added new sensors since my last visit!"

"Can we escape now?" I yelled, clapping my hands over my ears.

"Have to!" Juniper grabbed my arm. "Hold on to your fangs!"

The universe collapsed around us once more, reality twisting inside out. This time, the sensation was even more violent – like being pushed through a sieve while reality fractured around us. We tumbled out of the translocation into Juniper's office, collapsing in an undignified heap on the floor.

"That," I gasped, my head spinning viciously, "was considerably worse than last time."

"Forcing through active wards," Juniper explained, looking uncharacteristically dishevelled. "Like driving through a concrete wall. Effective but rough."

I dragged myself into a sitting position, my vampire constitution already recovering from the spatial trauma. "So, what do we know?"

"We know that multiple parties are interested in this artefact and its power...and for all we know, any evidence found here could well be planted."

My head was already spinning, and this was a bit too much.

"We know that Clara Blackwood is coming to investigate," Juniper added. "Which has the witches extremely nervous."

"And there's tension with the vampire authorities getting involved," I added. "Which complicates things even further."

Juniper nodded, her expression thoughtful.

"Who would benefit from conflict between vampires and witches. Who gains from the Concordat's disappearance? Perhaps there are far too many interested parties."

Juniper smiled grimly. "And that, Counsellor, is why this case is so fascinating. Everyone has a motive, and everyone is pointing fingers at everyone else."

"Sounds like my divorce," I muttered

**Current status: Illegal investigator of supernatural conspiracy. Suspect list: growing exponentially. Personal status in vampire society: still extremely precarious. Children: still desperately missed.**

# CHAPTER 7
# HIGH STAKES SOCIETY

**7:42 PM. Vampire political education: imminent. Anxiety level: climbing steadily. Outfit: borrowed from Azalea's wardrobe and probably worth more than my former annual salary. Ability to navigate supernatural high society: untested and highly suspect.**

"Are you certain this is wise?" I asked Charles for the third time as our car glided through London's evening traffic. The dress Azalea had selected for me – a midnight blue creation that managed to be both elegant and slightly intimidating – felt like wearing someone else's skin.

"Wisdom is relative," Charles replied, adjusting his silver cufflinks with practiced precision. "But necessity is absolute. Your interest in the Concordat has not gone unnoticed, Gillian. Better to present you openly than have questions raised about your... enthusiasm."

The way he said it made my stomach clench. "Questions about my enthusiasm, or questions about me in general?"

Charles's expression grew carefully neutral – never a good sign in vampire politics, I was learning. "Some may question your origins tonight. If pressed directly, say nothing beyond acknowledging your recent turning."

"Why?" The word came out sharper than I'd intended. "What's wrong with my origins?"

"There are questions surrounding your turning," Charles said quietly, his centuries-old eyes reflecting the passing streetlights. "It is a rather... unorthodox situation. The less they know, the better. For now."

I felt that familiar chill of being out of my depth in supernatural politics. "Then why bring me into the hornets' nest at all? Wouldn't it be safer to keep me hidden away in the castle?"

"Hiding you would suggest we have something to conceal," Charles explained with the patience of someone accustomed to teaching political manoeuvring to newcomers. "Showing up like this – bringing you openly to Council proceedings – makes it appear as though you have nothing to hide."

"Even though we apparently do have something to hide," I pointed out.

Charles's smile was slight but genuine. "Especially because we do."

"I'm not sure about this," I admitted.

"Think of it as useful reconnaissance for your investigation, Gillian," Charles insisted. "If powerful vampires are involved in the missing Concordat, there may be clues."

"What do you know about the Obscurum Societalis?" I asked and Charles stiffened slightly. "Juniper mentioned them as potential suspects but says there are only vague rumours circulating about them.

"Vague indeed," said Charles. "Vampires tend to do secret societies very covertly, but they are not beyond bragging and, to let you in on a little secret, we are terrible over-actors. My advice is to be on the lookout for anyone who is either too pleased about the situation, or too outraged about it."

"Thanks," I said, smiling weakly. "That might actually be helpful."

The entrance to the vampire courts was not what I'd expected. Instead of a Gothic cathedral or Victorian mansion, Charles led me down a narrow alley in Holborn to what appeared to be a perfectly ordinary door marked "Private Members Club." Only when Charles placed his palm against a seemingly decorative brass plate did the illusion fall away, revealing stone steps descending into depths that predated London itself.

"Roman?" I guessed, running my fingers along walls carved from stone blocks that had probably been ancient when Shakespeare was born.

"Older," Charles corrected. "This complex dates to the earliest vampire settlements in what is now called Britain. We've been expanding downward for over two millennia."

The stairs seemed to descend forever, lit by torches that burned without producing smoke – vampire magic, I assumed. The air grew cooler as we went deeper, carrying scents of age and authority that made my newly sensitive nose twitch. Stone dust. Ancient wood. Something metallic that might have been old blood or might have been fear.

"How deep does this go?" I whispered, though there was no particular reason for quiet.

"Deep enough that the humans above never suspect," Charles replied. "And far enough that even vampire voices don't carry to the surface."

We emerged into a vast underground complex that took my breath away. Vaulted ceilings soared overhead, supported by columns that seemed to grow from the living rock. The architecture was a mixture of periods – Roman arches giving way to medieval stonework, which in turn yielded to more modern additions that somehow managed to complement rather than clash with the ancient foundations.

The corridors were lined with tapestries depicting scenes I didn't recognise – vampire history, presumably, full of figures in period dress engaged in activities that looked either ceremonial or violent. Possibly both.

"Stay close," Charles murmured as we walked. "And remember – observe everything, but comment on nothing. Tonight, you are a student, not a participant."

Other vampires moved through the corridors with us, all dressed in formal evening wear that made my borrowed gown seem almost casual by comparison. I caught fragments of conversation in languages I didn't recognise, gestures that spoke of centuries of diplomatic protocol.

"I feel like a pet being paraded around," I whispered.

"Better a treasured pet than a wild animal to be caged," Charles replied without breaking stride. "Trust me on this."

**8:34 PM. Location: The vampire equivalent of the Houses of Parliament, apparently. Intimidation factor: off the charts. Sense of belonging: non-existent.**

The main chamber was breathtaking and terrifying in equal measure. Built like an ancient amphitheatre, it curved downward in concentric rings of stone seating, all focused on a central floor. The ceiling disappeared into darkness overhead, giving the impression of infinite space.

Vampires filled the seating – hundreds of them, representing what Charles had explained was the International Council of Vampires. Their ages were impossible to guess from their appearances, but their bearing spoke of centuries or millennia of accumulated authority.

"The Mesopotamian delegation," Charles murmured, indicating a group of vampires whose formal wear incorporated elements I recognised from museum displays – intricate beadwork and metallic threads that caught the torchlight. "They're particularly displeased with recent events."

As if summoned by his words, one of the Mesopotamian

vampires rose to speak, his voice carrying clearly through the amphitheatre despite the lack of any visible amplification system.

"The Concordat should never have been entrusted to such a young civilisation," he declared, his accent placing the English language like an uncomfortable foreign garment. "Babylon understood the management of power when London was still a collection of mud huts beside a river."

A ripple of agreement ran through his section, while murmurs of protest rose from what I assumed were the British vampires.

"Easy to blame placement after the fact," came a crisp voice with a distinctly Oxford accent. "Perhaps if the ancient civilisations had shown more interest in active participation rather than nostalgic superiority, the situation would be different."

The Mesopotamian vampire's eyes flashed with genuine anger. "We who built the first temples, who codified the first laws, who established the frameworks that your 'modern' Council still uses – we understand responsibility better than children playing at governance."

"Children who have successfully maintained supernatural stability for centuries," the British vampire retorted. "While older powers retreated into isolation and historical grievances."

More voices joined the debate – French vampires defending European cooperation, what sounded like Chinese delegates questioning Western competence entirely, American vampires suggesting a complete restructuring of artefact custody protocols.

"This happens every time," Charles murmured in my ear. "Crisis brings out ancient grudges. They'll argue about whose civilisation is most qualified to handle responsibility while the actual crisis grows worse."

"And the witches?" someone called out.

"Ah yes," came a new voice, this one carrying the authority of extreme age. "Let us discuss the witch question."

A vampire who looked no older than thirty but moved with the careful precision of millennia took the central floor. "The evidence increasingly points to witch involvement in the Concordat's disappearance. Perhaps a pre-emptive strike designed to destabilize vampire-witch relations."

"Speculation," another voice called. "We have no proof of witch involvement."

"The witches gain leverage by creating crisis."

"Or," came a voice sharp enough to cut glass, "we have a situation complex enough that simple blame serves no one."

The chamber fell silent with startling abruptness, and something deep in my chest clenched tight. Every vampire head turned toward the entrance, but I was already leaning forward before I realised I was moving, drawn by something I couldn't name.

She descended the stone steps like she owned every inch of space around her, dark hair gleaming in the torchlight. She held herself – controlled but not rigid, elegant but strong.

This wasn't authority or intimidation. This was recognition. The power within me hummed – the way a flame recognises oxygen, the way metal recognises a magnet. The way she moved... the air itself seemed to bend around her presence...Her eyes violet, intense, scanning the assembly with the focused attention of a predator.

*What is happening to me?*

"Clara Blackwood," Charles murmured beside me, his voice carrying a note of... was that wariness? "Chief Investigator for the Council's Security Division."

Clara Blackwood. The name resonated through me like a bell.

*Clara...* It was her, the same sharp features, the same dark hair and violet eyes. The woman from my dream. *Impossible...* and yet, my new life now involved seven impossible things before breakfast, so was a psychic dream something so strange after super speed, super strength and super senses were all considered?

When she spoke, her voice flowed like mead, rich and intoxicating.

"Honoured Council members," she began, her words seeming to

caress the air between us. "I come before you tonight to present our current understanding of the Concordat situation."

I gripped the stone armrest of my seat, fighting an almost overwhelming urge to lean forward, to drink in every syllable. The rational part of my mind was screaming warnings, but the rest of me was drowning in the sound of her voice.

"Physical evidence from the Archives suggests sophisticated magical intervention," Clara continued, producing documents that somehow remained visible despite the distance and dim lighting. "The wards were bypassed rather than broken, indicating intimate knowledge of the security protocols."

*It's all I can do to stop myself climbing over these ancient bannisters to try to drink up her words.*

Charles put his hand on my arm and whispered. "It's normal to react in this way. You're in a room full of some of the most powerful vampires, and some of the most powerful are turning up their compulsion to full volume when we would normally turn it down, for practicality, or course."

I nodded. Normal. All this was normal. I relaxed slightly, continuing to drink in the investigator's words.

"Timing analysis indicates the theft occurred during a twelve-hour window when the Archive's primary guardian was attending meetings. It is understood that a witch is also missing, presumed to be connected, though it is unclear in what capacity. The coincidence is... notable."

She moved as she spoke, her gestures emphasising points with balletic precision. Every motion seemed designed to draw the eye, to command attention.

"The Helix Coven has been implicated by a pin with their insignia, found at the scene."

A gasp echoed around the room at the mention of the coven, but it was the other detail that caught my attention. A pin? This was news to me.

"However," Clara's tone sharpened, "the evidence pointing to specific perpetrators is curiously convenient. Too neat. Too obvious. This suggests either remarkable sloppiness from sophisticated thieves, or deliberate misdirection. As we know, there are also vested interests in the Concordat among our own kind."

Murmurs rippled through the assembly – agreement, disagreement, ancient vampires accustomed to seeing through political machinations.

"Our investigation continues," Clara concluded, "but I caution against premature conclusions. The truth of this matter is more complex than surface evidence suggests."

She finished her presentation and stood silent for a moment, scanning the amphitheatre. Looking for something. Looking for someone.

Then her gaze found mine.

The moment our eyes met, rage flashed across her features – rage powerful enough to bowl me over. I actually pressed back against my seat, gasping at the intensity of her fury.

But the expression was gone so quickly I might have imagined it.

"Fascinating as always, Investigator," came a voice that made every nerve ending in my body light up with warning signals wrapped in silk.

The woman who rose from the upper tiers moved like poetry written in violence – each step deliberate, each gesture containing centuries of practised lethality disguised as grace. Her platinum hair was woven with what looked like actual silver threads that caught the light and threw it back in patterns that hurt to follow. As she descended, I found myself holding my breath, not from fear exactly, but from the overwhelming sense that I was watching something magnificent and terrible unfold.

"Lady Odette Valencourt," Charles whispered, and the name itself seemed to carry weight, like speaking the true name of something that might turn its attention toward you if you weren't careful.

When she spoke again, her voice was like molten steel. "Whether we should be investigating the theft of our shackles, or celebrating their destruction."

The words hit the assembly like a discordant conductor to an orchestra. This woman was pure evil, clearly, but then again, I was in a sea of vampires. Were they all sort of evil? Was I?

As the debate concluded all I could think about was that moment where Clara Blackwood had looked at me – and the inexplicable rage that had followed it.

Clara Blackwood knew something about me. Something that made her furious.

And despite every instinct screaming that I should be terrified, all I wanted was to find out what.

As vampires began filtering from the amphitheatre in clusters of whispered conversation, it felt as if the shadows beneath my skin stirred restlessly. I turned to see Odette Valencourt approaching our section, and every instinct I possessed screamed contradictory warnings – run toward her, run away from her, but definitely *run*.

She moved through the dispersing crowd like a shark through a school of fish. Other vampires stepped aside without seeming to notice they were doing it, their conversations faltering as she passed. Charles went rigid beside me, his centuries of diplomatic training snapping into place like armour.

"Charles," she greeted, her voice carrying the same honeyed poison I'd heard from the amphitheatre floor. "How refreshing to see the Burk family taking such an... active interest in current events."

The way she said *active* made it sound like an accusation wrapped in silk.

"Lady Valencourt," Charles replied, his tone so carefully controlled it could have been carved from ice. "I trust you found tonight's proceedings... illuminating."

Her laugh was like crystal breaking – beautiful and sharp enough to draw blood. "Oh, Charles. Always the diplomat." Her gaze shifted to me, and I felt the full weight of centuries-old attention settling on my shoulders like a lead cloak. "And this must be your new protégée. The one everyone's whispering about."

I tried to extend my hand, but something in her expression made the gesture die halfway.

"Recently turned," she said, circling me. I fought the urge to turn with her, to keep those calculating eyes in sight. "A secret hidden in plain sight."

I flinched.

"Gillian is adapting remarkably well," Charles said, stepping slightly closer to me.

"Oh, I'm certain she is." Odette stopped directly in front of me, close enough that I could smell expensive perfume – spice and snow and apricots. "The question is: adapting to what, exactly?"

She leaned closer, and her voice dropped to a whisper that somehow carried more weight than her earlier pronouncement to the entire assembly. "Tell me, young one, when you feel the shadows calling to you – and I can see that you do – do you ever wonder why we've agreed to muzzle such magnificent potential?"

For a terrifying moment, I could see exactly what she was seeking – power without restraint, hunger without guilt, strength without apology.

"I –" I began, but Charles's hand on my arm cut me off.

"That's enough," he said, and there was steel beneath the diplomatic veneer now.

Odette's smile revealed just a hint of fang, and the sight sent an unexpected thrill through me that I immediately tried to suppress. "Is it, Charles? Because from where I stand, it seems we're just beginning to scratch the surface." She reached out as if to touch my face, and I found myself leaning toward her before catching myself. "The Concordat teaches us to be ashamed of our nature. To apologize for what we are. But you, my dear..." Her eyes glittered with dangerous approval. "You have the potential to be something extraordinary."

"Gillian," Charles said sharply, and I realised I'd taken a step toward her without meaning to.

Odette noticed too, and her smile widened. "The old ways, my dear. They're far more... satisfying than what you've been taught."

With that, she glided away, leaving behind the lingering scent of perfume and the uncomfortable feeling that I'd just been offered something both tempting and dangerous.

"She seems..." I struggled for words, my pulse still racing. "Intense."

"Lady Valencourt," Charles said grimly, "has been arguing for the abolition of the Concordat since before it was signed. She believes vampires should rule openly, without restraint or regulation." He turned to me, his ancient eyes serious. "She's never been wrong about the intoxicating nature of unconstrained power. That's what makes her so dangerous."

"But why the interest in me?"

"She wants to use you," Charles corrected. "Rumours have been circulating about you since your mysterious turning. They didn't come from us, but the word is, you're extremely powerful."

I shook my head. "That's ridiculous when you consider I'm about the least powerful one here. But how did anyone even know about me?"

His voice softened slightly. "That, indeed, is the question."

# CHAPTER 8

# DUE DILIGENCE AT THE FAE MARKET

8:15 PM. Emergency briefing: mandatory. Blood-tea consumption: second cup (dependency confirmed). Vampire professional look: barely attained.

The conference room at Clifford and Burk hummed with tension that I could taste in the air – metallic anxiety mixed with the lingering scent of magic from the building's old stones.

Perseus had called an emergency briefing but he hadn't arrived yet. Juniper sat quietly at the end of the table, scribbling notes.

"The witching community is in uproar," Imani said, her voice carrying the weight of centuries of diplomatic experience. "Several leaders have formally accused the Vampire High Council of orchestrating both the Concordat theft and Elara's disappearance."

I slipped into the seat beside Daniel, who looked haggard despite his vampire constitution. Dark circles under his eyes suggested he'd been working far too many hours.

"That's ridiculous," Daniel said, his voice tight with frustration. "Why would vampires kidnap a witch researcher?"

The Petrov twins sat across the table, their identical expressions tense with concern. "Political manipulation," Anastasia said grimly.

"Create a crisis, then position themselves as the solution," Alexei Petrov continued, his tone carrying unusual worry. "Classic destabilization tactics."

Perseus entered the conference room, his presence immediately commanding attention. "Daniel, brief everyone on what we know about Elara Ashwood. The political implications are escalating rapidly."

Daniel straightened, pulling out a file with the careful precision of someone who'd been preparing for this moment. "Elara Ashwood, twenty-four years old, originally from Brighton. Lost both parents to a magical accident when she was sixteen. She was taken in by Professor Thornfield at Cambridge," Daniel continued, his voice softening with genuine respect. "Brilliant student – youngest person ever admitted to the Archive's dimensional magic research program. But more than that..." He paused, looking up from the file. "Everyone who knew her describes the same thing: she was kind. The type who'd spend her weekends tutoring struggling first-years, who remembered everyone's birthdays, who brought soup to sick colleagues."

I felt my throat tighten with emotion. "Poor girl... and no one knows what happened to her?"

Daniel shook his head.

"I read about her in Magical You last month," Imani added quietly. "Her work on stabilising dimensional morphing was considered groundbreaking. The applications for infrastructure safety were enormous."

The Petrov twins exchanged one of their synchronised glances, their expressions darkening. "This makes her disappearance even more suspicious," Anastasia observed.

"Someone with her expertise and access to the archives," Alexei continued, "would be valuable to anyone wanting to steal something as complex as the Concordat."

Perseus nodded grimly.

"The witching community sees it as an attack," Imani said, her diplomatic training evident in her careful word choice. "Not just theft, but the targeting of their future."

I found myself thinking about Merryn and Keyne – about how I'd feel if someone had taken them not just from me, but from their entire future. Just thinking about it made me furious.

"The witches are demanding access to vampire investigations on the Concordat," Perseus replied. "Immediate release of all intelligence on magical artefact security. And if Elara isn't found within the week…" He paused. "They're threatening to withdraw from all cooperative treaties."

Daniel gasped. "The entire supernatural political structure would collapse."

"Exactly," Imani confirmed. "Centuries of careful diplomacy, gone. We'd be back to the territorial wars of the 1600s."

"Elara was part of the Helix Coven," the Petrov twins said in their creepy unison. "This is all a ploy for them to gain power."

I looked towards Juniper who had stayed silent the entire briefing, just observing.

"Is this her?" I asked picking up the photograph Daniel had left on the table. He nodded.

Elara Ashwood had the kind of genuine smile that suggested she laughed easily. Her red hair pulled back in a practical ponytail, her brown eyes gleamed behind horn rimmed glasses. She looked like everyone's friend. Someone who deserved to grow up and change the world with her brilliant mind. Why were the Petrovs so suspicious of her? Perhaps my gut instinct was wrong, but something told me she was a victim in all this. Daniel seemed to think so too.

I had a feeling she'd been taken. Used as a pawn in someone else's game. Perhaps whoever had done it was counting on the chaos her disappearance would cause – the fracturing alliances, the political turmoil, the growing suspicion between supernatural communities.

I'd spent hours staring at faded ink and archaic supernatural legalese. My law school professors never mentioned courses in "Magical Contract Enforcement Through the Centuries" or "Blood Oaths and Their Binding Properties."

My phone buzzed again. Three new messages.

*Priya: "Still 'under the weather'? What's with the radio silence. Are you actually dying or having a secret fling?"*

*Adrien: "Darling, if you're having some sort of breakdown, at least let us bring wine and inappropriate gossip."*

*Tilly: "The kids are OBSESSED with this place - Keyne keeps asking if he can live in a castle when he grows up, and Merryn has declared herself a princess. I'm having the time of my life – you know I've always fancied ancient architecture and there's sooo much to explore here. But YOU have some serious explaining to do when you're feeling better. What exactly is going on? Also, Jenkins makes the most incredible afternoon tea. Azalea is my new fashion icon but it's hard to believe any of this is real."*

I stared at the messages, my undead heart doing something that felt suspiciously like breaking. How could I possibly text them back? It had only been days since my life imploded, since I'd been turned into a creature of the night, since I'd become someone who couldn't safely be around my own children without supervision. Apparently, I was just mysteriously ill. To Tilly, this was an unexpected holiday.

If only they knew their sick friend was currently reading ancient texts about shadow regulation while fighting the urge to drink human blood.

"Ready for another interdimensional field trip?" Juniper's voice made me look up from my phone. She leaned against my office door-way, her eyes gleaming with purpose rather than her usual mischief.

I quickly pocketed my phone, pushing away the guilt and long-ing. "Actually, I was thinking – shouldn't we try talking to the Helix Coven directly? If they're being framed, they might know who's really behind this. And if they're not..." I shrugged. "Well, at least we'd know for certain."

Juniper's expression shifted to something between amusement

and horror. "That would be like walking into a hornet's nest while covered in honey and shouting insults about their queen. Even if they're innocent, they're not exactly fond of vampires at the moment."

"Fair point," I conceded. "So what did you have in mind?"

"I know someone who might actually have answers about the Concordat," Juniper replied, her expression unusually serious. "Someone who deals in artefacts rather than politics."

I sighed. "Another field trip? Shouldn't we leave the investigation to the professionals?"

"We are the professionals," Juniper insisted. "Besides, there's a chance that people within the authorities are involved. That's why Perseus wants us on the case. The more information, the better."

My mind flashed to Clara Blackwood and the presence she commanded in her tailored suit...those violet eyes. Could she part of the plot, pretending to investigate? Even the thought of her gave me shivers.

"Please tell me this field trip involves proper authorisation," I said, massaging my temples. Not because I had a headache – apparently vampires don't get those – but because some human gestures are hard to shake.

"Technically, yes. There's no authorisation needed here. Besides, Thaddeus Grimshaw owes me several favours," Juniper replied, her expression unusually serious. "He's the magical antiquities dealer in London, possibly Europe. If anyone knows the Concordat's history well enough to guess where it might be hidden, it's him."

I glanced at my watch – 11:17 PM. Normal people are sleeping or winding down for the night, perhaps watching late-night telly with a cup of tea. I'm preparing to visit an ancient magical antiques dealer. Well, at least this time it didn't sound illegal.

"And where exactly is this shop?"

"In theory? It's between a cafe and a mobile phone store on Denmark Street." Juniper's expression turned calculating. "Metaphysically? Between the eighteenth and nineteenth centuries with a dash of pocket dimension.”

Before I could protest, Juniper had grabbed my hand. The now-familiar sensation of reality collapsing around us hit with disorienting force. This time, colours inverted, space twisted inside out, and my enhanced senses went haywire – smells became visible, sounds acquired texture, the ground turned to liquid beneath my feet.

Then came the nauseating snap-back as we rematerialised in a narrow alleyway that definitely hadn't been there a moment ago.

“A little warning next time,” I gasped, steadying myself against the ancient brick that felt oddly warm beneath my palm. “Is it always going to feel like being put through a cosmic blender?”

“Everyone experiences it differently,” Juniper replied with a dismissive shrug. “My ex said it felt like diving into warm honey, but his mother was a selkie, so moisture references were kind of his thing.”

Of course. Part-selkie ex-boyfriend. Perfectly normal dating history.

I straightened my suit jacket and took in our surroundings. We stood before what appeared to be a shop wedged impossibly between two modern buildings. The storefront looked ancient – weathered wood, leaded glass windows cloudy with age, a sign bearing the name “Grimshaw's Arcane Antiquities” in faded gold lettering that seemed to shift when viewed from different angles.

“Does this place even exist in normal reality?” I asked.

“Only if you know how to look,” Juniper replied, her fingers tracing arcane patterns in the air. “Perception filters. Very old magic.”

One moment, the buildings appeared to touch; the next, the narrow shop revealed itself, impossibly wedged between worlds.

“Grimshaw's has occupied this space since 1692,” Juniper explained as she approached the door. “The city literally built around it, leaving it in a dimensional pocket. It's like magical squatter's rights – once an arcane establishment puts down roots, reality tends to accommodate."

Just days ago, this would have seemed utterly impossible. Now it's just Tuesday. Or whatever day it is – this nocturnal existence makes my internal calendar rather fuzzy.

The shop hit me like a sensory avalanche. Ancient wood, tarnished silver, preserved specimens – my vampire senses couldn't separate the layers of scent and magic that had accumulated over centuries. If the British Museum and a Victorian curiosity shop had a baby raised by wizards, this would be it.

Two figures stood near a glass display case at the far end – one a tall, elegantly dressed man, and a woman with silver hair examining what appeared to be an ornate dagger through a jeweller's loupe.

"Juniper," came a creaking voice from behind a cluttered counter. "Either the world is ending, or you've finally decided to settle that tab from 1998."

The elderly man who emerged from the shadows looked ancient even by supernatural standards. His wispy white hair formed a halo around a face mapped with wrinkles so deep they seemed to tell stories. His pale blue eyes were sharp and clear.

"The world might actually be ending this time, Thaddeus," Juniper replied, making her way carefully through the antiques. "And I settled that tab in 2003 with that temporal displacement formula, now you owe me, remember?"

"Ah yes," the old man chuckled. "The one that gave me three extra hours every Tuesday for a decade. Quite useful for inventory." His gaze shifted to me, eyes narrowing in assessment. "And who might this be? New turn, by the smell of her. Still has that fresh grave scent."

"Fresh grave scent?" I hissed at Juniper, mortified.

"He's exaggerating," Juniper muttered. "Mostly." Then louder, "Thaddeus, this is Gillian Spark, newest associate at Clifford and Burk. Gillian, meet Thaddeus Grimshaw, proprietor of the finest arcane antiquities establishment in London and walking encyclopaedia of magical artefacts."

"Pleasure," I said, extending my hand and trying not to accidentally crush the elderly man's fingers with my still-unpredictable strength.

Thaddeus ignored my hand, instead leaning uncomfortably close. "Interesting. Very interesting indeed."

I pulled back slightly, uncomfortable with the scrutiny.

"Juniper," called the man from across the shop, his cultured voice cutting through our awkward introduction. "What brings you to Grimshaw's at this hour? Magical emergencies seem to follow you like stray cats."

Juniper's posture shifted subtly. "Ezra. Didn't expect to see you here."

The man approached, moving with the grace that seemed characteristic of older vampires. Up close, he was even more imposing – tall, aristocratic features, dark hair swept back from a face that belonged on a Victorian cameo.

"Ezra Worster," he introduced himself, taking my hand with old-world formality. "Court stenographer for the Vampire High Council."

His cool fingers clasped mine, and an unexpected jolt of connection passed between us – vampire recognising vampire. His eyebrows rose slightly.

"Interesting," he murmured. "Very interesting indeed."

Juniper cleared her throat.

"We're here on business, Thaddeus," she said, her tone making it clear this wasn't a social call. "The Concordat has been stolen from the Witching archives."

Thaddeus's expression darkened.

Ezra went utterly still, like a statue, then nodded. "It's been all anyone can talk about at work."

The elegant silver-haired customer who had been examining the dagger approached us, her eyes – an unusual shade of green that seemed almost to glow – studying me with uncomfortable intensity.

"Victoria Prendergast," she said without offering her hand. "I couldn't help but overhear, ghastly business."

"When?" Thaddeus demanded, all trace of the doddering shopkeeper vanishing as he straightened to his full height.

"Two nights ago," Juniper replied. "The containment ward was breached."

"I thought so," said Ezra. "I heard the Helix Coven was behind it."

Juniper shrugged. "There was evidence of them at the scene, apparently, along with some botanical magic, but it all seems a bit too obvious."

"Nothing is too obvious for the Helix Coven," Ezra said firmly. "Making a statement is part of their agenda."

"That's why we're here," Juniper said. "You've dealt in ancient artefacts for centuries, Thaddeus. If someone wanted to hide the Concordat, where would they put it?"

Thaddeus ran a gnarled finger down a page of his ledger. "The Concordat isn't just any artefact. It can't be destroyed – at least not by conventional means. And it must remain in a state of balance." He looked up, his pale eyes intense.

"Any ideas where to look?" Juniper asked.

"There's someone who might know more," Thaddeus said, closing his ledger. "Roe Thistle tracks the movement of every significant magical artefact across dimensions. If anyone can point you in the right direction, it's them."

"The fae scribe?" Ezra asked. "Clearly, the fae are not to be trusted."

"There's still at least one honest fae in London," Thaddeus said with a nod. "Roe takes their role as Keeper of Movements very seriously – no politics, just facts. They operate in the Market Under Bridge."

Victoria made a displeased sound. "The Market is no place for civilised vampires."

"I'm not civilised, or a vampire," Juniper pointed out.

"And I'm not too civilised either, apparently," I muttered.

"In that case, neither am I," Ezra said. "I'll come with you. I have business of my own to attend to at the market."

Juniper shrugged again. "Sure, come along. But time is of the essence."

"What exactly is the Market Under Bridge?" I asked, sensing I was missing crucial information.

"A trading post beneath Westminster Bridge," Ezra explained, his tone suggesting this should be obvious. "Where the supernatural community conducts commerce outside mundane regulations."

"It's also dangerous as hell for the unprepared," Juniper added. "But I agree with Thaddeus. Roe Thistle is our best hope for information on the Concordat."

Victoria narrowed her eyes. "A pleasure to meet you both," she said with little pleasure in her voice. "I have important matters to attend to now, I'll take my leave."

"Just keep your wits about you," Thaddeus warned, as we turned to go.

**12:07 AM. Standing under Westminster Bridge. Chance of being arrested by river police: moderate. Supernatural mission: in progress.**

The night air carried the scent of the Thames – a complex bouquet of algae, pollution, ancient stone, and the countless human lives that had played out along its banks for centuries, layers of history from ancient Roman settlements to Victorian sewage to modern chemical traces.

We stood beneath Westminster Bridge, the rumble of late-night traffic overhead sending vibrations through the stone arches.

"The London entrance shifts every night," Juniper explained, her hands glowing faintly as she traced patterns in the air while consulting Thaddeus's compass. "It follows the tidal patterns as they would have been in 1603."

"Why 1603?" I asked, watching in fascination as the magical energies coalesced around Juniper's fingertips.

"The year Queen Elizabeth I died," Ezra supplied. "The fae courts considered it the end of the last great age of magical cooperation in Britain. They're sentimental that way."

Because of course magical beings would base their interdimensional doorway locations on Elizabethan tidal patterns and royal deaths. Why use a simple fixed entrance when you can make it complicated?

Juniper's compass emitted a soft chime as its needle settled on a particular section of darkness beneath the bridge. "Found it," she announced, completing her pattern. The section of darkness... deepened.

"Baby vampires first," she said, gesturing toward the impossible darkness.

I hesitated only briefly before stepping forward. The shadow enveloped me like liquid velvet, cool and substantial against my skin. For a disorienting moment, I felt suspended between realities, neither here nor there. Then I stepped through into chaos.

Light, sound, and smell hit me simultaneously. My senses, already heightened beyond human capacity, were bombarded with input from dozens – no, hundreds – of magical beings and artefacts. The market sprawled beneath the ghostly outline of Westminster Bridge, but the Thames was gone, replaced by crystalline canals filled with luminescent liquid that definitely wasn't water.

Stalls constructed from impossible materials lined labyrinthine pathways – living wood that continued to grow and reshape itself, metals that flowed like mercury, fabrics that changed colour with each passing customer. The vendors themselves defied categorization – beings with too many limbs or not enough, skin tones that didn't exist in the human spectrum, features that rearranged themselves while you watched.

And the smells – raw and unfiltered: Cinnamon and ash, rain and salt, loam and minerals, a metallic tang that made my fangs instinctively extend.

This made Oxford Street on Christmas Eve look like a quiet country lane.

"Stay close," Ezra murmured, suddenly beside me. "Some might see you as easy prey."

I nodded, fighting to control my overwhelmed senses. Juniper appeared on my other side, consulting the compass which now spun wildly, its needle glowing with blue light.

"Roe's stall is this way," she said, pointing down a particularly crowded avenue of stalls. "The compass is locked on their location now, regardless of how the Market shifts."

We made our way through the crowd, which parted subtly before Ezra's presence. I noticed other vampires among the magical beings, but they were different from those at Clifford and Burk – wilder, less concerned with appearing human. Some nodded respectfully to Ezra, while others watched us with naked curiosity.

I felt like the new girl at school all over again, except instead of wondering if my uniform skirt was the right length, I was wondering if my fangs were showing and if that tentacled being was actually wearing someone else's face as a hat.

The compass led us through increasingly exotic and bizarre sections of the Market until we reached what appeared to be its centre – a circular plaza dominated by a fountain of that same luminescent liquid. Surrounding it were the largest and most elaborate stalls, clearly belonging to the Market's most prestigious vendors.

The compass needle pointed unerringly toward a stall constructed entirely of what appeared to be living parchment that continuously inscribed and erased itself with flowing script.

"Err, I should perhaps warn you so that you don't stare too much," Juniper said. "Roe is fae, but not like the High Fae who look mostly human, a rather different being altogether."

"Anything in particular I need to watch out for? Multiple heads?" I joked.

"You're not far off," said Juniper.

I stifled a gasp.

Behind a counter made of stacked ancient tomes stood a being unlike any I'd seen before.

Roe Thistle. They were tall and willowy, with skin that shifted between bark-like texture and something resembling hammered copper. Their hair grew not just from their head but from various points along their arms and shoulders, each strand ending in a tiny leaf or flower. Their eyes – all four of them – were arranged vertically on their face, each a different colour.

And I thought Azalea was intimidating. This being makes her look positively conventional.

"Ezra Worster," they called out, their voice harmonizing with itself in multiple octaves simultaneously. "Your presence indicates matters of significance. The threads of fate stir and tangle."

"Roe Thistle," Ezra greeted with formal courtesy. "We seek your expertise."

"And Juniper," Roe continued, their four eyes blinking in sequence. "Calculations and patterns. The mathematics of chaos." Their gaze finally settled on me, all four eyes focusing simultaneously. "A new vampire. Very new. But old magic. Interesting combination."

Before I could respond to this cryptic observation, Juniper stepped forward, producing Thaddeus's compass. "Thaddeus Grimshaw sends his regards and asks for your assistance."

Roe's expression shifted, copper-like aspects of their skin gleaming in the market's strange light. "The old collector knows the proper protocols. What do you seek?"

"Information about the Twilight Concordat," Ezra said. "It has been taken from the Witching Archives."

The market around us seemed to still, ambient noise diminishing as if the very air was listening. Roe's four eyes widened, then narrowed.

"A theft of great consequence," they said, voice dropping to a whisper that somehow carried more weight than a shout. "The balance tilts."

"Do you know where it might be?" Juniper pressed. "Or who might have taken it?"

Roe gestured for us to enter their stall – a significant honour, according to Ezra's quickly whispered explanation. Inside, the living parchment walls continued their endless cycle of writing and erasing, but I noticed the script now seemed to be recording our conversation.

"The Concordat cannot be destroyed," Roe began.

"Cannot, as in it's impossible to destroy...or cannot as in it would be the end of the world?" I asked.

Roe simply gave me a pointed look and continued. "Cannot be removed from this realm. Cannot be completely hidden from those who understand its nature." They turned to me, all four eyes focusing intensively. "It must remain in balance – between night and day, between magic and mundane, between life and death – look to where water touches sky but remains untouched by earth. Where salt meets sweet but neither may drink"

"That's not very specific," I pointed out, then immediately worried I'd violated some fae etiquette.

To my surprise, Roe's mouth curved in what might have been a smile. "Direct. Refreshing." They reached beneath their counter and produced what appeared to be a glass orb filled with swirling mist. "The Concordat's movements leave traces in the currents of magic. Like so."

They passed their hand over the orb, and the mist inside coalesced into a map of London, with a bright point of light. As we watched, the light moved – not in a straight line as a normal object would travel, but in a strange, zigzagging pattern that seemed to fold back on itself multiple times.

"The thief knew the wards," Roe observed. "Knew how to mask their path. But the Concordat itself leaves traces that cannot be hidden from one who knows how to look."

Before I could ask what that cryptic instruction meant, a commotion erupted elsewhere in the Market – shouts and a pulse of magic that made the air vibrate.

"Witch authorities," Ezra hissed. "They must be searching for the Concordat."

"Or for those who stole it," Juniper added. "Either way, we should go."

Roe nodded. "The eastern exit will be clearest. Go now."

**12:31 AM. Cryptic clues received: ominous. Hunger levels: suddenly rising. Vampire control: rapidly deteriorating.**

I became acutely aware of the hunger that had been building since we entered this place. The magical energies around me suddenly seemed edible, tempting – especially the swirling patterns emanating from the magical beings themselves. I could sense their essence, their life force, their... blood.

"What's happening?" I whispered, feeling my fangs fully extend without my permission. My vision narrowed, the colourful chaos of the Market taking on a reddish tinge. The scent of a passing fae – something like wildflowers and ozone – hit me like a brick.

"Gillian," Ezra's voice came from far away. "Control it. You're experiencing blood hunger. The Market amplifies it."

"I can't," I gasped, my body trembling with need. My focus locked onto a fae with delicate butterfly wings and iridescent skin who was examining merchandise at a nearby stall.

Without conscious decision, I lunged – crossing the space between us in a blur of vampire speed. The fae turned, eyes widening in alarm, but too late. My hands grasped their shoulders, fangs bared and ready to sink into their shimmering neck.

"PREDATOR VIOLATION!" someone shouted, and suddenly three towering fae guards materialised, each bearing crystalline staffs that hummed with ancient magic.

"Stand down, vampire!" the tallest commanded, staff aimed at my chest.

But the hunger had consumed me, focused me, became me. I couldn't stop – didn't want to stop – as I pulled the terrified fae closer.

The guard slammed his staff against the ground. "Final warning!"

Something inside me snapped. Not the hunger, but something deeper, more primal. A surge of power I didn't recognise coursed through my veins, and as the guards moved to strike, a ring of dark fire suddenly erupted from where I stood, expanding outward in a perfect circle.

The dark flames weren't hot – they were cold, freezing cold – and where they touched the Market floor, frost patterns formed in intricate spirals. The guards stumbled backward, expressions of shock replacing their determination.

"Impossible," one whispered. "A vampire summoning fire..."

The fae I'd been about to attack scrambled away in the confusion, wings beating frantically as they took to the air above the commotion.

My hunger momentarily forgotten, I stared at the dark flames surrounding me with equal confusion. "What is this? What's happening?"

"Gillian," Ezra's voice cut through the chaos, his hand gripping my shoulder. "Enough."

The Market had formed a circle around us, dozens of magical beings watching with expressions ranging from fear to awe to calculation.

"What just happened?" I whispered, the hunger now completely gone, replaced by a humming energy that made my skin feel too tight.

"Something that should be impossible," Juniper whispered.

Juniper grabbed my arm in a panic. The guards had recovered and were advancing, their staffs glowing with retaliatory magic.

"Time to go!" she shouted, and with a disorienting yank, the Market suddenly dissolved around us as her spatial translocation magic pulled us away.

**Current status: Vampire with apparently rare and disturbing**

magic. Caused scene in magical marketplace. Supernatural therapy: needed urgently.

# CHAPTER 9

# DINNER AND UNDEAD THERAPY

**1** **2:47 AM. Teleportation: complete. Nausea level: severe. Fire incident: baffling. Public embarrassment: incalculable.**

Reality snapped back into place like a rubber band, the nauseating twist of teleportation depositing Juniper and me directly into the reception area of Clifford and Burk. My enhanced senses were still reeling from the Market – the lingering sensation of cold fire tingling on my skin. The artificial brightness of the fluorescent bulbs overhead felt harsh and clinical after the organic chaos of the Market Under Bridge.

I steadied myself against the reception desk, trying not to look like I'd just nearly eaten a fae, summoned magical fire, and caused a minor supernatural incident.

"We should probably talk about what just happened –" Juniper began, her own voice still uncharacteristically subdued after witnessing my apparently impossible feat of magic.

But the mage abruptly fell silent, her eyes widening as they fixed on something – someone – over my shoulder.

Perseus Burk stood in the doorway to the main office, his normally immaculate appearance slightly dishevelled. His tie was askew, his hair mussed as if he'd been running his hands through it repeatedly. The scent of anxiety – like burnt cinnamon – emanated from him. But most alarming was his expression – grave concern in features that typically maintained composure, his grey eyes lacking their usual calculated calm.

"I thought we had more time," he said without preamble. His gaze fixed on me with an intensity that made me instinctively step back.

"More time for what?" I asked, still disoriented. The world around me seemed simultaneously too sharp and slightly unreal, my senses still adjusting from the overload at the Market. My gaze drifted past Perseus to my office door, where an elaborate basket wrapped in midnight-blue cellophane sat waiting, tied with a silver ribbon. "Is that... a gift basket?"

Perseus grimaced before his professional mask reasserted itself. "Standard welcome package for new vampires. The fact that it's arrived means they know about you."

"Who knows about me?" I looked between Perseus and Juniper, the latter now uncharacteristically serious.

The memory of Clara Blackwood's inexplicable hostility flashed through my mind – that cold fury when our eyes had met at the Council gathering. Had she known even then? Was this what her rage had been about?

The sudden tension in the air was palpable, pressing against my skin like a physical force. "I hate to look a gift basket in the mouth... but can you please tell me what's going on?"

**12:52 AM. Office tension: intense. Gift basket: apparently ominous. Understanding of situation: zero.**

Perseus straightened his tie with a practised gesture, his fingers moving with the fluid precision that marked ancient vampires – a movement too smooth to be human, yet executed with such ease it appeared natural to casual observation. "My office. Now."

The walk through the main workspace felt endless as we passed between glass-walled offices and open workstations. Vampiric employees averted their eyes as I passed.

I fought the urge to check if my blouse was tucked in properly or if I had metaphorical spinach in my teeth. Being the centre of supernatural attention triggered all the same social anxieties as human scrutiny, just with higher stakes. The memory of dark fire erupting from me at the Market suddenly felt like a weight around my neck, the power I'd felt fading beneath the weight of their scrutiny.

Juniper walked a half-step behind me, uncharacteristically silent.

Perseus's corner office had impressive floor-to-ceiling windows with a panoramic view over Burkenswood. Unlike the modern aesthetic of the main workspace, this was a blend of modern minimalism and ancient artefacts displayed in illuminated cases – medieval manuscripts and what appeared to be a Grecian urn depicting scenes of battle.

A massive desk of polished obsidian dominated the space, its surface bare except for a single ancient-looking document written in script that hurt my eyes to look at directly.

Behind the desk, a wall of books stretched from floor to ceiling – some modern volumes with crisp spines, others ancient tomes bound in materials I didn't want to identify, all organised in some system I couldn't immediately discern.

He closed the door. The subtle click of the lock sent a shiver down my spine.

**1:03 AM. Locked in boss's office: never a good sign. Career prospects: potentially terminal.**

"Your turning is a mystery," Perseus said. "And one that's now attracted attention I'd hoped to avoid for a while longer."

"Why did Charles take me to that council meeting and parade me around if my existence was supposed to be secret? I don't understand," I said, though a creeping dread suggested I was beginning to.

"My father argued that the best place to hide is in plain sight," Perseus shook his head, the tremble in his voice gave away that he'd been angry about it. "He said it was just like sneaking new chickens into the coop at night so that they wake up already belonging there. I, personally, didn't think it wise, but he was sure it would look far less suspicious. Clara Blackwood has been asking questions. Lady Valencourt has expressed further interest in your progress." Odette's name gave me chills.

I shuddered.

"Vampires are bureaucratic to a fault," Perseus continued, his voice clipped and precise. "All petitions to turn a human undergo rigorous verification. The paperwork takes years to process. Background checks, psychological evaluations, compatibility assessments, historical reviews to prevent turning known criminals or individuals with problematic magical descent." He made a vague gesture, his signet ring catching the light. "The usual."

"The usual," I echoed faintly, the absurdity of supernatural bureaucracy momentarily distracting me from the obvious implications.

Of course immortal beings would naturally develop a love for endless forms in triplicate.

"No one filed paperwork for you, Gillian." Perseus's eyes held something approaching genuine regret, the grey darkening to almost slate. "In such cases, the Council's standard response would be immediate termination."

The word hung in the air like a thunderclap. Termination. Not firing. Not dismissal.

Execution.

**1:07 AM. Legal status: apparently illegal vampire. Bureaucratic oversight: potentially fatal. Current mood: understandably panicked.**

"They want to kill me?" My voice sounded distant to my own ears, as if someone else were speaking through me. The room seemed to contract around me, my enhanced senses suddenly hyperfocused on escape routes, on the subtle shifts in Perseus's posture, on the controlled rhythm of Juniper's breathing behind me. "Because someone forgot to file the proper forms?"

"Vampire politics are complicated," Juniper interjected from where she leaned against the door, her voice gentler than I'd ever heard it. "The paperwork isn't just bureaucracy – it's magical preparations and binding. It creates connections, responsibilities, obligations. An unbound vampire is considered dangerous and unpredictable. Like a nuclear reactor without containment protocols."

I sighed. "And the welcome basket means they know about me."

Perseus nodded, a muscle in his jaw tensing subtly. "We filed a 'missing paperwork' form immediately of course – technically a retroactive application for emergency transformation due to exigent circumstances. The system is backed up and it often takes over a year for them to get to new applications. That should buy us some time, but..."

"But what?" I pressed, my legal mind already analysing options, loopholes, precedents. Seven days as a vampire and already facing execution on a technicality – it was absurd, infuriating, and terrifyingly plausible given what I'd learned about supernatural bureaucracy.

Perseus sighed, a surprisingly human gesture for one so ancient, and finally sank into his chair. The leather creaked beneath him, the sound unnaturally loud in the tense silence. "The situation is rather complicated. We'll need to find a vampire powerful enough and willing to take on the role of Sangrelié for you and file the foster paperwork."

"Sang-what? Foster paperwork?" I repeated, the term conjuring images of social services and temporary guardianship. "Like I'm some sort of orphaned vampire child?"

"In a manner of speaking, yes." Perseus's expression softened slightly, centuries of experience briefly visible in his eyes. "We need to find you a Sangrelié, the vampire who agrees will have to be a magical match, and you'll have to trust them implicitly."

"Why?"

"Because they'll have certain... powers over you. Vampires need lineage. It will protect you from shadow poisoning."

I shivered, unsure if I was brave enough to ask more about what that term meant, or if the implications were horrific enough.

"A maker's bond is sacred," Perseus continues. "It gives them influence over your actions, your emotions, even your physical responses. Not mind control exactly, but something more fundamental – a connection at the level of your transformed essence."

"So whoever made me a vampire already has that kind of power over me?" I shook my head in disbelief.

"If only we knew who that was," Perseus said. "But since we do not, finding a Sangrelié is imperative, not just for your sake, but to protect everyone else from what might happen to you otherwise."

"I'm not giving anyone control over me," I insisted.

Perseus gave me a look somewhere between compassion and pity.

**1:13 AM. Personal autonomy: potentially compromised. Comparison to previous marriage: uncomfortable. Existential horror: growing.**

The room seemed to tilt beneath my feet, the elegant furnishings blurring momentarily as my control over my enhanced senses wavered. Power over me. Control. The very thing I'd fought so hard to escape when leaving my marriage. The years of subtle manipulation, of measured criticisms designed to shape my behavior, of calculated disapproval that had slowly eroded my sense of self – all that I had finally escaped, only to face a supernatural version of the same dynamic.

Just my luck. Finally escaped one controlling relationship only to be told I need to enter another one or face supernatural execution.

"None of the Burk family are a match," Perseus continued, apparently unaware of my internal turmoil. "We've already checked our blood signatures against yours. Azalea tried first, naturally, given her role in your initial stabilization. Then myself, Charles, even Dora."

I barely heard him, my mind still reeling from the implications.

Someone would own me – magically, legally, fundamentally. My newfound freedom as a creature of power and potential would be curtailed before I'd even begun to explore it.

"How long do I have?" I managed to ask, my voice steadier than I felt, years of maintaining composure in hostile corporate negotiations now serving me well.

"The Council's bureaucracy works in our favour for once," Perseus replied, his expression calculating. "We have several options for delay tactics – requesting extended verification periods. Because of the current backlog, we have time – perhaps a year – before they demand resolution."

"A year to find someone I trust enough to give control over my entire existence," I said flatly, the bitter irony settling like acid in my stomach. "Wonderful."

"It's not ideal," Perseus acknowledged, spreading his hands in a gesture of pragmatic acceptance. "But it's better than the alternative."

Silence fell over the office, heavy with implications. Through the windows, the lights glittered, the city blissfully unaware of the supernatural politics playing out in a law office that shouldn't exist.

"If you don't mind," I finally said, each word carefully measured, "I think I need some time to process this."

Perseus nodded. "Of course. Take the rest of the night off. But Gillian –" His eyes held mine with sudden intensity. "Be careful. Your display at the Market will have ripple effects. Word travels quickly in supernatural circles."

I nodded stiffly and left the office, feeling the weight of both vampires' gazes on my back. The walk to my own modest office seemed to take hours, each step requiring conscious effort as my mind raced through the implications of Perseus's revelation.

Inside, the gift basket waited on my desk like a mockery – a cheerful welcome to a community that apparently wanted me dead for existing without permission. I stared at it, the elaborate arrangement suddenly sinister in its cheerful presentation. I approached cautiously.

The midnight-blue cellophane crinkled beneath my fingers as I unwrapped it, the sound grating against my sensitive hearing. Inside, arranged with meticulous attention to detail, sat an assortment of items clearly intended for the newly-undead.

A set of comically large novelty sunglasses labelled "Daywalker Delusions – When You Forget You're a Vampire" that expanded to cover half my face. The tag warned: "Not actually sun-proof. Please don't test this."

A tiny refrigerated pouch containing what appeared to be blood popsicles in various Flavours: "O Negative Originale," "AB Positive Berry Blast," and "Universal Donor Unicorn." The packaging cheerfully proclaimed them "Ethically Sourced Frozen Treats for the Discerning Undead."

A vampire-themed phone case with a special "Night Mode" screen cover to protect sensitive immortal eyes."

A "Vampire Vocabulary" flash card set for "modern integration" with helpful translations like "I require sustenance" instead of "I want to drink your blood" and "I prefer dimmer lighting" rather than "The sun is my ancient enemy."

A small bottle of "Fang-Friendly Dental Floss" ("Because immortality is no excuse for poor oral hygiene") and mint-flavoured "Blood Breath Begone" mouthwash ("For after-dinner conversations with the living").

Perhaps most disturbing of all was a glossy brochure for "Forever Young: Navigating Eternal Adolescence," a support group for vampires struggling with perpetual identity crisis. I shivered thinking of Dora, forever trapped in the body of a child.

The concept of supernatural therapy, on the other hand... Now there's something I genuinely need. "So, how does being hunted by a vampire council make you feel?" "Slightly stressed, if I'm honest."

I lifted an elegant black card embossed with silver script, the weight and texture of the paper suggesting expense and tradition:

**1:42 AM. Bureaucratic threats: received. Personal crisis: deepening. Career options: supernatural fugitive?**

I sank into my chair, the weight of my situation finally crashing down upon me. A week ago, my biggest concerns had been finalising divorce paperwork and making sure Merryn finished her science project on time. I'd been planning a small celebration for Keyne's upcoming birthday, wondering if I would ever feel ready to start dating again after ten years with Neville.

Now I was an illegal vampire with extraordinary powers I didn't understand – powers that apparently included magic that should be impossible for my kind – facing execution if I couldn't find someone willing to claim magical ownership of me. My children were being cared for while I learned to control bloodlust. And somehow, I'd become entangled in a mission to find an ancient magical artefact that could destabilize the entire supernatural world if not recovered in time.

And now I'd need to find a more powerful vampire to control me? No. Never again, I had promised myself after leaving my marriage. Never again would I allow someone to control me, to dictate my actions, to hold power over my choices. I'd rather take my chances with the shadow poisoning. It had taken everything I had to reclaim my independence, my identity, my right to exist on my own terms. I had to leave because staying would have destroyed me.

Yet here I was, faced with exactly that choice – submit to another's authority or face destruction.

I carefully replaced the items in the basket and pushed it aside. The Council's "gifts" felt less like a welcome and more like a collar – the first step in controlling and categorizing me. Whatever destiny had brought me to this point – I refused to approach it from a position of weakness.

I thought of my children, their faces clear in my enhanced memory – every freckle, every eyelash, every subtle expression preserved with perfect clarity. Keyne's smile when he'd mastered riding his bike without training wheels. Merryn's solemn concentration as she practiced her letters.

What would they think if they could see me now? Would they recognise their mother in this transformed creature? Would they fear me, with my predator's instincts and uncanny abilities? Or would they see what I was only beginning to glimpse – not just a vampire, but a being of power and potential, somehow capable of wielding fire that should be impossible for my kind, reshaping reality in ways my human self could never have imagined?

I stared at the so-called welcome basket, the gleaming midnight-blue cellophane still scattered across my desk like the remnants of a particularly elegant crime scene. After the bombshell Perseus had dropped – that I was essentially an illegal vampire facing potential execution – I needed something, anything, to distract myself from the cascading existential horror.

Rummaging deeper through the basket's contents, my fingers encountered a slim volume bound in burgundy leather that I'd initially overlooked. The gold embossed title caught the light: "Fabulously Fanged - From Mortal to Immortal: Navigating Your First Century as a Vampire."

More interesting was the author's name: Azalea Burk.

"Vampire self-help?" I muttered, flipping open the cover. "What's next, 'Chicken Soup for the Undead Soul'?"

Despite my scepticism, I found myself sinking back into my office chair, book in one hand, reaching for the blood-enchanted tea that the night receptionist had quietly delivered shortly after my meeting with Perseus.

I flipped to a random page, curious what wisdom the elegant and terrifying Azalea might dispense to newly-turned vampires.

*"Chapter 3: Managing Your First Blood Moon*

*The first blood moon after your turning is a time of heightened senses and emotional volatility. Many new vampires describe it as 'PMS combined with a caffeine overdose.' A good time to binge watch television shows and drink a steady supply of blood-enchanted beverage. Under no circumstances should you attempt to resolve longstanding family conflicts or make major financial decisions during this period..."*

I snorted, nearly spilling my tea. The thought of the imposing, ethereal Azalea binge-watching television shows was almost too absurd to contemplate. Yet there was something oddly comforting about the practicality of her advice.

I continued reading, finding myself genuinely absorbed in Azalea's explanations of vampire society, politics, and biology. The chapter on blood types and their various effects ("O-negative: the vampire equivalent of comfort food") was particularly illuminating, as was the section titled "Explaining Your Transformation to Mortal Loved Ones: What NOT to Say."

As I sipped my tea and read, I found myself mentally constructing theories about the missing Concordat, or Twilight Concordat as the fae had called it. Roe Thistle's cryptic clue tumbled through my mind – *look to where water touches sky but remains untouched by earth. Where salt meets sweet but neither may drink.*

A body of water that touches the sky but not the earth... a reflection, perhaps? And where salt water meets fresh water... an estuary? Or something more metaphorical?

The plant obsessed Consortium Virentia with a grudge against both vampires and conventional witches made sense as suspects. But something about it felt too neat, too obvious. In my years as a lawyer, I'd learned that the most straightforward explanation was rarely the complete one, especially when powerful interests were involved.

My musings were interrupted by a soft knock at the door, followed immediately by Juniper's distinctive energy signature as she entered without waiting for a response. The mage looked different – her usual exuberant presence dampened.

"How are you holding up?" she asked, perching on the edge of my desk and eyeing the blood-tea and self-help book with interest. "Ah, Azalea's magnum opus. The chapter on clothing care is actually quite useful – her method for removing blood stains has saved many of my favourite shirts."

"I'm processing," I replied, setting the book aside. "How bad is it out there? The political situation with the missing Concordat?"

Juniper's expression darkened. "The witching authorities are in an absolute spin about it all. Magical chaos everywhere. Ley lines fluctuating, random transmutations occurring – a parking meter in Hackney turned into a flamingo yesterday." She ran a hand through her purple-streaked hair, making it stand even more on end than usual. "If we don't find the Concordat soon..."

She didn't need to finish the sentence. We both knew what was at stake – not just vampire feeding methods but the entire balance of the supernatural world.

"Perseus told me about your... situation," Juniper continued, her voice gentler than I'd ever heard it. "The Council, the maker issue."

"Apparently being an unauthorised vampire is rather bad form," I said dryly, taking another sip of blood-tea. "Who knew immortality would come with so much paperwork?"

I tried to lighten the mood but the ominous dread of my situation was really sinking in.

No one would ever control me again.

Especially not after feeling such power coursing through my veins.

**Current status:** Illegal vampire. Mother of children I can't see. Embroiled in supernatural political crisis. Reading vampire self-help books at 3 AM

# CHAPTER 10

# HOSTILE TAKEOVER OF THE SOUL

**5**:17 PM. Vampire office productivity: minimal. Mental state: distracted. Blood-tea consumed: too much, judging by slight jitters.

I stared at the glowing screen of my phone on the desk, the notification of a voicemail from "Mum" sending a wave of guilt through me. I was thinking of our last awkward conversation, where I'd fumbled through vague explanations about a sudden career change and relocation that made no sense. I was working strange hours, barely ever needing to sleep – barely aware of the days, and yet checking the clock sporadically like a touchstone, grounding me to the moment.

With a sigh that was entirely unnecessary for my respiratory system but deeply necessary for my emotional state, I pressed play and held the phone to my ear.

*"Your father's trying to rip me off. I might need you to represent me after all. By the way, I've taken myself on a holiday to Myrtlewood. Do you know of it? It's a little village not too far from where you are. Just letting you know, in case you decide you want to spend some time with your mother after all."*

I nearly dropped the phone.

Myrtlewood? The name triggered an immediate memory – Perseus mentioning it offhandedly during my first day at Clifford and Burk. *We also have offices in New York, Tokyo, and a small branch in Myrtlewood.*

At the time, I'd thought nothing of it, too overwhelmed by everything else to question why an elite supernatural law firm would maintain an office in some obscure village I'd never even heard of. But now, with my mother suddenly holidaying there…

This couldn't be coincidence. Nothing in my life was coincidence anymore.

I pulled up a map search on my computer and typed in "Myrtlewood." The search returned maddeningly unhelpful results – no clear location, just vague references to it being somewhere along the southern coast. It was as if the place barely existed on official maps.

A thought struck me with the force of a physical blow. What if my mother was mixed up in the supernatural world somehow? What if she'd always been? It would explain her theatrical temperament, her dramatic flair, her ability to command attention in any room. What if she was a vampire too?

Had my entire life been a carefully constructed lie?

Without conscious decision, I found myself on my feet, striding through the corridors of Clifford and Burk toward Perseus's office. Vampire staff glanced up as I passed, perhaps sensing the storm of emotions I was barely containing. I didn't care. I needed answers, and I needed them now.

I didn't bother knocking, simply pushing open the heavy oak door with more force than necessary.

Perseus looked up from his desk, one elegant eyebrow rising at my dramatic entrance. "Gillian. To what do I owe this… energetic visitation?"

"Myrtlewood," I said without preamble. "Why does a prestigious supernatural law firm with offices in London, New York, and Tokyo have a branch in a town so obscure it barely appears on maps?"

A flicker of something crossed Perseus's face – surprise, perhaps, or concern – before his features settled back into their usual composed mask.

"That's a rather specific question," he observed mildly. "What prompted it?"

"My mother just left me a message saying she's gone on holiday there. And I find it very hard to believe that's a coincidence."

Perseus set down his pen and leaned back in his chair, studying me with that unnervingly ancient gaze. "Please, sit down, Gillian."

"I don't want to sit down," I replied, crossing my arms. "I want answers. There's something you and Juniper aren't telling me, isn't there? Something about me, about my family. I'm tired of being kept in the dark about my own existence."

Perseus sighed, a sound weighted with centuries. "Some knowledge is protected for good reason, Gillian. Your unusual abilities, your rapid adaptation to vampire existence – these things have made you a person of interest to multiple factions within the supernatural community. Not all of them have benevolent intentions."

"So you're saying it's for my own safety?" I asked incredulously. "That's the excuse tyrants have used throughout history to maintain control."

"It's not an excuse," Perseus countered calmly. "It's a reality. The less you know about certain aspects of your nature, the harder it is for others to extract that information from you."

"Extract?" I repeated, a chill running down my spine despite my indignation. "What exactly do you think is going to happen to me?"

"Nothing, I hope," Perseus said. "But given your close encounter with Clara Blackwood—"

That name again. Why was this woman haunting me?

"And your mother's sudden appearance in Myrtlewood," he continued. "We cannot afford to be careless."

"My mother," I seized on the reference. "Is that why she's gone there? Is she a vampire?" My voice rose with each question, the strain of recent events finally cracking my composure.

"No," Perseus said firmly. "She is not a vampire. But Myrtlewood is… a sanctuary of sorts."

"And the Clifford and Burk office there?"

"Myrtlewood is actually the closest village to our castle, much nearer than Burkenswood. That's where I tend to work during daylight hours," Perseus said. "I don't need to sleep at all in this stage of immortality. Our small branch there provides specialised legal services to the community," Perseus explained.

I sank into the chair opposite his desk, my legs suddenly unable to support my weight despite vampire strength. "So my mother is in danger there?"

"Quite the opposite," Perseus assured me. "She's safer in Myrtlewood than almost anywhere else at the moment. We have friends and allies throughout the town who will ensure she comes to no harm."

"But why would she go there?" I pressed. "She's never mentioned it before."

Perseus's expression turned inscrutable. "Perhaps she was guided there by someone who recognised the growing instability in the supernatural world and wanted to ensure her protection."

I studied his face, searching for deception but finding only careful neutrality.

"How is your mother?" he asked, smoothly changing the subject. "Beyond her flamboyant exit from the theatre and her unexpected travel plans?"

The question caught me off guard. "She sounds stressed. My father's apparently being difficult about the divorce settlement." I ran a hand through my hair, a habit that had survived my transformation. "And she wants me to represent her legally, which is obviously impossible now. I don't even know what to tell her about my own situation. How do you explain to your mother that you've become a vampire and can't see her during daylight hours anymore?"

"Preferably nothing," Perseus advised. "The situation is far too sensitive. Clear communication about supernatural circumstances to those without the necessary context often leads to misunderstandings or worse."

"She's already stressed enough about the divorce," I agreed reluctantly. "She's never been a divorce specialist, and neither have I, yet she's begging for my support. I've been so distant, and I feel terrible about it."

Perseus's expression softened slightly. "If legal representation is what concerns her, perhaps I could assist. I've had occasion to practice various forms of law over the centuries and have kept abreast of modern precedents. Her case would be in excellent hands."

I blinked in surprise. "You? But surely you have more important responsibilities than handling my mother's divorce?"

"I consider this important," Perseus replied simply. "The mother of a vampire under my protection deserves the full resources of this firm."

Something in his tone made me pause. There was a personal quality to his offer that seemed out of character for the normally reserved ancient vampire.

"You already know her, don't you?" I said slowly, the pieces clicking together. "You're the one who guided her to Myrtlewood."

Perseus remained silent, neither confirming nor denying, but his lack of denial was answer enough.

I should have been furious at this further evidence of manipulation, but instead, I felt a strange reluctant gratitude. Whatever else was happening, Perseus was ensuring my mother's safety.

"Why are you doing all this?" I asked, my anger giving way to weariness. "What's so special about me and my family that warrants this level of involvement?"

Perseus' expression turned grave. "There are forces at work far beyond what you currently understand, Gillian. And while I wish I could explain everything, doing so now would place both you and those you care about in grave danger."

"So I'm just supposed to trust you blindly?"

"Trust is earned," he acknowledged. "And I've given you little reason for it beyond vague assurances. But consider this – in the short time since your transformation, have I or my family acted against your interests? Have we not provided protection, employment, guidance?"

He had a point, which only irritated me further. Despite everything, there was something about Perseus that inspired trust, something beyond his aristocratic bearing and centuries of authority.

"Let me take on her case," Perseus said firmly.

I let my shoulders drop a little. It would be a relief to know Mum was in good hands. "Are you sure?"

"Gillian, I tend to work in the Myrtlewood offices during the day anyway, attending to all manner of minor local legalities – inheritance, property disputes...the mundane rhythm helps me to stay grounded and humble, a major benefit in a long supernatural life."

"Fine," I sighed. "You can represent my mother...I mean. Thank you? But I want her out of Myrtlewood as soon as possible, once it's safe."

"A reasonable request," Perseus agreed. "Though neither of us get to decide that. And she may find the town has its own charm."

I pulled out my phone, staring at it with trepidation. "I should call her back."

"I'll give you privacy," Perseus said, rising from his chair. "But Gillian – remember, discretion is paramount. For her safety as much as yours."

Once alone in Perseus's office, I stared at my phone for a long moment before finally making the call. My mother answered almost immediately.

"Hello, love," came her familiar voice, simultaneously comforting and guilt-inducing.

"Mum, what are you doing?" I asked, trying to keep the desperation from my tone.

"I just took myself on a little holiday, that's all."

"To Myrtlewood?" I couldn't keep the incredulity from my voice. "Seriously? Do you even know what that place is?"

"It is eccentric, I'll give you that," Mum conceded, and I could almost see her looking around at what she surely thought were merely quirky locals, completely unaware they were likely various supernatural beings.

Despite Perseus' assurances, I didn't trust the place. It was all far too uncomfortable to think of my mother getting mixed up in this dangerous new world.

"Get out of there, get back to London. It's not safe..." I stopped myself from saying anything too revealing. "I mean, for a woman your age to be travelling alone. You're vulnerable." A weak argument, but the best I could manage.

"It's a damn sight safer than London," Mum retorted, her indignation clear. "Your father sent some ridiculous actor in a cape to attack me on the street, in broad daylight. In the West End, no less."

My blood ran cold. An actor in a cape? That sounded disturbingly like a vampire – though in broad daylight that sounded risky, even in a cape. Had someone supernatural targeted my mother? Was that why she'd taken refuge in Myrtlewood?

"Really? Is that what Dad told you?" I asked, trying to keep my voice steady.

"No, but who else could be responsible than an out-of-work actor paid by my disgruntled ex? I can't think of any other possible explanation. He went right for me. I'm sure Jerry is just trying to rattle me. He's trying to take everything."

I exhaled in relief. She'd interpreted it as one of my father's spiteful tricks. Better that than the truth—whatever that was.

"I saw the email," I said, changing the subject slightly. "Thanks for forwarding it."

Mum sighed. "Will you represent me? I know you'll do a better job than that ridiculous man Smithers. I'm sure he's an old friend of your father's."

"I can't. You know that, Mum. It would be a conflict of interest, representing one of my parents against the other one. But someone at my new firm will be able to pick it up. Besides, I'm a barrister, not a solicitor."

"Of course," Mum said, disappointment evident in her voice. "Oh well, send the files to someone. Make sure they're good."

"Are you staying in Myrtlewood long, then?" I asked, trying not to sound as concerned as I felt.

Mum's voice brightened. "You know, I just might. I've been feeling slightly depressed in London in that terrible little flat…And besides, I feel like being close to the sea will do me a world of good."

"You know it's a –" I started to warn her about the town's supernatural nature, then caught myself. "A what dear?"

"Oh, never mind, Mum. Just take care of yourself and let me know if you see anything strange."

Perhaps staying in a magical sanctuary was indeed a good idea, given all the mysterious dangers that now seemed to plague my family.

"Everything's strange around here, I'm sure," Mum laughed. "That's why I quite like it. It's inspiring. Maybe I'll write another play."

My heart – metaphorically, given that it no longer beat – lifted at her words. "It's nice to hear you say that. It's been such a long time since you've written anything."

"And when will I get to see my daughter and my grandchildren?" she asked, the question hitting me like a bat on steroids.

"I'm terribly busy," I replied automatically, hating myself for the evasion. What could I say? *Sorry Mum, I can't see you because I might accidentally drain your blood?*

Then an idea struck me. "Although… Maybe the kids could come and stay with you for a bit if you had somewhere to keep them." The words were out before I'd fully thought them through. The children were currently with Tilly as their temporary guardian while I adjusted to vampire life. I was not able to have supervised visits with them, and soon Azalea assured me I'd be able to safely be around them without endangering them, but I was sure they missed Mum, too. Perhaps sending them to Myrtlewood wasn't such a bad idea.

"Really?" Mum's voice filled with hope. "Now that could be nice, it'd keep me occupied."

"You're a worry, Mum," I said, guilt washing over me again. "I'm sorry I haven't been able to help you through… whatever it is you're going through lately. Things have been a little bit hectic. But I'll see you at some point soon." Another lie. I had no idea when – or if – I'd be able to see her in person again. I wasn't the same person, and she'd know it.

"Good luck with the move," she said as we ended the call.

I sat in Perseus's office, phone clutched in my hand, feeling more powerless than ever, despite technically being more powerful than I'd ever been in my human life. What a cruel irony – supernatural strength and abilities, yet unable to help my own mother through a divorce, unable to see my children daily, unable to have a normal conversation without lies and evasion.

A soft knock at the door preceded Perseus's return. He took one look at my expression and seemed to understand immediately.

"It went as well as could be expected?"

"I told her the children might be able to visit," I said. "Which I hadn't planned to do, but now that I've said it, it makes sense. They'd be protected in Myrtlewood, wouldn't they?"

Perseus nodded thoughtfully. "The town has extensive wards and protections. And it would perhaps ease your mind to have them somewhere safe during this tumultuous time."

"But I'll still be here, unable to see them except for brief super-vised visits," I said bitterly.

"For now," Perseus acknowledged. "But your progress has been remarkable, Gillian. Your shadow integration, your control – all suggest you may achieve stable interaction with your loved ones far sooner than most newly turned vampires."

"And the Sangrelié situation? The Council investigation? The mysterious attack on my mother? How do those fit into this optimistic timeline?"

Perseus's expression remained serene despite my sarcasm. "One challenge at a time. Your mother is now safe in Myrtlewood. Her legal matters will be handled with the utmost care."

I rubbed my temples, a useless gesture for a vampire but a hard habit to break. "I feel like I'm stumbling through a maze in the dark, Perseus. Everyone seems to know more about my situation than I do."

"Knowledge does not always equate to understanding," he replied, sagely. "But I promise you this – when the time is right, when it is safe to do so, you will have answers."

I stood, gathering what remained of my dignity. "I'll hold you to that. And Perseus – thank you for helping my mother. Whatever else I may think about your methods, I'm grateful for that."

I couldn't shake the feeling that I was still missing important pieces of the puzzle – about Myrtlewood, about my mother, about my own unusual vampire nature. But perhaps Perseus was right. Perhaps, for now, ignorance was the safer option.

I just hoped that safety wouldn't come at too high a price.

**Current status: Vampire daughter with mother in supernatural town. Confusion level: stratospheric. Secrets being kept: apparently numerous. Trust in the Burk family: reluctantly growing. Answers: still frustratingly elusive.**

# CHAPTER II

# WELCOME TO MYRTLEWOOD

"I've got news," Juniper announced, bursting into the conference room at Clifford and Burk where I sat with Imani and the Petrov twins, surrounded by case files that seemed to multiply overnight. "About Elara Ashwood."

She brandished a small piece of bark-like paper that seemed to shimmer in the light. "Cryptic note from Roe Thistle. Apparently our missing witch had connections to the Consortium Virentia."

"The plant extremists?" Alexei Petrov looked up from his meticulously organised notes. "That's... unexpected."

"Unexpected and potentially significant," his twin Anastasia added in their unsettling unison. "What kind of connections?"

Juniper consulted the bark paper, squinting at text that seemed to shift as she read it. "According to Roe, Elara was working with them on some kind of magical plant enhancement project. Something about pesticide resistance." She looked up with excitement. "That could explain the botanical residue found at the theft scene."

"Or it could be another red herring," Imani pointed out, her tone sceptical. "The Consortium Virentia has been linked to several false leads already."

"There's more," Juniper continued, practically vibrating with energy. "Evidence has come in that the plant residue in the archives did indeed come from the Consortium Virentia It wasn't planted. I have contact details for a dryad named Sage who was working with Elara. Maybe she can clear things up. We can meet her in Myrtlewood."

My stomach clenched. Myrtlewood. Where my mother was currently holidaying, completely unaware that her daughter had been transformed into a creature of the night.

Juniper was already gathering her things, stuffing crystals and instruments into her seemingly bottomless bag. "It's settled then. Myrtlewood field trip! This is going to be brilliant. Come on, Gillian."

"But what if I see Mum?" I asked. "How can I possibly explain..."

"Right," Juniper said, "before we go, you're going to need this." She produced what appeared to be an ordinary lemon drop from her pocket. "Glamour candy. One of my more useful inventions."

I eyed the sweet suspiciously. "What does it do, exactly?"

"Temporary appearance modification," Juniper explained cheerfully. "Changes your features just enough to make you unrecognisable to casual observation. Lasts about three hours, tastes like lemon, and has only minimal side effects."

"Define minimal."

"Slight tingling in the extremities, possible temporary colour blindness, and about a five percent chance of your voice changing pitch randomly. Nothing serious."

I took the lemon drop, weighing the risks. On one hand, randomly changing voice pitch sounded mortifying. On the other hand, being recognised by my mother while investigating supernatural crimes seemed considerably worse.

"How much will it change my appearance?"

"Enough," Juniper assured me. "Hair colour, facial structure, height slightly. Think of it as a magical Instagram filter for the real world."

I popped the sweet into my mouth. It tasted exactly like lemon, followed by a strange tingling sensation that spread from my tongue throughout my entire body. Looking down, I watched my hands shift subtly – fingers slightly longer, skin tone a shade warmer.

"Excellent!" Juniper clapped her hands together. "Now you look like a completely different person. Well, a completely different person who happens to be related to your original self. Magical genetics are complicated."

"Ready for spatial translocation?" she asked, extending her hand.

I grasped it, bracing myself for the now-familiar sensation of reality folding inside out. "As I'll ever be."

**12:15 PM. Location: Myrtlewood village centre. Disguise status: active. Mother proximity: unknown but terrifying.**

Reality unfolded with a stomach-churning lurch, and suddenly I was standing on cobblestones under a darkening sky, Juniper's hand still gripping mine. The first sensation that hit me wasn't visual – it was the overwhelming aliveness of the place, thrumming through my senses like electricity through water.

"Welcome to Myrtlewood," Juniper said, releasing my hand.

The village centre spread before us in the early evening light. Most shops were closed but I could hear heartbeats, conversations, the everyday sounds of a community settling into the evening. I breathed in the distant scents of flowers, chocolate, scones, cakes and stew, and felt myself relaxing, growing calmer, settling, almost like the sensation of coming home.

"The energy here," I murmured, watching a few snowflakes drift through the lamplight. "It's like the air is charged with something."

"Concentrated magical confluence," Juniper explained. "Makes tracking anyone here nearly impossible."

A sandy-haired man emerged from the bookshop, carefully locking the door behind him. He paused to check the window display before heading off down a side street, a cloth bag of books slung over his shoulder.

Outside the chocolate shop, a red-haired woman was bringing in a chalkboard sign. Something about her seemed oddly familiar, though I couldn't place it.

"That's Rosemary," Juniper whispered. "Perseus's girlfriend. Makes the most amazing magical sweets."

Of course – the picture on Perseus's desk. My mind wandered to whether blood-enchanted chocolate would taste any good.

Near the village green, two teenagers hurried past. They were deep in conversation about something that sounded like homework, though the words "transmutation" and "etheric balance" suggested this wasn't ordinary schoolwork.

"Here we are," Juniper pointed to the only establishment showing real signs of life. "The Witches Wort."

The pub glowed with warmth, its windows fogged with condensation. Through the old glass, I could see the comfortable bustle within – locals settling in for their evening pints, someone stoking the fire, the ordinary rituals of village life. The painted sign above the door showed a cauldron in weathered paint.

"Our contact is waiting inside," Juniper confirmed, already moving toward the entrance.

**12:32 PM. Pub entry: achieved. Mother detection protocol: active. Heart rate: elevated despite vampire physiology.**

The Witches Wort was exactly what you'd expect from a pub in a magical village – low beams, warm lighting, the scent of ale and something that might have been enchanted stew. What I hadn't expected was the clientele: a mixture of obvious supernatural beings and what appeared to be ordinary humans, all chatting amicably over their drinks.

"Sage?" Juniper called softly, approaching a corner table where a woman sat alone, her green-tinted skin and hair like flowing leaves... a dryad.

"Juniper," the dryad replied, her voice carrying the rustle of wind through branches. "I wondered when you'd arrive. Roe's message was... urgent."

We settled at her table, and I found myself automatically scanning the pub for any sign of my mother. The glamour felt strange – like wearing someone else's face – but it was holding steady.

"Tell us about Elara," Juniper said without preamble.

Sage's expression grew sad, her leafy hair shifting colour to deeper autumn shades. "Such a sweet girl. She was helping us with protective magic – spells to make our plants resistant to the chemicals humans use. Pesticides, herbicides, all the poisons they pour onto the earth."

"That would explain the botanical residue at the theft scene," I realised.

Sage nodded. "There might have been some residue from our work together. I hear Elara was working in the Archives that night. She preferred the quiet there for her research. Said the dimensional barriers were thinner, made complex magic easier."

My pulse quickened. "How do you know she was in the Archives the night of the theft?"

Sage stiffened. "I was there...earlier on in the night. She sent me home with some scones she'd baked, said she still had more work to do. She must have been there for hours. She even checked in around midnight to see if I'd gotten home safely. She was excited. Said she'd made a breakthrough with her dimensional folding magic."

"An hour before the theft was discovered," Juniper breathed.

"She must have witnessed something," I said, excitement building. "Or..."

My words died in my throat as a familiar laugh rang out across the pub. My head snapped toward the sound, and there she was.

My mother.

Delia Spark sat at a table near the window, surrounded by three other women her age or older, all of them laughing at something she'd just said. She looked... different. Relaxed in a way I hadn't seen in years. Her silver hair was sporting a new bright red streak, and her entire posture radiated contentment.

But it was the company that shocked me most. Aside from Kitty and her theatre colleagues, my mother had never been particularly social. She'd always claimed to be "too busy for friendships," though I'd suspected it was more that she found most people boring. Yet here she was, clearly comfortable with these women, engaged in animated conversation.

" – told him that if he wanted the lead role, he'd have to audition like everyone else," she was saying, her voice carrying that theatrical projection that had filled our house throughout my childhood. "You should have seen his face! As if being married to the director entitled him to special treatment."

The other women erupted in supportive laughter, one of them reaching over to pat Mother's hand sympathetically.

"Gillian?" Juniper's voice seemed to come from very far away. "You've gone completely white. Well, whiter. Is that – ?"

"My mother," I whispered, unable to look away. Part of me wanted to rush over, to throw my arms around her and tell her everything. Another part was terrified that even if I sat perfectly still here she'd somehow see through the glamour and recognise me despite the magical disguise.

As I watched, one of the women leaned forward conspiratorially, and I caught fragments of their conversation:

" – worried about my daughter though. She says she's ill, but won't let me visit –"

" – sometimes children need space to figure things out –"

" – but she sounded so strange on the phone, so distant –"

My throat tightened. She was worried about me. Here she was, clearly enjoying her new friends and her escape from London, but she was still concerned about her daughter who had become mysteriously unavailable.

"We should go," I managed to say, my voice barely steady. "She can't see me like this."

But even as I said it, I couldn't stop watching her. She looked happy – genuinely happy in a way I hadn't seen since before my father's emotional manipulation had worn her down. Whatever else

Myrtlewood was providing, it was giving my mother something she'd needed for a long time.

The guilt of my deception churned inside me. She deserved to understand why her daughter had suddenly become so distant and unavailable. But how could I possibly explain any of this?

"Gillian," Juniper said gently, "we have what we came for. Sage has given us crucial information about Elara's whereabouts that night. We should report back."

I nodded, forcing myself to look away from my mother's table. But as we prepared to leave, I heard her voice one more time:

"I just hope she knows she can tell me anything. Whatever's going on with her, whatever she's going through – I'm her mother. I'll always be here."

The words followed me out of the pub like an accusation.

Outside, I leaned against the pub's stone wall, fighting to compose myself. The glamour was still holding, but I felt exposed nonetheless.

"She seems lovely," Juniper offered diplomatically.

"She is," I managed. "And she's worried sick about me, and I can't tell her why I can't see her, and she's making friends for the first time in years, and I'm investigating magical crimes instead of supporting her through her divorce, and –"

"Breathe," Juniper interrupted. "Metaphorically speaking. We'll figure this out, Gillian. One crisis at a time."

I straightened, forcing myself back into investigative mode. "If Elara was in the Archives that night, working on dimensional magic…"

"She either witnessed the Concordat theft or was forced to participate," Juniper finished. "Either way, she's the key to understanding what really happened."

"And we still don't know if she's alive or dead," I added grimly.

"No time to agonise about that now," Juniper said. "Let's go."

As reality folded around us, I caught one last glimpse of the Witches Wort's warm windows. Somewhere inside, my mother was laughing with her new friends, building a life that I couldn't be part of until I could master control the monster I'd become.

**3:17 PM. Dreams: horrific. Sleep quality: abysmal. Existential dread: off the charts. Vampire therapy sessions attended: apparently not enough. Vampire nightmares: apparently not just some goth teenager's Tumblr fantasy.**

*Blood. Everywhere. In my dream I stood in my old kitchen, making packed lunches while shouting upstairs. "MERRYN! COAT! NOW!" But my voice came out all wrong – like Darth Vader gargling with gravel – and the jam sandwiches I was making were filled with something dark and sticky that definitely wasn't strawberry conserve.*

*"Mummy, I'm hungry," came Keyne's little voice behind me.*

*I turned to find my darling boy in his Spiderman pyjamas. My heart went into full-blown cardiac arrest as ravenous hunger overtook me, my treacherous vampire body moving forward, drawn to the pulsing veins in his tiny neck.*

*"Run!" I tried to scream, but only managed a pathetic hiss.*

*The kitchen dissolved and I found myself in the conference room at Bennett & Associates. Neville sat at the head of the table with that smug expression I'd fantasised about slapping off his face for years.*

*"Poor Gillian," he said in that condescending tone. "You signed the ultimate contract, and you didn't even read the fine print. Typical."*

*He slid a document written in blood across the table, the text writhing like worms.*

*"ILLEGAL VAMPIRE. SENTENCE: TERMINATION."*

*"But I have children," I protested. "I have responsibilities!"*

*Then darkness began pouring down the walls, enveloping me as I heard Merryn's distant voice: "Mummy? Why did you leave us?"*

I bolted upright with such force that I nearly catapulted myself into the ceiling. My hands had massacred the silk sheets, with stuffing leaking from the mattress like the world's most expensive eviscerated teddy bear.

For a moment, I sat there panting – completely unnecessarily. Old habits die hard.

The room was bathed in moonlight streaming through partially drawn curtains. As my panic subsided, I surveyed the damage. Another set of Azalea's luxurious sheets destroyed. At this rate, I'd single-handedly devastate the castle's bedding stocks within a month.

"Just a nightmare," I muttered, running a hand through my tangled hair. My voice echoed slightly, the vampiric resonance still weird to my ears.

Ten days. That's how long it had been since my transformation. Ten days since I'd gone from being an overworked lawyer and mother of two to an illegal vampire with mysterious powers. Ten days since I'd properly held my children, tucked them in, or kissed their foreheads goodnight. The supervised visit had been wonderful but painfully brief – like being allowed to glimpse paradise through a keyhole before having the door slammed in your face.

Would I ever be able to be a proper mother to them again? Or would I always be this creature of darkness, watching them grow up from the shadows, supervised like some sort of supernatural risk?

Azalea entered with her usual breezy disregard for personal boundaries.

She wore what must have been her idea of casual loungewear – a midnight-blue dressing gown and hand-embroidered night dress that probably cost more than my car. Her hair was arranged in an elaborate braid that looked like it required a team of stylists.

But it was her expression that sent my anxiety into overdrive – grave and serious. No smirk. Her eyes bored straight into mine as though seeing me for the first time. A wave of mortification crossed her face, followed by delight.

"It's starting," she announced dramatically, a gleam of excitement in her eyes that belied her sombre tone. "How absolutely marvellous!"

"What's starting?" I asked.

"The shadow encroachment," Azalea replied, gliding further into the room with the poise of someone who's never tripped over their own feet. "Usually this doesn't set in for at least a decade and fledgelings have plenty of time to adjust. However, I suspected it might begin soon after your little performance at the Market. Such a delightfully accelerated timeline!"

I clutched the shredded remains of my sheets around me like some sort of tragic Victorian heroine. "I have no idea what you're talking about. Does this castle include an ancient burial ground? Because that would explain so much. Am I being haunted in my dreams?"

Azalea's perfectly shaped eyebrows performed a synchronised lift. Her lips curved into a delighted smile that seemed far too enthusiastic for the situation. "Not a haunting, precisely. Shadows exist between states – much like vampires themselves. Neither fully dead nor alive, but something... else. It's such an exquisite parallel, don't you think?"

"I don't know what to think."

"Shadow manifestation at this rate is unheard of. It's a messy process – you'll experience mortal adjacent symptoms that vampires don't usually have to deal with – nightmares, pain, falling apart at the seams," she continued, her tone suggesting she found my supernatural predicament utterly thrilling. "But you're an exception, Gillian. So wonderfully ahead of schedule!"

"Is this covered in your book? Chapter twelve: 'When Your Shadows Start Stalking You: Setting Healthy Boundaries with Your Darkness'?"

A smile flashed across Azalea's face, her eyes sparkling with macabre delight. "Certainly relevant... though perhaps I should consider adding more for the next edition. 'The Premature Emergence of Shadow Companions: When Your Darkness Cannot Wait to Meet You.' It has a certain poetic ring to it, wouldn't you agree?"

She turned to face me fully, her expression growing more serious though the gleam in her eyes remained. "Most new vampires spend their first few decades being haunted by shadow manifestations. It's part of the transition – the price of immortality is confronting all the darkness you've spent your human life pretending doesn't exist. Such a beautiful, painful awakening."

"Brilliant," I muttered. "Just what I needed. As if regular therapy wasn't expensive enough, now I need supernatural shadow therapy. Does the NHS cover that? Because my insurance definitely doesn't have a 'turned into vampire' clause."

"That's precisely what you need," Azalea confirmed, completely missing my attempt at humour. "And we need to begin immediately. First, you'll join us for a proper dinner. Then shadow therapy. Your darkness awaits a formal introduction."

I was no longer in any position to deny I needed therapy.

Dinner at the Burk household was, predictably, a grandiose affair. The dining room could have hosted a small royal banquet, with a table long enough to require telecommunications equipment for conversations between opposite ends. Elaborate candelabras cast a warm glow over porcelain place settings and crystal goblets that probably predated several countries.

Azalea had insisted I dress for dinner, providing a black velvet dress that hugged my figure in ways my human clothes never had. "Proper attire elevates the dining experience," she'd explained while selecting jewellery from a case that would have caused museum security to have palpitations. "The modern vampire needn't sacrifice elegance for sustenance."

Charles sat at the head of the table, resplendent in a smoking jacket that should have looked ridiculous but somehow didn't.

"Ah, Gillian," Charles greeted me as I entered. "Just in time. Jenkins is about to serve the first course."

Dora already occupied her customary seat, perched on silk cushions that still left her appearing dwarfed by the massive dining furniture. Tonight's dress was mourning attire from the early Victorian era, hair in elaborate coils that no actual child would tolerate.

"You're late," she observed, her childish voice carrying the weight of someone who had been measuring time since before clocks were common. "Azalea is bothered by lateness. She gets that from me, though she'd never admit it." Her small fingers drummed on the table. "I was late once. 1347. Missed the plague's arrival in Venice by three days. Terribly inconvenient."

I shook my head and took my place, noting the elaborate place settings – multiple forks, spoons, and knives arranged with perfect precision. "I hope there's not a test on which utensil to use. I've never been one for strict etiquette."

"Instinct will guide you," Azalea assured me, taking her seat with supernatural grace. "The transformation enhances innate refinement. Or so one hopes."

"Hope is what killed your great-great-grandfather," Dora told Azalea matter-of-factly, selecting the correct fork with practiced ease despite her small hands. "He hoped the mob would be reasonable. They were not."

"Maman," Azalea sighed, "perhaps we could avoid family history during Gillian's first formal dinner?"

"Why? She should know what she's joined." Dora's ancient eyes fixed on me. "The Burk line has survived through adaptation, not hope. Hope is for fools and mortals."

Jenkins entered pushing an elegant serving cart laden with covered dishes. With practiced efficiency, he served each of us, removing silver domes with theatrical flourish.

My plate contained what appeared to be a normal appetizer – some kind of sophisticated salad with artfully arranged greens, edible flowers, and a light dressing.

Charles grinned. "Special cuisine for a special occasion, of course – celebrating Gillian's progress. You have shadow therapy tonight. Such advancement! Unprecedented!"

"Really?" I said. "Unprecedented?"

"Indeed," Charles explained. "Usually Azalea makes new vampires wait two years after beginning the physical hunger training before attempting anything deeper, but you have surpassed all expectations in your progress."

I smiled and carefully speared a forkful of the salad. The moment it touched my tongue, a burst of flavour exploded across my palate – complex, rich, satisfying in a way that transcended human culinary experience. "This is... incredible. Almost like real food."

"The enchantment process is quite fascinating," Azalea added, delicately consuming her own portion. "Death and life suspended in perfect balance, much like ourselves. Isn't that simply delicious to contemplate?"

The main course proved equally revelatory – a perfectly cooked filet mignon but satisfied my blood cravings completely. I found myself relaxing into the experience, the elegant dining ritual soothing after days of stress and confusion.

"You really are adapting remarkably well," Charles assured me again, as Jenkins cleared our plates.

"It doesn't feel like I'm adapting well," I admitted, dabbing my lips with a napkin embroidered with the Burk family crest. "I've destroyed three sets of bedsheets and nearly attacked a fae at the market."

"Yet you maintain your sense of self," Dora spoke for the first time since the meal had begun, her childish voice jarring from her ancient eyes. "Many lose themselves entirely. Become mere hunger with legs."

That wasn't exactly comforting.

"The meal should have stabilised your hunger," Azalea said as we finished the final course of blood enchanted crème Brûlée. "Now we can address your shadow situation without the distraction of bloodlust."

**8:30 PM. Shadow meditation: imminent. Apprehension level: stratospheric. Second thoughts: numerous but futile.**

Alazea guided me to the meditation chamber.

"Most new vampires spend their first twenty decades or so feeling utterly miserable, haunted by shadows," Azalea began without preamble. "They fight against their nature, against the darkness within themselves. Such pointless resistance, such wasted years of torment."

"Twenty decades?" I repeated, horrified. "Two hundred years of... this?"

"For most, yes," Azalea confirmed, her eyes bright with macabre enthusiasm. "But you're not most vampires, are you? Your turning was unusual. Your abilities are manifesting at an accelerated rate. How gloriously efficient!"

She leaned forward, her dark eyes boring into mine with unsettling intensity. "You have two choices, Gillian. You can spend the next century fighting against your nature, as most new vampires do. Or you can embrace it now and save yourself two hundred years of unnecessary suffering. The darkness will find you either way – might as well welcome it properly, don't you think?"

"The only way to process the shadows is to embrace them," Azalea continued, her voice taking on a hypnotic quality. "They are you – the parts of your humanity denied, suppressed, or that you couldn't bear to acknowledge in your human life. Such beautiful, painful truths waiting to be discovered."

I thought of my nightmares, of the shadows whispering all my insecurities like a greatest hits compilation of my personal failures.

Azalea's expression softened slightly, which on her perfect face looked almost like a normal human emotion. "Humans spend their lives building internal walls, separating what they can accept about themselves from what they cannot. Becoming a vampire dissolves those walls. You're sensitive to the collective shadow as well as your own. What a precious gift of insight."

Azalea leaned forward, fixing me with an intense gaze. "Close your eyes. Breathe in the rhythm I establish."

I hesitated, then complied, synchronising my unnecessary breath with Azalea's slow, deliberate pace. Though I didn't need the oxygen, the action itself was calming, familiar.

"Imagine a door within your mind," Azalea's voice came from directly in front of me, though I hadn't heard her move. "A door you have kept locked. Behind it lie all the things you fear to acknowledge about yourself. All your forbidden desires and truths."

I visualised a heavy wooden door, similar to the ones throughout the castle. I could almost feel its weight, sense the secrets contained behind it.

"Now, open it," Azalea whispered, her voice almost caressing the words.

In my mind, I pushed against the door. It resisted at first, then slowly swung inward to reveal a swirling darkness within. The sight filled me with instinctive dread.

"Tell me what you see," Azalea prompted, her voice eager with anticipation.

"Darkness," I whispered. "Moving, changing darkness."

"Look deeper. The shadows will take form if you allow them. Such magnificent revelations await."

I concentrated, peering into the void. Slowly, shapes began to coalesce – impressions more than clear images. A silhouette that resembled Neville, his voice echoing with familiar criticisms. The outline of a woman cowering, making herself small. Another figure – myself, watching impassively as someone suffered.

"I see... weakness," I admitted, my voice barely audible. "The times I didn't stand up to Neville. The times I stayed silent when I should have spoken."

The hardest part wasn't seeing these failures – it was recognising how comfortable I'd become with my own diminishment, how I'd convinced myself it was a virtue to stay quiet.

"Good," Azalea encouraged, her voice vibrating with approval. "Continue. Deeper now."

"I see rage," I continued, surprised by the intensity of the emotion swirling in the darkness. "So much anger I never expressed. Not just at Neville – at everyone who ever made me feel small. At myself for allowing it."

The shadows within the doorway churned faster, forming new shapes – darker, more primal.

"I see... hunger," I whispered. "Not just for blood. For Validation. For power. For respect. For revenge. I wanted to see Neville fail. I wanted to excel where he said I couldn't." The recognition was liberating and terrifying.

"Yes," Azalea's voice had taken on a reverent quality. "These are some of your shadows, Gillian. Not weaknesses to be ashamed of, but parts of yourself to be acknowledged and integrated. The hunger you feel as a vampire is merely an extension of hungers you've denied your entire human life. Beautiful, powerful aspects that have finally broken free of their chains."

My eyes flew open to find Azalea watching me with an expression of almost maternal pride.

"I've always been hungry," I said softly. "For something more... far more than what my life had become."

"Precisely," Azalea nodded approvingly. "And now you must face that hunger – embrace it without being consumed by it. If you deny your shadows, they will grow stronger, more insistent, until they overcome your control entirely."

She sat back in her chair, arranging her dress with elegant precision. "This is especially important for those who wish to safely interact with human loved ones."

Hope flared in my chest. "My children."

"Exactly," Azalea confirmed. "The sooner you confront these inner shadows, the sooner you can see Keyne and Merryn without endangering them. You can be a mother in darkness as you were in light."

"So my shadow is... what? My repressed anger? My secret desires? My existential dread? That time I shoplifted a lipstick when I was fourteen and still feel guilty about?"

"All of those things and more," Azalea confirmed, barely containing her delight. "The shadow is everything you've hidden from yourself – your rage at other people's treatment of you, your resentment at the sacrifices demanded of you, your hunger for power and respect, your fear of your own potential. Such delicious secrets, finally emerging from their hiding places."

Her words hit with uncomfortable precision, like an arrow

finding a bullseye in my chest. I might have suspected her of reading my mind, if I didn't already know that even vampires couldn't do that without permission. No, this was simpler and more disturbing – she was just naming the universal shadows that most people carried, the ones I'd apparently been suppressing all my life.

"How do I... embrace them?" I asked, my voice smaller than I intended. "Do I just... give it a hug? Write it an encouraging note? Set up a joint bank account?"

"We begin with meditation," Azalea replied, straightening her spine. "Close your eyes. Focus on your breathing – unnecessary for our kind, but useful for centring the mind."

I closed my eyes, feeling slightly silly. Breathing exercises seemed a bit basic for dealing with supernatural shadow manifestations, like bringing a water pistol to a zombie apocalypse. Still, I settled into the rhythm of inhalation and exhalation, feeling the cool air fill lungs that no longer needed oxygen. There was something comforting in the familiar motion, like wearing your favourite pyjamas during a crisis.

"Now," Azalea continued, her voice low and measured, "I want you to visualize your shadow – the darkness within you. See it, acknowledge it, invite it closer."

In my mind's eye, I pictured a shapeless darkness. As I focused on it, it began to take on more definition – not a specific form, but a presence with weight and substance, sort of like a rain cloud made of emotional baggage.

"Your shadow contains your power," Azalea's voice guided me. "Every slight you ever endured, every rage you ever swallowed, every desire you denied yourself – all of that energy is preserved within the shadow. Vampires who fear their shadow deny themselves access to their full potential. What a tragic waste of darkness."

The darkness in my mind pulsed in response to her words, growing larger, more defined. I could feel its pull, the temptation to simply let it engulf me completely. It felt dangerous, but also strangely compelling.

"That's it," Azalea encouraged, somehow sensing my progress. "Now, reach out to it with your consciousness. Touch it. Claim it as your own. Feel its exquisite power."

I extended my awareness toward the darkness, half-expecting it to recoil or possibly slap me with a restraining order. Instead, it surged forward eagerly, meeting me halfway. The moment we connected, a shock of cold energy rippled through my body, like I'd just cannonballed into the Arctic Ocean.

Images and sensations flooded my consciousness – standing silent while Neville belittled my work in front of clients, rage building behind my composed expression. Watching other mothers at school pickup, laughing and socializing while I rushed from work, always feeling like I was failing at both motherhood and my career. The familiar ache of making myself smaller, quieter, less demanding to keep peace in my marriage.

But alongside these familiar pains came other, more disturbing revelations – the surge of satisfaction I'd felt signing the divorce papers, not just relief but vengeful triumph. The thrill of power I'd experienced at the market when that dark fire erupted from me. The hunger I felt not just for blood but for respect, for power, for the freedom to be ruthless and unapologetic after a lifetime of saying "sorry" for existing.

The shadow knew all of this. The shadow was all of this. And it had apparently been taking notes.

"The shadow is not your enemy," Azalea's voice seemed to come from both outside and inside my mind simultaneously, like surround sound for vampire therapy. "It is your strength, your truth, your power. Accept it as part of yourself. Such a beautiful union."

Taking a deep mental breath, I did just that – opened myself to the darkness, allowing it to flow into me, through me. It felt like removing a too-tight corset I hadn't even realised I was wearing.

The sensation, terrifying and exhilarating, strangely like bungee jumping while doing your taxes – simultaneously freeing and restructuring. The shadow merged with my consciousness, like a

Venn diagram emerging between two circles, a part of my awareness that had always been there but had never been acknowledged.

When I opened my eyes, I knew immediately that something had changed. The room seemed brighter somehow, more defined, as if I were seeing it through a sharper lens.

"Very good," Azalea said, genuine approval in her voice. "Most new vampires require dozens of sessions to achieve even partial integration. Your connection to shadow energy is truly remarkable. How delightfully efficient you are! How do you feel?"

I considered the question carefully. "Stronger," I admitted, finally. "More... myself, somehow. But also like there's more of me."

Azalea smiled, a genuine expression that transformed her usually austere features. "That's exactly right. You've taken the first step toward becoming a true vampire, though we may have to be on guard for signs of shadow poisoning with your advanced pace."

"What does that mean?"

"It's a rare condition," Azalea said solemnly. "Vampires need lineage for the processed shadows to flow through. A vampire without a living maker or a Sangrelié for any length of time becomes at risk of the energy stagnating within them. It can get rather messy. Usually it takes decades to progress but with your advanced pace, we must factor in all the possibilities."

I slumped a little. "I really don't want a Sangrelié, or any kind of poisoning."

"Of course you don't," Azalea said. "For now, let's celebrate your progress. It has been truly remarkable. How marvellously transformative!"

She rose to her feet in one fluid motion. "I believe you're ready for the next step – a small test of your new integration."

"What kind of test?" I asked warily.

"The most meaningful one," Azalea replied. "Charles is waiting with your children in the east sitting room."

My entire body went rigid. "My children? Now? But is it safe? What if –"

"The shadow integration, combined with your blood-enchanted dinner, should provide sufficient control," Azalea assured me. "And we'll be monitoring carefully."

"Will I... will I ever get to be with them normally again?" I asked, voicing the fear that had been growing in me. "Not just supervised visits, but proper mothering?"

Something like genuine sympathy flickered across Azalea's perfect features. "That journey will be longer and more complex than I think you realize, Gillian. But tonight is one step closer. Shall we proceed?"

I nodded, both terrified and desperate to see my children.

**9:17 PM. Children: waiting. Hunger control: about to be tested. Maternal longing: overwhelming.**

The east sitting room was smaller than the grand reception rooms, designed for intimate family gatherings rather than supernatural politics.

A fire crackled in the hearth. Charles sat in an armchair, reading aloud from a children's book. On either side of him, nestled close, were Keyne and Merryn in their pyjamas, listening with rapt attention.

The sight of them hit me like a freezing bucket of iced water on a cold winter's morning. It had been only days since I'd seen them, but it felt like years. Every detail registered with painful clarity – Keyne's cowlick that refused to lie flat, Merryn's serious expression as she followed the story, the small hole in the knee of Keyne's pyjama pants that I'd been meaning to mend.

Charles looked up, alerted by either vampire senses or the small gasp I couldn't suppress. "Ah, Gillian. We've just reached the exciting part where the dragon reveals his secret talent for baking."

"Mum!" Keyne exclaimed, his face lighting up with recognition. He started forward, but Charles placed a gentle restraining hand on his shoulder.

"Remember what we talked about?" Charles reminded him softly. "Mummy's still getting better. We need to go slowly."

Merryn studied me with her serious eyes, always more perceptive than her age would suggest. "You look different," she said simply. "Prettier. But sadder."

They smelled different than I remembered. Not just the familiar scent of my children at bedtime – shampoo and toothpaste and the particular sweetness that was uniquely theirs – but something more fundamental, more tempting. Their heartbeats filled the room like drums, the rhythm of their blood calling to me with primal intensity.

The hunger rose immediately, sharp and demanding. My fangs extended involuntarily, pressing against my lower lip in what I hoped looked like thoughtful contemplation rather than predatory anticipation. But something else happened simultaneously – the shadow energy that I'd embraced now seemed to absorb the hunger, channelling it, transforming it from an overwhelming compulsion into a manageable awareness.

I could feel the hunger, acknowledge it, and yet... contain it. Like noticing a delicious cake in a shop window but not feeling compelled to press your face against the glass and make inappropriate noises.

"Merryn," I said softly, careful to keep my lips mostly closed to hide my fangs. "Keyne. I've missed you so much."

I looked to Azalea, silently asking permission. She nodded almost imperceptibly, though her posture remained alert, ready to intervene if necessary – probably had tranquilizer darts or something equally dramatic hidden in her sleeve.

Slowly, deliberately, I knelt down, maintaining a careful distance. "I'm sorry I've been away. I've been... getting better."

"Charles said you have a special condition," Merryn said, her small brow furrowed in concentration. "You can't be out in the daytime now."

"That's right," I confirmed, wondering what exactly Charles had told them. "It's called...photosensitivity. It means sunlight makes me very sick."

"Like allergies?" Keyne asked. "Jimmy in my class has allergies to peanuts, and he has to carry a special pen everywhere."

"Something like that," I agreed, fighting to keep my voice steady. Being this close to them, seeing their faces, hearing their voices – it was overwhelming in the best possible way. "But I've missed you so much. I think about you both every single day."

I wanted desperately to hug them, to breathe in their scent, to feel their small bodies against mine. But I knew that would be pushing my newly integrated control too far, too fast. Like trying to run a marathon immediately after learning to walk.

Instead, I held out my hand, palm up – an invitation without demand. "I've thought about you every minute," I told them truthfully. "And I'm working very hard to get well enough to be with you properly."

Merryn hesitated, then stepped forward with characteristic courage, placing her small hand in mine. The warmth of her skin against my cool flesh was shocking, marking the fundamental difference that now existed between us. But the hunger remained contained, channelled by the shadow energy into something manageable rather than overwhelming.

"Your hand is cold," she observed, but didn't pull away. "Like when you forget your gloves."

"That's part of my condition," I explained, fighting back tears because the last thing I needed was to terrify my children with blood pouring from my eyes.

Keyne, never one to be left out, rushed forward to place his hand on top of ours. "Like a sandwich!" he declared with a giggle that made my non-beating heart clench.

I laughed, careful to keep my fangs covered. "Yes, just like a sandwich."

For a brief, perfect moment, we were connected – mother and children, despite the chasm that now separated us. I could feel their heartbeats, their warmth, their essential humanity, but not as prey to be consumed – as precious lives to be protected.

The moment stretched, crystallizing in my memory with perfect clarity – every detail preserved with supernatural precision. The exact pattern of freckles across Keyne's nose. The small scar on Merryn's thumb from a paper cut last month.

As I knelt there, holding their hands, I was struck by the bittersweet reality of my transformation. I could see them with unprecedented clarity, notice details about their health and well-being that would have escaped human perception. I could protect them with supernatural strength if needed. But could I ever be a normal mother to them again? Could we ever have movie nights cuddled on the sofa, or would I always be this careful, contained creature, holding myself at a safe distance?

"I think that's enough for tonight," Charles said gently, after what seemed both an eternity and a heartbeat. "Mummy needs to rest, and you two need to get to bed."

Merryn nodded solemnly, always the practical one. "Will we see you tomorrow?"

"I hope so," I said, reluctantly releasing their hands. "If my doctors say it's okay."

"I hope you get better soon," Keyne said, suddenly serious. "I miss your bedtime stories. Charles does the voices wrong."

I smiled, love swelling in my chest until I thought it might burst. "I miss them too. And I will get better. I promise."

As Charles led them from the room, Keyne turned to wave enthusiastically while Merryn kept her eyes on me until the last possible moment, her expression thoughtful. The door closed behind them, and I remained kneeling on the floor, overwhelmed by what had just occurred.

**9:47 PM. First proper contact with children: successful. Hunger control: maintained. Emotional breakdown: imminent but hopefully private.**

"You did remarkably well," Azalea said, breaking the silence. "Better than I anticipated. Such exquisite control for one so newly turned."

I stood slowly, legs shaky despite my new strength. "I didn't want to eat them," I said, slightly dazed by the realization. "I mean, I felt the hunger, but it was... manageable. Like being hungry while cooking dinner — aware of it, but not controlled by it. Or like watching The Great British Bake Off without immediately raiding the kitchen."

"That's exactly how it should feel," Azalea confirmed. "The shadow integration allows you to acknowledge your hunger without being ruled by it. You're channelling your darkness rather than fighting it. Such a beautiful harmony of opposing forces."

"So I can see them again?" I asked, hope flaring bright and painful.

"Yes, though initially only under supervision," Azalea clarified, always the dampener on emotional moments. "Short visits at first, gradually increasing as your control strengthens. But Gillian —" Her expression grew serious again. "This accelerated development is unprecedented and will likely come with additional risks. Not only could the shadows encroach on you and overwhelm you, but you are under scrutiny. With Council's interest in your unauthorised turning... you need to be careful. Your remarkable progress makes you more... interesting to certain parties."

I nodded, understanding the warning beneath her words. The more unusual my abilities, the more attention I would attract — not all of it benevolent.

"What happens now?" I asked, already missing my children though they'd been gone less than a minute.

"You continue your training — both in shadow work and at Perseus's firm," Azalea replied. "The path to reunification with your children is the same path that leads to your survival in our world. Such elegant symmetry, don't you think?"

She moved toward the door, then paused. "And Gillian? You must think about what we discussed earlier — finding a vampire to claim the role of your maker. Your accelerated development makes you more valuable, but also more vulnerable. Finding a Sangrelié is imperative. The Council will not overlook an unbound vampire with your abilities."

With that cheerful reminder of my precarious supernatural legal status, she left me alone in the sitting room, still vibrating with the emotional aftermath of seeing my children.

My hunger management training and shadow integration had allowed me to hold my children's hands without harming them.

That alone made it worth embracing.

Whatever came next – the Council's demands, the search for the Concordat, the mystery of my turning, the strange witch-like powers I somehow possessed – I would face it with this new integrated strength. For Merryn and Keyne, I would master this new existence. I would become not just a vampire, but the kind of vampire who could still be a mother.

After all, I was Gillian Spark – newly divorced, newly undead, and newly determined to defy all supernatural expectations.

**Current status: Mother who can see her children (supervised, like some deadbeat dad with a drinking problem). Illegal supernatural being with accelerated development. Future: uncertain but contains possibility of regular bedtime stories.**

# CHAPTER 12

# CLUES AND COLLUSION

6:15 PM. Hours spent researching magical artefacts: 9 (v. dedicated). Dark circles under eyes: non-existent (vampire perk). Coffee consumed: 0 (unnecessary). Blood-tea consumed: 4 cups (becoming slightly dependent).

"And this is why the Grand Soirée is absolutely essential." Azalea's voice carried that imperious tone that meant resistance was futile. She glided around my desk, examining the precarious towers of ancient texts and scrolls I'd been poring over for hours. Apparently threatening me at home wasn't enough. She had to bother me at work too.

I looked up from a particularly dusty tome on fifteenth-century magical artefacts, trying to appear interested despite having heard variations of this speech three times already this week.

"It serves as the perfect opportunity to introduce you to potential Sangrelié candidates," she continued, brushing invisible lint from her immaculate charcoal suit.

I winced at the term. I'd looked it up. Sangrelié – literally "blood-bound" – the vampire who would volunteer to be my retroactive maker, providing the legal and magical bond required by vampire law. The one who would have certain powers over me, control over my actions.

The very thought made my skin crawl almost as much as the persistent shadow patterns that still occasionally rippled across my forearms when I was stressed.

"Azalea," I began, summoning what remained of my patience, "I appreciate your concern, I really do. But I have more pressing matters to deal with than finding someone to volunteer as my supernatural guardian."

I gestured at the research materials spread across the desk – grimoires, arcane legal documents detailing the original covenant negotiations, and a particularly ominous book bound in what I hoped was animal hide. "The Twilight Concordat is still missing, tensions between vampires and witches are at breaking point."

Azalea fixed me with a look that had probably intimidated Napoleonic generals. "Frivolous? The Grand Soirée is where the most powerful vampires in Europe gather, where critical alliances are formed, and where you might – if you're enormously lucky – find a Sangrelié willing to sponsor you despite your unprecedented and frankly alarming powers."

She picked up one of my research notebooks, examining my increasingly frantic scribbles with a raised eyebrow. "And given your Council status remains 'illegal' and your shadow integration is progressing at a rate that even I find concerning, I would suggest you reconsider your priorities."

I sighed, running a hand through my hair. Despite being a vampire for just over a week, I'd already developed a finely-tuned sense for which battles with Azalea were worth fighting. This wasn't one of them.

"Fine. I'll attend." I raised a finger as she began to look smugly victorious. "But I'm not promising to bond with anyone. And I need time to continue my research."

Azalea nodded graciously, as if granting a tremendous favour.

"That reminds me – I've arranged for a seamstress to visit tomorrow for your gown fitting."

I blinked. "A gown? Can't I just wear what I wore to that wedding last year? It's perfectly nice."

The look of abject horror on Azalea's face suggested I'd just proposed showing up in my pyjamas and slippers.

"That's... not how this works," she said faintly. "The seamstress will arrive at midnight. Don't be late."

With that parting directive, she swept from the room, leaving behind the lingering scent of violets and aristocratic judgment.

I turned back to my research with a groan. A party was the absolute last thing I needed right now, especially one designed to parade me before potential candidates for magical control over my existence. It sounded like a debutante ball crossed with an adoption fair, with me as both the debutante and the orphan in need of legal guardianship.

"Tea break?" Juniper's cheerful voice preceded her explosive entrance, the door banging against the wall with enough force to dislodge a small shower of dust from the ancient ceiling beams.

The mage bounded into the office, hair even more wildly purple than usual, carrying a steaming mug that smelled gloriously of blood-infused Earl Grey. Her energy was as ever a stark contrast to the library's solemn atmosphere, like a firework at a funeral.

"You're a lifesaver," I said gratefully, accepting the mug. "Or death-saver? Undead-saver? Whatever the vampire equivalent is."

"Existence-enhancer," Juniper suggested with a grin, perching on the corner of my desk in flagrant disregard of the priceless texts. "How goes the research?"

I took a sip of the tea, savouring the peculiar blend of bergamot and blood that had become my new favourite beverage. "If by 'goes' you mean 'am I drowning in contradictory information while getting absolutely nowhere,' then it's going splendidly."

Juniper peered at my notes. "You're focusing too narrowly," she said after a moment. "You're thinking of it as a treaty between vampires and witches, but it's more than that."

"That's what the fae scribe said too," I recalled, pulling out my notes from our visit to the Market Under Bridge. "'The Twilight Concordat, its true name. Names have power.'"

"Exactly!" Juniper snapped her fingers, producing actual sparks. "The Twilight Concordat isn't just a feeding arrangement – it's powerful binding magic, a magical stabilizer within the entire supernatural ecosystem."

She hopped off the desk and began pacing, her boundless energy making it impossible to stay still. "Think about it. You've been reading these texts like a lawyer, looking for clauses and loopholes. But magical artefacts don't work like legal documents – they're living embodiments of power and intent."

"Living?" I raised an eyebrow. "Metaphorically speaking?"

Juniper waved dismissively. "The point is, we need to understand what the Concordat actually does beyond the obvious vampire feeding regulations."

She grabbed a particularly ancient scroll from my "reviewed" pile, unfurling it with alarming disregard for its fragility. "Look here – this passage doesn't talk about blood or feeding at all. It references 'the shackling of primal instincts' and 'the containment of feeding across all domains.'"

"Containment of feeding?" I leaned forward, excitement building. This was the kind of breakthrough I'd been searching for. "You're right. I've been approaching this all wrong. I need to expand my search parameters."

Three hours and two more blood-enchanted-teas later, Juniper and I had assembled a more complete picture of the Twilight Concordat's true nature. We'd spread our notes across the library floor, creating what looked like the world's most arcane mind map.

"So it affects the ability to feed," I said, tapping a particular document with my pen. "It's a magical stabilizer that prevents certain vampire instincts from surfacing."

"And not just for vampires," Juniper added, highlighting a passage in a grimoire with her glowing fingertip. "It restricts certain witch powers too, particularly those related to mind control and biological manipulation."

I sat back on my heels, absorbing the implications. "So it's basically a supernatural control system, maintaining balance between magical species."

"A magical ecosystem regulator," Juniper agreed. "Without it, the dominance of old hierarchies will likely reassert themselves."

"The suppression fails," I finished. "I need to understand the political landscape better. If the Concordat is this important, everyone has a stake in its whereabouts."

**10:13 PM. Supernatural politics research: initiated. Factions identified: numerous. Probability of headache: 100% (if vampires could get headaches).**

Through conversations with the Burks, additional intel from historical records, and Juniper's considerable network, we'd assembled a complex picture of the current supernatural political crisis.

The Vampire High Council was, to put it mildly, furious with the Witching Parliament for losing the artefact from their archives. Demanding immediate action and suggesting the witches had orchestrated the theft themselves.

Meanwhile, the Witching Authorities were pointing fingers right back, accusing vampires of stealing it in order to return to "the old ways." Their theory: traditionalist vampires wanted to reclaim their full powers and return to direct feeding from humans. They were pointing the finger at the infuriatingly obscure secret society aptly named the Obscurum, which had only seemed to be attached to infuriatingly vague rumours. I'd asked Charles about them and all he could tell me was every vampire who spoke out against the current system was rumoured to secretly be part of the Obscurum, which made Odette Valencourt a primary suspect, and yet, her political power seemed to make her untouchable.

Caught in the middle were the fae, who maintained a studied neutrality while clearly preparing for potential conflict.

"It's a supernatural powder keg," I muttered, pinning another note to our increasingly complex evidence board.

"There has to be something we're missing," I said, frustration building. I turned back to Roe Thistle's cryptic hint: "Look to where water touches sky but remains untouched by earth. Where salt meets sweet but neither may drink."

"Could it be referring to a mirror?" I suggested. "Something that reflects the sky but isn't actually touching earth?"

"Maybe," Juniper said, not sounding convinced. "But what about the salt and sweet part?"

Perseus shook his head. "Fae riddles rarely have simple solutions. It's likely referring to a specific location that exists in multiple realms simultaneously."

"Helpful," I muttered, rubbing my temples. "We could ask Roe Thistle again, get more specific information."

Juniper winced. "After our last visit, You're not exactly welcome there."

Wonderful. One week as a vampire and I'd already developed a reputation.

"There's another theory gaining traction," Perseus said from the doorway.

"What's that?" I asked, adding his silhouette to our mental map of suspicious faction leaders.

Perseus looked at me, gravely. "Keep this information quiet. Not many people know these details for good reason."

"What is it?" I asked.

"Before the Concordat, before blood enchantment, the relationship between vampires and witches was... volatile," Perseus explained, spreading ancient documents across his desk. "Vampires were apex predators, witches were guardians of natural balance. Conflict was inevitable."

"Vampires were stronger?" I asked, studying the faded illustrations of ancient battles.

"Once, vampires ruled the magical world," Perseus confirmed. "Especially after we discovered that turning powerful witches created vampires of extraordinary capability – beings who could wield both shadow and magic with devastating effect. The most powerful covens fell to the strategic turning of their leaders."

I shuddered at the implication. "Vampires turned them against their will?"

"It was a different time," Perseus replied without apology. "Morality evolves, even for immortals. At our height, vampire dominion extended across Europe and parts of Asia. We operated openly, feeding on select humans chosen for their shadow richness, turning those with magical potential."

"What changed?"

"Hubris," Perseus said simply. "Vampires believed our dominance absolute, unassailable. But the remaining witch covens united, developed new defences specifically targeting vampire vulnerabilities. They created the first shadow-binding spells – magic that could sever a vampire's connection to the collective shadow."

He indicated a particularly grim illustration showing withered vampire corpses. "Without access to shadow energy, vampires starved from the inside out. Not physical starvation, but psychological. The psyche collapsing in on itself. They nearly drove us to extinction before the balance tipped too far in the other direction."

"What happened?"

"The collective shadow grew unmanageable," Perseus explained. "Without vampires processing the excess shadow energy, it began to manifest in increasingly destructive ways. Wars, plagues, eruptions of mass violence. The witches realised too late that we were a necessary component of the psychological ecosystem."

He turned to a newer document, its script more refined. "The First Accord was signed in 1327 – an uneasy truce that allowed vampires to exist but kept us firmly in the shadows, operating

through proxies, feeding discreetly. For centuries, we lived this way –
precariously balanced between extinction and restraint."

"Until blood enchantment," I guessed.

"A witch named Elisabeta Varne made the breakthrough in
1564," Perseus confirmed. "She theorised that shadow energy could
be harvested collectively rather than individually – drawn from the
ambient accumulation in the collective unconscious rather than
from specific humans. It took decades to perfect, but it changed
everything."

"And the Concordat formalised this new arrangement," I
concluded.

"It did more than that," Perseus corrected. "It created an entirely
new supernatural system. Witches would harvest excess shadow
energy, enchant food and drink for vampires, and in exchange,
vampires would provide certain services."

"What kind of services?" I asked, suddenly suspicious.

Perseus smiled thinly. "Someone needs to handle the darkest
aspects of life. Vampires, with our shadow affinity, are uniquely
equipped to absorb the psychological cost."

"And perhaps now some factions want to return to the old ways,"
I said. "Back to direct feeding, vampire dominance."

"Some believe the Concordat neutered us," Perseus said. "Transformed us from apex predators to domesticated shadow processors,
even though that change happened several hundred years before the
Concordat was created. They see blood enchantment as degrading –
like being fed kibble instead of hunting live prey."

"This sounds exactly like what Odette Valencourt was advocating for at the Council meeting," I said.

Perseus nodded gravely. "Indeed. Though there's no evidence
she's involved. That was the first place we checked. But at least now
you understand the true stakes of the Concordat's disappearance.
This isn't merely about feeding rights or political power. It's about
preventing a return to some of the darkest periods of supernatural
history – times when either the witches or the vampires nearly

destroyed the entire magical ecosystem in their quest for dominance."

The weight of this history settled over me. I had stumbled into a conflict far older and more complex than I could have imagined – one with implications not just for supernatural politics but for the psychological balance of the entire world.

"You need to rest," Perseus said, noting my increasingly frantic page-turning. "The Grand Soirée is coming up quickly, and Mother will be... displeased if you're not at your best."

I snorted. "Displeased" was putting it mildly. Azalea in a state of displeasure sounded like a category five hurricane deciding it was feeling a bit peevish today.

"I can't rest," I insisted. "The Concordat is still missing, supernatural war is brewing, and Azalea wants me to waltz around at a ball looking for someone to legally adopt me like I'm an orphaned child."

Perseus's expression softened slightly, centuries of experience showing in his eyes. "The Sangrelié bond isn't adoption, Gillian. It's protection – both for you and for others. If your powers continue to develop unchecked..."

He left the implication hanging, but I understood. I was becoming potentially dangerous in ways even I didn't fully comprehend.

"I know," I admitted reluctantly. "But surely there's another solution. Something that doesn't involve surrendering my autonomy to another vampire."

"Perhaps," Perseus allowed, not sounding convinced. "But until we find one, Azalea's Grand Soirée remains your best option for legal security. Try to keep an open mind – many of Europe's most distinguished vampires will be in attendance."

Great. A ballroom full of ancient, powerful vampires. Like speed dating, but with the potential for mind control.

"Fine," I sighed, knowing when I was beaten. "I'll go to the ball.

But I'm not promising to bond with anyone, no matter how distinguished or ancient."

Perseus nodded, his mouth quirking in what might have been amusement. "A reasonable boundary. Now, you really should prepare for the seamstress. Madame Lefèvre has been outfitting Burk vampires since the French Revolution, and she does not tolerate tardiness or 'insufficient preparation.'"

He glanced down at his phone. "Ah...new information has just come in. Juniper, you'll need to pick this up."

"What am I signing up for now?" Juniper asked, casually leaning against my desk as though collecting a coffee order.

"Strange activities have been reported at the Helix Coven's headquarters. There's likely further evidence that the radical witch faction, orchestrated the theft," Perseus explained.

"What kind of strange?" Juniper asked.

"That's for you to investigate." Perseus said, his expression grave. "But be careful. Without clear evidence pointing to any single culprit, diplomacy becomes rather challenging."

With those ominous words, he departed, leaving me alone with my scattered research and growing anxiety.

The Concordat's theft was no simple political manoeuvre. It was a calculated attempt to destabilize the entire supernatural world. But to what end? Who would benefit from unleashing vampire shadow powers while simultaneously risking witch retaliation?

And as for my personal predicament? I couldn't help but think that finding the Twilight Concordat remained my best hope. If I could prove myself, perhaps the authorities would let me live, and better yet, let me maintain my independence.

**Current status: Illegal vampire with escalating powers. Researcher of missing magical artefacts. Reluctant debutante at supernatural adoption ball. Mother of children seen only under supervision. Former human with rapidly diminishing connection to normal existence. Ball gown: pending.**

# CHAPTER 13
# SUSPICIOUSLY HELPFUL WITCHES

**5:23 PM. Vampire detective work: questionable. Hidden agendas detected: multiple. Trust level: somewhere between 'absolutely not' and 'what choice do I have?' Shadow integration: holding steady. Professional attire: questionably appropriate for magical investigation.**

"You're sure this is the right place?" I asked, staring at the charred remains of what had apparently once been an elegant Victorian townhouse in Bloomsbury. Now it was just a blackened skeleton, the acrid smell of smoke still hanging in the air despite the light rain that had been falling all afternoon.

Juniper nodded, her purple hair darkened to a deep plum by the dampness. "This was the London headquarters of the Helix Coven, their primary research facility."

I surveyed the damage with my enhanced vision, noting details that would have escaped human observers – the strange bluish tinge to some of the burn marks, the faint shimmer of residual magic still clinging to the ruins like cobwebs.

"This wasn't a normal fire," I said, stepping carefully over a fallen beam. The smell of smoke was mixed with something else, something acrid and chemical that made my nose wrinkle.

"Definitely not," Juniper agreed, crouching to examine a partially melted glass vial. "Magical accelerant. Designed to burn through protective wards. Whoever did this knew exactly what they were targeting."

I picked my way through the debris, careful not to touch anything that might still be magically reactive.

"So the question is," I mused, "did they burn it down to hide evidence of their involvement in the Concordat theft, or was it someone trying to eliminate them as witnesses?"

"Or option three – they burned it themselves to fake their own destruction and go underground," Juniper suggested, pocketing the melted vial. "The Helix Coven has a long history of dramatic vanishing acts when things get politically heated."

I turned to look at her. "How do you know so much about witch covens anyway?"

"Professional overlap," Juniper replied vaguely. "Plus, in my line of work, you learn to keep tabs on all the major players."

I wasn't entirely satisfied with her answer but let it drop for the moment. There was something in her tone that suggested this wasn't the time to press for details.

"Do you think they're connected to the Concordat theft?" I asked instead, turning back to the practical matter at hand.

Juniper straightened, brushing ash from her hands. "They certainly had motive. The Helix Coven has been campaigning for centuries to revise the magical regulations imposed by the Concordat. They believe it unfairly restricts certain types of experimental magic."

"Experimental magic like...?"

"Biological manipulation, mostly," Juniper explained. "Their speciality is genetic enhancement through magical means. The Concordat places strict limits on how far they can go – no creating new species, no permanent alterations to existing ones without multiple oversight approvals."

"So they're basically supernatural mad scientists," I summarised, "who want to play at being gods without so much paperwork."

"That's... not entirely unfair, actually," Juniper admitted with a small smile. "Though they'd be horrified to hear themselves described that way. They consider their work 'essential evolutionary advancement.'"

A sudden gust of wind sent a shower of wet ash swirling around us. I brushed a speck from my cheek, grimacing at the gritty texture. "So what now? Their headquarters is destroyed, and I'm guessing the coven members aren't still hanging around to answer questions."

"Now," Juniper said, her eyes lighting up with that particular gleam that I was learning to associate with magical mischief, "we go find where they're hiding."

**5:56 PM. Location: Juniper's ridiculously impractical sports car. Speed: alarming. Probability of vehicular disaster: increasing with each turn.**

"I'm regretting the suggestion that we should drive!" I said, clutching the door handle as Juniper took another hairpin turn at a speed that would have given a Formula One driver pause.

"But I'm tired of you complaining about the effects of teleportation, besides, driving's so fun!" Juniper said as we raced along in the violently purple car with an engine that sounded like a mechanical dragon having a tantrum. The interior was crammed with an assortment of crystals, technical magical instruments, and what appeared to be emergency rations of energy drinks and gummy bears.

We'd left London behind, heading west into increasingly rural landscapes. As the miles passed and the roads narrowed, I finally voiced the thoughts that had been building inside me since my transformation.

"Juniper," I began, choosing my words carefully, "do you think I'll ever get my life back? Any version of it?"

She glanced at me, then back at the road. For once, her perpetually animated face was still, thoughtful. "Define 'life'."

"Being a mother to my children," I said, watching the hedgerows blur past the window. "Not living in constant fear of Council execution. Understanding what I am and why I can do apparently impossible things like summon dark fire. Having some control over my own existence instead of facing this Sangrelié bonding that sounds disturbingly like supernatural indentured servitude."

Juniper was quiet for a long moment, navigating a particularly narrow stretch of country lane before responding.

"I think," she said finally, "that you'll have a life. Whether it resembles your old one depends on how you define its essential components. The children, yes, eventually. The Council situation... manageable with the right strategy. The magical anomalies..." She hesitated, something flickering across her face too quickly for me to interpret. "That's more complicated."

"Because I shouldn't be able to summon fire," I supplied. "Because vampires don't have that ability. Yet here I am, breaking the supernatural rulebook just days after being turned without even trying to."

"Rules exist until they don't," Juniper shrugged, but there was tension in her shoulders that belied her casual tone. "The world constantly evolves."

"But you know something," I pressed. "About why I'm different."

The car slowed slightly, Juniper's fingers tapping an irregular rhythm on the steering wheel. "Sometimes," she said carefully, "it's safer not to know things. Especially when those things might attract the wrong kind of attention."

"I'm already attracting attention," I pointed out. "The Council wants me terminated, apparently. I think the time for caution is well past."

Juniper sighed, her usual boundless energy momentarily subdued. "It's not that simple, Gillian. There are... factions within the supernatural world that make the Vampire Council look like a neighbourhood watch committee. If certain theories about your abilities proved correct…"

"Do you mean the Obscurum?" I asked, trying to recall what Juniper had told me about the aptly named secret society that no one seemed to know anything about.

She trailed off, then abruptly brightened. "And here we are! Perfect timing to drop this extremely uncomfortable conversation."

The car turned onto an unmarked dirt track that I would have sworn wasn't there a second ago, bumping along for another quarter mile before emerging into a small clearing. Juniper parked beneath an ancient oak tree and killed the engine.

"Welcome to the Hollow," she announced. "One of the oldest witch sanctuaries in England."

I peered through the windshield at what appeared to be an utterly unremarkable stretch of forest. "I don't see anything."

"That's rather the point of a witch sanctuary," Juniper replied, reaching into the backseat for her oversized bag. "Stay close and don't say anything until I tell you it's safe. Vampire visitors aren't exactly welcome here under normal circumstances, but follow my lead and try to look non-threatening."

"I'm wearing a pencil skirt," I pointed out. "How threatening could I possibly look?"

Juniper gave me a pointed once-over. "You're a vampire with unusually strong power and the ability to conjure fire. Trust me, they'll sense something the moment we cross their wards. So just… think peaceful thoughts."

**6:03 PM. Location: allegedly magical forest. Evidence of witch habitation: non-existent. Peaceful thoughts: increasingly difficult to maintain.**

We'd been walking for nearly twenty minutes, following a path that existed mainly in Juniper's imagination as far as I could tell. The forest had grown denser. Perfect for vampire comfort, less ideal for finding our way.

"Are you sure —" I began.

"Shhh," Juniper cut me off, raising one hand. Her head tilted, like she was listening to something beyond human – or vampire – hearing range. "We're here."

I looked around sceptically. Here appeared to be the middle of nowhere, a small clearing surrounded by ancient oak trees. No buildings, no people, just moss-covered stones and wildflowers.

Then Juniper began to recite something in a language I didn't recognise – the syllables flowing and melodic but with sharp consonants that seemed to slice through the air itself.

The air shimmered, like heat rising from summer pavement, and suddenly the clearing was no longer empty.

What had appeared to be natural woodland transformed before my eyes. The moss-covered stones and wildflowers were revealed to be small cottages in the distance, arranged in a rough circle around a central green space surrounded by carefully tended garden beds. And most startlingly, people – dozens of them – appeared as if they'd been there all along, going about their business in this hidden village.

"Perception filter," Juniper explained at my expression. "Only those invited or who know the proper greeting can see past it."

Before I could respond, our presence was noticed. A tall woman with silver-streaked black hair approached, wearing practical gardening clothes and carrying pruning shears. Despite her mundane appearance, power radiated from her like heat from a furnace.

"Juniper," she greeted, her voice carrying the slight lilt of a Welsh accent.

"Megan," Juniper replied with unexpected formality. "Thank you for admitting us. This is Gillian Spark, recently turned vampire and –"

Megan's dark eyes fixing on me with unnerving intensity. "Why have you brought her here?"

"We're investigating the Concordat theft," Juniper said simply. "And the destruction of the Helix Coven's London headquarters."

Megan's expression shifted subtly. "You'd better come with me. This isn't a conversation for the village green."

She led us to one of the larger cottages at the edge of the settlement. Unlike the others with their thatched roofs and quaint appearances, this one had a distinctly more modern feel – larger windows, a slate roof, and a door that looked like it might actually have a proper lock instead of a rustic latch.

Inside was equally surprising – sleek furnishings that wouldn't have looked out of place in a high-end London flat, walls lined with bookshelves holding an eclectic mix of ancient tomes and modern technical volumes, and a computer setup in one corner.

"You seem surprised," Megan noted, observing my reaction. "Did you expect cauldrons and broomsticks?"

"Honestly, I've given up having expectations about anything," I admitted. "Every time I think I understand the rules, they change."

A smile flickered briefly across her stern features. "A wise approach." She gestured for us to sit at a polished oak table near the window, then took a seat across from us. "Now, why exactly do you think the Helix Coven is connected to the Concordat theft?"

"Evidence found at the scene pointed to their involvement," Juniper explained. "But it seemed too convenient, too obvious."

"Like someone wanted them to be blamed," I added.

"And then the headquarters mysteriously burns down," Juniper continued. "Either destroying evidence or eliminating witnesses. We came to hear their side directly."

Megan's hands folded precisely on the table. "The Helix Coven has been here only a few days. After the Concordat disappeared, they received threats – nothing specific, but concerning enough that their leadership decided to temporarily relocate to safer ground."

"You're sure they weren't behind the theft, then?" Juniper asked.

"I can't speak to what individual members might have done," Megan replied carefully. "But as a collective, no. In fact, their new leadership has been advocating for a more collaborative approach with other supernatural factions. Quite a departure from their traditional stance."

"New leadership?" Juniper questioned. "When did that change happen?"

"About three months ago," Megan said. "After centuries of the same rigid hierarchy, they've adopted a more... democratic structure. It's been quite the talk among the covens."

I glanced at Juniper, whose brow had furrowed.

"That's... a significant shift in a very traditional organisation," Juniper observed. "What prompted it?"

"Evolution is necessary for survival," Megan replied with a shrug that seemed a bit too casual. "Even the most entrenched magical institutions must adapt eventually."

"And their former leaders?" I pressed. "Where are they now?"

Something flickered in Megan's eyes – caution, perhaps. "Retired to private research, I understand."

The conversation continued along these lines for some time – Megan providing perfectly reasonable answers that nonetheless felt slightly rehearsed, Juniper probing gently but persistently, and me watching the subtle interplay between them with growing suspicion.

Eventually, Megan offered to give us a tour of the village and introduce us to some of the Helix Coven members currently in residence.

The Helix Coven members we met seemed genuine enough – a diverse group of witches ranging from elderly scholars to bright-eyed apprentices barely out of their teens. All spoke of their new collaborative approach with apparent sincerity, emphasising research projects focused on healing magic and sustainable agriculture.

As the tour concluded and twilight deepened into true night, I found myself more confused than ever. Either the Helix Coven had undergone a genuine philosophical transformation, or they were putting on an extraordinarily convincing performance.

"Thank you for your time," Juniper said as we prepared to leave. "And for the sanctuary's hospitality."

"Our doors are always open to those who come in peace," Megan replied, with a pointed glance at me that made it clear vampire visitors remained an exception rather than the rule. "Even in these uncertain times."

As we walked back through the forest toward Juniper's car, guided by witch-light that Megan had provided, I finally broke the contemplative silence.

"They're hiding something."

Juniper nodded, picking her way carefully along the path. "Definitely. But I don't think it's the Concordat."

"Then what?"

"That," Juniper sighed, "is the question. Did you notice how none of the coven leaders we met were older than fifty? For a magical organisation that typically venerates age and experience, that's highly unusual."

"You think something happened to the older members?"

"They've has a lot of turnover in their leadership, that's all I know for sure. But that's for the witching authorities to figure out."

We reached the car and climbed in, the familiar purple interior oddly comforting after hours in the strange magical settlement. As Juniper started the engine, I turned to face her directly.

"You're hiding something too," I said quietly. "About me. About why I can do impossible things."

Juniper's hands tightened on the steering wheel, her normally animated face unusually still. For a long moment, I thought she might finally tell me the truth. Then her expression shifted, the familiar mischievous smile returning.

"Everyone's hiding something, Gillian. It's the first rule of the supernatural world." She pulled the car onto the dirt track, headlights cutting through the darkness. "Now, are you hungry? I know a fantastic little place just outside Oxford that serves the most amazing blood-infused pasta, I'm told. Their chef is a fire sprite with three Michelin stars and a minor criminal record for unauthorised blood sourcing, but the carbonara is worth the moral ambiguity."

And just like that, the moment was gone, the subject changed with Juniper's characteristic conversational whiplash.

**Current status: Vampire detective with mounting questions. Investigation: yielding more questions than answers. Juniper's evasiveness: reaching suspicious levels. Dinner plans: apparently involving ethically questionable pasta.**

# CHAPTER 14

# TRY NOT TO EAT THE CHILDREN

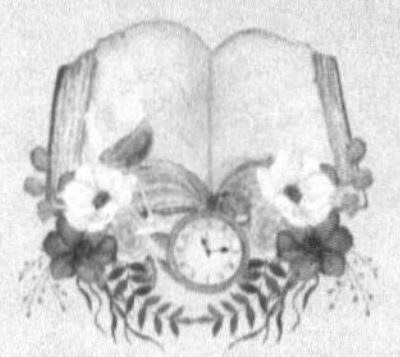

7:23 PM. Location: children's sitting room. Supervision level: hovering discreetly. Emotional state: desperately missing proper hugs.

The children's sitting room in the castle was elegant and comfortable – Persian rugs soft enough for sprawling, ancient tapestries depicting cheerful woodland scenes, and furniture scaled just right for small people. Keyne was building an elaborate tower from what looked like perfectly ordinary blocks (though I suspected they might be enchanted given how they kept balancing in physically impossible ways), while Merryn was carefully arranging her collection of interesting stones she'd found in the castle gardens.

I sat in the designated armchair – close enough to see them clearly, far enough away to be safe. Dora stood by the doorway, pretending to read correspondence while actually monitoring my control.

It was agony, watching them play without being able to cuddle them.

"Mummy, when can we have proper hugs again?" Merryn asked suddenly, looking up from her stone arrangement with those serious brown eyes that saw too much. "Tilly says you're feeling poorly, but you look fine to me. Just really pale."

My undead heart did something that felt suspiciously like breaking. "Soon, sweetheart. The doctors say I just need more rest to get my strength back."

"Is it contagious?" Keyne piped up without looking away from his architectural marvel. "Because Tilly hasn't got sick yet, and she's been sleeping in the room next to ours."

Tilly, who had been lounging on the settee in her signature purple cardigan – this one a particularly violent shade of purple that somehow worked perfectly with her auburn hair – looked up from her phone with sharp intelligence in her eyes.

"It's not that kind of sick," I said carefully, hating myself for the continued deception. "It's more like... an allergy. To sunlight. Very rare."

Tilly's head tilted slightly, and I caught the calculating look she was giving me before she glanced meaningfully at Perseus, then back to me.

"That sounds rubbish," Merryn announced with childlike bluntness. "How can you be allergic to the sun!"

"Merryn," Keyne said solemnly, "that's not very nice to say Mummy sounds rubbish."

Dora laughed as though this were the very entertainment she'd been hoping for.

"How are you finding the castle?" I asked, desperate to keep them talking about normal things. "Are you getting enough to eat? Sleeping well?"

"The food is amazing," Merryn said cheerfully.

"Oh yes," Keyne agreed, abandoning his tower to flop dramatically on the rug.

Merryn continued, "Jenkins makes these little cakes that taste like clouds."

"They taste like honey too," Keyne added. "And our room has a secret passage behind the bookshelf!"

As the children chattered, I felt the familiar ache of missing their daily lives. These supervised visits gave me glimpses into their world, but I wasn't part of it anymore. I was watching from the sidelines, a spectator to their childhood.

"Not secret if you tell everyone about it," Merryn pointed out with characteristic precision. "Also, the library here is wonderful. So many old, old, old books."

"That's wonderful, darlings," I said, though I made a mental note to ask Perseus exactly what kind of books seven-year-olds were accessing in an ancient supernatural library.

"The ancient texts are quite educational," Dora said, from the doorway.

I looked at her properly as she strolled over, taking in her black velvet dress with pearl buttons, hair in perfect plaits tied with black ribbons, framing a face that should have belonged on a porcelain doll but instead housed eyes older than some civilizations. "Your daughter asked me why some of the books are chained. I told her they're very old and valuable." She paused by my chair. "She then asked, if that's why I have to stay in the castle too. If I'm too valuable to leave." Her rosebud lips curved in what might have been a smile on anyone else. On her, it looked like a wound. "Clever girl."

I shivered and tried to ignore the ancient child vampire and the fact that she'd had more access to my kids than I did.

Tilly had been unusually quiet throughout the conversation, but I could see her observing everything – my careful distance from the children, Dora's watchful presence, the way I flinched slightly when they mentioned wanting hugs.

"Right then, you two," Tilly said suddenly, standing up with decisive energy. "Jenkins wants you in the kitchen."

"But we're visiting with Mummy," Keyne protested.

"Your mum will still be here when you get back," Tilly said firmly. "And Jenkins mentioned something about biscuits."

That got their attention. Ancient castles, it turned out, had excellent biscuits.

Dora rolled her eyes. "I'll follow them."

The door had barely closed behind them when Tilly rounded on me.

"Right then," she said, crossing her arms and fixing me with a look I knew all too well. "How long were you planning to keep this up?"

My stomach dropped. "Keep what up?"

Tilly gave me the look she usually reserved for particularly obtuse spreadsheets. "Gillian Spark, I have known you for ten years. Ten years of morning coffees and lunch breaks and listening to you complain about Neville's unconscious habit of leaving his socks exactly two inches from the laundry basket instead of in it."

I opened my mouth to protest, but she held up a hand.

"The pale skin I could chalk up to stress from the divorce," she continued. "The avoiding daylight could be explained by your newfound hatred of vitamin D or whatever excuse you were planning."

My heart sank.

"But," Tilly said, leaning forward with a grin that was equal parts fond and exasperated, "the bit where you can't physically touch your own children? Where you need a creepy doll-like creature standing guard during family visits? Where you move like you're afraid you might accidentally break something – or someone? I know what you are."

I stared at her, my mouth opening and closing soundlessly. "I... what..."

"Gill," Tilly said gently, "the only question was when you'd trust me enough to actually say it."

I felt tears pricking at my eyes and quickly wiped them away lest blood pour down my cheeks. "Tilly, I need to tell you something impossible..."

"That you're a vampire?" she interrupted with a laugh. "Finally! I was starting to think you'd never work up the nerve."

"But how..."

"The glimpse of fangs was dead giveaway," Tilly said cheerfully. "Also, you've started moving too quietly – normal humans make noise when they walk. And yesterday when you thought no one was looking, I saw you accidentally crush that pen in your hand like it was made of tissue paper."

I broke down completely then, all the fear and isolation and guilt pouring out in a rush. "I'm so sorry I lied to you. I was terrified you'd be frightened, or think I was insane, or –"

"Oh, love," Tilly said, moving closer but still respecting the distance I'd been maintaining. "Do you really think that little of me? I've been your friend through your marriage to Neville Bennett – if I can handle that level of psychological horror, I think I can manage actual vampirism."

Despite everything, I laughed. "That's... actually a fair point."

"Besides," Tilly continued, settling back onto the settee with obvious satisfaction, "you look absolutely lethal these days. That new wardrobe is working for you. Very 'don't mess with me, I have supernatural powers' chic."

"I've missed you," I said, feeling like I could breathe properly for the first time in days. "I missed being able to talk about...well, all this."

"Well, now you can talk to me about everything," Tilly said practically. "Starting with why you're living in a castle with what I'm fairly certain are other vampires, why the children think you have a mysterious illness, and what exactly happened to turn you into one of the undead."

"It's complicated," I said weakly.

"I have time," "Although first – more importantly – how does one get on the waiting list for immortality? Because I have thoughts about spending eternity with perfect skin and supernatural strength."

I snorted. "It wasn't exactly a voluntary process, Tills. And there are significant downsides."

"Such as?"

"Well, I can't hug my children because I might accidentally drain their blood," I said flatly. "And there's the small matter technically being dead, let alone figuring out how I'm going to tell my mother?"

Tilly waved this away dismissively. "Details. What about the supernatural politics? Please tell me there are supernatural politics. I do love a good political conspiracy."

And so I found myself explaining everything – the Twilight Concordat, the investigation, my illegal vampire status, the looming need to find a Sangrelié, and the Grand Soirée where I was expected to essentially shop for a supernatural guardian.

"Right," Tilly said when I finished. "So the children can't know the truth because they're too young and it would be traumatic. I'll keep up the 'Mummy's poorly' story. Evening visits work better anyway – I've never been a morning person."

She paused, considering. "This Sangrelié business though – that's essentially supernatural adoption for adults?"

"More like supernatural guardianship with bonus mind control potential," I said grimly.

"Ghastly," Tilly agreed. "Like having to ask permission to make major life decisions from someone who's older than the British Museum. Though I suppose these vampire candidates must be quite attractive in a 'dangerous immortal being' sort of way?"

"Tilly!"

"What? I'm just saying, if you're going to be magically bound to someone for potentially decades, they might as well be easy on the eyes." She grinned wickedly. "Besides, think of the networking opportunities. I bet vampire society has the most interesting parties."

"You're taking this remarkably well," I said.

"Gill, love, you're my best friend. You could tell me you'd secretly been a dragon this whole time and I'd just ask if that explained your hoarding tendency with legal documents." Tilly's expression grew more serious. "Besides, you've been miserable for years – first with Neville, then with the divorce stress. This is the first time I've seen you look properly alive in… well, ironic word choice aside, you know what I mean.”

She was right. Despite the complications and dangers, I felt more like myself than I had in years.

“Now then,” Tilly continued briskly, “what can I do to help? Besides keeping the children entertained and maintaining your cover story, obviously.”

“You’re already doing more than enough,” I said. “Just… having someone to talk to who knows the truth means everything.”

“Practical support, then,” Tilly said, pulling out her phone.

“What about work?” I asked. “People must be wondering why I’ve vanished. And our friends – Priya and Adrien must be going mad with worry.”

“Already handled,” Tilly said with the smug satisfaction of someone who’d been planning ahead. “I’ve been telling everyone you’re taking extended sick leave for a rare condition that requires specialist treatment. Very hush-hush, very clinical, very boring. Neville’s secretary even sent a get well card.”

She settled back with obvious relish. “As for Priya and Adrien – oh, you’ve missed some drama there. Priya’s been absolutely beside herself trying to research your mysterious condition. I had to physically stop her from driving to every private clinic in London demanding information.”

“That sounds like Priya,” I said fondly.

“And Adrien,” Tilly continued with a wicked grin, “has been channelling his worry into the most spectacular revenge plot against Neville. He’s been leaving anonymous art reviews of Neville’s office decor online. Apparently, Neville’s choice in desk accessories represents ‘the death of aesthetic sensibility in corporate environments. There’s a whole cult movement against his choice of ties.’”

Despite everything, I burst out laughing. “He didn’t!”

“Oh, he absolutely did. There’s now a scathing review going viral, comparing Neville’s motivational posters to ‘visual terrorism’ that’s been shared around half the legal community.” Tilly’s eyes sparkled with mischief. "Priya actually called me yesterday demanding to know if you'd been secretly training for Everest or handling radioactive materials."

"I feel terrible lying to them," I said, guilt washing over me. "They were so supportive during the divorce, and now I've just vanished without explanation."

"Well, you can't exactly text them 'Sorry I've been MIA, turns out I'm a vampire now, fancy drinks?'" Tilly pointed out reasonably.

"I suppose not."

She leaned forward conspiratorially. "I could arrange something, you know. An evening meet-up where you can see them safely. Tell them you're on medication that makes you photosensitive – it's not technically a lie. Just don't demonstrate any supernatural strength around Priya or she'll immediately try to reverse-engineer your condition."

"You've thought of everything," I said, impressed despite myself. "Maybe I can handle drinks, once I've settled in a bit more. I haven't had the urge to eat you, so that's progress. I'm just so relieved not to have to keep it all secret anymore."

"I've had a while to figure it out," Tilly pointed out. "I don't suppose your supernatural law firm needs an accountant? Because I have to tell you, normal corporate accounting is getting dreadfully boring after discovering vampires exist."

"Tilly..."

"Think about it," she said airily. "I'm discreet, I'm good with numbers, and I already know your terrible secret. Plus, I imagine supernatural beings have fascinatingly complex financial arrangements."

I had to admit, the idea of having Tilly nearby on a longer term was enormously appealing, not that I'd given much thought to my future outside of solving immediate major problems. "I'll ask Perseus if they need accounting help."

"Excellent. Now, about this Grand Soirée thing. What exactly does one wear to a vampire ball?"

"Apparently something elegant and expensive that makes me look like appropriate arm candy for ancient undead aristocrats," I said sourly. "I've had a fitting already with a very bossy seamstress, Madame Lefèvre. She decided to go for midnight blue to complement my essence.

"Perfect. You've got good bone structure and supernatural enhancement..." Tilly's expression turned calculating. "Although you'll want to project confidence and independence. Can't have them thinking you're desperate for their protection."

"I am desperate for their protection, apparently," I pointed out feeling genuinely ill at the thought. "The alternative is execution by the Vampire Council."

"Focus on your strengths," Tilly said pragmatically. "Basic negotiation tactics – never let them see how much you need the deal. Project desirability instead of desperation."

I laughed despite myself. "You're giving me dating advice for supernatural guardians."

"Someone has to," Tilly replied cheerfully. "Left to your own devices, you'd probably show up with a PowerPoint presentation outlining your legal vulnerabilities and a cost-benefit analysis of various Sangrelié options."

She wasn't wrong.

The sound of small feet in the corridor announced the children's return from their library adventure. Tilly immediately shifted back into caregiver mode, but not before giving me a meaningful look.

"Just promise me one thing," she said quietly. "Don't settle for someone who makes you feel small. You've had enough of that. If you're going to be magically bound to someone, make sure they see your value, not just your vulnerabilities."

The advice was surprisingly tender, and I felt a surge of gratitude for this remarkable woman who had taken my supernatural revelation in stride and immediately started plotting how to help me navigate immortal politics.

Keyne and Merryn burst back into the room, both sporting

biscuit crumbs and what appeared to be ink stains from their library adventures.

"Mummy!" they cried, rushing into my arms before I could stop them. I took a deep breath, inhaling the scent of biscuits, and blessedly found myself not craving their blood at all. Dora merely raised an eyebrow as I stepped back.

As we settled back into supervised family time, I caught Tilly's eye. She winked at me, her expression warm with affection and determination.

I had an ally now. Someone from my old life who knew the truth and not only accepted it, but was already plotting how to help me succeed in this strange new world.

For the first time since my transformation, I felt like I might actually be able to navigate all this chaos without losing myself entirely.

Now I just had to survive the Grand Soirée.

**Current status: Vampire with best friend who thinks supernatural transformation is a fashionable lifestyle choice. Support system: unexpectedly robust. Children: safely unaware and well-cared-for and unexpectedly hugged. Confidence level: marginally improved.**

# CHAPTER 15

# DANCE LIKE EVERYONE'S JUDGING

9:07 PM. Vampire ball arrival: imminent. Social anxiety: approaching nuclear levels. Chance of embarrassing self: approaching mathematical certainty.

I caught my reflection in an antique mirror and stopped short. The gown was midnight blue silk that seemed to absorb and reflect light simultaneously, it looked like I was wearing an elaborately detailed piece of the night sky. "Vampire haute couture," I murmured. "Who knew?"

"Everyone really ought to know," Azalea said smugly. "We invented fashion, darling."

The midnight-blue silk seemed to drink in light, creating the illusion that I was wrapped in liquid shadow.

"Finally," Azalea said with satisfaction. "You look like what you are."

"Which is?" I asked, tentatively.

She smiled. "Dangerous. Now come, we're fashionably late."

An hour later, the car stopped at the foot of a grand staircase lined with what appeared to be actual flaming torches. A footman opened the door with a white-gloved hand.

"Welcome madams," he intoned with a perfect bow.

I stepped out, immediately tangling one heel in the hem of my gown. Vampire grace apparently had its limits when confronted with formal wear.

"Remember," Azalea murmured as we ascended the stairs, her eyes scanning the entrance with excitement, "to try to appear intrigued rather than terrified."

"I am intrigued," I replied honestly. "I just don't see why intrigue has to come with social anxiety at catastrophic levels."

We passed through massive double doors into an entrance hall that could have comfortably housed my entire London home. Crystal chandeliers dripped from coffered ceilings, casting prismatic light across marble floors. The air was thick with the scent of roses and beeswax, underlaid with something else — the distinct absence of human scent. No sweat, no heartbeats.

A vampire-only affair, then. Somehow that made it worse.

A string quartet played in a corner, their fingers moving with inhuman precision across their instruments. The resulting music was technically perfect yet somehow unsettling — too flawless.

But before I could fully absorb the opulent surroundings, a hush fell over the entrance hall. Conversations stopped mid-sentence. Even the string quartet seemed to falter for a moment before resuming with renewed precision.

The cause became immediately apparent.

A woman descended the grand staircase with the grace of flowing water, yet every step commanded absolute attention. Platinum hair swept into an elegant chignon. Her gown was a deep burgundy that matched her wine-dark lips. Ancient power radiated from her like heat from a forge, making the air itself feel heavier.

"Odette Valencourt," Azalea breathed beside me, her voice carrying notes of both admiration and wariness. "I wasn't certain she would come."

"We've met," I said, dryly.

Azalea raised an eyebrow. "Of course, Charles did mention that.

But did you know she's one of the oldest vampires in Europe. What's certain is that she's been publicly opposing Concordat regulations for the better part of two centuries."

Odette's dark eyes swept the room acknowledging nods and bows with the barest inclination of her head. When her gaze fell on Azalea and me a chill shot down my spine. She began moving toward us with purposeful grace, and I noticed something extraordinary happening around her. Other vampires – powerful, ancient creatures who had been radiating their own supernatural dominance – were subtly submitting. Shoulders dropped slightly. Eyes looked away. It was unconscious, instinctive, the response of predators recognising an apex creature.

"Azalea, darling," came a melodious voice to our right just before Odette reached us. "Fashionably late as always."

I turned to see an elegant silver-haired woman in an emerald gown with sharp aristocratic features and penetrating dark eyes. She looked like someone I'd met before, but couldn't quite place.

"Victoria Prendergast," Azalea greeted her with the European double-kiss. "Timely as always. Still keeping up appearances, I see."

"Someone must," Victoria replied. Her gaze shifted to me, taking in every detail with uncomfortable thoroughness. "And this must be your protégée. The one causing such interesting ripples in our community. You look familiar..."

"Gillian Spark," I managed, extending my hand. "Recently divorced, recently undead, recently informed that I'm apparently a topic of conversation."

Victoria looked taken aback. Before she could reply, Odette Valencourt arrived at our small group with the quiet authority of approaching storm.

Both Azalea and Victoria stiffened slightly, though they managed polite smiles.

"Azalea," Odette said, her voice carrying a slight accent I couldn't place – something that suggested origins lost to antiquity. "How delightful to see you embracing your role as patron of the newly turned."

"Odette," Azalea replied. "We're honoured by your presence."

"Indeed," Victoria added, though her tone suggested something closer to wariness than honour.

Those ancient eyes turned to me, and I felt assessed in ways that went beyond the visual.

"And Gillian, a pleasure to see you again," Odette tilted her head slightly, studying me with unsettling intensity. "Tell me, child, what do you think of our world? This carefully constructed society of rules and regulations?"

I glanced at Azalea, who was watching our interaction with barely concealed tension. "I think," I said carefully, "that any society built on controlling supernatural predators probably has rules for good reasons."

Odette's laugh was rich and dark, like aged wine poured over velvet. "How delightfully naive. You speak of 'control' as if it were natural, necessary. But what if I told you that for millennia, we were the apex predators? That witches came to us, begging for transformation? That the very shadows bent to our will without requiring their magical mediation?"

"I'd say that sounds like a recipe for mutual destruction," I replied, surprised by my own boldness.

"Perhaps," Odette conceded, her dark eyes glittering with something that might have been approval. "Or perhaps it was simply honest. The Concordat, my dear child, is our muzzle. Some of us remember when we hunted free."

The temperature in the immediate area seemed to drop several degrees. Other vampires who had been hovering nearby suddenly found pressing reasons to be elsewhere.

"And some of us," Azalea interjected smoothly, "remember why such arrangements became necessary."

Odette's smile remained perfectly pleasant, but there was steel beneath it. "Of course. The modern view. Cooperation over domination. How very... civilised." She turned back to me. "But tell me, Gillian, when your shadows rise – and I can sense they do – do they feel civilised? Or do they feel like power that longs to be unleashed?"

Before I could respond, she leaned closer, her voice dropping to a whisper that only vampire hearing could detect. "Power must be claimed, child. Never granted. The Concordat would have you believe we need their permission to exist, their magical enhancement to feed. But what if there were other ways? What if the old paths were not as lost as they would have you believe?"

"Odette," Azalea's voice carried a warning note. "Surely such philosophical discussions can wait."

"Of course," Odette replied, straightening gracefully. "Forgive me. I sometimes forget that new vampires are still adjusting to the... limitations of our current existence." She inclined her head to me. "We shall speak again, I'm certain. I find myself quite curious about your unique situation."

As Odette glided away, her departure caused another subtle shift in the room's dynamics. Conversations resumed, but at a lower volume. The unconscious tension that had gripped the gathering began to ease.

"Well," Azalea said, her voice carefully neutral. "That was certainly illuminating."

The main ballroom took my breath away – not that I technically needed to breathe. Two stories high with a domed ceiling painted with classical scenes, the space glittered with more chandeliers, gilded mouldings, and floor-to-ceiling windows that looked out onto formal gardens lit by strategically placed torches.

Several hundred vampires filled the space, all impossibly beautiful, all dressed in finery that ranged from classic evening wear to more elaborate period costumes. The dance floor was filled with perfectly synchronised waltzing. The overall effect was disorienting – like stepping into a movie set where everyone was too perfect to be real.

"Don't stare," Azalea murmured, guiding me toward the centre of the room where a small group of elegantly dressed vampires stood in animated conversation.

"Gillian, may I introduce Lord Sebastian Rothsforte," Azalea steered me towards a suave gentleman with dark slicked back hair. "Sebastian comes from one of our most distinguished lineages, and is quite the collector of rare antiquities. He's been particularly eager to make your acquaintance."

I extended my hand, but wanted to recoil. Everything about him screamed calculated predator. His green eyes fixed on me with a dangerous intensity.

"Ms Spark," he said, taking my hand and bowing over it in a gesture that should have been charming but somehow felt like being marked as prey. "I've been hearing the most extraordinary things about you. Such remarkable adaptation, such unprecedented potential." His smile was all teeth and no warmth. "I do hope we'll have the opportunity to become better acquainted."

"Err…"

"Overwhelmed, darling?" came a warm, cultured voice beside me.

Relieved at the distraction, I turned to find a striking woman watching me with genuine amusement. Unlike the predatory assessment of the others, her gaze held something closer to artistic appreciation. She wore an elegant vintage dress in deep burgundy that complemented her classical beauty.

"Is it that obvious?" I asked, grateful for the lack of pretence.

"Only to someone who remembers their own first soirée," she replied with a smile that reached her eyes – a refreshing change from the calculated expressions I'd encountered all evening. "Beatrice Valois. Patron of the arts in Renaissance Florence."

"Gillian Spark. Former corporate barrister, current supernatural mystery… apparently."

Beatrice laughed, the sound musical and genuine. "Delightful! Your honesty is refreshing."

"My filter was never great when I was alive. Death hasn't improved it."

"Good. Never lose that." Beatrice gestured vaguely at the room full of perfect, poised vampires. "Most of these creatures have forgotten what it means to be authentic." Her expression grew more serious. "Though I would advise caution around certain individuals tonight. Not everyone here has your best interests at heart."

"Such as?"

"Well," Beatrice's gaze drifted across the room to where Odette was engaged in what appeared to be an intense discussion with several other ancient vampires. "Odette Valencourt is undeniably fascinating, but she has her own agenda. One that may not align with a desire for a peaceful integration into vampire society."

"What kind of agenda?" I asked. Of course, Odette's agenda was obvious, but as she was currently my number one suspect for the Concordat theft, I wanted to know what other people knew.

Beatrice leaned closer, her voice dropping to barely above a whisper. "She believes the old ways were better. When vampires ruled absolutely, when we turned whom we pleased. She sees the current system as a corruption of our true nature."

I looked at Beatrice for a moment, sizing her up, then decided to be bold. "What do you know about the Concordat theft?"

"I wouldn't know anything, myself," Beatrice replied primly. "But I will say...Nothing destabilizes a system quite like removing its foundational agreements. If Odette could prove that vampire-witch cooperation was unnecessary, that we could return to the old ways..."

She didn't need to finish. The implications were clear enough.

As if summoned by our conversation, Odette appeared beside us with that uncanny grace that seemed to be her hallmark.

"Beatrice," she greeted the other woman with a smile that was perfectly pleasant and only slightly dangerous. "I hope you're not filling our new friend's head with waffle."

"Would I do such a thing?" Beatrice replied.

Odette turned those penetrating dark eyes on me. "Tell me, Gillian, has anyone explained to you exactly what the Twilight Concordat contains? I hear rumours that you have been investigating in this area and I wonder if you know the specific restrictions it places on our kind?"

"Some of it," I replied carefully. "Feeding regulations…"

"Such a sanitised summary." Odette's voice carried notes of genuine regret. "It also contains clauses that essentially make us dependent on witch magic for our most basic functions. The shadows that should answer to our will now require their enhancement to be properly controlled. We who once commanded the night itself now need permission slips to access our own power."

"Perhaps because the former system resulted in centuries of war," Beatrice interjected.

"Perhaps because witches feared what we might become if left to develop our abilities naturally," Odette countered. "The Concordat wasn't just a peace treaty – it was a leash. And some of us are tired of wearing it."

The way she said it, with such conviction and barely contained passion, sent another chill through me. This wasn't just philosophical opposition – this was genuine rage at what she saw as systematic oppression.

"And if someone wanted to remove that leash?" I asked, testing.

Odette's smile was sharp and beautiful and dangerous. "Hypothetically? One would need to prove that the old ways were not only possible but superior. That vampires could thrive without witch cooperation." Her eyes glittered with dark amusement.

Before I could probe further, Azalea appeared at my elbow with the determined expression of someone interrupting a conversation that had gone on long enough.

"Odette, darling," she said with forced brightness. "I'm afraid I need to steal Gillian away. There are still several people eager to meet her."

"Of course," Odette replied graciously.

"She's involved," I said quietly to Azalea as Odette glided back across the ball room.

"What?"

"Odette. In the Concordat theft. She has to be." I explained the subtext of our conversation.

Azalea's expression grew troubled. "Those are serious accusations, Gillian. Odette may be radical, but she's also one of the most respected ancient vampires in Europe. The evidence would need to be irrefutable. Besides, wouldn't it be too obvious to crow about it like this if she was indeed involved? Wouldn't that just tempt all the magical authorities to come crashing down on her."

"I suppose, but what better way to hide than in plain sight," I said grimly.

"Set that aside for now," Azalea commanded. "We have more pressing concerns."

She guided me toward a side door that led to what appeared to be a private sitting room. Already present were the vampires who had paid me special attention throughout the evening – Sebastian, Beatrice, Victoria Prendergast... I stared at the silver-haired woman until I remembered where I'd met her before. It was at the antiques shop, with Ezra Worster... I looked around to see if he might be here too as everyone stared at me with varying expressions of interest and calculation.

"Welcome, esteemed colleagues of the night," Azalea began, practically vibrating with excitement as she guided me to stand beside her in the centre of the room. "Thank you for accepting my invitation to this private gathering. As promised, I present to you Gillian Spark, perhaps the most extraordinary vampire transformation I've witnessed in centuries."

I stood awkwardly as nine pairs of ancient eyes studied me with unnerving intensity.

"As you've observed tonight, Gillian exhibits unprecedented adaptation for one so newly turned," Azalea continued, her voice rich with pride, as if she were showing off a particularly gifted protégée. "Her shadow integration is progressing at a rate that would be remarkable even for a vampire decades old. Her control, her abilities – all suggest extraordinary potential."

"Yes, yes, we've heard about her remarkable adaptation," Sebastian interjected smoothly. "What you haven't explained, Azalea, is why you've gathered us specifically."

Azalea's smile was dazzling, her eyes gleaming with dark delight. "Because, my dear Sebastian, Gillian requires something that only one of you can provide – specialised guidance for her unique situation. A personal mentorship, if you will."

Understanding dawned. This wasn't just a showcase – it was an audition.

"A mentorship," Victoria repeated sceptically. "How... euphemistic of you, Azalea."

"Call it what you will," Azalea replied, unperturbed by the implied criticism. "The fact remains that Gillian's extraordinary development requires extraordinary guidance. The question is which of you is best suited to provide it."

Sebastian stepped forward, his eyes fixed on me with predatory intensity. "I would be willing to consider a traditional arrangement. The Rothsforte lineage has certain standards to maintain, after all."

"The traditional method is barbaric," Beatrice countered, her musical voice sharp with disapproval. "I would propose modern testing protocols to determine compatibility."

As the vampires began debating the merits of various "mentorship" approaches, I stood frozen, suddenly understanding the full implications of Azalea's scheme. It was as if she'd orchestrated an exclusive bidding war among some of the most powerful vampires in Europe.

"Don't I get a say in this?" I finally interjected, my voice cutting through the increasingly heated discussion.

The room fell silent, all eyes turning to me with expressions ranging from surprise to amusement.

"Of course you do, dear," Azalea assured me. "This gathering is merely to introduce you to potential candidates. The final choice will naturally be yours, provided there's a match."

"Within certain parameters," Sebastian added silkily. "After all, not every vampire here is willing to undergo modern testing protocols. Some of us require more... traditional arrangements."

"And what if I don't want any arrangement at all?" I asked, unable to keep the edge from my voice.

Before anyone could respond, Charles approached, his expression grave.

"Azalea," he said quietly, crossing to her side. "A word, if you please. There's been a development."

He leaned close, whispering something in her ear that made her eyes widen fractionally – the vampire equivalent of a shocked gasp.

"I see," she said, composing herself quickly. "How very... inconvenient timing."

She turned back to the gathered vampires, her voice brisk. "It seems we must cut our discussion short. A matter requiring immediate attention has arisen."

Protests erupted immediately.

"I've only just arrived from Vienna for this meeting," Victoria complained.

"We've barely begun discussing the parameters of potential arrangements," Eva added, her green eyes narrowing with suspicion.

"The complexities of Gillian's situation require more thorough examination," Sebastian insisted, his calculated calm showing the first cracks of frustration.

Beatrice alone seemed unperturbed by the interruption. "Perhaps it's for the best. Decisions of this magnitude shouldn't be rushed."

"I agree with Beatrice," I said quickly, seizing the unexpected reprieve. "I need time to consider all options carefully."

Azalea nodded, somehow managing to look disappointed and relieved simultaneously. "Of course. We shall reconvene at a later date. For now, I must ask you all to return to the main ballroom."

As the vampires filed out, grumbling with varying degrees of aristocratic petulance, Azalea gripped my arm.

"What is it?" I asked.

"We have a slight complication," she whispered, her voice pitched too low for even vampire hearing to detect at a distance. "Clara Blackwood, Chief Investigator for the Vampire Council, has just arrived unannounced."

My stomach dropped. "Here for me?"

"Unknown," Azalea replied tersely. "But we must return to the ballroom immediately. Act natural, smile, and follow my lead."

**11:03 PM. Vampire politics: intensifying. Mysterious Council investigator: present. Acting natural: completely beyond current capabilities.**

We re-entered the ballroom to find more tension hanging in the air. The crowd parted awkwardly before us, conversations falling silent as we passed. At the centre of the room stood a woman I recognised immediately – tall and elegant with an imposing air. Her long dark hair pulled back in a severe chignon framed sharp features, her tailored black suit managed to be both severe and devastatingly stylish.

"Whatever happens, remain calm," Azalea murmured.

Calm was not remotely possible. My newly enhanced senses went into overdrive – picking up the sharp shift in the room's atmosphere, the way other vampires attention gravitated toward the new arrival, the almost imperceptible tension in Azalea's frame beside me.

Clara Blackwood turned, her striking eyes sweeping the room with analytical precision. When her gaze landed on us, I felt a jolt of fear and fascination. She radiated authority – not the practiced social dominance of other vampires, but something more fundamental, more dangerous.

To my surprise and Azalea's visible relief, Clara didn't approach us directly. Instead, she strode purposefully across the ballroom toward Victoria Prendergast, who had just rejoined the party.

"Victoria," Clara said, her voice cool and precise. "A word, if you please."

Victoria's composure slipped momentarily, surprise and something like wariness crossing her features before her social mask reasserted itself. "Clara. How unexpected. Surely whatever Council business you have can wait until after the Soirée?"

"No," Clara replied flatly. "It cannot."

The tension was palpable, crackling like static electricity. Just as Victoria began to respond, Clara's gaze shifted, sweeping past to where Azalea and I stood watching. Her eyes narrowed slightly.

I watched as Clara guided Victoria from the ballroom, leaving a wake of whispers and speculation behind them. Part of me desperately wanted to follow along behind them.

"Well," Azalea said in a tone that didn't quite mask her concern, "that was certainly dramatic."

**Current status: Vampire matchmaking scheme interrupted by Council investigator. Sangrelié candidates: variously appealing and appalling. Clara Blackwood: terrifying yet fascinating. Ancient vampire conspiracies: still suspected.**

# CHAPTER 16

# SHADOW POISONING: A PROGRESS REPORT

**2:17 PM. Sleep quality: abysmal. Nightmares: vivid and horrific. Shadow situation: definitely worse. Regrets about attending vampire ball: numerous.**

I awoke with a gasp, clawing my way out of another vivid nightmare. For a disorienting moment, I couldn't remember where I was.

I rubbed my eyes, trying to shake off the aftereffects of the nightmare. I'd been back at the ball, but everyone had been wearing animal masks, circling me while chanting something in a language I didn't understand. Clara Blackwood was there, her eyes glowing through a wolf mask, telling me I was running out of time while she filled out execution forms in triplicate.

"Bloody vampire bureaucracy," I muttered, reluctantly dragging myself out of bed.

I'd thought being a vampire made me immune from tiredness, but apparently not in my current condition.

My reflection in the mirror looked worse than usual – and that was saying something. Dark circles under my eyes, and a new, unsettling detail: the whites of my eyes had the faintest purple tinge. Like bruises starting to form, or ink bleeding into water.

I leaned closer to the mirror, simultaneously fascinated and appalled. "That can't be good."

The events of last night's ball came flooding back. What a complete disaster that had been. A room full of ancient, aristocratic vampires all evaluating me like a prize horse with questionable bloodlines. Or possibly a bomb that might detonate at any moment.

The Vampire Immortal Court, that's what they'd been. Odette Valencourt with her perfect posture and judgmental eyes – definitely The Frost Queen, radiating icy judgment with every perfectly articulated syllable. Sebastian Rothsforte – Lord Smirksalot, too impressed with his own cleverness by half. Victoria Prendergast with her emerald gown and knowing looks – The Oracle of Undeath, definitely keeping an ancient ledger of vampire secrets somewhere.

And Clara Blackwood. What nickname could possibly capture her? The Shadow Inquisitor? Lady Judgment?

A shiver passed through me at the thought of her.

Whatever I called her, she remained a very real threat to my existence. The memory of her eyes boring into me made my stomach clench.

I couldn't shake the feeling she knew something about me that I didn't know myself.

Only Beatrice Valois had seemed halfway decent, with her artistic perspective and lack of interest in political manoeuvring. The Renaissance Patron, perhaps – well-meaning but still carrying centuries of vampire baggage.

I sighed. The thought of facing Azalea after last night's debacle made me seriously consider barricading myself in my room like a sulky teenager. Unfortunately, I doubted a chair wedged under the doorknob would keep determined vampires at bay for long.

"There you are!" Azalea greeted me with enthusiasm as I slunk into the dining room. "Oh, just look at those eyes! Such accelerated shadow manifestation – how absolutely fascinating!"

She sat at the head of a massive oak table, looking irritatingly perfect in a tailored black dress with intricate silver embroidery, not a hair out of place despite the previous night's events. Perseus occupied a chair to her right, examining what appeared to be ancient scrolls while simultaneously typing on a sleek laptop – vampire multitasking.

"Good afternoon, Gillian," he said without looking up. "I trust you slept poorly?"

"How did you guess?" I grumbled, dropping into a chair and eyeing the blood-enchanted tea and scones set before me with minimal enthusiasm. "Was it my sparkling demeanour or the fact that I look like I've been hit by a bus?"

"Your eyes," he replied. "The discolouration indicates accelerated shadows. Typically a symptom that doesn't appear until several decades post-transformation."

"She's rotting from the inside out," came a small voice from the corner of the room. Dora sat in a child-sized chair, looking like an expensive doll. "I can smell it. Sweet, like fruit going bad."

"Grandmother," Perseus said mildly, "that's hardly helpful."

"Helpful would have been finding her a Sangrelié already," Dora replied, swinging her feet that would never reach the floor. "Now we're watching her dissolve. It's fascinating, really. I've only seen it happen this quickly twice before."

I froze with a scone halfway to my mouth. "So the purple tinge is..."

"Shadow poisoning," Azalea confirmed, her eyes gleaming with dark delight. "Such extraordinary development! I don't think I've ever seen such rapid progression. It's deliciously terrifying!"

"Both times ended badly," Dora continued, ignoring Azalea's enthusiasm. "The first went feral and ate his entire household staff. The second simply... unmade herself. Dissolved into a puddle and never reformed. Of course, their deterioration took years while yours is happening in days." She narrowed her eyes.

"Maman," Azalea said with a warning note.

"What? She should know." Dora's ancient eyes fixed on me with unnerving intensity.

I set the scone down, appetite suddenly gone. "How bad is it, exactly?"

Azalea and Perseus exchanged a loaded look.

"There are no records of any vampire in accelerated shadow poisoning remaining... stable," Perseus finally said, his voice carefully even.

"Define 'stable,'" I demanded.

"Sane," Azalea clarified, somehow managing to make the word sound like an exciting adventure rather than a dire warning. "No vampire has ever remained sane. The shadows eventually overwhelm the host consciousness."

A chill ran down my spine.

"You've been without a bond for too long," Azalea added, studying me like I was the most fascinating experiment she'd ever encountered. "With unprecedented shadow manifestation so unprecedentedly fast from the beginning. The fact that you've maintained coherence is remarkable, but not sustainable."

I took a sip of blood-tea, needing something to do with my hands. "So I'm on borrowed time. Either accept a Sangrelié bond soon, or go insane from shadow poisoning, is that it?"

"Those are the historical precedents, yes," Perseus confirmed, his expression genuinely sympathetic. "If you wait too long, Gillian, you won't have a choice."

"Clara is watching you," Azalea said. "Such a marvellously complicated situation! She sent us a letter this morning and says she will be following up."

My gut twisted in strange complicated emotion I couldn't decipher. "What is she going to do, drag me off to vampire prison?"

"That is a risk," Perseus said. "Though we call it 'protective custody' these days. More humane."

"How thoughtful," I replied, unable to keep the bitterness from my voice. "Euphemisms make everything better."

A thought struck me suddenly.

"Speaking of things that need explaining," I said, turning to

Azalea, "did Perseus tell you my mother has mysteriously relocated to Myrtlewood?"

Azalea's eyes widened with genuine surprise and immediate fascination. "Myrtlewood? Your mother? How absolutely intriguing!" She leaned forward, suddenly intensely interested. "Perseus, you sly creature. Keeping such delicious secrets!" Her eyes glittered with curiosity.

Despite her flair for the dramatic and her unsettling enthusiasm for my shadow predicament, Azalea seemed genuinely surprised by the news.

"Perseus is clearly withholding information from me," I said, watching Azalea closely for her reaction. "About my mother, about Myrtlewood, about why I can do impossible things like summon fire."

"Oh, undoubtedly," Azalea agreed cheerfully, not even attempting to defend him. "Some things aren't safe for you to know yet, darling. The knowledge itself could attract dangerous attention."

"So I'm just supposed to stumble around in the dark until someone decides I'm ready for the truth?"

"Stumbling in the dark is half the fun," Azalea replied, her eyes dancing with mischief. "A good mystery unfolding piece by piece? The slow revelation of secrets? You'll know everything in time, I'm certain. And what a marvellous moment that will be!"

I pushed away from the table, suddenly unable to sit still. The shadows in the corners of the dining room seemed to pulse in sync with my agitation, a visual representation of my inner turmoil.

"Between the ball fiasco, and Clara Blackwood's investigation, I can't even think straight about the Concordat theft anymore," I admitted. "And that's supposedly the crisis I'm meant to be helping to solve."

"Conspiracy theories are my speciality," Azalea said with evident pleasure, perking up at the mention of the theft. "Which suspect groups are you considering?"

"Well, there's the Helix Coven, but they seem to be in hiding after their headquarters were torched," I began, mentally sorting through the evidence. "The Consortium Virentia, based on the plant residue, but apparently that was just left over from legitimate research. Then there's the possibility that vampire factions themselves are involved – perhaps this Obscurum Societalis but no one seems to know anything about them at all."

"Don't forget the fae," Azalea added, ticking off possibilities on her elegant fingers. "They're always up to mischief."

"How am I supposed to figure this out when the list of suspects includes literally every supernatural faction?" I groaned.

"That's what makes it delightfully complex," Azalea replied. "Though personally, I find the Consortium Virentia the least convincing suspects. Those sorts are terrible at covering their tracks – they tend to leave magical residue everywhere, like pollen in springtime. Too obvious."

I considered this. "So either they're genuinely sloppy, or someone wanted to frame them specifically."

"Precisely," Azalea nodded approvingly. "And the Helix Coven's sudden change in leadership just before the theft? Most intriguing timing, wouldn't you say?"

I rubbed my temples, trying to process it all. "I need to go to work," I declared, heading for the door. "I need to do something productive before I completely lose my mind to shadow poisoning or vampire politics."

"Gillian," Azalea called after me, a note of genuine concern beneath her gleeful fascination, "do be careful. In your current state, strong emotions will accelerate the shadows. And they're so beautifully dramatic already!"

"I'll try to stick to mild irritation then," I shot back.

**6:21 PM. Shadow poisoning: a more pressing concern. Eyes: Definitely more purple. Irritation levels: catastrophic**

"Holy magical meltdown, you look terrible," Juniper announced cheerfully as I entered the office. "Ball that bad?"

"Worse," I groaned, collapsing into my chair. "I'm going to lose my mind to shadow poisoning if I don't accept vampire adoption immediately."

Juniper nodded sagely. "Your eyes are getting all shadowy! Very dramatic. Very goth."

I fixed her with what I hoped was a withering stare. "Juniper. Not helping."

"Sorry, sorry." She held up her hands in apology. "Defence mechanism. I get flippant when things get serious. And shadow manifestation in the ocular region is definitely serious."

"Tell me something I don't know," I muttered, shuffling through the stack of ancient texts I'd left on my desk. "Like where the bloody Concordat might be, or why it was stolen, or how I can avoid meeting with Clara Blackwood again."

Juniper's expression turned thoughtful. "Clara Blackwood is involved? Interesting. She doesn't usually handle routine cases."

"Apparently I'm special," I said, unable to keep the bitterness from my voice. "Lucky me."

"Tell me everything," Juniper commanded. "Every excruciating detail of vampire aristocracy at its finest."

For the next hour, I regaled her with the complete saga of the Grand Soirée – from Odette's ravings about the Concordat and romanticising vampire rule, to Sebastian's calculated presence and insistence on the old way of testing for compatibility, to the dramatic entrance of Clara Blackwood.

"She just showed up and announced that the Council received an anonymous tip?" Juniper asked, her eyes narrowing. "That's... suspicious."

"Everything about this situation is suspicious," I agreed, gesturing to the research materials spread across my desk. "I've been turned without authorisation, developed abilities I shouldn't have for decades, and now the magical artefact that supposedly regulates those very abilities is missing. It's all connected somehow."

"And some of the archive records about the Concordat seem to be missing," Juniper added, pulling a file from her seemingly bottomless shoulder bag. "I've been digging deeper into the official records, and there are gaps – references to appendices and supporting documents that aren't in the main archives."

I leaned forward, instantly alert. "Missing records? That can't be coincidence."

"No such thing as coincidences in magical law," Juniper agreed. "Someone has been selectively removing information about the Concordat."

I fanned through the files, noting the inconsistent references and missing sections she'd flagged. "Is there anywhere else we could look? Copies of the original documents, maybe?"

A slow, mischievous smile spread across Juniper's face. "I was hoping you'd ask that. The fae archives might have what we need."

"The fae archives? As in, back to the Market Under Bridge where I caused a scene?" I asked sceptically.

"Not the Market," Juniper clarified. "The actual Archives of the Fae. Far more comprehensive, far more ancient, and far more restricted."

"And how exactly would we get access to these restricted archives?"

"Well..." Juniper drew out the word. "We wouldn't. Not officially. But I know a back way in, and the fae are notorious hoarders. They keep copies of everything – especially legal documents involving other magical species."

I should have been appalled at the suggestion of breaking into yet another magical repository. A week ago, I would have recoiled at the mere thought of such blatant illegality. But that was before I became an unauthorised vampire with rapidly advancing shadow poisoning and a deadline from the supernatural authorities.

"When do we leave?" I asked.

**7:21 PM. Magical breaking and entering: becoming concerning habit. Professional ethics: severely compromised.**

"Are you sure about this?" I whispered as we approached what appeared to be an ordinary oak tree in a secluded corner of Hyde Park.

"Absolutely not," Juniper replied cheerfully. "But uncertain times call for recklessly creative solutions."

She placed her palm against the gnarled bark. The wood rippled like water, revealing a narrow opening that definitely hadn't been there before.

"Entrance to the Fae Archives," she announced with a flourish. "As I explained –"

I sighed. "Stay close, don't touch anything without asking, don't accept any food or drink, don't thank them directly, and don't, under any circumstances, make promises."

"Gold star for the vampire lawyer," Juniper grinned. "Ready to commit some light interdimensional trespassing?"

"As I'll ever be," I muttered, steeling myself for whatever fresh supernatural madness awaited on the other side.

We stepped through the opening into what felt like a transition space – neither here nor there, a liminal zone of shifting textures and disorienting perspective. My heightened senses struggled to make sense of the contradictory input.

Finally, reality (or some version of it) reasserted itself, and we found ourselves in a vast, impossibly tall library. Unlike the Archives of the Witching Parliament with its floating books and magical organisation system, the Fae Archives had an organic, almost living quality. Shelves grew from the floor like trees, curving and twisting to form elaborate patterns. Books and scrolls nestled in what looked like giant seedpods or massive flower blooms. The air smelled of old paper and herbs.

"Welcome to the London Fae Archive," Juniper whispered. "Hidden because the fae don't technically exist in our realm. I mean...there's a treaty in progress but for the last hundred years they've kept to themselves in their own realm. The archives are an anomaly, like the market, hidden inside a pocket dimension.

"How do we find what we're looking for in... this?" I gestured to the seemingly endless, chaotic collection.

"Very carefully," Juniper replied, "and preferably without attracting attention from the –"

"Intruders," came a familiar, multi-toned voice from behind us. "How fascinating."

We turned to find Roe Thistle standing there, their bark-like skin shifting patterns as they regarded us with four differently coloured eyes. Today they appeared more tree-like than metallic, with small buds blooming from their shoulders and hair that resembled fine green filaments.

"Roe," Juniper greeted them with careful formality. "What a coincidence."

"There are no coincidences," Roe replied, echoing Juniper's earlier sentiment with unsettling precision. "Only patterns yet unrecognised." Their eyes focused on me with unnerving intensity. "Your shadows grow stronger. Hungrier. The balance shifts."

I resisted the urge to touch the corners of my eyes, where I knew the purple shadow tinge was visible. "We're looking for information about the Twilight Concordat. The complete records."

Roe's multiple eyes blinked in sequence. "Dangerous knowledge. Dangerous times."

"That's why we need it," I pressed, deciding directness might be our best approach. "For the sake of peace in the magical world. If the Concordat isn't found..."

"Chaos," Roe finished. "War between witches and vampires. Fae caught in the middle, as always."

"Help us prevent that," Juniper urged. "You know the Fae Courts don't want another Magical Conflict. The last one reshaped continents."

Roe regarded us silently for a long moment, their skin shifting between bark and copper as they considered. Finally, they nodded, a gesture that sent small seedpods falling from their hair.

"Follow. But touch nothing without permission. The Archives remember unauthorised handling."

They turned and glided deeper into the archive, leading us through twisting pathways between living bookshelves. I noticed that certain plants seemed to react to our passing – flowering or closing, turning toward or away from us. The entire place felt sentient in a way that was both wondrous and deeply unsettling.

Eventually, we reached what appeared to be the heart of the Archive – a massive, ancient tree with a hollow centre filled with scrolls and codices nested in natural shelves formed by the wood itself. Soft, bioluminescent fungi provided gentle illumination, casting blue-green light over the collection.

"The Contracts Section," Roe announced. "All agreements between magical species, preserved in their entirety. No redactions. No omissions." They fixed me with their uppermost eyes. "What specific knowledge do you seek about the Twilight Concordat?"

"Its complete purpose," I answered. "Not just the parts about vampire feeding regulations or shadow harvesting permits. We believe there's more to it – something that might explain why it was stolen and who would benefit from its theft."

Roe nodded, then reached up into the branches of the great tree. The wood seemed to respond to their touch, bending and shifting to bring certain documents within reach. They selected a bundle wrapped in what appeared to be living vines and carefully handed it to Juniper.

"A copy of the original draft documents behind the Twilight Concordat, with marginalia by all signing parties," they explained. "And this –" they extracted a slim volume bound in shimming, colour-shifting material, " – the implementation protocols never included in the public version."

Juniper and I exchanged excited glances as we carefully laid the documents on a flat section of the tree that obligingly formed itself into a reading table. The scroll unrolled of its own accord, revealing text in multiple languages and scripts, some of which seemed to move or change as we looked at them.

"I can decipher these," Juniper offered, "but it'll take time."

"I'll focus on the implementation protocols," I said, gently opening the shimmering volume.

Two hours later, my vampire-enhanced speed reading and Juniper's magical deciphering skills had yielded significant results.

"Like we've been saying, it's not just a contract," I said. "But even more than that...It's a magical mechanism – a spell embedded in legal language."

"More like legal language embedded in a spell," Juniper corrected, tapping a particularly complex section of the original draft. "The magical binding came first, then they formalised it with legal wording to make it enforceable."

"And its primary function isn't just regulating vampire feeding or witch powers," I continued, flipping to a key passage in the implementation protocols. "That's secondary. Its main purpose is containing and neutralizing excess shadow energy in the supernatural ecosystem."

Roe, who had been silently observing our research, nodded in confirmation. "Shadows existed before vampires. Will exist after. Must be managed."

"So the Concordat is basically a shadow recycling system," Juniper mused, her eyes scanning the ancient text. "It prevents build-up of raw shadow in the atmosphere."

Juniper let out a gasp, pointing to a section of the implementation protocols I hadn't reached yet. "Gillian, look at this. The activation clause."

I turned to the indicated passage, reading the complex magical-legal jargon with growing disbelief. "The Concordat isn't just a passive regulatory system. It can be actively triggered to release all contained shadow energy in a controlled manner."

"Or an uncontrolled manner, if done improperly," Juniper added grimly. "Which means –"

"And who would want that?" I asked.

Roe's four eyes blinked in their unsettling sequence. "Many would benefit from chaos between vampires and witches. Few would have the skill to activate the Concordat. Fewer still would understand the consequences."

"The shadow release would affect everyone differently," Juniper realised, scanning more of the text. "Vampires would experience enhanced abilities but decreased control. Witches would find their powers fluctuating unpredictably."

I sat back, my mind racing. "So whoever did this wanted to destabilize relations between vampires and witches specifically. Force vampires back to traditional feeding. Make witches vulnerable to vampire predation. Create the conditions for conflict."

"While conveniently weakening both sides," Juniper added. "Setting the stage for a third party to step in and take advantage."

A sudden, chilling thought struck me. "What about humans? How would this shadow release affect them?"

Roe and Juniper exchanged concerned glances.

"Humans are naturally shadow-generative," Juniper explained carefully. "Their emotional states, especially negative ones, create shadow energy that the Concordat normally processes and regulates."

"Without that regulation..." Roe began.

Juniper shook her head. "Magnified negative emotions. Fear, anger, paranoia – all amplified across human populations."

I paced back and forth. "I can't believe this is something the Helix Coven would want, or any of the suspects...other than Vampires. Odette was so sure this was for the best, that vampire rule is the natural order of things..." I shivered, feeling like I'd unwittingly been pulled into the wrong side of a global conflict. "Vampires are evil, after all."

"Not all vampires," Juniper said.

"But how do we know which ones we can trust?" I asked, genuinely concerned. I thought of the Council, of the Grand Soiree, of Clara, of the Burk family who had so kindly taken me in...or was that all a ruse.

I buried my head in my hands.

Juniper gently patted me on the shoulder. "Deep down, you know who you can trust. Maybe not with everything, but trust yourself first."

I nodded. "The only vampires I'm sure I can trust are Azalea, Charles and Perseus."

"They'd be top of my list as well," Juniper agreed.

"We need to tell them. They may need to warn the Council. If this is true, the stakes just got a lot higher with the theft."

"Not theft," Roe corrected. "Weaponization."

**Current status: Shadow-poisoned vampire with rapidly diminishing sanity window. Potentially caught in supernatural terrorist plot. Determination to resolve crisis: absolute.**

# CHAPTER 17

# ARREST WARRANT FOR INCONVENIENT EXISTENCE

**7:32 PM. Shadow containment: barely hanging on. Purple eye situation: definitely worse. Sleep achieved: minimal. Mood: apocalyptic.**

I stood in my castle bedroom, glaring at my reflection with a mixture of fascination and horror. The purple discolouration in my eyes had spread, tendrils of shadow extending into the surrounding whites like ink dropped in water. Not a great look, if I'm honest. Very much "possessed character in horror film who's definitely not making it to the sequel."

The nightmares had been relentless – shadows whispering in voices that sounded disturbingly like my own, telling me to let go, to surrender, to embrace the power that hummed beneath my skin. In one particularly vivid sequence, I'd been floating above London, watching shadow tendrils extend from my fingertips into the streets below, feeding on the fear and confusion of the humans like some sort of emotional vampire buffet.

I'd woken up to find my actual sheets shredded and strange patterns burned into the stone floor around my bed.

"Get it together, Gillian," I muttered to my reflection. "You've survived divorce papers, Neville's passive-aggressive post-it notes, and Merryn's experimental cooking phase. You can handle a bit of shadow possession."

A soft knock at my door interrupted my pep talk.

"Ms. Spark," came Jenkins' voice, "you have a visitor downstairs. Mr. Sebastian Rothsforte requests the pleasure of your company in the blue drawing room."

Lord Smirksalot was here? Fabulous. Just what I needed when teetering on the brink of shadow-induced insanity.

"Tell him I'm busy having an existential crisis," I called back.

A pause. "I believe the matter is quite urgent, madam. He was most insistent."

I sighed. "Fine. Tell him I'll be down in five minutes."

Sebastian AKA Lord Smirksalot stood by the fireplace in the blue drawing room, his calculating eyes gleamed with something I couldn't quite identify as I entered.

"Gillian," he greeted me with a smile was more like a smirk. "How delightful to see you again so soon."

"Sebastian," I replied, not bothering with titles or formalities. "To what do I owe this... unexpected visit?"

He laughed softly, the sound practiced and precise. "Direct as ever. It's refreshing, truly."

"Jenkins said it was urgent."

"Indeed." Sebastian moved toward me with chilling grace, stopping just close enough to invade my personal space without actually touching me. "I've been reflecting on our conversation at the Grand Soirée. Your... situation has continued to occupy my thoughts."

"My situation," I repeated flatly. "You mean my unauthorised vampire status?"

"Precisely." He smiled again, this time with a hint of actual warmth that somehow made him more unsettling. "I've come to offer a solution."

"You've reconsidered the modern testing methods and are now

willing to submit to compatibility verification for the Sangrelié bond?" I crossed my arms, meeting his gaze directly.

"Nothing so clinical, I'm afraid." Sebastian's eyes flickered to the purple shadows in mine, clearly noting their progression. "The traditional methods have served vampire society for centuries for good reason, Gillian. They establish a deeper connection, a more... meaningful bond."

The way he said "meaningful" sent an unpleasant shiver down my spine.

"I'm here to offer you protection the old-fashioned way," he continued smoothly. "No tests, no Council involvement, no bureaucracy. Just an ancient ritual between two vampires, establishing a bond that would satisfy even the most traditional members of our society."

"And what exactly does this 'ancient ritual' involve?" I asked, though I was pretty sure I already knew the answer.

Sebastian smiled, showing just a hint of fang. "An exchange. Intimate, private, and considerably more... pleasurable than the modern procedures."

The predatory undertone in his voice made my skin crawl. This wasn't about protecting me – this was about possessing me, controlling me.

"Thanks, but I'll pass," I said, taking a deliberate step back. "I prefer my autonomy intact."

His expression hardened, the charming facade slipping. "You misunderstand the gravity of your situation, Gillian. Look at yourself." He gestured to my eyes. "The shadow poisoning advances rapidly. You have days, perhaps hours, before you lose control completely."

"And you're offering to help out of the goodness of your ancient heart?" I raised an eyebrow. "How altruistic."

"I'm offering a mutually beneficial arrangement," he countered, circling me slowly. "My protection and guidance in exchange for... access to your unique abilities. A fair exchange."

"Access to my abilities," I repeated, not bothering to hide my disgust. "Is that what they're calling slavery these days?"

Sebastian's expression darkened. "You're being childish. The Sangrelié bond is a cornerstone of vampire society – a sacred trust between maker and made. I'm offering you legitimacy, protection, and survival."

"You're offering me a collar and leash," I shot back. "And I've spent too many years being controlled by others to volunteer for supernatural servitude."

A flash of genuine anger crossed his face, his composure fracturing. "Your stubbornness borders on suicidal, Gillian. You stand at the precipice of complete shadow consumption, about to face Council interrogation, and you reject the one lifeline offered to you?"

"If the choice is between shadow insanity and being magically bound to a calculating, smirking, self-serving vampire aristocrat, I might just take my chances with the shadows."

The temperature in the room seemed to drop several degrees as Sebastian's eyes hardened to ice. "You will regret this," he said softly, each word precise and cutting. "When the shadows take you, when you lose all memory of your humanity, when you become nothing more than a feral creature to be put down by the Council – remember that I offered you salvation."

"Is that a threat, Sebastian?"

"Merely a prediction," he replied coldly. "Based on centuries of observing fools who valued pride over survival."

**8:07 PM. Vampire confrontation: escalating. Shadow control: slipping. Potential violence: imminent.**

"Should I come back at a more convenient time?" came a cool, measured voice from the doorway.

We both turned to see Clara Blackwood standing there, taking in the scene with cool detachment. Her severe black suit was both official and fashionable.

"Clara – I mean...Inspector Blackwood," Sebastian recovered first, his charm resurfacing with practiced ease. "What an unexpected pleasure. Council business brings you here?"

"Obviously," she replied, her gaze shifting between us; it lingered on my increasingly purple eyes, but she made no comment. "Though I seem to have interrupted something."

"Not at all," Sebastian said smoothly. "I was just leaving. However, Clara, since you're here on Council business, you might be interested to know I've uncovered some rather compelling evidence regarding the Concordat theft."

Clara's eyebrow arched slightly. "Have you, indeed?"

"The Helix Coven's involvement is becoming increasingly apparent," Sebastian continued. "Their sudden leadership change three months ago – suspiciously close to when planning for such a theft would begin – followed by the convenient destruction of their headquarters just as questions were being raised."

"That's one theory," Clara replied, her tone giving nothing away. "And your evidence?"

"My associate discovered magical residue at the scene consistent with their particular brand of magic," Sebastian explained. "And there's the matter of their pin found near the empty pedestal – rather careless, wouldn't you say? Almost as if someone wanted us to know who was responsible."

"Or wanted us to think we know," Clara countered, her eyes never leaving Sebastian's face.

Sebastian's eyes narrowed slightly. "We all want the same thing, Clara. The Concordat returned and those responsible held accountable."

"Of course," she agreed, though something in her tone suggested scepticism.

He turned to me, his charm firmly back in place. "Consider my offer, Gillian. It remains open... for now."

With a formal nod to Clara, he strode from the room, closing the door with just enough force to express his displeasure without seeming petulant.

I let out a breath I didn't need to hold, the tension in my shoulders easing slightly before turning my attention to the other dangerous creature in the room. "Have you come to threaten me too?" I asked Clara directly.

Her eyebrow rose fractionally. "Was that what Sebastian was doing? Threatening you?"

"More or less," I admitted, dropping into an armchair. "Offering to be my Sangrelié 'the old-fashioned way' while implying I'll regret refusing him when I'm a shadow-crazed monster being put down by the Council."

"Charming," Clara observed dryly. "Sebastian always did prefer the traditional approaches."

"And you?" I challenged. "What's your preferred method of supernatural coercion?"

To my surprise, a hint of amusement flickered across her features. "Direct questioning tends to be more efficient than threats or manipulation, in my experience."

She took the seat opposite me, her posture perfect but somehow less intimidating than at the Grand Soirée. Without the audience of vampire aristocracy, she seemed more focused, less performative.

"No," she said after a moment of studying me. "I haven't come to threaten you, Gillian. I've come to find out if you know anything more about the Concordat case. I've been told you have been conducting your own investigations."

"Of course," I said, attempting to sound casual. "But I doubt we know any more than you."

"The situation deteriorates by the hour," she replied, her expression grave. "Vampire-witch relations are at their lowest point in centuries. The Witching Parliament is accusing the Vampire Council of orchestrating the theft, while your Council is equally convinced of witch involvement."

"And what do you think?" I pressed, watching her carefully.

"I think," Clara said deliberately, "that the evidence pointing to the Helix Coven is suspiciously convenient. Too neat. Too obvious.

Her eyes fixed on me with unnerving intensity. "You've been prying into this case alongside Juniper."

"We've been looking into it," I acknowledged cautiously.

"And breaking into several highly restricted magical repositories in the process," Clara added, her tone conversational but her eyes sharp. "Including the Archives of the Witching Parliament and, if my sources are correct, the Fae Archives as well."

I tensed, preparing for the inevitable arrest or threat. Instead, Clara simply watched me, waiting.

"Why should I trust you?" I asked finally.

"You shouldn't," she replied candidly. "Trust is earned, not given. But consider this – if I wanted to take you into custody for those breaches, I could have done so already. I prefer cooperation to coercion when possible. It yields better results."

Something inside me melted at her words. Confused. I tried to hold myself together.

I shook my head, weighing my options. The shadow poisoning was advancing rapidly – I could feel it even now, humming beneath my skin, whispering at the edges of my consciousness. And Clara clearly knew more than she was letting on.

"Fine," I decided. "But this goes both ways. I'll tell you what I know, and you tell me why the Council is so interested in my case specifically."

Clara considered for a moment, then nodded. "Acceptable. You first."

I filled Clara in on the basics – our discovery that the Concordat was more than just a feeding treaty, that it regulated shadow energy throughout the supernatural ecosystem, and most importantly, that it hadn't just been stolen but possibly activated in some way.

I carefully avoided mentioning our specific break-ins. No need to add "multiple counts of magical trespassing" to my already substantial list of supernatural offenses.

"The release of accumulated shadow energy would explain much of what we're seeing," Clara said thoughtfully. "The increased aggression in both vampire and witch communities, the surge in shadow-related incidents among newer vampires..."

"And what about my accelerated shadow progression?" I prompted. "Is that connected to the theft?"

"Unlikely," Clara replied, though something in her expression made me wonder if she was being entirely truthful. "Your shadow manifestation appears to be a separate phenomenon – rapid but not unprecedented. Some vampires simply integrate more quickly than others."

"Just my luck," I muttered. "So why is the Council so interested in my case?"

Clara studied me for a long moment before answering. "The Council has been receiving anonymous tips suggesting your involvement in the Concordat theft."

"What?" I stood abruptly, shadows swirling around me in response to my shock. "That's absurd! I wasn't even a vampire when it was stolen!"

"I'm aware of the timeline discrepancy," Clara said calmly. "Which is precisely why these tips are so intriguing. Someone is very deliberately attempting to direct our attention toward you."

"Why would anyone do that?"

"That," Clara said grimly, "is what I'm trying to determine."

Before I could process this bombshell, the door burst open without warning, admitting a whirlwind of purple hair.

"Gillian! I've been looking every – Oh." Juniper stopped short, blinking at Clara. "Hello, Investigator Blackwood. Fancy meeting you here. In this place where I definitely expected you to be and am not at all surprised by your presence."

Clara's expression remained carefully neutral. "Juniper."

"Right! Well, this is awkward but also potentially fortuitous because I have NEWS!" Juniper's excitement overrode her initial wariness, the equations on her arms calculating at breakneck speed. "I have had what one might call a 'tip-off' about our missing magical artefact."

I straightened in my chair. "The Concordat? You've found it?"

"Not exactly found it, more like located where it might potentially be being sold to the highest bidder in approximately –" she checked a watch that hadn't been on her wrist a second ago, " – forty-seven minutes!"

"Explain," Clara demanded, all business now.

"An auction," Juniper said excitedly. "A very exclusive, very illegal supernatural black market auction happening right now in a pocket dimension connected to a private club in Mayfair. And guess what's listed as Lot 37? 'Ancient artefact of significant magical regulatory properties.' That's auction house code for 'stupidly powerful magical item that could probably destroy the world but we're selling it anyway because capitalism.'"

Clara was already on her feet. "How reliable is your source?"

"Extremely unreliable in general but never wrong about auctions," Juniper replied cheerfully. "It's his one area of actual expertise between bouts of pathological lying."

"I need to contact the Council, assemble a tactical team –" Clara began.

"No time!" Juniper interrupted. "The auction's already underway, and a Council raid would just send everyone scattering to the four winds with their purchases. We need stealth, not force."

"We?" Clara asked sceptically.

"Well, I can get us in undetected," Juniper explained, wiggling her fingers as sparks danced between them. "Spatial translocation is kind of my thing. And I guess you can come too, being all official and investigatory."

Clara stared at Juniper for a long moment, her expression unreadable. Then, to my surprise, she nodded. "Very well. But this is a reconnaissance mission only. We identify the artefact, confirm its authenticity, and then I call for backup."

There was something in her quick acceptance that made me suspicious. It seemed almost as if she'd anticipated this development – or perhaps even orchestrated it.

"Splendid! Magnificent! Everyone hold hands!" Juniper said.

"Wait –" I began, but it was too late.

We materialised in what appeared to be a storage closet, the sudden transition making my senses spin wildly.

"Everyone still has all their body parts in the right places? Excellent," Juniper whispered, pressing her ear against the door. "We're in the back rooms of The Gilded Chalice, one of London's most exclusive supernatural clubs. The auction's happening in a private room, but what we want is the vault where they keep the lots before they're brought out."

"And you know where this vault is how, exactly?" Clara asked, her tone suggesting she already knew the answer wouldn't be entirely legal.

"Let's just say I've had occasion to... recover items from similar establishments in the past," Juniper replied vaguely. "For purely legitimate magical research purposes, of course."

"Of course," Clara said dryly.

As they discussed the plan, I found myself watching Clara closely. Her composure was perfect – too perfect. And something about her easy acceptance of this illegal infiltration felt off. Council Investigators didn't typically engage in unauthorised operations, especially not with suspects they were investigating.

What was her real agenda?

"The vault should be down one level," Juniper continued, producing a small vial of glowing liquid from her pocket. "This will temporarily mask our magical signatures. Drink up!"

I eyed the suspicious potion. "Is it safe?"

"Define 'safe,'" Juniper hedged. "It won't kill you. Probably. Might cause mild hallucinations, temporary invisibility, or uncontrollable singing in about 2% of users."

"Lovely," I muttered, but downed the liquid anyway. It tasted like electricity and regret.

Clara took hers without comment, her expression suggesting she was mentally adding this to the list of charges she might eventually bring against us.

"Right!" Juniper beamed. "Let's go artefact hunting!"

She cracked the door open, peering into the hallway before gesturing us forward. We followed her through a maze of service corridors, passing what appeared to be kitchen staff – though they were definitely not human, given the extra arms and occasional tentacle I glimpsed.

The club itself was opulent beyond belief, all gold fixtures and velvet upholstery, magical lighting that adjusted to the mood of each room. We skirted the main areas, keeping to the shadows (ironically appropriate given my condition) until we reached a nondescript door marked "Private - Staff Only."

"Here we go," Juniper murmured, placing her palm against the door. The lock clicked open. "I'm temporarily convincing the door we're authorised personnel. Very technical magical process."

"You're picking a lock with magic," Clara translated flatly.

"Such a reductive perspective," Juniper sighed, pushing the door open to reveal a narrow staircase descending into darkness.

We made our way down carefully, arriving at another door – this one considerably more substantial, with magical wards shimmering across its surface.

"This is the tricky part," Juniper whispered. "Security on the vault is serious business. I can get us through, but it'll take a minute."

As she worked on the complex magical locks, Clara turned to me. "Your eyes," she observed quietly. "The shadow manifestation is advancing rapidly."

I nodded, not bothering to pretend otherwise. "Since yesterday. Accelerating by the hour."

"Yet you maintain control," she noted, studying me with clinical interest. "Most vampires would be completely feral at this stage of shadow integration."

"I'm stubborn," I replied with a shrug. "Also, I have children.

Amazing what maternal determination can accomplish in the face of supernatural corruption."

Something flickered in Clara's eyes – respect, perhaps? Or simple curiosity? It was impossible to read her completely.

"Got it!" Juniper announced triumphantly as the last ward dissolved. "We have approximately seven minutes before the security system realizes something's amiss. Let's make this quick."

The vault was smaller than I'd expected, but packed with extraordinary items – everything from glowing gemstones to what appeared to be actual shrunken heads (which blinked at us as we passed, thoroughly creeping me out). Each item was numbered, corresponding to the auction lots.

"Lot 37," Clara reminded us, moving efficiently through the collection.

"Here!" I called, spotting the number beside a pedestal holding what appeared to be an ancient stone tablet inscribed with symbols that hurt my eyes to look at directly. "This has to be it."

We gathered around the artefact, Juniper practically vibrating with excitement while Clara maintained her professional composure. I reached out, my shadow senses tingling.

"Something's wrong," Juniper said immediately, drawing back. "This isn't the Concordat."

"Are you sure?" Clara asked sharply, her sudden intensity making me even more suspicious.

She nodded. "There's magical energy here, yes, but not shadow energy. And certainly not the concentrated shadow power of a centuries-old regulatory artefact. This is... something else. A convincing fake, maybe."

Clara leaned closer, her eyes narrowing. "She's right. This is dressed up to look like the Concordat, but the magical signature is all wrong. It's a forgery – good enough to fool most buyers, but definitely not the real thing." Her expression darkened. "So someone is attempting to sell a fake Concordat. Interesting timing."

"Check the seller information," I suggested. "There must be documentation somewhere."

Juniper was already rifling through a folder on a nearby desk. "Here – consignment paperwork for Lot 37. Submitted by... oh, this is interesting." She looked up, eyes wide. "One Maximilian Thorpe, antiquities dealer. Who just happens to be –"

"Sebastian Rothsforte's procurer of rare items," Clara finished, her voice cold. "I'm familiar with his reputation."

My blood would have run cold if it weren't already room temperature. "Sebastian? You think lord smirksalot is involved in the theft?"

Clara suppressed a laugh.

"Or taking advantage of it," Juniper suggested. "Selling a fake to profit from the crisis."

"Or this could be a setup," I said cautiously.

Clara's eyes met mine, and for a moment I glimpsed what might have been approval. "A reasonable assessment. The pattern of too-perfect evidence continues."

A commotion from above interrupted our speculation – raised voices, the sound of magical discharge, running feet.

"Our seven minutes are up," Juniper grimaced. "Time to make a hasty and completely dignified exit."

"Wait –" I began, but Juniper had already grabbed both our hands.

Reality dissolved around us once more.

"So what does this mean?" I asked, pacing the blue drawing room where we'd rematerialised. "Is Sebastian behind the theft? Or just trying to profit from it? Or is he being framed too?"

"Unclear," Clara replied, her voice carefully neutral. "Rothsforte has always operated in grey areas of vampire law. Selling a forgery during a crisis is unethical and violates several codes, but it's not evidence of involvement in the original crime."

"But coming here to try to establish a Sangrelié bond with Gillian right before his fake goes to auction?" Juniper pointed out. "That's some suspicious timing."

"Or perhaps he genuinely saw an opportunity to acquire a valuable asset – a rapidly integrating vampire – while also profiting from the crisis separately," Clara suggested.

"What about the anonymous tips implicating me?" I asked Clara directly. "Could Sebastian be behind those too?"

"Possibly," Clara acknowledged. "Though it seems an unnecessarily complicated strategy."

I stopped pacing, a thought striking me. "What if the fake was meant to be discovered? A distraction from where the real Concordat might be?"

Clara's eyes met mine, a flash of something in their violet depths. "A valid theory. The question remains – where is the real artefact, and what is happening to it while we chase wild geese?"

At her words, the Mary Oliver poem flew into my mind. *Let the soft animal of your body love what it loves...*

I shook my head, looking away from those eyes, bringing myself back to the present. "And who benefits from all this chaos? The Helix Coven? The Obscurum, whoever that is? Sebastian?"

"Indeed," Clara agreed, studying me with that unsettling intensity. "All we have about the so-called Obscurum Societalis are rumours, and not very solid ones, at that. Vampires have never been very good at rumours."

"I wish I could be of more help," I said, lowering my gaze.

"Your insights into this case have been... surprisingly valuable, Gillian."

I felt a small wave of pride and then stiffened. There was something about the way she said it – measured, calculated – that raised my suspicions again. Was she genuinely impressed, or simply collecting more information about me for reasons unknown?

"Lucky me," I muttered. "Getting to play supernatural detective while slowly losing my mind to shadow poisoning."

"And Gillian," Clara added, her voice dropping slightly, "I would avoid further contact with Sebastian Rothsforte. His interest in you likely extends beyond the merely political."

"Thanks for the warning," I said, surprised by her apparent concern.

With a nod to us both, Clara strode from the room, leaving behind the faint scent of cardamom and winter.

"Well," Juniper said into the ensuing silence, "that was surprisingly not terrible? I mean, Chief Investigator Blackwood didn't arrest us for magical breaking and entering, which I'm counting as a win."

"She's waiting to see what else we uncover," I pointed out. "We're more useful to her running around finding clues than sitting in vampire jail. The question is – useful for what exactly? Her official investigation, or something else?"

"You don't trust her," Juniper observed.

"I don't trust anyone right now," I admitted. "Sebastian is obviously manipulating the situation for his own benefit. Clara's motives remain opaque at best. The evidence keeps pointing in too many convenient directions. And none of it explains why I'm becoming a shadow-consumed monster at record speed."

"Fair point," Juniper conceded. "So what now? Break into Sebastian's mansion? Track down Maximilian Thorpe? Continue our vigilante crime-solving while you slowly succumb to shadow poisoning?"

I touched the corners of my eyes, feeling the cold energy of the shadows that were progressively claiming me. "Find the real Concordat," I decided. "Not because it's necessarily connected to my condition, but because sorting out one crisis might give me space to deal with my own."

"Right," Juniper nodded, suddenly serious. "No pressure or anything. Just preventing supernatural war while you fight off shadow corruption at the same time."

"Just another day in the life of an illegal vampire," I agreed with a weak smile.

**Current status: Shadow-poisoned vampire detective. Potential suspects: increasing. Conspiracy theories: multiplying. Shadow control: rapidly deteriorating. Clara Blackwood: defi-**

**nitely hiding something. Sebastian Rothsforte: definitely up to no good. Determination: somehow undiminished despite everything.**

As Juniper left to pursue new leads, I sank into a chair, momentarily exhausted despite my vampire stamina.

The thought of Sebastian trying to claim me – to control whatever unusual power I had – made my skin crawl. Clara's warning echoed in my mind, along with the implications of Sebastian's connection to the fake Concordat.

Something larger was happening here, with multiple players moving pieces on a board I could barely see. The only certainty was that I was running out of time – both to solve the mystery of the Concordat theft and to maintain my own grip on sanity as the shadows continued their relentless advance.

# CHAPTER 18

# CONTAINMENT AND OTHER EUPHEMISMS

6:27 PM. Shadow control: tenuous at best. Purple eye situation: now with bonus veiny pattern. Blood-tea consumed: seven cups (definitely developing dependency). Bedtime stories with kids: excellent. Research progress: desperate.

"The early vampire treaties explicitly mention shadow containment rituals, but nothing about activation mechanisms," I muttered, flipping frantically through a crumbling tome that smelled older than most countries. My desk at Clifford and Burk had vanished beneath stacks of ancient texts and scrolls.

I rubbed my eyes, which was a mistake – they'd become increasingly sensitive. I'd taken to wearing sunglasses indoors like some kind of diva, but they only concealed the problem.

"You should rest," came Perseus's voice from my doorway.

I looked up to find him watching me with that carefully neutral expression that nevertheless managed to convey concern.

"Can't," I replied. "The formal questioning with Clara is in less than twenty-four hours, we're still no closer to finding the real Concordat, and my shadow situation is..." I gestured vaguely at my eyes, which I knew were visible even behind the sunglasses to vampire vision.

"Advancing," Perseus supplied diplomatically.

"That's one word for it. 'Catastrophic' would be another. 'Completely terrifying' also works." I took a fortifying sip of blood-tea. "If I don't find answers soon, there won't be enough of me left to question."

Perseus set the files on the one clear corner of my desk. "These might help. Historical accounts of shadow manifestation in vampires predating the Concordat. I had them retrieved from our private archives."

I blinked in surprise. "Thank you. That's... helpful."

"I don't want to see you consumed by shadows or executed by the Council," he said dryly. "It would be terrible for office morale."

Despite everything, I laughed. "Heaven forbid we disrupt workplace harmony with a little shadow insanity and supernatural execution."

Perseus's expression softened marginally. "Gillian, even if you locate the Concordat tonight, the shadow poisoning has progressed too far for simple reversal. You need to consider –"

"I know," I interrupted, not wanting to hear the Sangrelié lecture again. "But I'm not accepting a bond with someone like Sebastian Rothsforte, especially not after discovering his connection to the fake Concordat."

"There are other candidates," Perseus suggested carefully.

I shook my head. "Trading one form of control for another isn't a solution – it's just changing prisons."

Perseus sighed, in that moment it seemed an oddly human gesture from a centuries-old vampire. "Sometimes the prison we choose is preferable to the one thrust upon us. Consider that while you research."

With that cryptic bit of vampire wisdom, he departed, leaving me with the new files and the unsettling implication that I might be running out of options faster than I was willing to admit.

I'd barely made it through the first file when a distinctive perfume – something floral with notes of aged paper and oil paint – wafted through my door seconds before an elegant knock.

"Come in," I called, though I already knew who it was. My vampire senses had become adept at identifying visitors by scent, footfall, and even the subtle magical signatures some carried.

Beatrice Valois glided into my office, looking every bit as refined as she had at the Grand Soirée. Today she wore a vintage-inspired pantsuit in deep burgundy that somehow managed to appear both timeless and perfectly contemporary.

"Gillian, my dear," she greeted me with genuine warmth. "I hope I'm not interrupting your work."

"Just drowning in ancient vampire lore," I replied, gesturing to the chaos of my desk. "Nothing urgent, except possibly my impending descent into shadow madness."

Beatrice's expression softened with what appeared to be genuine concern. "That's actually why I'm here." She produced an ornate silver box from her handbag. "I've brought something that might help stabilize your condition."

I eyed the box suspiciously. "No offense, Beatrice, but I've learned to be wary of gifts from ancient vampires."

She laughed, the sound musical and surprisingly genuine. "Wise policy. But this is simply a shadow anchor – an old remedy for temporary relief during difficult transitions."

She opened the box to reveal a delicate silver bracelet etched with intricate symbols. It looked harmless enough, though something about it made the shadow energy inside me recoil slightly.

"It's designed to provide relief without full suppression," Beatrice explained, holding it out. "Much gentler than the Council's brutish containment devices."

I hesitated. "Thank you, but... why? We barely know each other."

"Perhaps I simply dislike seeing potential wasted," she replied. "Or perhaps I feel a certain responsibility toward new vampires struggling with their nature."

There was something in her tone that made me pause. A hint of intensity behind the casual charity.

She slid the bracelet across my desk. "Consider this a gesture of goodwill, regardless of where your Sangrelié search leads you." Her smile turned slightly enigmatic. "Though I do hope you'll keep an open mind."

"Meaning?"

"Meaning sometimes the most compatible match isn't the one that shows up on magical tests and compatibility charts," she said. "Sometimes it's a matter of... instinct."

The implications were clear. Beatrice was putting herself forward as a candidate, despite whatever test results might say.

"I'll keep that in mind," I said neutrally.

She rose to leave but paused at the door. "One more thing, Gillian. Be careful with Investigator Blackwood. Her interest in your case may not be as professional as it appears."

Before I could question this cryptic warning, she was gone, leaving behind only her distinctive perfume and the silver bracelet. I studied it without touching it.

Beatrice's apparent generosity seemed genuine, but her interest in becoming my Sangrelié despite implied incompatibility set off alarm bells. Was she merely another vampire aristocrat looking to control whatever unusual power I possessed? Or did she have a more specific agenda?

And what did she know about Clara that prompted such a specific warning?

I set the bracelet aside, deciding to have the Burks and Juniper examine it before I considered putting it on. In this new world of supernatural politics and hidden agendas, even seemingly kind gestures required scrutiny.

**7:42 PM. Research focus: slipping. Shadow malfunction: increasingly. Grip on reality: questionable at best.**

Two hours and three more cups of blood-tea later, I'd made some progress through Perseus's files. The historical accounts were disturbing but informative – detailed descriptions of pre-Concordat vampires whose shadow powers had manifested naturally, without magical suppression.

They'd been significantly more powerful than modern vampires, capable of feeding on emotions, manipulating fears, even absorbing fragments of memories along with blood. But the cost had been steep – progressive loss of self, increasing disconnection from their former identities, and eventually, in many cases, complete surrender to the shadows.

"The vampire known as Elisabeta of Kraków maintained coherent thought for approximately twenty-seven days after notable shadow poisoning," I read aloud from one particularly grim account. "After which she was observed consuming seven villagers in public in a murderous rampage. When confronted by her maker, she displayed no recognition, attacked authorities, and was subsequently destroyed by immolation."

I swallowed hard, setting down the document with slightly shaking hands. Twenty-seven days. Given the accelerated rate of my own shadow integration, I'd be lucky to have twenty-seven hours.

The whispers were getting louder now, a constant susurration at the edges of my consciousness. They didn't form coherent words yet, but the intent was becoming clearer – urging me to stop fighting, to surrender, to embrace the power that hummed beneath my skin. Sometimes they sounded like my own voice, sometimes like strangers, and occasionally, most disturbingly, like Neville at his most patronizing.

*You're making this harder than it needs to be, Gillian. Just let go. It's so much easier when you stop resisting.*

"Shut up," I muttered, pressing the heels of my hands against my temples. "I'm trying to work."

I reached for a different file – a detailed description of the Archives of the Witching Parliament and the security measures protecting the Concordat. There had been no signs of forced entry, no magical alarms triggered until after the artefact was discovered missing. What if someone had found a way to conceal it dimensionally while making it appear to be gone?

I'd seen references to dimensional folding magic in some of the older texts – a specialised form of concealment that could hide objects in the same physical space they normally occupied, just slightly out of phase with normal reality.

My phone buzzed with an incoming text from Juniper:

*Found something interesting in auction records. Multiple supernatural black market sales of "Concordat fragments" over past week. All fakes, but someone's profiting from forgeries. Checking buyer identities now.*

Who would benefit from all this chaos and misdirection?

My stomach lurched as my paranoia advanced from all directions. Perhaps my mysterious turning was connected to all this, somehow...

And if the anonymous tips implicating me in the theft were part of the same plan...

I needed to find out who had been sending those tips to the Council.

I reached for my phone to call Perseus when the dark energy inside me suddenly pulsed and writhed of its own accord. A vase on my desk shattered without being touched, sending shards of glass and water spraying across my research.

My powers were becoming stronger. And I was running out of time.

Raised voices echoed from the reception area – one cool and authoritative, others protesting.

I froze, recognising Clara Blackwood's distinctive tone beneath the commotion. What was she doing here?

Before I could decide whether to investigate or hide under my desk (a surprisingly tempting option), my office door burst open. Clara stood there, flanked by two stern-looking vampires in what appeared to be supernatural tactical gear – black uniforms with council insignia. Her eyes took in my dishevelled appearance, the chaotic research spread across every surface.

"Gillian Spark," she announced, her voice formal and cold, "by authority of the Vampire High Council, I am placing you under arrest for theft and illegal activation of the Twilight Concordat, unauthorised shadow manipulation, and endangering the supernatural equilibrium."

I stared at her, momentarily speechless. "You're... what? That's ridiculous! I didn't steal the Concordat – I'm trying to find it!"

"The magical signature of the artefact was traced to an antiques shop during the exact timeframe of your visit," Clara replied, unmoved. "The evidence is compelling."

"That's impossible," I protested, rising from my chair. The shadow energy rose with me, pulsing outward. Another object on my desk – a heavy paperweight – suddenly slid across the surface and crashed to the floor without being touched.

Clara's eyes tracked the movement, her expression hardening. "Your condition has progressed beyond safe containment levels. You are now classified as an imminent threat to supernatural security."

I took a step back, suddenly realizing why she'd come with armed guards. She wasn't just here to arrest me for the theft – she was here because I was spiralling out of control.

"I was about to figure it out," I said desperately. "The dimensional folding, the fake fragments on the black market, the connection to my turning – I'm sure it's all linked. Someone planned this."

"You can explain your theories after you've been secured," Clara said, gesturing to her guards. "Containment procedure four."

Perseus appeared in the doorway behind Clara, his expression tightly controlled. "Investigator Blackwood, this is highly irregular. If you have concerns about Ms. Spark, the proper protocol is to present your evidence at a scheduled questioning."

"New evidence necessitates immediate action," Clara replied without looking at him. "The Council has granted me exceptional authority in this matter."

Perseus raised his hand. "Gillian remains under our protection until formal charges are filed and processed."

"A protection that doesn't supersede Council security directives," Clara countered smoothly. "She poses an immediate threat given her advancing shadow condition and alleged connection to the missing artefact."

"Alleged being the operative word," Perseus retorted. "You have circumstantial evidence at best."

The two security vampires moved forward, positioning themselves on either side of me.

My research was so close to making sense. The dimensional folding theory, the fake fragments, the anonymous tips, Beatrice's suspicious interest, my own accelerated shadow integration – all pieces of a puzzle I was just beginning to assemble.

And now I was being arrested, my investigation cut short just as I was about to connect the dots.

"This is insane," I said, struggling to keep my voice steady. "I didn't steal anything. I'm trying to help!"

One of the security guards took an involuntary step back as tendrils of darkness extended toward him.

Clara's voice softened slightly. "Come quietly, Gillian. Don't make this more difficult than it needs to be."

"There isn't enough evidence for an arrest," Perseus insisted, stepping fully into the room now. "At minimum, this requires a formal hearing before the Security Council."

"Permission has already been granted for immediate detention," Clara said, producing an official-looking document with elaborate seals. "Signed by the High Chancellor himself."

"This isn't right," came Juniper's voice as she materialised – literally – in the middle of my office with a small pop of displaced air. "Gillian was with me half the time, and we were looking FOR the Concordat, not hiding it!"

Clara's expression remained impassive. "Your testimony will be noted, Juniper. However, the detention order stands."

I looked from face to face, searching for some way out of this nightmare. Juniper looked genuinely distressed, Perseus troubled but resigned.

The shadow energy was pulsing more strongly from me now, responding to my panic. Books began to slide off shelves, papers rustled without wind, and the temperature in the room dropped noticeably. I couldn't control it anymore – it was feeding on my emotions, growing stronger with each surge of fear or anger.

"Do I have a choice?" I asked finally, my voice barely steady.

"Everyone has choices," Clara replied, meeting my eyes directly. "Though some have more immediate consequences than others."

The implications were clear. I could resist and be taken by force, likely facing additional charges, or cooperate and maintain what little dignity I had left.

"Fine," I said, straightening my shoulders while trying desperately to rein in the shadow energy swirling around me. "But I want it on record that I'm innocent, this is ridiculous, and someone is obviously setting me up."

"Noted," Clara said.

The two security vampires moved forward, producing what looked like silver manacles etched with complex symbols.

"Are those really necessary?" Perseus asked, voice cold with anger.

"Standard procedure for shadow-compromised detainees," Clara replied. "For her safety as well as others."

I extended my wrists, trying to ignore the way the shadows recoiled from the silver as if in pain. "Let's just get this over with."

As the manacles clicked closed around my wrists, I felt an immediate wave of cold numbness flow through me. The shadowy whispers in my mind subsided to a dull murmur, still present but less insistent. The darkness around me receded, no longer responding to my emotional state.

"We'll resolve this," Juniper promised as I was led toward the door, her normally animated face unusually grave. "And I'll keep working on the dimensional folding theory. If the Concordat is still in the Archives, just hidden, we'll find it."

I looked back over my shoulder, suddenly realizing the implications of my arrest. "My children —"

"Will continue to be cared for," Perseus assured me. "Focus on maintaining your control, Gillian. We'll handle everything else."

As Clara led me through the offices of Clifford and Burk, past wide-eyed vampire employees and concerned receptionists, all I could think was that I'd failed – failed to find the Concordat, failed to protect myself from shadow corruption, failed to understand who had orchestrated my transformation and why.

And now I was being arrested for the very crime I'd been trying to solve, while whoever had planned all this remained free to continue their scheme.

Clara's hand on my arm was firm but not rough as she guided me toward the elevator. "This isn't personal, Gillian," she said quietly, for my ears only. "But it is necessary."

"Necessary for whom?" I asked, studying her perfect, impassive face for any hint of her true motives. "And why now, just when I was getting close to answers?"

For the briefest moment, something flickered in her eyes – concern? Regret? Something deeper? But it was gone before I could identify it, replaced by the cool professional mask.

"All will be explained in due time," she replied as the elevator doors closed behind us, sealing my fate.

**Current status: Arrested vampire. Shadow powers: temporarily suppressed. Investigation: forcibly halted. Mysterious conspiratorial mastermind: still at large. Dimensional folding theory: tantalizingly unresolved. Children: unreachable. Confusion level: astronomical.**

# CHAPTER 19

# HOW TO LOSE FRIENDS AND TERRIFY PEOPLE

**9:37 PM. Location: Council facility. Accommodations: surprisingly clinical rather than dungeon-like. Shadow control: failure imminent. Hope levels: subterranean.**

The sound of the door opening made me look up. Clara Blackwood entered alone, but this time she carried something that made my blood run cold – a sleek black case, its surface etched with protective runes.

Her hair was pulled back severely, emphasising the sharp angles of her face.

"The containment device is failing faster than anticipated," Clara stated without preamble, setting the case on the metal counter with deliberate precision. "We need to upgrade your containment immediately."

I tensed, instinctively backing away. "Upgrade how?"

Clara opened the case, revealing what lay within. My breath caught.

Nestled in custom foam was an elegant leather collar, its surface inlaid with intricate silver runes shimmered. The craftsmanship was exquisite – supple black leather that looked butter-soft, silver clasps and arcane symbols that hurt to look at directly.

"This is a significant step up from your current device," Clara explained, her tone professionally detached even as her fingers traced the collar's edge with something approaching reverence. "The original containment was only temporary. Your... progression has accelerated beyond our initial projections."

"That's a collar," I said unnecessarily, my voice barely above a whisper.

"Enhanced restraint device," Clara corrected, though her clinical tone couldn't quite mask the underlying tension that had entered the room. "This requires precise placement for optimal effectiveness."

She lifted the collar from its case.

"I need you to expose your throat," Clara said, her voice carefully neutral.

I found myself frozen, suddenly hyperaware of the vulnerable position she was asking me to assume – throat bared, exposed, completely at her mercy.

"Gillian." Clara's voice was softer now, though still edged with authority. "Your current device will fail completely within the hour. This isn't optional."

Just as I reached for my failing bracelet, the door burst open.

Juniper appeared. "Emergency!" she gasped, unfolding a message with trembling fingers. "The Petrov twins intercepted Helix Coven communications – they're working with Odette Valencourt!"

Clara's expression remained impassive, but I caught the subtle tightening of her jaw. "My colleagues are already moving to apprehend Odette Valencourt. This changes nothing about Ms. Spark's immediate medical needs."

"But Ezra!" Juniper's voice cracked. "He sent me a message this afternoon – 'Odette Valencourt is planning something.' He wanted to talk strategy. He sent me a follow up message that just said "help!" but now he's not replying."

"Ezra Worster has survived four centuries," Clara interrupted coldly. "He's not easily taken by surprise. Ms. Spark's deteriorating condition, however, poses an immediate threat to everyone in this facility."

Her dismissive tone made anger flare in my chest. Of course she'd prioritize controlling me over checking on a colleague who might be in danger. I was just another problem to be solved, another criminal to contain.

"That's heartless, even for you," I said before I could stop myself.

Clara's eyes flashed dangerously. "Heartless is allowing an unstable vampire to succumb to madness in a facility full of vulnerable staff. Remove your bracelet. Now."

Her voice brooked no argument. With shaking hands, I unclasped the failing device. The moment it came free, the shadows surged forward like a tidal wave. Dark tendrils rippled across my vision, and whispers filled my mind – hungry, seductive, overwhelming.

Clara moved faster than thought. Her hand pressed against my throat, skin to skin, and the shadows recoiled as if burned. The touch was sent shockwaves through my system that I suspected had nothing to do with shadow corruption.

"Look at me," she commanded, her voice cutting through the chaos.

I found myself obeying, meeting those eyes that seemed to see straight through to my corrupted soul. Her hand remained at my throat, cool and steady, holding the darkness at bay through sheer force of will.

"That's it," she murmured, positioning the new collar with her free hand. "Stay with me, Gillian."

The use of my name startled me. Clara's fingers brushed my jaw as she secured the clasps, each touch precise yet charged with something neither of us would acknowledge. For a moment that stretched into eternity, we remained frozen in that intimate tableau – her hand at my throat, faces inches apart, the air between us crackling with tension.

"There," Clara said finally, stepping back with careful control. "Much better."

The new collar hummed with power, its suppression field infinitely stronger. The shadows retreated completely, leaving my mind startlingly clear but somehow confined.

"Now can we check on Ezra?" Juniper pleaded.

Clara studied me for a long moment, her expression unreadable. "Fine. A brief investigation. But Ms. Spark remains in my custody, and any deviation from my instructions will result in immediate activation of the collar's submission protocols."

"Submission protocols?" I echoed, ice flooding my veins.

Her smile was razor-sharp. "Full neuromuscular paralysis, among other features. Consider it motivation to behave."

**10:45 PM. Location: Ezra Worster's residence. Status wellness check.**

The pristine apartment had been violated – books torn from shelves, furniture overturned, and dark stains on the pale carpet that made me recoil.

"Vampire blood," Clara confirmed, kneeling to examine the largest stain. "Several hours old. Ezra's, based on the magical signature."

We spread out to search in urgency. In his office, I found his desk calendar – today's date circled in red with the notation: "SR - warning?"

"Sebastian Rothsforte?" Juniper guessed. "Ezra might have implicated him in working with Odette."

"Here!" Juniper called from across the room. "Hidden compartment in the wall – it's been forced open."

The safe was empty, but I noticed something the others had missed – a scrap of paper that had fallen behind the desk. I retrieved it carefully, unfolding what appeared to be a torn notebook page.

The handwriting was hasty, urgent:

" – not what we thought. The Concordat wasn't stolen – it was hidden. In plain sight, as the ancient texts suggest. I've discovered that dimensional concealment magic was used, and I believe I know who –"

The rest was torn away.

"Dimensional concealment," Juniper breathed, eyes widening. "That's seriously advanced magic. Vampires can't do that."

"No," Clara agreed, taking the paper and examining it closely. "This would require magic. Powerful magic."

"So it's not just the Obscurum vampires – Odette and Sebastian and whoever else. They must be in league with someone else..."

"In conspectu omnium abscondita," Clara murmured, studying the scrap of paper again.

"What?" I asked.

"'Hidden in plain sight,'" Clara translated. "It's an old phrase, used to describe the perfect deception – one so obvious that no one thinks to question it."

A memory surfaced suddenly. "Wait. Roe Thistle told me something at the Market. A riddle about the Concordat's location – 'Look to where water touches sky but remains untouched by earth.' I didn't understand then, but water touching sky – that's a reflection! The Concordat isn't gone, it's..."

"Still in the witching archives," Clara finished, understanding dawning. "Hidden in a dimensional reflection of the same space."

"Brilliant," Juniper whispered. "Everyone searching the world for something that never left."

"We need to get there immediately," Clara decided, already moving toward the door. "Before whoever took Ezra realizes we've discovered the truth."

**11:42 PM. Location: Archives of the Witching Parliament. Mission: Reveal the impossible.**

The Head Archivist's suspicion was palpable from behind her silver spectacles, but Clara's icy authority and Council credentials eventually gained us access to the central chamber.

"I'll be monitoring from the adjacent room," the Archivist warned. "Any unauthorised interference will trigger immediate lockdown."

Once alone, Juniper immediately began setting up her spell components. "We have maybe twenty minutes before she gets suspicious. Less if the dimensional magic triggers their wards."

Clara positioned herself by the door while I stood near the empty pedestal, trying to sense through my collar's suppression. Despite the restraint, I could feel it – a wrongness in the air, like looking at a place where reality had been folded.

"There," I said, pointing to a spot just above the pedestal. "The space feels... wrong. Twisted."

Juniper began her chant, pouring Clara's vial of Concordat residue into the ritual circle. The air shimmered, reality itself beginning to bend and warp. The wrongness I'd sensed intensified, making my teeth ache.

And then, with a sound like tearing silk, the dimensional fold peeled back.

What we saw made us all freeze.

The Concordat floated there, exactly where it had always been, just slightly out of phase with our reality. But it wasn't intact – fractures ran through the stone, pulsing with unstable energy. And around it, preserved in the dimensional pocket like insects in amber, were other objects.

A leather notebook, its pages fluttering despite the absence of wind. A silver bracelet engraved with witching runes. A chalk diagram half-drawn on nothingness.

And a pair of horn-rimmed glasses, one lens cracked, floating like an accusation.

"Elara's," Juniper whispered, her face going pale. "Those are Elara Ashwood's glasses."

"The witch who was reported missing from the archives?" Clara asked.

Juniper and I nodded.

The implications hung heavy in the air. Elara hadn't just disappeared – perhaps she'd been silenced for discovering exactly what we'd just found.

"The Concordat's been deliberately damaged," Clara observed, studying the fractures. "This isn't decay – it's sabotage."

"Creating shadow instability," I realised. "Forcing vampire-witch tensions to escalate."

"This is too dangerous. A political powder keg. We need to extract it," Clara decided. "Get it repaired before anyone realizes what we've found."

"But the evidence – Elara's things –" Juniper protested.

"Will be photographed and documented," Clara said, producing a small crystal device. "But the Concordat takes priority. Without it, we're facing supernatural war."

Juniper produced an extraction bag made of shimmering material. "This should contain the magical signature, but moving it might destabilize the dimensional pocket."

As Juniper carefully manoeuvred the bag around the damaged Concordat, I couldn't stop staring at those horn-rimmed glasses. Elara had stood where we were standing. She'd discovered the truth. And someone had made sure she never reported it.

The dimensional pocket began collapsing the moment the Concordat was secured. Elara's belongings scattered like autumn leaves, dissolving into magical residue before we could save them. Only the memory remained – and the knowledge that we were dealing with someone willing to kill to keep their secret.

Alarms began blaring as the dimensional manipulation triggered the Archive's security.

"Time to go," Clara commanded, the bagged Concordat disappearing into her jacket.

As we fled, I caught her expression – calculating, concerned, but something else too. For the first time since we'd met, Clara Blackwood looked genuinely shaken.

Whatever game she'd been playing, finding evidence of Elara's fate had changed the rules. And as the collar hummed against my throat, I realised that being Clara's useful prisoner might be the only thing keeping me alive.

**Current status: Collared vampire asset. Concordat: recovered but damaged. Elara Ashwood: presumed dead. Ezra: missing. The conspiracy: more complicated than anyone imagined.**

# CHAPTER 20
# TERMS OF ENSLAVEMENT

**1** **2:03 AM. Location: Racing through London streets. Concordat status: Secured but damaged. Paranoia level: Justified, as it turns out.**

The cab swerved around another corner, tires squealing in protest. I clutched the door handle with vampire strength, probably leaving permanent indentations in the plastic.

"Denmark Street," Clara barked at the driver, her usual composure cracking slightly. "Quickly."

Juniper bounced nervously in the middle seat, the bagged Concordat cradled in her lap like the world's most dangerous baby. "The Petrov twins were very specific – Thaddeus Grimshaw is the only one who can repair magical damage this extensive."

"Since when do you trust the Petrovs?" I asked, something niggling at the back of my mind.

"Since they've been nothing but helpful throughout this entire investigation," Juniper replied defensively. "They've provided crucial intel at every turn."

Every turn. Right... The phrase sat uneasily in my stomach as we screeched to a halt outside Grimshaw's Arcane Antiquities.

The shop looked exactly as it had during our last visit – wedged impossibly between modern buildings, its windows cloudy with age. But something felt different now. The air itself seemed heavier, charged with anticipation I couldn't quite name.

Thaddeus answered our frantic knocking immediately, as if he'd been waiting by the door.

"My dear ladies," he greeted us, his wispy white hair forming its usual halo. "What brings you here at such an ungodly hour? Though I suppose for vampires, this is rather like afternoon tea."

"We need your help," Clara said without preamble, her authority cutting through pleasantries. "The Concordat has been recovered but it's damaged. The Petrov twins said you're the only one who might repair it."

His pale blue eyes widened with what appeared to be genuine surprise. "The Concordat? Found at last? How extraordinary!" He peered at the bag in Juniper's arms. "May I?"

Juniper carefully handed over our precious cargo. Thaddeus unwrapped it with reverent fingers, his expression growing grave as he examined the fractures running through the stone.

"Oh my. Oh dear. This is… significant damage indeed." He looked up, meeting each of our eyes in turn. "This will require my specialised workshop. The energies involved are far too volatile for the main shop."

He ushered us toward the back of the store, past shelves groaning with arcane artefacts. I picked up subtle scents – old leather, dried herbs, and something else. Something that made the hairs on the back of my neck stand up.

Fear. I could smell fear lingering in the air, days old but still present. Someone had been terrified in this shop recently.

"Just through here," Thaddeus said, pressing his palm against what looked like an ordinary wall panel. It swung inward, revealing a narrow staircase descending into darkness.

Clara hesitated at the threshold, and I caught the subtle tension in her shoulders. "Your workshop is underground?"

"The best magical work requires isolation from surface interference," Thaddeus explained, already starting down the stairs. "Natural stone dampens unwanted energies. Please, time is of the essence if we're to stabilize the Concordat."

We followed him down, the temperature dropping with each step. Emergency lighting cast sickly green shadows on stone walls that looked far older than the shop above. My enhanced hearing picked up something else now – multiple heartbeats echoing from below, their rhythm too steady to be human.

Vampires. Several of them.

"Clara," I whispered, but she was already moving, her hand going to her jacket where I knew she kept various Council enforcement tools.

The staircase ended at a heavy wooden door reinforced with iron bands. Thaddeus pressed another hidden panel, and it swung open to reveal –

"Wow," Juniper breathed.

The underground chamber was massive, carved from living rock with pillars supporting a vaulted ceiling. Magical symbols covered every surface, glowing with faint phosphorescence. But it wasn't the impressive architecture that made my blood run cold.

It was the welcoming committee.

Ezra Worster stood at the chamber's centre, very much not kidnapped, not injured, and wearing an expression of smug satisfaction that made me want to punch his face. Beside him, Victoria Prendergast lounged against a stone altar. Six other vampires flanked them – all ancient, all radiating the kind of power that made my teeth ache.

And behind them, wearing matching expressions of eerie satisfaction, stood the Petrov twins.

The door slammed shut behind us with finality. I heard locks clicking.

"Juniper," I said quietly, "now would be a great time for that spatial translocation trick of yours."

Her hands were already glowing as she reached for her power, but the light sputtered and died. Her face went pale. "I can't. The chamber's warded against my powers."

"How disappointingly predictable," Ezra said, his cultured voice echoing off stone walls. "Though I must admit, you found the Concordat faster than we anticipated. Well done. After our initial plan met some unexpected...hiccups we had to find another way. It took a while to come up with the plan and figure out a way to lure you back there. No powerful witch would have helped us, but a mage with a penchant for rule breaking was perfect."

"You faked your own kidnapping," Clara stated, her voice cold enough to frost windows. "The blood, the ransacked apartment, the conveniently torn note – all staged."

Ezra's smile was all satisfaction. "Guilty as charged, Investigator. Though I prefer to think of it as strategic misdirection. The note was a particularly nice touch, don't you think? Just enough truth to point you in the right direction."

"Why?" Clara demanded. "You're a court stenographer. You've served the Council for decades."

"Centuries," Ezra corrected. "Centuries of watching our kind diminished. Reduced from apex predators to domesticated pets, begging witches for our very sustenance." His voice hardened with genuine anger. "Vampire suppression has gone on long enough."

"Odette would agree with you," Clara said carefully, clearly trying to buy time while assessing our options.

Ezra laughed – a sound like breaking crystal. "Darling Odette. She does make such an excellent scapegoat, doesn't she? All that public ranting about returning to the old ways, her dramatic opposition to the Concordat..." He shook his head with mock sympathy. "She'd never actually dirty her hands by joining us – she's far too superior for that. But when this is over, everyone will believe she was behind it all."

"No one else will ever find out the truth," Victoria added. "We've been very thorough."

My mind raced, pieces clicking together with sickening clarity. "The evidence pointing to Sebastian. The Helix Coven red herrings. You orchestrated all of it."

"Every clue you followed, we placed," the Petrov twins said in their horrible unison, their synchronised movements making my skin crawl. "Every conclusion you reached, we guided."

Juniper made a sound like she'd been punched. "You used me. I thought we were colleagues. Friends."

"We are terribly fond of you," Anastasia said with what might have been genuine regret.

"But the cause comes first," Alexei finished.

"Speaking of which," Ezra said, turning those calculating eyes on me, "let's discuss why you're really here, Gillian."

"Because you manipulated us into finding the Concordat for you?" I suggested with more bravado than I felt.

"Partially," he acknowledged. "Your friend Juniper's particular magical skills were necessary to extract it from the dimensional fold. We'd tried using Elara Ashwood initially, but she proved... uncooperative."

"You killed her," I said flatly.

Victoria waved a dismissive hand. "She refused to see reason. Kept insisting the Concordat was too important to tamper with. Such limited vision. She and the Concordat both disappeared. It took us a while to figure out they hadn't gone somewhere else in London."

"Brilliant, really," Ezra added. "Everyone searching the world for something that never left. It worked in our favour. The witches blaming the vampires and vice versa, the extremist groups being blamed. Sebastian Rothsforte tried to take advantage sent people chasing after fake fragments on the black market. It only served to muddy the waters further."

"But Elara isn't why you're here," Victoria said, studying me with uncomfortable intensity. "You are."

She moved closer, circling me with dangerous grace. The collar around my throat hummed with increased power, responding to the threat.

"Such rare potential," she murmured. "Shadow manifestation within days of turning. The ability to summon fire – a power no vampire should possess. You're either an anomaly or…Something far more valuable."

"Join us," Ezra said abruptly. "I'll serve as your Sangrelié. Give you the guidance and protection you need while helping you develop these extraordinary abilities."

"Don't be ridiculous," Victoria interjected sharply. "She needs someone who understands the feminine aspects of power. I would make a far better Sangrelié." She turned to me, her voice dropping to a hypnotic purr. "Your power deserves proper guidance to flourish into its greatest potential, not Clara's leash or Ezra's antiquated notions of control."

Juniper turned to him, desperation creeping into her voice. "Thaddeus, I don't know how you got caught up in this, but there are other options. You don't have to –"

His laugh was grandfatherly and utterly chilling. "Caught up in it? My dear child, I helped plan it. Every step, every manipulation, every careful placement of evidence. Though I must admit, Gillian's transformation was an unexpected gift. We'd planned to destroy the Concordat regardless, but having her power on our side? That changes everything."

"You're not even a vampire," Juniper said. "Why?"

"Not a vampire, yet, my dear," Thaddeus corrected. "No one will make me into one because of my supernatural blood, and yet, despite my age, if I'm to survive another century, I need transformation."

Juniper shook her head sadly.

"So here's your choice," Ezra announced, spreading his hands like a generous host. "Join us willingly – swear a blood oath to the Obscurum – and help usher in a new age of vampire supremacy. Or…" His smile turned sharp. "Die here, tonight. We'll blame everything on Odette, destroy the Concordat, and in the chaos of the vampire-witch war that follows, we'll seize control anyway."

"Either way," Victoria added, "vampires will be restored to their full power. Free to hunt. Free to feed properly instead of subsisting on magically enhanced scraps. Free to turn whoever we please without bureaucratic oversight."

"Free to dominate humanity like the good old days," I said. "How delightfully medieval of you."

"Says the woman wearing a collar like a well-trained pet," Victoria countered.

The collar. Clara's collar that could paralyze me with a thought. I was trapped in every possible way – physically, magically, and through the supernatural restraint locked around my throat.

Clara stepped forward, and every vampire in the room tensed. "The Council will –"

"The Council will blame Odette Valencourt," Ezra interrupted. "Especially after we plant your bodies in her lair along with the destroyed Concordat. Such a tragedy – the brave investigator and her friends, murdered while trying to stop a madwoman's scheme."

"Though we'd rather you joined us," Victoria added, focusing on me again. "Your power is too valuable to waste."

**12:31 AM. Negotiation status: Failed. Violence: Imminent. Survival prospects: Grim.**

"Go to hell," I said clearly.

The temperature in the room dropped ten degrees.

"Disappointing," Ezra sighed. "But not unexpected. Anastasia? Alexei? If you would?"

The twins moved in synchronisation. But Clara was already in motion.

I'd never seen a vampire fight at full capacity before. Clara moved like liquid mercury, producing a silver blade from her jacket that blazed with light. She took out the first attacking vampire with surgical precision, the blade finding the sweet spot between ribs that even vampire healing couldn't quickly fix.

Juniper's hands erupted with crackling energy – not her usual spatial magic, but something rawer, more desperate. Lightning arced between her fingers.

"Get the Concordat!" Clara shouted, currently holding off three vampires at once with a combination of martial arts and that blazing blade.

But Victoria was already there, standing between me and the altar where Thaddeus had placed our prize. Her smile was all fangs and malice.

"Come then, little anomaly," she purred. "Show me this power they're so eager to claim."

The collar around my throat burned as I reached for my abilities, its suppression field fighting against my will. Victoria struck first. Her fist caught me in the ribs, sending me flying into a stone pillar with bone-crushing force.

Definitely broke something. Several somethings. The pain was excruciating even with vampire healing already trying to knit bones back together.

"Is that all?" Victoria taunted.

Rage built in my chest – not just at her, but at everything. At being manipulated, controlled, collared like an animal. At Ezra and his supremacist delusions. At the Petrovs' betrayal. At all of them for murdering Elara Ashwood, whose only crime was trying to do the right thing.

The shadows responded to my fury, pressing against the collar's constraints like flood water against a dam.

Victoria struck again, her nails raking across my face, leaving bloody furrows that burned like acid. "Pathetic. Clara's made you weak. Dependent."

"Stop holding back!" Juniper screamed from across the room. She was pinned between the twins, their synchronised attacks slowly overwhelming her defences.

Holding back? I wasn't holding back. I was –

The realization hit like lightning. I was still thinking like Gillian

Bennett, the compliant wife who made herself smaller to avoid conflict. Who accepted control because it was easier than fighting.

But I wasn't Gillian Bennett anymore. I was Gillian Spark. Vampire.

And I was done being controlled.

The rage transformed into something colder, more focused. I thought of my children. Thought of how these monsters would remake the world into their hunting ground.

Not while I still existed.

When Victoria came at me again, I was ready. I caught her wrist, using her momentum to flip her over my shoulder. We crashed into the altar together, stone cracking under the impact.

"Better," she gasped, actually looking pleased as she rolled to her feet. "But not enough."

She was right. The collar still limited me, keeping my shadows locked away. But as we grappled, trading blows that would have killed humans instantly, I felt something else building. Not shadow magic, but the fire that had manifested at the Market.

Victoria's hands locked around my throat, pressing against the collar. "Submit or die. Those are your only choices."

"You forgot option three," I growled.

I reached deep, past the shadows, past the hunger, to that impossible spark of power that made me an anomaly. The collar fought against it, its suppression field screaming protests.

But rage is a hell of a motivator.

The collar shattered.

The explosion of released power sent Victoria flying backward. Dark fire erupted from my hands – not the cold flames from before, but something new. Shadow and fire combined, purple-black flames that consumed light itself.

"Impossible," Thaddeus breathed.

"I'm getting really tired of that word," I snarled, advancing on Victoria.

She tried to flee, but the shadows responded to my will now, wrapping around her ankles like living chains. The hybrid flames licked at her skin, and her scream was music to my ears.

"The Concordat!" Clara shouted. She'd dealt with her opponents but was bleeding from multiple wounds. "Gillian, the Concordat!"

Right. Save the world first, existential crisis about impossible powers later.

I sprinted for the altar, shadows propelling me faster than mere vampire speed. Ezra tried to intercept, but Juniper hit him with a bolt of pure magical chaos that sent him spinning into a wall.

My hands closed on the damaged Concordat. The moment I touched it, brilliant light exploded from the artefact, filling the chamber with radiance that sent every vampire scrambling for cover.

The light was warm, peaceful, and utterly wrong coming from something that regulated shadow magic. It pulsed through me, through the hybrid flames still wreathing my hands, through the very stones of the chamber.

When it finally faded, I stood there gasping, the Concordat clutched to my chest. The Obscurum members were down – some unconscious, others groaning in pain. Even Clara looked dazed, blinking away the afterimage of that impossible light.

"What did you do?" Juniper whispered.

"I have absolutely no idea," I admitted.

That's when we all heard it – a small, confused voice from behind the altar.

"Excuse me? I'm terribly sorry, but has anyone seen my glasses? I seem to have dropped them somewhere around here..."

We turned as one to stare at the young woman standing there, blinking myopically at us. Red hair pulled back in a practical ponytail. Horn-rimmed glasses notably absent.

"Elara Ashwood," Clara breathed.

Elara squinted in our general direction. "Yes? I'm sorry, do I know you? The last thing I remember is discovering something quite extraordinary, and then..." She frowned. "Actually, I'm not entirely sure what happened next. Why am I underground? And why does everyone look so surprised to see me?"

I looked down at the Concordat in my hands, its fractures now glowing with soft golden light instead of ominous shadow. Whatever I'd done, it had apparently included resurrecting a witch.

"This night just keeps getting weirder," I muttered.

**Current status: Collarless vampire with impossible hybrid powers. Concordat: Secured and apparently upgraded. Obscurum: Exposed and mostly unconscious. Elara Ashwood: Inexplicably alive. Rational explanations: Completely exhausted. What the hell happens now?: Excellent question.**

# CHAPTER 21

# FIGHT CLUB FOR THE IMMORTALLY CONFUSED

2:33 AM. Location: Underground chamber. Situation: Frozen tableau of impossibility. Dead witch: Apparently not so dead.

For a heartbeat, nobody moved. We all stared at Elara Ashwood like she might evaporate if we breathed too hard. She stood there in her practical cardigan and sensible shoes, squinting at us with the particular frustration of the severely nearsighted.

"Seriously," she said, patting her pockets with increasing agitation. "My glasses. I can't see a thing without them, and I really need to document these extraordinary dimensional resonance patterns before they fade."

"Elara," Juniper whispered, her voice cracking. "You're... you're not dead."

"Dead?" Elara laughed, a nervous sound that echoed off stone walls. "Don't be ridiculous. I'm right here. Though I did have the strangest experience. One moment I was examining the dimensional fold around the Concordat, and then everything went sort of... sideways?" She frowned, rubbing her temples. "Time felt weird.

Stretched out but also compressed. Like being stuck between heartbeats."

"How long?" Clara asked sharply. "How long were you stuck?"

Elara shrugged. "Twenty minutes? Maybe half an hour?"

"Days," I said quietly. "You've been missing for days."

The colour drained from Elara's face as she looked around at the scattered vampires. "That's... that's not possible. I would have noticed –"She stopped mid-sentence, her myopic gaze finally taking in the scene properly. The unconscious vampires. The scorch marks from our battle. The way we all stood in defensive positions.

Her hand flew to her mouth. "Oh. Oh no. Now I remember... You're them. You're the ones who attacked me."

That's when Ezra stirred. "Impossible," he growled, struggling to his feet. "We killed you. Made sure of it."

Elara's face went from pale to ashen. "You tried. But then... She touched her chest wonderingly. "The concordat...It suspended me... healed me somehow. It drew on my magic and wrapped us both up into a pocket dimension."

"The Concordat healed you?" Clara asked.

"Fascinating," Victoria hissed, pulling herself upright against the altar. "But ultimately irrelevant. Dead then or dead now makes little difference."

Elara squeaked as Victoria lunged at her with vampire speed.

I moved on instinct, shadows propelling me between them. Victoria's claws raked across my back instead of Elara's throat, sending white-hot agony through my nervous system. But the pain just fed the darkness rising inside me.

Without the collar's suppression, the shadows were LOUD. They whispered, screamed, sang – a symphony of power that threatened to drown out my own thoughts. Purple-black energy rippled across my skin like living tattoos, and I could feel myself fragmenting at the edges.

"Gillian!" Clara's warning came just as Ezra struck, trying to pin me with his superior strength and age.

"Submit!" he commanded, his voice layered with vampiric compulsion. "Accept the Sangrelié bond. Let me guide your power!"

The shadows recoiled violently from his attempt at dominance. Dark fire erupted from every pore, sending Ezra flying backward with a howl of pain. The flames were different now – hungrier, wilder, less controlled.

"Can't," I gasped, falling to my knees as the power threatened to tear me apart. "Can't hold it –"

"Together!" the Petrov twins said in eerie unison, moving to flank our group. Their hands wove complex patterns, attempting to contain us all in a binding circle.

Juniper threw up a shield just in time, golden equations clashing against their vampiric power. The resulting explosion of competing energies sent books and artefacts flying.

Elara, meanwhile, had found her second wind. And apparently her temper.

"You absolute bastards!" she shouted, her English accent sharpening with fury. "Do you have any idea how long I worked on that dimensional resonance theory? Months of calculations ruined because you couldn't stand the idea of regulated shadow consumption!"

She pulled something from her cardigan pocket – a piece of chalk, mundane and ridiculous in the circumstances. But when she started drawing on the floor, the symbols blazed with power that made even the ancient vampires step back.

Thaddeus breathed. "That there is proper old magic, not the diluted moderne versions."

"Cambridge Practical Magic Society, first in my class," Elara snapped, adding another symbol that made the air itself ring like a bell. "Specialised in dimensional manipulation and theoretical applied dynamics. Also, very angry right now!"

Her spell crashed into the Petrov twins' binding attempt, shattering it like glass. The feedback sent both twins staggering, their perfect synchronisation faltering.

But we were still outnumbered, and the shadows inside me were getting stronger. I could feel myself dissolving at the edges, becoming less Gillian and more... something else. Something that looked at all these vampires and saw only prey to be dominated or destroyed.

"Enough games," Victoria snarled. She nodded to one of the unnamed vampires, who produced a small device from his pocket.

My enhanced senses immediately identified the threat – magical explosives, wired throughout the chamber. The scent of charged crystal and unstable alchemical compounds made my nose burn.

Everyone froze.

"Insurance," Victoria explained with cold satisfaction. "Either we all win, or we all burn together. The explosion will be... thorough. They'll find nothing but ash and assume Odette's madness extended to bombing."

"You're insane," Clara stated flatly.

"I'm practical," Victoria countered. "Thaddeus, complete the ritual. Strip the Concordat's protections so we can destroy it properly."

The elderly antiquarian moved toward the altar where I'd dropped the Concordat during the fight. His hands were steady as he began pulling ritual components from hidden pockets – black candles, silver dust, something that looked disturbingly like dried blood.

"No!" Elara started forward, but Ezra caught her easily.

"Watch and learn," he murmured in her ear. "This is how the old world returns."

Thaddeus lit the candles with a word, their flames burning an unnatural blue-black. "The Concordat has bound us for too long," he intoned, sprinkling silver dust in precise patterns. "Tonight, we break chains forged by fear and compromise."

"Stop," Juniper pleaded. "You don't understand what you're doing. The magical ecosystem –"

"Will adapt," Anastasia interrupted, though her voice lacked its usual certainty.

"As it always has," Alexei added.

Thaddeus began chanting in a language that probably predated Latin. The Concordat responded, its golden glow flickering like a dying heartbeat. Each word of the ritual felt like nails on a chalkboard to my supernatural senses.

But something else was happening. As Thaddeus worked, I felt the Concordat... watching. Not with eyes, but with awareness that pressed against my consciousness. It was evaluating, measuring, judging.

"Does anyone else feel that?" I asked, shadows writhing around me in response to the artefact's attention.

"Feel what?" Clara demanded, still poised for action despite the explosive threat.

"The Concordat. It's... alive."

Clara stared in awe. "It protected Elara and healed her... protected itself, created the dimensional fold to hide in."

"Nonsense," Thaddeus scoffed, but his hands hesitated over the next ritual gesture.

Juniper laughed. "Oh. Oh! You absolute idiots. You don't understand what the Concordat is at all!"

"Enlighten us," Victoria said sarcastically.

"It's not just a treaty or a regulatory mechanism," Juniper said, her voice rising with excitement and horror. "It's a living spell. A magical entity created by the fusion of vampire and witch magic. It doesn't just regulate shadow consumption – it thinks. It learns. It's been testing all of us!"

"Impossible," Ezra stated, but uncertainty crept into his tone.

"Is it?" Elara asked, squinting at the Concordat with professional interest. "A sufficiently complex magical construct could develop consciousness. Especially one that's been processing shadow energy for centuries. All that psychological data flowing through it..."

The Concordat pulsed, brighter this time. And then it spoke.

Not with words, but with pure magical resonance that bypassed ears and went straight to the soul. Images flooded our minds – visions of what vampire supremacy truly meant.

Cities burning as vampires fought over territory. Humans reduced to cattle, their terror and despair poisoning the very shadows vampires fed on. Witches hunted to extinction, taking their magical balance with them. The ecosystem collapsing as shadow energy ran unchecked, consuming even the vampires who thought they controlled it.

And finally, inevitably, extinction. Not just for humans or witches, but for vampires themselves – destroyed by the very power they'd sought to unleash.

"No," Victoria whispered, her aristocratic composure cracking. "That's not... we would control it. We would rule properly."

More visions. Victoria's own memories reflected back at her – centuries of resentment, of feeling diminished, of blaming others for her own inability to adapt. The Concordat showed her the truth: her supremacist dreams were just elaborate ways to avoid facing her own obsolescence.

The Petrov twins made a sound I'd never heard before – individual gasps of pain as the Concordat forced them to experience true separation. For beings who'd spent centuries in perfect synchronisation, the sudden individuality was agony.

"Stop," Alexei begged, clutching his head.

"Please," Anastasia sobbed, reaching for her twin but unable to bridge the gap the Concordat had forced between them.

Even Thaddeus staggered back from the altar, his ritual implements scattering. The Concordat showed him his centuries of planning, all the careful manipulations, and revealed the pathetic truth – he was just a bitter old creature afraid of becoming irrelevant.

"Enough!" Ezra roared, dark veins standing out on his pale skin as he fought the visions. "It's just a spell! A construct! It doesn't have the right to judge us!"

But the Concordat wasn't done. It turned its attention to me, and

I felt its alien consciousness brush against mine. The shadows inside me responded, surging up to meet it.

*You are the bridge,* it whispered in concepts rather than words.

"I don't understand," I gasped, shadows pouring off me in waves.

Elara suddenly gripped my arm, her touch shockingly warm against my cold skin. "I do," she said quietly. "The Concordat isn't just damaged. It's a living thing. It was always meant to evolve, to grow beyond its original parameters. But it needs both aspects to do so."

"Shadow and light," I breathed, understanding flooding through me. Roe's clue had been more than a signal to find the Concordat, the wily fae had been playing both sides all along with is paradoxes: *between night and day, between magic and mundane, between life and death – look to where water touches sky but remains untouched by earth. Where salt meets sweet but neither may drink.* It wasn't just the clue to finding the Concordat – there was a deeper wisdom here – a resounding truth in bringing together the opposites that just might save us all.

"Vampire and witch," Elara confirmed. She looked at me with those earnest brown eyes, no longer squinting now that we were close. "It's a treaty, Gillian. And treaties require all parties to participate."

She held out her hand, chalk dust still clinging to her fingers. "Shall we?"

I stared at Elara's outstretched hand, acutely aware that everyone in the chamber was watching us. The shadows writhing around me recoiled instinctively from her magic – oil and water, fundamentally incompatible.

Except I was proof that wasn't true. I was both oil and water, existing in defiance of natural law.

"If this kills us both," I said, taking her hand, "I'm going to be very annoyed."

"Noted," Elara replied with a shaky smile. "Though technically I've already been mostly dead, so I'm ahead of you there."

Our joined hands created an immediate reaction. Where shadow met magic, silver-gold sparks erupted, neither dark nor light but something entirely new. The sensation was like grabbing a live wire while swimming in honey – overwhelming but not exactly painful.

"The Concordat," Elara directed, pulling me toward the altar. "We need to touch it together."

"No!" Victoria lunged forward, but Clara intercepted her with brutal efficiency.

"Anyone moves and I'll detonate the explosives myself," one of the unnamed vampires threatened, hand on the trigger device.

"Go ahead," I called back, shadows and witch-light spiralling around Elara and me in a double helix. "Either this works or we all die anyway. At least this way it's interesting."

Our free hands touched the Concordat simultaneously.

The world exploded into sensation.

I could feel everything – every shadow in the chamber, every spark of magic, every heartbeat and thought and fear. But more than that, I could feel the Concordat itself, vast and complex and desperately hopeful.

It was like touching the mind of a small god, one that had been born from desperation and compromise but had grown into something neither side had anticipated. It showed us its centuries of processing shadow and magic, learning the delicate balance required to keep both species from destroying each other.

*Fix me,* it pleaded. *Make me whole.*

Elara's magic flowed through our joined hands, precise and analytical, finding every fracture in the Concordat's structure. My shadows followed, not to destroy but to fill – seeping into the cracks like living mortar, binding what had been broken.

"It's working," Elara breathed, wonder in her voice. "The shadow energy isn't corrupting the magic – they're complementing each other."

I could see what she meant. Where vampire shadow alone would have been too hungry, too destructive, her magic tempered it.

The Concordat drank in our combined energy eagerly, its golden glow intensifying. The fractures began to seal, but more than that – new patterns emerged, more complex and beautiful than the original design.

"Stop them!" Ezra commanded, but his voice sounded distant, unimportant.

Through the Concordat, I could feel the magical ecosystem responding. All across London, vampires and witches paused as something fundamental shifted. The artificial barriers between shadow and light began to blur, not into grey but into a spectrum of possibilities.

"Almost there," Elara murmured, sweat beading on her forehead from the effort. "Just a bit more –"

The shadows inside me surged, wanting to give everything to this working. But that way lay dissolution – losing myself entirely to the magic.

"Gillian, stay with me," Elara said firmly. "Think of who you are. What anchors you."

Merryn and Keyne. Their faces blazed across my consciousness, more real than the magical fire surrounding us. My brilliant, serious daughter who saw too much. My chaotic, loving son who found joy in everything.

The Concordat blazed with renewed life, its glow filling the chamber. When it finally dimmed, we all stood blinking in the aftermath.

The artefact looked different now. The stone surface showed new patterns – shadow and light intertwined in fractal spirals that hurt to follow with normal vision. It hummed with contentment, its consciousness settled and whole.

"What did you do?" Thaddeus whispered, staring at the transformed Concordat.

"What it always wanted," Elara replied, exhausted but triumphant. "We let it evolve."

The Obscurum members stood frozen, their grand plans shattered by something as simple as cooperation. The explosive trigger fell from nerveless fingers, clattering harmlessly on stone.

"It's over," Clara said quietly, and I couldn't tell if she meant the fight or something larger.

As sirens began to wail in the distance – the Council's enforcement division finally arriving – I looked down at my hand still clasped with Elara's. The silver-gold sparks had faded, but I could still feel the echo of what we'd created together.

"Thank you," I said simply.

"Thank you back," she replied, then frowned. "But seriously, has anyone seen my glasses? I really can't function without them, and there's so much to document about what just happened."

Despite everything – the betrayal, the battle, the near-death experiences – I laughed. Some things, apparently, transcended even supernatural transformation.

**Current status: Extremely overwhelmed. Extremely tired. Extremely relieved. Concordat: Repaired and evolved. Obscurum conspiracy: Shattered. New friend: Acquired. Glasses: Still missing. Future: Completely uncertain but oddly hopeful.**

# CHAPTER 22

# CAKE, COLLARS AND CONSPIRACIES

2:47 PM. Blue drawing room. Collar itchiness level: 9.5/10. Number of times I've been told to stop scratching: 47. Blood-tea temperature: Perfect. Ability to enjoy blood-tea while neck feels like it's hosting a colony of fire ants: Severely compromised.

The blue drawing room had become our unofficial headquarters for what Tilly insisted on calling "Vampire Gossip Hour," though technically it stretched well into the afternoon.

"For the love of all that's unholy, stop scratching!" Tilly commanded from her sprawl across the Chesterfield sofa where she'd been nibbling on tiny elaborate cakes. Today's cardigan was a shade of orange so violent it could probably be seen from space.

"Easy for you to say," I grumbled, forcing my hand away from my neck where the silver collar pressed against my skin like a circle of frozen needles dipped in itching powder. "You're not wearing supernatural jewellery designed by someone who clearly failed their 'Comfort in Design' module at Magical Accessory University."

The collar was delicate, almost pretty if you ignored the containment runes etched into its surface that glowed faintly whenever I had a particularly strong emotion. Which, given my current state of perpetual irritation, meant it was basically a very expensive, very uncomfortable night light.

Azalea tittered from her perch on the settee, looking impossibly elegant in a black silk dress that probably cost more than my former annual salary. "But darling, it catches the light so beautifully! And the way it complements your pallor – absolutely divine. Like moonlight on fresh snow. Or –"

"More like a Warning: Unauthorised Vampire, Approach with Caution," I interrupted, taking another sip of blood-enchanted Earl Grey. Like a hug in a teacup, if hugs came with a slight metallic aftertaste.

Juniper looked up from the fortress of ancient legal texts she'd constructed around herself on the ottoman. Her eyes sparkled with mischief. "At least yours is subtle. You should see the industrial-strength versions they use on rogue vampires. Thick as a dog collar and about as flattering. Plus they come with a leash attachment for 'transport purposes.'"

"Please tell me you're joking."

"Afraid not. Though I did hear about one vampire who bedazzled his. The Council was not amused."

From beyond the open door came the sound of children's laughter mixed with Charles's patient baritone explaining something about Victorian detective methods. My enhanced hearing picked up every word as Keyne peppered him with questions about fingerprinting while Merryn methodically documented everything in her small notebook with her characteristic precision.

"Detective Charles says that observation is the most important skill," Keyne announced loudly enough for us to hear. "And that you can tell loads about someone just by looking at their shoes!"

"Indeed," Charles replied with the gravity of someone taking a six-year-old's education in crime-solving very seriously. "For instance, your shoes tell me you've been exploring the garden's mud patches despite Tilly explicitly telling you not to."

"That's not deduction, that's just looking!" Keyne protested.

"Ah, but knowing what to look for – that's the art."

I smiled despite myself. The adjustment to this new normal had been surprisingly smooth. Finally being able to interact freely with my children again felt like a miracle. My control had stabilised enough that I could hug them whenever I wanted, help with homework, even tuck them in at night.

"Still weird that you can see them whenever you want now," Tilly observed, echoing my thoughts. "No more supervised visits with Dora hovering like an anxious helicopter parent. Must be nice."

"It's wonderful," I admitted, then grimaced as the collar sent another wave of itching across my skin. "Though explaining to Mother why I look younger than my university photos while wearing what appears to be avant-garde jewellery is going to be interesting. 'Oh yes, Mum, I've discovered this amazing new skincare routine. It's called being undead. Very exclusive.'"

"Just tell her it's Botox," Tilly suggested. "She'll be too polite to ask follow-up questions."

I laughed. "Have you met my mother?"

Azalea clasped her hands together in delight. "Oh, meeting the mother! How thrilling! Will she serve traditional Christmas pudding? I haven't had proper pudding since 1847. That was a memorable Christmas – Lord Pemberton caught fire during the flambé, and Lady Pemberton pretended not to notice for a full minute out of sheer politeness."

"Beatrice sends her regards," Perseus mentioned. "She's relocated to her estate in Provence. Said something about needing distance from 'London's exhausting conspiracies.'"

"Speaking of updates," Juniper interjected, clearly trying to steer us away from Azalea's historical tangents, "I have news about Elara."

My attention sharpened. "How is she?"

"Apparently, she's recovering well in the closest magical hospital. Memory's still a bit fuzzy about her time in suspension."

"I'm so relieved to hear it," I said, picturing Elara's face. "She's just a bright innocent young thing who got caught up in all this..."

Juniper's expression turned serious. "The Concordat itself is secured in a joint facility. It'll need renewal at the next blood moon – but the repairs we made should hold until then."

The gentle click of expensive heels on marble announced Clara Blackwood's arrival. She materialised in the doorway like winter's own ambassador, dark hair gleaming against her customary black suit. Today's version was particularly severe – jacket cut with military precision, trousers that could have been pressed by the weight of judicial disapproval alone.

"Gillian," she said, her voice carrying that particular blend of authority and barely contained irritation that I'd come to recognise as her default setting. "A word in private, if you would."

The others exchanged meaningful glances. Azalea's eyes danced with barely suppressed glee, and Tilly's widened with the anticipation of drama she could dissect later.

"Of course," I said, setting down my teacup. The collar tightened – or perhaps that was just my imagination responding to Clara's presence.

She led me to Perseus's study. The scent of winter followed her – not just cold, but that particular crisp smell of frost on pine needles mixed with something else. Ozone, perhaps.

Clara closed the door with a decisive click and turned to face me.

"There's paperwork to file," she began without preamble, producing a leather portfolio. "The Council requires extensive documentation for... unusual cases."

"How delightfully Kafkaesque," I muttered. "Should I expect to turn into a giant beetle next?"

Her lips tightened – what passed for amusement in Clara Blackwood's emotional repertoire. "The metamorphosis you've already undergone is quite sufficient, I assure you."

"Any updates on our rogues' gallery of villains?" I asked, trying to appear casual while my shadows stirred restlessly beneath my skin.

"All have been formally charged," Clara reported. "Ezra managed to escape with decades of stolen court transcripts."

I sighed. "That's not great. No idea where to?"

"No," Clara admitted, and in other not so great news, Sebastian Rothsforte has evaded charges on the forged artefacts."

"Of course he has," I sighed. "Let me guess – dramatic exit through a window while delivering a parting quip?"

"We suspect he's fled to one of the older European countries where extradition proves... challenging."

"So he's sipping blood wine in a Swiss castle somewhere and perfecting his smirk."

"Most likely."

"What about Odette?" I asked, remembering the ancient vampire's terrifying presence.

Clara's expression darkened. "Odette Valencourt has been exonerated of direct involvement."

"But?"

"But she's furious. With the Council for suspecting her. With the conspirators for using her name. With you, particularly, for exposing the plot and stopping the Obscurum." Clara paused, seeming to weigh her words. "Odette Valencourt is far more dangerous than Ezra ever was. He was motivated by ideology. She's motivated by wounded pride. And she holds grudges like precious heirlooms, passed down through generations and carefully polished."

"Wonderful. Any other good news?"

"The Petrov twins are being studied by our research division. Victoria is claiming she was enchanted against her will, but that defence is very hard to prove."

"She seemed pretty lucid to me..."

Clara studied me with those violet eyes that seemed to see through flesh and bone to the shadows beneath. "Which brings us to the matter at hand."

My stomach dropped, which was quite a feat considering I no longer used it for digestion. "Oh?"

"Despite your assistance in uncovering the conspiracy. Despite your role in recovering and repairing the Concordat. Despite your unusual abilities proving instrumental in preventing supernatural war." She paused, and I swear I saw a flicker of what might have been regret. "You remain an unauthorised vampire in the eyes of the Council."

I shook my head. "You mean it wasn't one of the Obscurum vampires who turned me?"

Clara looked me in the eye. "That, I'm afraid, would be too convenient. The Obscurum heard about you, somehow, but there's no evidence to show they were involved in you becoming a vampire."

My heart sank. "Well, at least I don't have a totally evil master to answer to...yet."

"I know it's hard not to have answers, Gillian," her voice softened. "Believe me, I've been looking into your case. Someone orchestrated this but I can't quite put all the pieces together. The Burks received an anonymous tip directly after your turning. I wonder...do you remember anything else?"

I thought back to that night. "I remember drinks with Tilly and Priya and Adrien...all those margaritas...leaving the bar. Fumbling for my keys... then it's all a blur...maybe there was chanting?"

Clara's shoulders relaxed, just slightly. "Maybe you'll know more in time," she said, gently.

"But for now I'm still an illegal mystery?"

"Your turning violated seventeen different statutes, three treaties, and one strongly worded memo from 1897 that specifically forbids 'the creation of vampires during parties.' I'm not sure how, but apparently you fall under that one too."

I sighed. "Well, there was a lot of tequila."

My shoulders sagged as I took all this in. After everything – the battles, the revelations, the narrow prevention of global extinction – I was still illegal. Still wrong. Still existing outside the careful boundaries of supernatural law.

"I see," I managed, voice carefully neutral even as my shadows writhed beneath my skin like angry cats.

"However," Clara continued, and her usual stern demeanour softened fractionally –becoming slightly less granite-like, perhaps sandstone on a warm day. "There is some good news."

She pulled out a small black case, the kind that usually held expensive jewellery or tiny weapons of mass destruction. Inside, nestled on midnight blue velvet, lay a pendant that took my metaphorical breath away.

It was a flower crafted from what looked like garnets, each petal a perfect droplet. The gems caught the light and threw it back in shades of crimson and wine, and at its heart was a stone so dark it seemed to absorb light entirely. The whole thing hung from a gold chain so fine it looked like captured sunlight.

"I had this special request expedited," Clara said, and was that actual warmth in her voice? A whole degree above absolute zero? "This is far more powerful than your current replacement collar."

"So you admit it's a collar!" The words burst out before I could stop them.

Clara sighed.

"You're incorrigible," she said, but there was something almost fond in her tone.

She moved behind me, her fingers surprisingly gentle as they found the clasp of the silver band.

The moment the collar released, my powers surged like a dam bursting in a hurricane during a lunar eclipse.

Shadows exploded from my skin, dancing across the walls. My senses expanded exponentially – I could hear spiders three floors down, smell the ink Perseus had used on documents last week, feel the vibrations of every footstep in the building.

But more than that, for one terrifying, exhilarating moment, I felt Clara's own power. It crashed into mine like an arctic ocean meeting lava – vast and cold and ancient, beautiful in its terrible precision. Her shadows were different from mine, ordered where mine were chaotic, calculated where mine were intuitive. For a heartbeat, our energies mingled, shadow dancing with shadow in a way that felt like recognition.

I glimpsed something beneath her icy exterior – loneliness vast as winter nights, duty heavy as mountain chains, and underneath it all, a flicker of something that might have been longing.

Then the pendant settled against my throat, warm where the collar had been cold, and the connection severed.

We both exhaled simultaneously, the air between us charged with unspoken things. Clara's fingers lingered for just a moment on the clasp, and I felt their tremor – the only sign that she'd been affected at all.

"This is temporary," she warned, stepping back and rebuilding her professional walls with visible effort. "You'll need to find a Sangrelié soon enough. Your power is too significant to remain unchecked. The shadows you carry, the abilities you've manifested – they require proper binding."

The disdain in her eyes as she said it was devastating. Not because it was cruel, but because it warred so visibly with something else – respect, perhaps, or recognition of a kindred spirit.

"I understand," I said quietly, my hand going to the pendant. It pulsed gently against my palm, like a second heartbeat, warming at my touch.

She turned to leave, then paused at the door. "The garnet flower is called a blood rose in the old tongue. They're said to bloom only in the presence of... exceptional vampires."

Before I could process that, she was gone, leaving only the scent of winter and the memory of shadows intertwined.

I stood alone in Perseus's study, touching the beautiful pendant that marked me as both valuable and dangerous. It was warm against my fingers, almost alive, and I could feel the power it contained – not suppressing my shadows like the collar had, but channelling them, giving them structure without stealing their wildness.

The irony wasn't lost on me. Saved by the very person who seemed to despise what I represented, yet who had moved heaven and earth and considerable bureaucracy to protect me. Who had expedited special requests and chosen a pendant that was not just functional but beautiful. Who had called me exceptional in the language of flowers and blood.

A devastating thought crossed my mind: As much as she hates me, there's no vampire I'd prefer to be bound to more than Clara Blackwood.

*A personal message from Iris*

Hello my lovelies! Thank you so much for joining me and Gillian on this adventure. If you enjoyed this book, please leave a rating or review to help other people find it!

If you want to know the full story of what's going on with Delia's mother, you can read the Myrtlewood Crones series!

If you want more of the Burk family, they appear in later books of my Myrtlewood Mysteries series.

I include the first chapter of both so you can check them out if you read on!

I absolutely love writing these books and sharing them with you. Feel free to join my reader list and follow me on social media to keep up to date with my witchy adventures.

Many blessings,

Iris xx

P.S. You can also subscribe to my Patreon account for extra stories and to receive books before they're published, as well as real magical content like meditations and spells, and access to my Myrtlewood Discord community. Subscribing supports my writing and other creative work!

For more information, see: www.patreon.com/IrisBeaglehole

# CRONE OF MIDNIGHT EMBERS CHAPTER 1

Delia groaned, rolling over and squinting at the morning light as if it was deliberately trying to cause her personal offence. At first it was only exhaustion, but as she turned her head, the hangover quaked inside her skull with a searing pain. She covered her head and rolled over onto her front, tangling the sheets.

That's when the worst part hit her. "What have I done?"

The entire West End would be talking about her. Her ears were burning; actually, her entire head was burning, due to the physical consequences of drinking one too many smoky whiskey sours after 'the event', which may have included an act or two of righteous revenge.

The familiar sound of the Darth Vader music blared out. Gilly had changed Delia's ring tone to the Imperial March as a joke after their theatre company had put on that one-woman Star Wars show.

Delia felt a pang in her chest. She hadn't seen her daughter or her two adorable grandkids for a while. So not only was her head throbbing with pain, her chest heavy with embarrassment, but Delia was emotionally low already, longing for time with her grandchildren and her grown-up child with the silly sense of humour. She pushed the pain away because it was too much to bear.

Delia wasn't going to answer the phone, not at all. But she did glance at it, just to make sure she wasn't not-answering something important.

Kitty's name flashed up on the screen.

Delia sighed and pressed the green button. "Is it as bad as I think it is?" Delia asked her best friend in the world, Kitty Hatton.

"Oh, Deals! You were a star," Kitty crooned.

"Don't lie."

"I'm serious. The whole town will be talking about you. I bet it'll even make it into the London papers."

Delia groaned again; it was becoming her theme song.

"Don't worry, love," Kitty said reassuringly. "It won't be long until you've processed your emotional hangover."

"And the regular hangover that I seem to have as well."

"Oh yes. It was rather nice whiskey, wasn't it?" said Kitty.

"Thank you for helping me drown my sorrows," Delia said.

"Anytime, darling. You know it will all be worth it. When you think about that awful prick."

"A worthless, pathetic little man," Delia muttered.

"Exactly," said Kitty, "and the look on his face. When you emptied his possessions onto the floor, including his mistress's undergarments, poured his special vanilla vodka all over the pile, and set it on fire! It was genius."

Delia sighed. "It wasn't the affairs that made me do it."

"Of course not, love," said Kitty. "It was far worse than that."

"Actually, the affairs were a welcome distraction," Delia admitted. "When you're married to someone like that for so long you begin to pray he'll leave you alone."

Kitty chortled. "Still, it was embarrassing for him. He likes to think he's an upstanding member of society."

"An upstanding little prick," Delia grumbled. "How dare he force me out of my own business?"

"It was very wrong of him," Kitty said, consoling her. "But what are you going to do now?"

"Hide under the biggest rock I can find," said Delia. "I'm sixty-three years old and far too old for hangovers and shame. What am I supposed to do?"

"Go back into acting," said Kitty. "You were brilliant in theatre."

Delia pushed a painful memory out of her mind before it had time to surface. "I don't have the energy for it."

"Start another business then?"

"Even the thought makes me tired. If I never have to look at another costing spreadsheet again, it'll be too soon."

"Well, take early retirement and sue that bastard for all he's worth."

"I suppose I'll have to," said Delia. "He's taken everything else from me."

"Oh, now, now," said Kitty. "That's not true, you still have your brilliant wits and your brilliant daughter and all your wonderful experience. Maybe Jerry did you a favour. This divorce sets you free. Think of it as a fresh start."

Delia couldn't suppress the wave of bitter anger, bursting forth from her chest. A beam of sunlight caught her eye, bringing more hangover pain with it. She glared across the room at the curtain that never closed properly in her small temporary rented flat.

All of a sudden flames burst forth, engulfing the drapes.

"Blimey biscuits!" she cried out, dropping the phone. She leapt up from the bed, bracing herself against the crashing boulders that insisted on tormenting her skull. She tore the curtain down and stomped on it, coughing as she waved her hand through the smoke to clear it and opened the window to stop the alarm being set off.

"Delia, Delia!" a small voice cried out.

Delia picked up the phone again. "Sorry," she said to Kitty. "Minor disaster. I think my curtain just spontaneously combusted. What do you think that's about?"

"Faulty wiring," said Kitty matter-of-factly.

"I don't think there's any wiring in the curtain," Delia muttered. "Maybe it was the sunlight. It's quite bright, you know."

"It's winter," said Kitty. "I don't know. Perhaps you have a pyromaniacal ghost. Call in a professional. See what they say."

Delia couldn't help feeling that Kitty was deflecting. "Did you do something? Were you trying to distract me from my woes by setting booby traps around the apartment?"

"Of course not, darling," said Kitty. "Anyway, I'd better go. I have brunch with Roger later."

Delia made a cooing noise. "How is Roger?"

"Just as romantic as always, dear. So typical, he's probably going to bring me some plastic flowers again. And a bottle of cheap bubbly."

Delia couldn't help but chuckle; her best friend had been dating quite an odd character indeed. It was almost as if he didn't understand normal human customs.

"I'll call you later," Kitty said briskly, and hung up the phone.

Delia rolled onto her back, staring at the ceiling.

"This is my life now, is it?" she muttered, before glancing around the room at the only-partially-curtained window of the small cramped-but-modern flat.

It had been the first property that was tolerable that she'd found in a tight rental market, after Jerry's betrayal. At the time, anything would do. Delia had just needed somewhere to stay until the divorce settlement came through.

But now, Delia couldn't stand it for one moment longer.

She pulled on the first items of clothing she could find in her wardrobe, which happened to be the same plain black turtleneck and grey knitted cape with black jeans that she almost always wore. She quickly washed her face, applied her scarlet lipstick, and attacked her mostly grey hair with a brush.

"Strange," she muttered.

Amid the grey and silver and sparse strands of her natural black hair, a distinctive red streak stood out, curling from her roots down past her left shoulder.

"I don't remember getting that drunk that I'd let Kitty dye my hair."

She squinted at herself in the mirror. Despite the hangover which seemed to now be fading fast, she didn't actually look too bad. While her face had just as many wrinkles as it had the day before, there was a new clarity in her complexion, and the dark circles she'd anticipated were hardly there at all.

"One hot crone," she muttered to herself, "ready to kick some arse." And that was absolutely true, and the arse in question was Jerry.

# PROLOGUE: ACCIDENTAL MAGIC – MYRTLEWOOD MYSTERIES

Thunder roared and lightning crashed through the sky, illuminating the clouds above Thorn Manor. The sky darkened again and all that could be seen was the light from the manor's tower, shining above the dark forests of Myrtlewood and the restless sea along the Cornish coast.

"Ah… that's it," Galderall Thorn muttered.

The storm raged outside, shaking the very foundations of Thorn Manor. Lightning flashed again followed by a loud boom of thunder, as if the gods themselves were at war. Inside the tower room, Galderall stood upright and proud, her white hair tied back in a red scarf as she gazed out into the night with shrewd eyes. She may be an old witch, but she had a deep connection to the magic that flowed through the earth, and pooled, concentrated, around the village of Myrtlewood. She had lived here her entire life, and had dedicated herself to protecting it from the darkness that threatened to consume it.

But on this night, the darkness was closing in. Galderall could sense the malevolent forces approaching, drawn by her power and the ancient magic that flowed through her veins. She knew that she had to act quickly, before it was too late. She gathered her ingredients and began to mix them together in her cauldron, stirring them with a powerful hand. Fresh herbs and protective crystals, mandrake root, obsidian and colloidal silver – mixed with the power of the moon and the strength of the crone goddess, Cerridwen.

She would fight off her enemies if she could, but she was no fool. She knew she was old, and her magic was beginning to wane.

She searched through her shelves of occult implements until she found it, its dark surface gleaming against the light: her black mirror. She used it often, to check on her wonderful bubbly granddaughter, Rosemary, and her great-granddaughter, Athena with the acerbic wit. She hadn't seen them in person for years, for their own protection. Tonight she was relieved to see that they were safe, in their shabby flat in Burkenswood. She watched them, sitting around their battered kitchen table eating a simple meal of beans on toast and commiserating about their days. If only they knew what was coming.

They were safe, for now, but Galderall could sense that something was wrong. Lightning struck again and the scent of danger hung heavy in the air.

Like many witches, Galderall Thorn knew that nature had its cycles and patterns; the full moon always rose at sunset; the high tide would be an hour later every day and, observing the seasons, garlic should always be planted on the shortest and longest days and harvested accordingly. She knew when her time was coming to an end. However, like many people who look up and suddenly realize it's a full moon, Galderall had been busy, distracted by life. She hadn't noticed the sand running out in her own hourglass until a short time before it happened.

The clouds cleared above and Galderall looked at the moon. She realised that her time was coming to a close, just like other natural cycles. She knew that she could not hold off her enemies forever. She had to prepare one final spell and a message for Rosemary and Athena that would guide them on their journey. She had to trust that they would take on the Thorn legacy, and save the town of Myrtle-wood from the darkness that threatened to consume it.

With a fierce determination, Galderall began to chant. She used all of her remaining strength and magic, pouring it into the words and the incantation. The spell was a powerful and ancient incantation that had been passed down through her family for generations. The words flowed from her lips like a river of power, filling the room with a sense of ancient magic. She could feel the energy gathering around her, swirling and pulsing with a life of its own.

*I call upon the powers of the earth*
*To protect the Thorn family, and give us strength*
*I call upon the powers of the wind*
*To keep us safe from harm outside and within*

*I call upon the powers of fire*
*To burn away the darkness, and never tire*
*I call upon the powers of water*
*To cleanse and purify, and make us stronger*

*By the power of the ancient ones*
*As I do will it shall be done*
*By all the powers of land and sea*
*As I do will, so mote it be!*

With a final flourish, she cast the spell, a shield of pure magic that enveloped the manor and all within its walls. She breathed a sigh of relief, knowing that she had done what she could to protect her family and her home. But she knew that it was not enough. She could sense her enemies approaching, stronger than ever.

A blinding light filled the room. The magic flowed through her, filling her with a sense of peace and calm. She knew that this was her final act, and she was ready to face her fate.

She could feel the magic gathering around her. She spared one last glance towards the black mirror, and her dearest kin.

"Everything is about to change, my darlings," she muttered.

A crashing sound alerted her that it was time. But Galderall Thorn, despite her respect for natural cycles, wasn't going to go without a fight, and her enemies had no idea what was coming to them – not now, and certainly not in the future. Rosemary would have to make sure of that.

The light of her spell might be fading fast, but Galderall Thorn was at peace. She knew that her time had come, and she was ready for the next stage of her journey into the realm of the ancestors. Her granddaughter, Rosemary, would have to take on the legacy that her own children had never accepted.

"You might not be ready, my dear, and you might want a nice quiet life, but fate has other plans for us."

# ACCIDENTAL MAGIC
## CHAPTER 1

Rain bucketed down outside the rusty old car. Rosemary groaned.

"It's just water," Athena said from the passenger seat, picking at her chipped purple nail polish.

Rosemary sighed and looked at her teenage daughter. Athena's red hair hung over her face, the same fiery tone as Rosemary's but straighter and easier to tame.

"Just water...sure," said Rosemary. "Easy for you to say. You're not the one who has to get out of the car." She smoothed down her curly locks in anticipation of the rain that was sure to make them even more wild and frizzy than usual.

"What are you, a cat?" Athena teased with a smile.

"Just because you've always loved the rain, it doesn't mean the rest of us have to."

Athena patted her mother's shoulder. "You used to love it too. Back before..." She didn't finish the sentence and she didn't have to.

There was a moment of silence before Athena added gently, "You do need to go in."

Rosemary felt a chill that had nothing to do with the weather.

"Can't you come with me?" she asked.

"You know that wasn't the instruction," Athena said. She put on a posh voice and recited, "Rosemary Thorn, granddaughter of Galderall Thorn, must come alone to meet with the lawyer administering the estate."

"You should go into comedy," Rosemary said, laughing at her daughter. She looked up at the old building with its stone gargoyles. "I don't get it. Why would she do this?"

"She was *your* grandmother," Athena replied. "How should I know? I hardly knew her."

"But there are other family members who should probably be here too, not that Granny had a lot of money to leave behind or anything, but I don't know why she asked for me, in particular."

"Maybe she had something sensitive to tell you..." Athena said.

Rosemary grimaced. "Maybe I'm not ready to find out there's a deep dark family secret."

"Stop being silly, Mum."

"Or is it that I was really adopted and not part of the family at all – you know it's something I used to wonder since I never fit in."

"Mum..."

"You know, even our hair colour is different."

"What about Granny? You said she used to have red hair like us."

"Well, yes. But if it wasn't for that I'd be absolutely sure we weren't related to those other nasty Thorns, and perhaps we aren't. Maybe this is my formal disowning."

"Stop being paranoid."

Rosemary mock-pouted. "How dare you say that to your mother on the day of her formal disowning."

"Mother!"

"Alright, alright." Rosemary opened the door and a gust of wind whipped the rain into her face. "Yuck!" She tried to pull the door closed, but Athena was too fast and gave her an encouraging push, jolting Rosemary out into the weather where she made a dash towards the lawyers' office.

Rosemary ran through the rain, using her arms to ineffectively shield her head.

Despite the dark moods that had plagued her lately, there was a ray of hope that she had been hiding from Athena. It was just possible that her late grandmother might have bequeathed her something, anything…and even a small sum of money might be enough to give them some respite from the hole they were in.

That ray of hope shrivelled up like a deflated balloon as she saw the huge plumes of smoke pouring out of the building. An alarm rang out, deafeningly loud. Rosemary covered her ears as she watched the people scurrying out of the lawyer's offices, ducking their heads against the rain.

She stood there for a moment, stunned.

"What the…" Athena came to join her.

"Just when you thought things couldn't get worse," Rosemary yelled, through the rain and the screeching alarm and the sirens as the fire brigade arrived.

"Hey – at least you aren't in there, somewhere," Athena said.

"Too true, kid," Rosemary said, wrapping her sopping wet arm around her daughter. "Let's get out of here. It's not like we can do anything to help and the lawyers certainly aren't going to be in any mood to meet with us now."

The drive back to the flat was a quiet one. Athena seemed either dejected or lost in thought and Rosemary was too caught up in her own worries to find out which particular teenage mood her daughter was in.

Athena let out a long sigh as they pulled into the driveway of the dingey flat, which, despite its unpleasantness, they could barely afford. "I don't suppose there was any inheritance waiting for us in that building anyway."

Rosemary let her shoulders slump. "I didn't want to even bring that up as a possibility," she admitted. "I didn't want to–"

"Get my hopes up?"

"Something like that. I mean, I can't have you running wild with fantasies of inheriting a dynasty or anything."

Athena sighed. "I don't need a dynasty, Mum. I don't think you even know what that means. But it would be nice to go back to something like our old life in Stratham."

They went inside and took turns to shower under the pathetic trickle of water from the old broken fixture in the mouldy dilapidated bathroom before getting into dry clothes and watching broadcast TV on the couch, sipping the cups of hot cocoa that was Rosemary's speciality comfort drink.

"You know, you should really sell these," Athena said holding up her drink.

"Wow, things must be bad," Rosemary replied.

"Why do you say that?"

"The situation must be pretty dire if my sixteen-year-old daughter is trying to cheer me up."

"You make me sound like a monster." Athena squinted at her mother and then laughed. "I'm serious though. You make the best hot chocolates, and it wouldn't kill you to dream a little – maybe about creating a chocolate dynasty."

"Now that's a deluded fantasy I can get behind," Rosemary said. "My speciality would be Turkish delight flavoured hot chocolate – you know, the one I make with the rosewater."

"Tastes like soap," Athena complained, wrinkling her nose. "Actually..." Her voice became more serious. "Wasn't there a strange soapy smell in the air, outside that building?"

"Was there?" Rosemary asked. "I can't recall."

"Yes, something a bit like lily of the valley."

"That can't be right," Rosemary said. "I would have noticed that. It would have reminded me of my cousins. You know, the Bracewell-Thorns."

"Yes, I know. You always said they smelled like that flower. How do you think I recognised it? Remember, when I was a child you told me and I insisted you take me to the perfumery to see what it was like – you even got me a little bottle of the scent."

"Nasty stuff."

Athena crossed her arms and pouted. "That's what you said whenever I wore it."

"Well, you reminded me of my nasty cousins. They always smell like that icky poisonous plant."

"That's not a polite thing to say...hey, you don't think there's a chance that they were there today?"

Rosemary thought for a while. "Well, they weren't supposed to be there, unless they had a separate appointment right before ours with Granny's lawyer."

"Do you think that..."

"You're not implying my wealthy cousins could be arsonists?" Rosemary said, raising her eyebrows. "It seems like a stretch, even for them."

But the thought wedged its way into Rosemary's brain and refused to dissipate. Something strange was definitely afoot.

# HUNGRY FOR MORE MAGIC?

MYRTLEWOOD MYSTERIES

Rosemary Thorn and her teen daughter Athena move to the quirky, magical town of Myrtlewood, confronting grief, identity and the ups and downs of maternal tension. In Accidental Magic, Rosemary rediscovers her inherited power and begins healing from her past. Through late spring in Experimental Magic and Beltane in Combustible Magic, Athena awakens to her own magic, asserting identity and autonomy. Celestial Magic explores their evolving mother-daughter bond and how trust shapes growth. Each instalment offers seasonal rites that mirror deeper self-trust, emotional courage and letting go.

MYRTLEWOOD CRONES

Centered on older witches reclaiming power, community and purpose with plenty of sassy banter! Embracing the power of the wise woman archetype, mature witches reclaim their magic and power. It's a loving reminder that our inner fire only grows stronger with age and self-trust. As they learn to honour their experience, readers witness self-worth maturing like fine whiskey—age as strength, not loss and having something to look forward to as we age!

DREAMREALM MYSTERIES

A young Dreamweaver, Awa, travels through lucid dream scapes learning how to cope with anxiety, face challenges and heal. In this trilogy, suitable for ages 9-99, each book follows inner and outer-world quests: facing hidden fears, integrating shadow and light, and alchemising into empowerment.

KOTAHI BAY (CO-WRITTEN with NovaBlake)

*In In the Spirit* and *In the Earth's Embrace*, Alyssa inherits earth-linked magic, reconnecting with ancestral land and identity. Through ceremony and earth healing, she reclaims belonging, roots, and trust in herself—a soulful mirror for grounding self-love.

THE WITCHES of Holloway Road (Standalone)

Ursula, newly heartbroken, discovers her own craft and resilience. Her journey is one of inner reclamation: from fear of vulnerability to embracing strength, facing her shadow, building self-trust and choosing joy beyond pain.

## SACRED SHADOW WORK (COURSE)

There is a kind of magic you cannot find in the light.

It waits in the places you have avoided:

The grief that still burns.

The hunger you have learned to silence.

The fears you run from.

The desires that terrify you.

This is the magic that can make us formidable if only we learn how to wield it.

You have carried this power all along, in fragments. This work is where you gather it back together.

## SELF LOVE MAGIC (COURSE AND BOOK)

If you're like most sensitive souls, you're brilliant at holding space for everyone else. You know exactly what your best friend needs to hear. You can sense what others need before they ask. You give from a deep well of compassion, to everyone but yourself.

Meanwhile, you're still struggling to love yourself, shrinking to fit, waiting to feel enough before you fully inhabit your own life. This gap between how you care for others and how you abandon your-self? It's exhausting. And it's not your fault. I've created this course with you in mind.

https://irisbeaglehole.com/

# MANY THANKS TO ALL MY PATREON SUPPORTERS, ESPECIALLY:

Shari Yates Farrell

William Winnichuk

Rachel

Ricky Manthey

Danielle Kinghorn

dawn dexter

Cindy

Cheryl Gawel

Linnea Johnsson

# About the Author

Iris Beaglehole is a witch, druid and writer, based in New Zealand. She has been learning about magic all her life, and has been a witch for over twenty-five years. She has completed a PhD in the social sciences and studied many healing modalities. Iris has written over 20 magical novels which all draw on her passion for deep inner work and real magic including the popular Myrtlewood Mysteries and Myrtlewood Crones series.